"The Vanishing Year is intimate, conversational company,
and its plot is strong, its closing twists superb."
—*NEW YORK TIMES BOOK REVIEW*

"A jaw-dropping thriller. Replete with unsavory characters,
buried secrets, and a bounty of unexpected twists
and turns, *The Vanishing Year* is a stunner."
—MARY KUBICA, *NEW YORK TIMES* BESTSELLING AUTHOR

"The tantalizing plot twists layered atop the juxtaposition of the
protagonist's troubled past and the opulence of her current life are
not only intriguing, they'll keep you reading far into the night."
—LESLEY KAGEN, *NEW YORK TIMES* BESTSELLING AUTHOR

"Dark, twisty, edge-of-your-seat suspense. I read
it in a single sitting and enjoyed every word."
—KAREN ROBARDS, *NEW YORK TIMES* BESTSELLING AUTHOR

"Fans of S. J. Watson, Lisa Unger, and Sophie Hannah
will enjoy this fast-paced psychological suspense novel."
—*BOOKLIST*

"In this gut-grabbing novel, Moretti creates a
glittery world of dreams and nightmares, moves and
counter-moves. You're going to be up all night."
—T. E. WOODS, AUTHOR OF THE JUSTICE SERIES

THE VANISHING YEAR

ALSO BY KATE MORETTI

Binds That Tie

Thought I Knew You

While You Were Gone (A Thought I Knew You Novella)

THE VANISHING YEAR

A Novel

KATE MORETTI

ATRIA PAPERBACK

New York London Toronto Sydney New Delhi

ATRIA PAPERBACK

An Imprint of Simon & Schuster, Inc.
1230 Avenue of the Americas
New York, NY 10020

First Atria Paperback edition September 2016

ATRIA PAPERBACK and colophon are trademarks of Simon & Schuster, Inc.

For information about special discounts for bulk purchases, please contact Simon & Schuster Special Sales at 1-866-506-1949 or business@simonandschuster.com.

The Simon & Schuster Speakers Bureau can bring authors to your live event. For more information or to book an event, contact the Simon & Schuster Speakers Bureau at 1-866-248-3049 or visit our website at www.simonspeakers.com.

Interior design by Kyoko Watanabe

Manufactured in the United States of America

10 9 8 7 6 5

Library of Congress Cataloging-in-Publication Data

Names: Moretti, Kate, author.
Title: The vanishing year : a novel / Kate Moretti.
Description: New York : Atria Books, 2016.
Identifiers: LCCN 2015050466
Subjects: LCSH: Upper class women—Fiction. | Secrecy—Fiction. | Identity (Psychology)—Fiction. | California—Fiction. | New York (N.Y.)—Fiction. | Psychological fiction. | BISAC: FICTION / Suspense. | FICTION / Romance / Suspense. | FICTION / Contemporary Women. | GSAFD: Romantic suspense fiction. | Mystery fiction.
Classification: LCC PS3613.O7185 V36 2016 | DDC 813/.6—dc23 LC record available at http://lccn.loc.gov/2015050466

ISBN 978-1-5011-1843-2
ISBN 978-1-5011-1844-9 (ebook)

To my mom.
This one should have enough plot for you.
Pretty sure.

THE VANISHING YEAR

CHAPTER 1

APRIL 2014, NEW YORK CITY

Lately, I've been dreaming about my mother. Not Evelyn, the only mother I've ever known, the woman who raised me and loved me and taught me to swim in the fresh water of Lake Chabot, bake a sticky sweet pecan pie, fly-fish. I've thought about Evelyn plenty in the five years since she died—I'd venture to say every day.

My dreams lately are filled with the mother I've never met. I imagine her at sixteen years, leaving me in the care of the neonatal nurses. Did she kiss my forehead? Study her baby's small wrinkled fingers? Or did she just scurry out, as fast as she could, hugging the wall, ducking the shadows to avoid detection until she burst through the doors, into the night air, where she could breathe again?

I could have been born in a bathroom stall at the junior prom or in the back of her parents' car. I prefer to imagine her as a scared young kid. The only thing I know about her at all is her name: Carolyn Seever, and that is likely a fake.

My dreams are disjointed, filled with bright colors and blinking lights. Sometimes Carolyn is saving me from a faceless killer and sometimes she is the faceless killer, chasing me with knives up winding staircases that never seem to end.

Even when I'm awake, chopping vegetables for a salad for lunch or taking notes for a board meeting, I'll drift off, lost in a daydream about what she might be doing right now or if we have the same dark, fickle hair or the same handwriting. Wonder what quirks, biologically, I've inherited from someone I've never met, and sometimes, I'll come to in the middle of the kitchen wielding a large butcher knife, the lettuce limping on the counter. I've killed quite a bit of time this way.

I wonder if she'd be proud of the woman I've become.

The benefit for CARE, Children's Association for Relief and Education, starts in an hour. I pace back and forth in the bedroom. I've never chaired before and I can't afford to be distracted, yet here I am, my brain run amok when I can least afford it.

"Relax, Zoe, you've done a fabulous job, I'm sure. Like always." Henry approaches me from behind. His large hands dance over my clavicle as he fastens the clasp of a single strand of freshwater pearls around my neck. I close my eyes and relax back into his lean frame, all sinewy muscle despite his forty years. He kisses my bare right shoulder and runs a hand down my side. His palm is hot against the fitted silk of my gown and I turn to kiss him. I step back and admire his tuxedo. His slick, blond hair and angular jaw give him an air of power, or maybe it's just the way he appraises people, even me. He is studying me, his head cocked to the side.

"What?"

"I think the single diamond would look stunning with that dress," he suggests softly, and I pause. He crosses the bedroom and opens the safe, retrieving one of many velvet cases and I watch him deftly remove a thin, sparkling chain, return the box to the safe, and give the dial a clockwise spin. I love the curve of his neck as he examines the necklace, the small dip behind his ear and the slope of his hairline, his hair curled slightly at the nape, and I want to run my nails up the back of his scalp. I love the long lines of his body and I imagine his spine beneath the layers of thick fabric, all hard-edged dips and valleys. I love his almost invisible smirk, teasing me, as he motions me to spin around. I comply and in one swift motion he removes the pearls and clasps the solitaire. I turn and gaze into the mirror and a small part of me agrees: *the solitaire looks fantastic.* It is large, five carats, and it rests above the wide band of the strapless dress, the bottom of the teardrop hinting seductively at an ample swell of cleavage. As always, I am divided with Henry. I love his authority, the strength he has that his opinions are not merely suggestions. Or maybe it's just that he's so different from me: decisive, definitive.

But I did love the pearls.

"Seems indecent somehow for a benefit, doesn't it?" I am tracing the outline of the diamond, watching him in the mirror. His eyes flicker over my reflected body. "The size of the diamond," I clarify.

He shakes his head slowly. "I don't think so. It's a benefit for children, yes, but only the wealthy attend these sorts of things. You know this. It's as much a display of the organizer as anything else. Everyone will be watching you." He rests his hands on my shoulders.

"Stop! You're making me nervous." I am already on edge, my mind swimming with details. I've done a few of these kinds of events as a second chair but never as a chairperson. There will be a large crowd, all eyes on me, and my heart flutters against my rib cage at the thought.

I've been in Henry's world more than a year now and the need to prove myself seems never-abating. This will be the first time I've taken any of the spotlight for myself. My debutante ball, if you will. And yet, I'm completely foolish. I'm risking everything for a slice of validation. These are things I can't say to Henry, or to anyone.

His palms are cool and heavy. We stand this way for an indefinite amount of time, our eyes connected in the mirror. As usual, I can't tell what he's thinking. I have no idea if he is happy or pleased, or what he feels beyond anything he says. His eyes are veiled and closed, his mouth bowed down in a slight frown. He kisses my neck and I close my eyes.

"You are beautiful," he whispers, and for a moment, his cheekbones soften, his eyes widen slightly, the tautness of his mouth, his chin, seems to loosen. His face opens up to me and I can read him. I wonder how many other women say this, that their husbands befuddle them? Most of the time, Henry is a closed book, his face a smooth plane, his bedroom face similar to his boardroom face, and I'm left to puzzle him out, to tease the meaning from carefully guarded responses. But right now, he looks at me expectantly.

"I was thinking about Carolyn." I wince, knowing this isn't the right time. I want to pull the words back. He gives me a small smile.

"We can talk later. Let's just have a nice time, please?" He reaches into his pocket and pulls out his cell phone. He strides out of the room and my back is cold, missing the heat of him. My shoulders feel lighter, and when I glance back to the mirror, my mouth is open as if to call him back.

It's not that he objects to my finding Carolyn necessarily, he's just impatient with the recent obsession. He doesn't think these things ever end well, and he is the kind of man who respects the current "state of affairs"—he may have used those words. He can't understand the need. *You have me*, he says when I bring it up. *You have us, our life, the way it is now. She rejected you.*

I think he takes it personally.

We have been married nearly a year and have the rest of

our lives to "complicate things." I think about couples who giggle and share their pasts, their childhood memories and lost loves. Henry thinks all these conversations are unnecessary, trivial. He is the kind of person whose life travels a straight path, his head filled with to-do lists and goals. Meandering is for slackers and dreamers. And certainly, mulling over the what-has-been is a fruitless effort; you can't change the past. I admitted once to having a journal in college, a place to keep scraps of poetry, quotes I'd picked up along the way, slices of life. Henry cocked his head, his eyebrows furrowed, the whole idea unfathomable.

And yet, here I am. This house. This man. This life. It's mine, despite the insecurities that seem to follow me around like a stray cat. I stare at my reflection. A thin, pink scar zigzags horizontally across the top of my right wrist, as I touch the diamond at my throat, the setting big as a strawberry.

His sure footsteps beat against the teak floor of the apartment and his deep baritone echoes as he calls for the car. Time to leave.

· · ·

I've always been attracted to elegance and I blame Evelyn's fascination with money. It's so easy to be consumed by it when you have none. But unlike Evelyn, I don't look for the glossy, airbrushed facade of celebrity, the flash of comfortable entitlement. I prefer the tiny details: clean lines and sleek design. I care about whether California rolls are passé, or if the gift bags properly reflect a theme. I love when bright spiky dahlias are arranged with classic white lilies, a contrast of classic and fun, and the resulting graceful style elicits a quiet gasp of "You know, I rarely notice the centerpieces, but this is exquisite." I muse over minutia, the table linen color—*will it match the butter yellow stamen that shoots from the center of the lily?*—the wine, the main course—*lamb is such an acquired taste.* Designing, whether it be a floral arrangement or decor for a benefit, is where I feel at home. It's where I feel like *me,* whoever I am at the moment. It's been the only constant.

The New York Public Library steps are lit with hundreds of flameless candles that flicker by design, with no regard to the wind. The white marble of Astor Hall is awash with deep blue lighting. Large light installations reminiscent of bare, budding trees are intermingled with six-foot-tall columns wound with bursting white and green lilies. White lights twinkle on almost every flat surface. The tables are spotlighted in soft blue and green lights. It's an enchanted forest, complete with hanging crystal butterflies. *Metamorphosis.* How apt.

Henry places his hand on the small of my back and leans down to my ear.

"Zoe, this looks incredible." His breath smells sweet like spun sugar.

"You were right, is that what you're looking for?" I tease. Henry had suggested the NYPL for the venue in the first place.

The rotunda looks better than I could have imagined, better than my silly sketches. I turn in place, absorbing the details, the *elegance* I desire so much—the six-person tables, perfect for intimate conversation, the crystal centerpieces that mimic the trees, white reaching branches thrust toward the ceiling, balancing a smattering of glass-winged butterflies. Each table is adorned with greens, small woody bundles nestled inside frosted mason jars, and blooming baby lilies. The overall effect is of being thrust into an enchanted forest, minus the wood sprites. Everything glittery, white and green, glass sparkling.

I think to call Lydia, the flowers look amazing. La Fleur d'Elise did the event, as a favor to me, although my conversations with Lydia had been all business. A familiar pang of loss hits me.

The walls are tastefully hung with information on CARE,

black-and-white photos of past events, less elegant but more *real*, as the wealthy often claim to want to be *real*, a concept that has always made me laugh. People claim to want *authenticity*, another word that is bandied about at these events, yet men like Norman Krable, on the short list of the richest men of New York, are never seen on the new playgrounds or at any orphan shelter, outside of the ribbon cutting. I try very hard not to let this bother me. But yet, the black and whites hang, *real and authentic*, with wide-open smiles of parentless children, black and white, Asian and Indian, Portuguese and Spanish. Children who don't understand racism or hate, only the cool rejection of a foster family's dismissal. Some of them I know by name, but not all, and at that juncture I have to wonder if I'm any better than the Norman Krables of the world.

"Zoe, I think everything has come together beautifully." Francesca Martin is walking briskly toward me, her heels clipping against the marble floor. "One thing, we had chosen white linens, but here, look." She leads me to a table in the corner and the white is stark, blinding and rough, in the blue lighting. The table next to it absorbs the blue effortlessly, the lights softened somehow by the linen, but I can't make out the color. "It's a lavender linen. I know!—" she holds up her hand and shakes her head. "Lavender is outdated, *believe me* I know. It's like three springs ago, and I honestly have no idea if it's ever coming back, but I think with the blue lighting the white is just too *much*! You can't even tell it's lavender. It's so offset by the green and blue."

"It's so late for a last-minute change." I'm skeptical, but Francesca isn't the event coordinator at NYPL without reason. Her instincts are sharp, impeccable. I agree and one of Francesca's hired hands changes linens. The brightness of the room softens to a deep, rich glow.

The benefit is a relatively small one—only two hundred

people. It's not a formal sit-down dinner, but a simple cocktail hour with a rotating array of hors d'oeuvres all chosen to reflect the enchanted forest theme of the party: wild mushroom ragout, spring pea puree on crostini, diver scallops with foie gras butter, bison tartare. The standing tables in the corner hold silver trays, lined with Stilton pastries and raspberry chutney, strawberry ricotta tartlets with apple blossom honey.

My mouth waters, but my stomach flips in nervous protest.

"Simply stunning, darling." Henry hovers next to the three-piece orchestra, a flute of champagne in each hand. He hands one to me and gives me one of his rare but dazzling smiles.

Proud. At this moment, he is proud.

The evening turns with unstoppable speed. I am shuttled from one table to the next, a conveyor belt for mingling. I stay mostly quiet, nod and smile. I recognize a few people but Henry knows everyone, his arm snaked protectively around my waist. It's my event, yet somehow, Henry still runs the show. I'm appraised always, the unasked question *why* hovering on everyone's lips. With every charm, every joke, every time the crowd rumbles with laughter at my husband, the women, *especially* the women, look at me, heads slightly cocked, a small flick of their eyes. Barely noticeable. *Why you?* The question is never verbalized. Now that I've assimilated, the men are more accepting.

Tonight, they're stunning in dark tuxedos, their faces clean-shaven and shiny; their dates, breathtaking in long draping gowns, their designers referred to only as *Carolina, Vera, Donna,* and *Oscar.* My own strapless gown, blue and adorned with white crystals, was bought off the rack at Bergdorf's. I swing wildly between my independence and my desire to be preened by Henry. His power and his money and his affection. He pretends not to notice, and I pretend I'm not in over my head here in this world. At the moment, we both find this silent agreement charming.

A reporter from the *New York Post* circulates, as I've invited him but requested that he not make a nuisance of himself. His ticket was a gift, much to the protest of the board of CARE, but in return I've asked for a front-page spread in the society pages. I am hoping for above the fold. I'm told that it will depend on Norman Krable's appearance.

The reporter, whose name I've forgotten, has strict instructions: *Photograph the event. The guests. The decor. Do not, under any circumstances, photograph me.* He laughed at that, mistakenly believing my adamancy derived from a woman's insecurity and I waved off his protests with a light flick of my hand. He spends the evening quietly snapping photographs, and I can't be certain, but I feel as though the camera is frequently aimed at me. I skim the shadows, avoid the spotlight, but too often, I catch the reporter's eye. He seems to be one of these men who wants to rescue a woman, a *she-doesn't-know-she's-beautiful* man, like he could be the one to show me. The whole idea is silly. Skirting the spotlight has become a way of life, and not all that long ago, a necessity. Maybe even still a necessity, but I avoid thinking about it.

Past donors and board members rotate on the podium. I've talked my cochair into being the MC. Public speaking is not my thing. The closing speaker is Amanda Natese, a twenty-year-old culinary student who was raised primarily on the money provided by CARE. She is a success story, we hope a harbinger of things to come. We'd like more stories like hers. When Amanda was eighteen she aged out of the system and was handed $4,000, courtesy of CARE. She's worked nights as a dishwasher and apprentice in various chain restaurants, and recently she enrolled in culinary school. Her speech is met with a standing ovation. The reporter is snapping madly. It doesn't hurt that Amanda is a stunning six-foot-tall black woman born with a grace the system was unable to take from her. I greet her offstage, in the darkened wing, and give her a hug. Up close she is teary, and I feel the edge seep away. *This matters.* I repeat it like a mantra, it's the best I can do.

I seek Henry. In public, I always seek Henry. I can't help it. He is only moderately tall, but his glossy hair is a beacon.

In a crowd, he is charming, erudite. His comments are thoughtful and he is well versed in current events and politics. His opinions are generally heavily considered and almost never debated. Something about the tone of his voice, floating above the din of the crowd. I find him in a circle, men nodding along with him as he waxes about tax benefits.

A redhead leans toward him, whispering in his ear, and he laughs. When he sees me, he reaches back, pulls me into the circle against his side, between him and the redhead, and she gives me a sly smile. There's that *why.* She relocates to his left, continues to lean toward him. She whispers clever commentary out of the side of her mouth, words I can't make out, bits of gossip I don't understand. She and Henry know the same people. I absently tend to a wayward strand of lights. Eventually, she wanders away.

Norman Krable shows up late, a blonde on his arm who is not Mrs. Krable, and the crowd buzzes with the slight whiff of scandal. As I catch the *Post* reporter's eye, he gives me a small wink. *Above the fold, it's all I'm asking for here.* He nods once, the blonde cementing the spot, and I sigh with relief.

The charity has never been featured in the Society section, but my goal this year was to bring it up to the celebrity level. Not for the glitz and the glamour of it, that's more of a liability than anything to me, but for the fact I am deeply attached to the cause of helping adopted and orphaned children.

Then again, I am one.

"Silly man," Henry murmurs from behind me. Henry

knows Norman and he's always been fairly vocal about his impatience with adulterers. It's easy for Henry to chide, as his wife is not yet thirty years old. I remind him of this, as a private joke, and he tells me what he always tells me. *I will love you when you're ninety.*

The buzz dies down, and later I hear that Norman's blonde is lovely to look at but dumb as a stone. Henry almost laughs at this, but not quite, the soft laugh lines around his mouth deepen and he gives a muffled *harrumph.*

The evening is ending, the number of guests leaving tipsy and laughing is a sign of success, I think. I have spoken with 90 percent of the people there and I am worn. Tired. I lean against Henry's shoulder.

"I'm sorry, we've been watching you all night and I have to ask," says a voice from behind me. I turn and stare. The woman continues as though my face has not drained of all color. "But you're Hilary Lawlor, aren't you? You are! We'd know you anywhere." The woman is round and soft and friendly and her husband is almost a mirror image of her—two Weebles standing side by side. I concentrate on breathing, but I'd know them anywhere, their happy laughter, their identical snub noses—hers freckled, his not. Her round bright blue eyes, framed with black spidery lashes. She's gained about twenty pounds in the past five years and, not surprisingly, so has her husband. I am hot and cold at once; my head is buzzing.

I'm overly aware of Henry's arm brushing mine, and I sense him straighten up, take interest.

"I'm sorry, you must have the wrong person. My name is Zoe Whittaker." I turn and grasp Henry's arm, too hard. Henry says nothing but wrinkles his brow, my back turned to the couple.

In five years, this has happened only one other time. One other incident of being discovered, of being found out, and it amounted to nothing. I saw an old college professor in a restaurant and tried to duck out before she could recognize me. I saw the dawning comprehension in her eyes, a slight turn of her head, her mouth opening to speak. I paid the bill and left.

It amounted to nothing, as I am sure this will, too. Yet I find that I can't catch my breath.

"Hilary, I can't believe this. Do you know everyone thinks you're dead!" Her voice is shrill and she's excited, inching around to face me again. I realize she's not going to let it go. Who would? I stare at a large, pink cubic zirconia pendant wobbling in her ample cleavage, a bead of sweat glistens there. She's about to hug me, I can tell. I want to tell her, Hilary *is* dead, you see? But I can't. I open and close my mouth and then, because I don't know what else to do, I cover my lips with my hand and murmur to Henry, "I've had too much champagne, I think. I feel sick."

Quickly, he grabs my elbow and leads me outside. The air is crisp, the way an April night should be, and the wind slaps my cheeks, bringing some of the blood back. I don't know when Henry called the car, but it idles out front and we rush into it, a tumble of silk swooshing against the leather seats. After we pile in, he pinches my chin, turns my head to him. Studies me. I involuntarily jerk my head away. He asks, "Are you okay? Are you going to faint?" I shake my head no.

We are quiet while I put the pieces together and I realize it's a bit amazing it's only happened twice. I mean, I went to college in California but it's not the other side of the world. This is New York, the city of millions of transplants a year. I take deep calming breaths and hope that tonight she will not call her girlfriends, her old sorority sisters: *You will not believe who I saw tonight!* No one will believe her. It's too crazy.

"That was the oddest thing," Henry says, looking out the window, his fingers absently tracing circles on the back of my hand. "They thought you were someone else, Hannah something?"

"I know. I have no idea who she was." I laugh but it sounds forced. "I must have drunk a ton of champagne."

"But did you know them?" Henry watches me now, his eyes narrowed. It's not like Henry to press an issue. He's generally too dismissive for that. His sharp, eagle eyes are fastened now on the idea, a field mouse in his sights.

I pause, weighing my options. I stare out the window at the receding steps of the library and I can see them at the top, watching us, their mouths agape and the man shaking his head, pointing with a thick index finger at the car as it pulls away. They must have followed us out. I have no options, I still protect my secret as though my life depends on it. "No, I didn't."

But I'm lying. Molly McKay was my roommate in college. Five years ago, in the throes of finals week, I left our small one-bedroom apartment on Williard Street in the middle of the night and never came back.

CHAPTER 2

I wake on Saturday, sweating and panicked with the vague notions of a terrifying dream tugging at my mind. Before it seeps away, I can only grasp large shadows and men with guns, chasing me down Forty-Second Street. I sit up, untangling my legs from damp sheets. The room has the eerie cast of early morning rain, bluish and depressing.

Henry is gone and that itself isn't unusual. He's usually up before five and out the door, even on a Saturday. Sundays are for sleeping in and espresso in the sitting room, but Saturdays are just another workday.

The night before comes back to me in a rush, followed by a heavy, clenching feeling in my stomach. I swing my legs over the side of the bed, and for a second, my vision clouds as the world shifts sideways. I push the heel of my hand into my forehead. I didn't drink but one glass of champagne—the pulsing behind my eyes can't be a hangover. I have a nebulous memory of Henry pressing a small white tablet into my palm the night before, kissing my forehead. "Tonight, you'll take this," he said, and I felt a quick flash of irritation. But I swallowed it down on instinct, the need to sleep, and to forget

Molly McKay. I hadn't protested, but quite honestly, I don't understand his penchant for pills, his fussing, trying to push this or that—a medication, a tablet, a drug. There's always *something* to cure any ailment and the bottles sit, lined up in Henry's medicine cabinet like soldiers waiting to battle the bulk of his ails: *alprazolam, zolpidem, lorazepam.* The thick, cottony coating of my tongue confirms it. Henry, unaware of my past or my reasons, always pushes aside my protests with a dismissive pat.

The shower is hot, the spray rinses away the remaining fog from whatever I'd been given. As I dry off and tie the towel around me, tucking one end into the other, I shake loose any resentment. *He's only trying to help.* Henry babies me and I waffle between secretly adoring it, the pampering and the idea of being this "kept woman," and childishly rejecting it, rebelling like a teenager to his silly rules and requests. Henry is a product of a traditional household and paternalism runs deep in his veins, which I find both charming and a little infuriating, depending on the day.

I check the clock. 8:58. I want to call Francesca, to find out exactly how I missed Molly McKay's name on the final guest list. *Of course!* She married her boyfriend, but his last name escapes me entirely. Then it clicks, like tumblers sliding into place. *Gunther!* Her boyfriend, now her husband, I was sure, his name was Gunther. Well, if I had seen Molly and Gunther on the guest list, I would have been on alert. I am used to watching my back this way. I've spent half of the last decade with a careful eye on the street behind me, although, to be honest, since marrying Henry, I've become increasingly sloppier about it. In our Tribeca penthouse, it is hard not to feel protected, insulated from evil, as though having money keeps you good, or wholesome. I'm not naïve: in many cases, aren't the rich the ones perpetuating evil?

I remember Molly from our college days, round and bubbly, with peering, hawk-like blue eyes. Even then, she'd fasten on to an idea—a boy one of us liked, a professor we hated, a piece of wayward gossip—and figure out how it could benefit her, turn it razor sharp. She was subtle in her manipulation, even then, and age and time hone natural skills. She was someone to fear, if she knew your secrets. I envision her now, working her pet Gunther into a full frenzy. We'd always called him that, meanly, behind their backs. Her trick dog.

The phone shrills, and I'm startled out of this thought. The clock reads exactly nine and I smile. Henry calls at exactly nine every day. Never a minute later or a minute earlier. I asked him once, what if he was in a meeting? Surely this could happen. At the time, he had only blinked at me and replied, "I can miss a few minutes of any meeting, regardless of the topic." And his answer was so definitive, I never questioned it again, at least not out loud. It still strikes me every single day as odd. Who can say that they can carve out time, no matter the length, at exactly the same time every day, without fail?

"Hello?" I half-sigh and half-laugh into the phone.

"Are you still sick?" His voice comes over the line, silky and deep like melted chocolate.

"No, I feel better. With enough sleep, I guess anyone would." I say this sarcastically, but with a smile in my voice.

Henry laughs softly. "Can't you ever just let me take care of you? I love to, you know. And you said you *do* feel better." I say nothing, because quite honestly, I do. When I'm quiet, he continues, "Okay, I'm sorry. I know you hate the sleeping pills. I try very hard not to recommend them. Am I forgiven? Meet me for lunch?"

"Maybe. I have some odds and ends to tie up from last night. Can I let you know?" I trace the pattern of the coverlet with my fingertip, a manicured red fingernail on the bright white spread like a blood spatter. I pull the towel tighter around me.

He harrumphs on the line, I can tell. I rarely say no to Henry. "You *will* eat, right? You'll eat regardless. Why not join me?"

"We'll see, okay? I'll call you. Don't worry. I love you."

We hang up and before I can second-guess myself, I call Francesca and request the final guest list. In thirty seconds, my email bings, I tap it open on my phone and scan it. It looks the same as it did the previous Wednesday, no mention of Molly McKay or Gunther What's-his-name. I call Francesca back and ask her if there is a way someone could have attended the benefit without being on the guest list. She is flippant.

"Sure, I think some sets of tickets were purchased as comps from corporations. That's pretty common, an out-of-town colleague, the boss wants to show him a nice event, *see how swanky New York can be?* Benefit events are used as networking opportunities all the time. Why?"

I say no reason and we hang up. I log on to the computer with my phone still in my hand. I Google *Gunther* and the *University of California, San Francisco,* and the first hit has a picture. *Gunther Rowe.* The picture is dated this year. His face is sloped into his neck and his smile is wide, too ingenuous for a man approaching thirty. His teeth are gapped and the overall effect is cartoonish. He looks slightly older than my memories of him, a bit more rotund, but there's no doubting who he is. A few more Google searches reveal Gunther and Molly were married a few years ago, a lavish west coast wine country wedding.

A few more searches, including Facebook, Twitter, and LinkedIn reveal Gunther is currently living in Mobile, Alabama, as a pharmaceutical sales representative for Gencor Pharmaceuticals. Another quick search shows me the home office of Gencor is on Lexington Avenue here in Manhattan. I puff out a breath. Okay, that mystery is probably solved. I contemplate calling Francesca back to confirm, but between my hasty exit last night and the phone call this morning, she probably thinks I've lost my mind. I feel irrationally stuck, claustrophobic. What if Molly and Gunther figure out who I am? It wouldn't be difficult, really, I've become shamefully carefree. I imagine them staking out my apartment, possibly chatting easily with Walter, the doorman. *How long have you known Zoe Whittaker?* I put my head between my knees and take a few deep, calming breaths. I'm thinking of the pictures, God, I was so stupid. I want to bring CARE up a notch—I said that! What was I thinking? What if my face ends up in the newspaper? It wouldn't be the first time.

Shortly after I came to New York, I was part of a feature that appeared in *New York* magazine for the flower shop where I worked, La Fleur d'Elise. I was a grunt, an intern. They stuck me in the corner of a group photo shoot, no matter that I tried to wriggle out of it altogether. I repeatedly turned my head at the last moment, until the photographer, exasperated, finally proclaimed he'd gotten a good one. Elisa had looked at me, rolled her eyes like she'd known I was the problem. When the feature ran, I sweat bullets for a month. But my face, my stupid, stretchy, involuntary grin was there, as recognizable as anything. Nothing happened.

I press my fist between my teeth. I've always had a problem with listening, even as a child. I was stubborn. *Hilary will do what Hilary will do.* A common singsong refrain from Evelyn, her round cherubic face, healthy and flush with color, tilted up, her mouth open, her finger wagging in front of my nose.

I remember something and fish through my purse. Pulling out a slip of paper, I dial the number scrawled on the back in my own hand. When the receptionist picks up and chirps *New York Post*, I ask for Cash Murray. His voice comes on the line after a small blip of hold music and I ask him to meet me for coffee. He agrees and picks a place a block from the office. I dress conservatively, in a white silk blouse and black pants, and I'm at the coffee shop ten minutes early. To my surprise, Cash is already there, seated in a corner booth, thumbing through the *New York Times*.

"Do you have to hide out in obscure diners to read that?" I say as I slide into the booth across from him. My pant leg catches on a ripped swath of red vinyl. I look down quickly and am relieved to see the fabric isn't torn.

He gives me a grin, and I realize he's much younger than I'd thought. He's my age—a beefy man, the kind that spends an hour in the gym every day, but probably not more than that, a simple effort to fight off genetics. His elbows rest on the table and his arms are thick, his nails bitten to the quick. He moves quickly, the jumpy, alert markers of a journalist.

"To what do I owe the honor, Mrs. Whittaker?" He sips from his mug, raising one eyebrow. I flush, feeling transparent.

"I need you to show me your pictures from last night?" I end the statement with a upward lilt, and silently curse myself. I think of Henry, who speaks with *gusto*, who would have thrown off the statement like a command, and Cash would be scrambling to meet it. I get raised eyebrows and a friendly smile.

"Oh! Yeah, I got some really great shots!" He's enthusiastic now, leaning back in his seat. "I'd love to run them by you. You know, you're easy to photograph." He picks at his nail.

"Well, that's what I wanted to tell you. I need you to not run any shots of me, in particular." I try for my *Henry* voice. "I did discuss that before the event, you know."

"Oh, that's almost impossible. I mean, you ran the show. The whole event was spectacular, and you were the shining star of the night. Really, if you're worried about the shots, I'm telling you, they were stunning. I say that professionally, you know?"

"No, Mr. Murray, listen, it's not that. I just can't have my picture in the paper, okay? I won't sign off on it."

"Well, to be honest, you don't have to. I was invited to the event *to take pictures.* If you want me to run the article, I need to use you. Frankly, photos of impoverished kids aren't selling the society pages. Beautiful women who care about impoverished kids are."

"Then don't run the article."

"But I already wrote it."

"I don't care, can't you just call the whole thing off?"

He eyes me suspiciously and I shift in my seat. I maintain eye contact, refusing to be the one who breaks first. Finally, he gives me a wry smile.

"Why don't I show you what I have and we can go from there?"

I nod slowly. Okay, fine.

"But my camera is at home. How about we meet here Monday, same time?"

"When is the article running?" I'm surprised, I'd expected it to run tomorrow.

"Oh, well, it's a write-up of the event but it's more a spotlight of the charity, so it'll run next Sunday."

I agree to meet him, then almost laugh out loud at a sudden thought. The reason behind my insistence is a better story than the one he's trying to protect. I realize then why Cash Murray is a journalist for the society pages. He lacks the nose for hard news.

I pull out my cell phone and call Henry.

"Zoe, I had a feeling you'd change your mind. I was headed to Gramercy Tavern. Join me."

By the time I get there, he is already seated. He has chosen a table in the center of the room with an eye on the door where he can view the comings and goings. He wears a casual Saturday dress shirt with pressed khakis and he flashes me a genuine smile. My heart catches.

"Sit, sweetheart. I've ordered you wine. How did you

spend your morning?" He eyes me keenly over his menu. He means to look nonchalant but how I spend my time is always of utmost interest to him. Sometimes, this irritates me. Today I do something I've never done before—I omit.

"Oh, I spoke with Francesca about last night." A technical truth.

"Ah, and she was thrilled, I imagine?" Henry studies the first courses. I don't know why he bothers—he'll order beef tartare with a single glass of Barolo.

"Completely thrilled. Thanks for all your help. Last night, the past few weeks."

Henry had been publicly supportive of the benefit, talking it up in conversations with colleagues and giving statements to the media. Above the menu I can see his eyes, crinkled at the corners. He looks older, somehow, than he did even last night.

"Why wouldn't I? What matters to you, matters to me. Is that so hard to believe?" He folds the menu and looks at me intently. This is his thing, this intense *you're-the-only-one-in-the-room* gaze. Everyone from investors to servicemen are equally charmed by Henry Whittaker. Which is mostly why he can order a bottle-only wine by the glass.

Henry motions to someone across the room and through the rest of lunch I sit silently while Henry discusses business—market dips and trades—with anyone who stops by our table. He makes attempts to include me, blathers on about last night, calls me brilliant to his friends. He receives polite nods in return; they're used to his posturing when it comes to me. I stay for an hour, enough time to placate him, and then excuse myself. I kiss his cheek and walk myself out.

In the afternoon, I nap. Later, I wander the penthouse as dusk settles, enveloping the apartment in darkness, almost without my realizing it, until suddenly I can barely see. I wander to the great room and flick on a single lamp. I love our home. You can see every inch of Manhattan, I swear. I've spent cumulative hours staring out the windows in each room, down to the street below, where the cars look like toys and the people scurry by, busy as mice.

The building is a converted textile warehouse, *prewar,* Henry drops in casual conversation. People seem impressed by this. The floors are deep cherry and the moldings are ornately carved. Everything is heavy and big, *big,* decorated by a man. Twenty-foot ceilings and elaborate archways give way to sleek furnishings with simple lines. The contrast is a designer's dream, and when I first moved in I explored every corner, ran my fingertips against every brocade carved mantel, every marble surface. The whole place looked dipped in shellac. I asked Henry once if I could redecorate it, maybe add some light, floral touches. He gave me a funny look: *Oh, but Penny does the decorating.*

Penny. Henry's right-hand woman—housekeeper, cook, life organizer, home decorator, retriever of lost keys and wallets, and finder of obscure late-century credenzas. She's in her sixties, I think, but looks older, weathered like she'd sat too long in the sun, browned like a raisin. I felt stung at the time. I majored in design in college, although I couldn't tell him that then. I wonder if I can tell him that now? I open my book.

I wait for Henry to come home.

CHAPTER 3

JUNE 2009, SAN PABLO, CALIFORNIA

The bar smelled like old men, the kind of permanent sweat stain that leaches into everything: the unfinished wood grain of the chairs, the thick, ancient varnish of the bar top, the heavy brocade drapes. The air felt hot-wet, like maybe the air conditioner had been on, and now it was condensing on every flat surface in the heat wave. Even the neon bar signs had given up, flickering on and off halfheartedly: *Max's Cocktail Lounge*. The name conjured up some kind of 1940s velvet-lined art deco salon, but the reality was shrouded in wood paneling.

I sat at the end of the bar, the beginning of a nightly ritual that started with vodka tonics and ended with whiskey. I had no place to go. Except this place.

I heard him before I saw him. "Well if it isn't little Hilary, who ain't so little." The voice cut through the smoke and the booze and gave me a chill. He stood next to me, his fingertips dancing across the back of my barstool, and all I could think was *don't you dare touch me*. The anger filled my throat.

"Mick." I faced him, and he seemed surprised. His blond

hair flopped in front of his green eyes. His face was tanned, lined, but in a broken, weathered way that made women want to fix him. One woman, in particular. "She's dead. But thanks for stopping by."

I watched his reaction through slitted eyes and he was appropriately surprised, then sad.

"Ah, I'm sorry, Peach. I knew she was sick."

"But you didn't come?"

"Your mama and I . . . I loved her, but we just aren't the same kind of people." He made a coughing sound, which almost sounded like a sob. For a second, I looked up. His eyes were dry.

"I don't know what that means."

"It's easy, sugar. She's a good person."

"Was." I pushed my glass away, the liquor sliding up over the lip and onto the bar top.

"What's that?"

"She was a good person. She's dead now. She's actually in the county coroner's office because I, her daughter, and possibly the only person who truly cared about her, can't afford to bury her."

He sat on the barstool next to me, his palms flat on the wood in front of him. "When?" His voice was soft, the swagger kicked out and his grief coming too late.

"A week ago, Sunday."

"Your mama had a million friends, H. Everyone loved her, she was a spirit, you know?" He said this to me, like I didn't know, and I wanted to kick his shins with both feet, hard. I pictured that, the toe of my high heel making small, pointed, bluish green marks, like the ones he'd left on Evelyn's arms, dotting his flesh like tiny fingerprints.

The truth was, she used to have friends. Before Mick. Before cancer.

"Yeah, well, where are they?" I pulled the corner of my

napkin back, pressing the pad of my finger into the puddle of whiskey and touching it to my tongue.

"I don't know. I have some phone numbers, we could call some people. Get help."

"Why don't you help? She loved you, you know."

He looked pained. "I was never good enough, that's all, Hilary. I'm sorry about Evelyn. I'm sorry about everything."

I waved my hand. It didn't matter. Mick had been in and out of our lives so much, he'd hardly been a stabilizer. I hadn't seen him in more than six months. Just enough time for Evelyn to get sick, really sick. For the cancer to come back with a vengeance and for her to die. Alone.

"I can help you. I can get money, what do you need?"

"Three thousand dollars."

"That's not a whole lot." He rubbed his jaw, his three-day stubble, flecked with new gray. "Can I give you a ride home?"

"Just go away, Mick." I rested my forehead on the back of my hand, which cupped the top of my glass. Everything felt so heavy. When I looked up he was gone.

• • •

The days had started to blend into each other. I ignored my phone, which rang incessantly with professors and friends, people I'd blown off when I left that night. When the call came from the care nurse: *Come home now. Evelyn won't make it through the night.* I hopped the BART to Richmond with little more than the clothes on my back and my pathetically near-empty wallet. Almost two hours later, I arrived home, too late. Evelyn had passed away before I could say good-bye.

Professors wanted me to come back to class, to take the final, to graduate. I listened to exactly three out of twenty-two voicemails. Molly: *Hilary, what the hell happened to you? Just call me.* And then, *Hilary, you have one final, that's it. Please don't throw it all away. Call me, we'll make arrangements for you.* That was Dr. Gupta, her delicate accent floating through the line, comforting only in its familiarity. I almost called her back, the one person who seemed to have some empathy, who had always been a presence for me, an ear. I sat with my finger on the button, thinking, but eventually hit delete. *Hilary, if you don't come back this week and take your final exam, you will not earn your degree. This is the last time I'm calling you.* Dr. Peterman. Asshole prick. I deleted them all. It all felt so hopeless.

I couldn't scrabble for money from within the walnut walls of an exam hall, especially since if I had any hopes of passing, I'd need to study. I had two weeks left to bury Evelyn, before the state intervened. But I had no real way of getting my hands on any money. I tried to apply for a credit card, but with no history, I'd been denied.

I went to see Evelyn's "estate" lawyer, a thin, rumpled sort of man who operated from his damp basement in Elmwood, and he'd laughed at me. There was nothing but debt. I had to pay the debt before I could pay for Evelyn. I was stuck in this quasi purgatory, hopeless and bottomless. The self-loathing felt like a thick, wet blanket. The haze of alcohol dulled the sharp edges. Just a little.

"Here's what will happen," he explained to me, his twitchy fingers ashing a cigarette so frequently, so nervously, he lost the cherry more than once and had to relight. "The state will do what's called a state-funded burial. It's not actually a burial. They'll cremate the body. You have time after that to claim the ashes, but then you owe the funeral home fees, as well as the state. Then they dispose of the ashes how they see fit."

A wave of intense nausea overtook me. "Dispose?" I squeaked, breathing through my mouth. His breath smelled like fish.

"I don't know the protocols. The funeral homes generally have individual protocols."

I left him in his office, the ashtray tilted up to his face, chasing the red hot ember around the glass with a broken Camel between his teeth.

Mick came back to Max's a week later, throwing a dirt-streaked manila envelope in front of me, thick with bills. I sat in the same chair, with the same drink, the same shoes, the same hatred on my tongue.

"There's a thousand there. I'll get more. How much time do we have?"

"Four weeks from the day she died, so that's only two more." I flipped the envelope back and forth between my index and middle fingers. "Don't even bother."

He sat on the stool next to me. "I failed Evelyn a lot. I failed you."

"You don't owe me shit, Mick." I needed to stave off some kind of misplaced daddy syndrome, which churned my stomach.

He ordered a whiskey. Then another. He clasped my shoulder and the gesture seemed almost paternal. Caring. He bought me another drink. I felt the tear work its way down my cheek, splashing on the bar top, and under his thumb he slid the white pill across the bar top. It didn't feel like exploitation. It felt like friendship. It melted on my tongue, acrid and bitter, and when I closed my eyes, I floated. That night, Mick took me home, left me in Evelyn's apartment, a three-story walk-up on Market with peeling paint and a useless front lock. I slept on her bed, in her nightgown.

When I woke up the next morning, I didn't feel bad. No real hangover, just the faded memory of happiness. It wasn't a high like I'd ever known, back in college we'd tested E, a warm liquidy pooling between my thighs and a bursting in my chest like we were in love with the whole world. This time, there were no hallucinations, no real elation, just a lighthearted easiness that I hadn't felt in months. I wanted it back. It tugged at me like physical craving, but as innocuous as caffeine.

I hung out at Max's every day after that, waiting for Mick, but telling myself otherwise. I'd turn and look at the door every time it opened. Truth be told, I was starting to like the smell of the place. Evelyn's apartment smelled like expired Calvin Klein. When he came back, the envelope in his hand was thin. He tossed it down and sat with a grumbled sigh.

He ordered us drinks without asking. "You're not taking care of yourself, Hilary."

I knew I looked like hell. I didn't know what to say. I was falling apart? I wondered how many of those little white pills I'd need to stay oblivious forever? I hadn't washed my hair in more than a week, and it shone wet with grease. I wore the same pair of jeans because everything else fell off. Evelyn didn't have a washer so I'd worn them in the shower, scrubbing shampoo into them with my fingernails and hanging them over the curtain rod to dry.

The landlord had started coming around, knocking. He hadn't heard Evelyn died, but he still needed his rent, cancer or not. I had begun sneaking in and out, looking furtively up and down the hall before darting down the steps and into the street. The bills were stacking up.

This time, he put the pill on the cocktail napkin. I almost didn't see it.

"What if I want more?"

"You don't have money, Peach." He picked something out of his molar. I stared at the envelope between us.

"I need money. I need to bury my mom. Pay her rent. Pay her credit cards." I licked my pinkie and pressed it to the pill, lifting it to my mouth.

Mick blew out hot, sour breath, leaned back, and dug in his jeans pocket. He came up with a small, white envelope, about the size of a playing card. He slid it under my thigh, his palm resting on my knee for a beat too long. "Unload these for ten each. We'll split the profit, you can keep one for every ten you get rid of."

I pulled the envelope out and pinched it open. Inside were ten little white pills. I gave him a look. "No." But my heart thumped in my chest.

"Okay, then. Got a better idea?" The smirk on his face made me want to slap him. I sealed the envelope back up and stuck it in my back pocket. All those little tickets to oblivion.

"See you in a week, Peach."

•   •   •

At first we met weekly, but then I started seeking Mick out, calling his phone. I needed more than one of those little tabs. They made me feel like I could solve my problems. I figured out that the stay-at-home moms in Berkeley loved "legal" pills. Oxy, Vicodin, whatever Mick gave me. It didn't matter. Plus, I didn't look like a drug dealer: I took a shower, washed my hair. I was "in college." I took the BART down a few times a week and hung out in Cragmont Park. It was all so fucking civil. I never felt weird or creepy hovering around playgrounds peddling pills to pristine little blonde women. I was one of them.

I'd watch them pay their ten bucks, pulling from stacks of green tucked inside Chanel purses. They parted with it so easily, and then they'd slip the pills between their teeth, swallow once, and kiss their fat, drooly babies, burying their noses in downy soft hair. They'd wander away, pushing Bugaboo prams, holding hands with their skipping six-year-olds, and I'd sit under the gazebo, watching them sway and giggle until I couldn't see them anymore.

I felt weird about selling to students, that somehow it was less destructive to supply professor's bored wives with "pep" pills. Besides, the students scared me. Their fresh-faced happiness was so familiar, it gave me a pain right below my breastbone. I couldn't look them in the eye, couldn't pull off being "one of them." No, the moms were easier. At least, if I didn't think about it too hard.

Sometimes, it was too tempting to take more than I was supposed to for myself. I started charging them double, literally eating the profits. What did they care? A twenty was as easy to hand over as a ten, and then at least they didn't have to worry about change.

I called Mick, needing almost double the supply, running a game with myself. Meanwhile, I was getting higher and higher every day. Two pills a day. Four. Then two at night. All the while spending my nights at the bar, my nose buried in a tumbler of vodka. I didn't even bother with the lemon anymore.

"What am I gonna do with my life, Mick?" I was whining.

"Bury your mom. Live in her apartment. Get a job." He shrugged, a toothpick between his teeth. "It's what people do, Hilary."

I didn't need life lessons from Mick. He was a bigger mess than me. I threw what little money I had on the bar and stood up and wobbled. Mick stuck his arm out and caught me. He led me out the door and we walked the four blocks to Evelyn's apartment.

In the morning, I crept out and vomited in the street. Maybe it was the booze, maybe it was the pills. Mostly it was just me and my self-loathing. In oblivion, the pain in my stomach went away. I could eat, albeit small amounts. If I stayed high enough, I no longer felt high. I felt normal. Functioning. I could conduct small talk with the sales clerks and passengers on the bus, cabdrivers and people in elevators. The pills became a necessity. They kept me feeling normal. They calmed my racing heart and the all-encompassing anxiety.

My money stack was growing, but it still wasn't enough to ward off the eventual eviction notice. I thought about throwing a few hundred dollars to the landlord, a fat, greasy bald man I'd seen lumbering around the hallways knocking on other deadbeat's doors. I thought about taping an envelope to the door in good faith. I worried it would get stolen. Sometimes details hang you up, propel you to inaction. More purgatory.

I started partying at night with Mick. We ended up at some guy's apartment, whose name I never knew, and they passed me a pipe and I smoked it. It was the easiest four hours of my life. I felt free, like it was all going to be okay. I felt beautiful. I felt accomplished, like I could just go back and finish college, maybe even *that night*. Everything felt so goddamn *possible,* where all I had gotten used to seeing was depressing impossibilities.

I woke up on the floor of Mick's room the next morning, sticky and sour and sweating. He was gone, but in his place, in his bed, sat a young girl. Had to be sixteen. Fifteen. Too young. My bowels churned. Whether it was from the comedown or the girl, I didn't know.

"Who the fuck are you?" I was pissed. She was so goddamn *young.* She shrugged, but she looked terrified, pressed her back up against the headboard, staring at me with bulging black-rimmed eyes.

I went to the living room and called Mick, left a colorful message. When I turned around, there she stood, all gamine and doe-eyed.

"How old are you?"

"Eighteen." Her mouth twitched.

"Bullshit," I hissed. She barely had breasts. I was struck with a stupid, irrational idea. "Come with me. Let's . . . go somewhere. Coffee. Whatever."

She looked at me like I'd lost my mind. Too jaded for her age. "You're a crazy bitch if you think I'mma go with you." But her shoulders rounded.

I could feel it: It wouldn't take much to convince her. How could I save someone when I couldn't even save myself? *Please,* I mouthed. She stepped away from me, her eyes wildly scanning the room.

"I need help," I said. It wasn't a lie. "What's your name?"

"How the fuck am *I* gonna *help you?* You'll get me killed."

"Let me help you, then. How old are you?"

"Fuck you," she whispered, and then pulled down her lower lip. A black brand on the wet, pink skin. One word: JAREd. Inked by an amateur, the lowercase *d* crooked and dangling off the corner like it could fall right out of her mouth.

There was a knock at the door and her eyes went wide, terrified. I flung it open to a hulk of a man who reared back, not expecting me. His wide, flat nostrils flared, his eyes slit, thin as razor blades. On the left side of his face, from chin to forehead, was a long, fat scar, as red and furious and flashing as his eyes. He leaned in close, smelled like cigarettes and weed. He had on a light black jacket, the silver glint of a gun on the inside.

"Who are you?"

I backed away from the door. My teeth ached, my jaw felt clenched shut. I pressed my palm flat against the door and reached my arm out to her.

The man grabbed my hand away, twisted it behind my back until I yelped in pain. "Don't you fucking touch her."

She scampered past me, shooting back one empty, haunted look. Dark eyes, still and deep as a quarry. She buttoned her shirt as she ran. The man followed her out and once they reached the dusty sedan, pushed her roughly into the backseat, where at least two other girls were waiting.

As the car sped away, I wrote down the license plate, sure it would get me nowhere. It was most likely stolen. I felt like I'd been doused with ice water. I looked around: a month's worth of newspapers, ashtrays, and cigarette boxes. Clothes everywhere. Garbage on every flat surface, flies buzzing around the mouths of sticky, empty liquor bottles. The filth. It all became crystal clear in that moment. I was part of this. I was as much a lowlife as Mick. Only steps away from being abused, like Evelyn, like that young girl. I saw, for the first time, my own greasy complexion, the whiteheads that dotted my hairline from the drugs, my ragged bitten nails from nerves, the dirt on the knees of my jeans.

I grabbed my purse and flung it over my shoulder. When I opened the front door, Mick was standing there, his key poised above the lock.

"Where ya headed, Peach?" he drawled. God, that smirk.

"I'm outta here, Mick."

"D'ja meet Rosie?"

The girl. "She's gotta be fifteen, Mick." I had to get the hell out of there.

He shrugged. "J says eighteen. I go by what he says."

"Bye, Mick." I hauled ass home, where I stayed for a week. No pills. No booze. I shook, I paced. I lay in bed, steeped in my own sweat, my breath coming in gulps. The days blended together, my body feeling like I'd just run fifty miles. My knees and ankles ached and popped when I walked to the bathroom.

Mick pounded on Evelyn's door, his deep voice filling the apartment, first worried, then desperate, then angry. Furiously angry. He came back every day.

When the worst of it passed, I checked my phone. Missed calls from the coroner's office and three voicemails. I eyed the half-full manila envelope on my dresser as I listened to weeks-old messages. Knowing I'd missed the deadline was more manageable without confirmation. His voice rattled in my ear. They had to make decisions without me. I knew what that meant. A state-funded cremation and a common burial.

Funny how they make it sound so nice. All it meant was Evelyn's ashes would be buried with any other "unclaimed body." Other lowlifes who couldn't afford funerals: druggies and drunks. I didn't even call him back.

I didn't know how much a person could hate herself until that moment. I couldn't get the image of Evelyn, lying in a mass grave, surrounded by other decaying corpses, out of my mind. Even though she was cremated. Even though the coroner had explained it wasn't like that, that it was more humane than that.

I had voicemails from friends at school, mostly Molly, wondering where I was, if I was okay. *Would I please call someone back?*

I couldn't get Rosie out of my mind. The fear on her face, the hopelessness in her eyes. That backseat full of Rosies, their long, skinny legs layered like pretzel sticks.

Days later, I found myself at the Richmond police department, filling out an incident report. I couldn't fit all my observations in the lines provided.

"I just want to talk to someone. Please." My nose wouldn't stop running and the receptionist just stared at me in disgust. Hadn't she ever seen a sick person? She worked in a police station for God's sake.

They led me to an interview room and a young, twenty-something officer set a cup of water on the table. He sat across from me with a legal pad and a digital recorder.

I told him everything. I gave him Mick's name, Jared's name, I told him what I did, the pills I sold and where, what I saw, about Rosie and the car full of girls. How young they looked. I didn't care if I went to prison, I had nothing to lose anyway. I gave them the license plate number and a description of the man at the door, tall, broad, greasy dark hair, thick beard.

I asked if I would go to jail.

The officer clicked the stop button on the recorder. "You sold drugs at a playground."

"Not to kids." I stuck my chin out, defiant, like this made it better.

"You're going to be under arrest." He was trying to be kind.

"I have bail money." Evelyn's funeral money. The proverbial nail in the coffin lid.

I wasn't allowed to leave. I was processed, strip-searched, and placed in a holding cell for two days, charged with sale of an illegal substance. But in the end, the playground moms wouldn't admit to buying anything from me. All they had was my "confession" of selling them. No evidence. I was led to a conference room, and the same young cop met me. I'd swear he had a crush.

"We've got bigger things to worry about," he said gravely. His hair stood straight up and he looked like he hadn't slept in two days. "Those names you gave me? That car? Those girls? You got mixed up in sex trafficking. There's a San Francisco PD task force for this, all the Bay Area PDs work with them. They've been tracking this guy for a long time. Your testimony, combined with the evidence they have, could bring it down. You told us something we didn't know. The brand."

"I can't testify." Mick was a dangerous dude, but the guy who picked up Rosie? Downright terrifying.

"You don't exactly have a choice." He reached out and touched my hand. His clean, square-cut fingernails against my dirty ragged ones. He smelled nice, like soap and after-shave. He wore a wedding ring. I wondered if his wife was as young as him. Perhaps pregnant with their first child, round and glowing, her days filled with baby "sprinkles" and pedicures. He probably rubbed her tired feet at night, massaged cocoa butter into her belly. She surely had many pairs of jeans that fit her and that she washed in a machine, swirling fresh with Tide and fabric softener. She'd surely never done heroin. Or sold drugs in the presence of children.

I pulled my hand away. I'd taken the right steps not to be scum. I had to finish the job.

When it all fell out, I told my story to a grand jury. I told the world, or at least my corner of it, what I did. The story never hit national media; the splash it made seemed large only to me and perhaps the eleven girls I helped to free, who may or may not ever thank me. Some of them seemed angry at their newfound freedom, but then again, at least under someone's thumb they were fed and clothed and kept appropriately high.

I found out through the court proceedings, and the kind Richmond cop, that Mick was involved, which surprised me. Jared was the ringleader but Mick worked for him. Jared sold drugs and girls and Mick did his bidding. I couldn't help but wonder if Evelyn knew the extent of his criminal activities. Doubtful. I felt dirty, like scum, like I'd helped. Like I'd let Evelyn down, somehow, yet again.

I was allowed to go home. To Evelyn's crap apartment in San Pablo. I slept in her bed, with her nightgown and her blankets and her perfume and pillows. Drug and alcohol free. I had every intention of staying there. I even used my drug money to pay the rent. I wanted to find a job.

I thought about calling my friends. But college felt like a million years ago. I had grown into a whole other person, one capable of hurting people, hurting myself, rescuing people. For a week after the trial, I woke up every day at a normal hour and made coffee, got the newspaper, checked the classifieds. Like a real and decent human being.

Eight days later, they came back for me.

CHAPTER 4

When I wake up on Monday morning at eight, Henry is gone. His side of the bed is smooth and made, complete with cream brocade throw pillows. The tassels feather kiss my cheek. I stretch, a deep arch, and my fingertips brush a slip of paper. A note. *I will be home for dinner tonight, please ask Penny to prepare something. There are croissants in the kitchen.* I let the paper flutter back to the bed. I can prepare dinner and I have on occasion, but he always insists we ask Penny, which irritates me. I have all day in this echoing apartment, my own voice bouncing off the sterile, bare walls and marble floors. Sometimes I wonder if uselessness can kill a person.

I have a waiting text message from Cash Murray. *How's ten?* I text back, *See you there.*

In the kitchen, I break off a piece of flaky pastry and let it roll around my tongue, melting smooth as butter. I have no idea where he got them. In my new life, I've grown quite accustomed to luxuries just appearing out of nowhere. This is what it is like to live with Henry. I once found a note and all it said was *Paris, tomorrow,* and when I woke the next day, the car was humming outside, the trunk packed with suitcases I didn't know we owned and clothing that wasn't mine. A black-and-white striped silk dress with wide-brim hats, and Hermès scarves. My grown-out bob flowing behind me in the breezy fog tumbling off the Seine. Henry's dazzling smile across the chartered cruise boat. *Are you happy?* And my dodging reply, *Who wouldn't be happy?* Because at least that part was true.

Later, I asked him, *Why Paris?* And he gave a casual, coy shrug. *I've never been here. I wanted to see Paris. With you. It's a city for lovers, you know.* His fingertips twisted my curls, tugging gently, a silent approval of letting my pixie cut grow. Then, his hot mouth, his tongue on my neck, the gold-leafed ceiling dancing and flickering in the candlelight.

Then, after midnight, I pushed, as I always do. Under the cloak of blackness, my fingers finding his under the covers, half-asleep, I whispered the questions into the air, like a puff of smoke, and they hovered there, between us. *Tara. His life before me.* He lay there, so still and so quiet for so long I assumed he'd fallen asleep. When he got up, the cold air whooshed under the blankets like an arctic blast. He crossed the room, clicked the latch on the bathroom door. I fell asleep before he came back.

It wasn't the first time I'd pushed him, my ideas of marriage formed by some hybrid of Lifetime Television and Disney movies. I longed for the intimate connection I felt sure was buried, beneath some surface hurt that only I could heal. I was the new wife consoling the widower, cajoling him into love again, almost against his will. There, in the most romantic city in the world, under the glittering lights of the Eiffel Tower, his rebuff didn't feel like rejection. It felt like a challenge. A rom-com conflict, scripted to a Peter Gabriel sound track.

My phone rings, jostling me out of the memory.

"G'morning, love." Henry's voice rolls through the line like a rumbling locomotive, and I close my eyes.

"Hey, you. How's your day?" I press my fingers to the white-and-black marble countertop and lick off the sticking crumbs.

"Busy, but I wanted to hear your voice. What are you doing?"

"I was eating a croissant and remembering Paris, for some reason."

"Oh God, I was just thinking about that the other day. That was an amazing trip, you were beautiful." His voice catches and I know he is remembering our nights, the long lazy nights in the Jacuzzi, our naked legs entwined. I give a soft giggle.

"Remember the rooftop?" My heart pulses and I feel the quick beat between my legs. I flash on the image of my back against the brick hotel, my dress hastily pushed up to my waist and Henry pressed up against me, my hands skimming his warm back, damp with perspiration from the July air. The clenching of his muscles as he came.

"I can't talk about this here." His tone is teasing, a low, breathy huff of pent-up frustration that breaks on the last word. "Tonight, we can remember it properly."

"Okay, okay."

"Did you call Penny?" He speaks in a normal register, a return to business as usual.

"Not yet, I will. Or I'll cook. I do that sometimes."

There is a pause. "Whatever you'd like." I hear voices in the background. "Tonight. See you then." He's gone, just like that.

I love making Henry weak. I love to see his stone face crack with a smile or his dark, clever eyes cloud with want. I love this idea of him: powerful and in control in his board-room, with its rich mahogany and skyline views, all steel peaks and clouds, and underneath his muscle and dominance, as he barks out orders that men scurry to fulfill, he is unfocused, thinking of me. He's said that before, *You drive me to distraction.* I tend to believe that's one of the nicest things he's ever said to anyone.

I dress quickly and I'm in a cab in less than a half hour. The diner is no fuller than it was two days ago, and Cash is seated in the same booth, two steaming cups of coffee in the center of the gray-and-blue-Formica-topped table. I slide into the booth across from him and he gives me a wide grin, folding his paper. He clicks open his laptop.

"These photos are amazing, I cannot *wait* to show you." His face is animated, his eyes wide, and voice hitches as he navigates the trackpad. His background is of a towheaded child, freckled and gap-toothed. I wonder if she's his and check his hand. *No ring.*

He clicks up a slideshow and turns the screen to face me. There are photos of Henry, breathtaking in his straight-cut suit and blond hair glinting under the ballroom lights. He is watching me, staring at me, smiling at me in almost every photo. The shots of me are less confident, my head turned, my expression unsure or nervous, candid shots where I am flicking back my hair or scanning the crowd, or laughing in a small group. He has captured me beautifully, though in fact, I can't even believe it's me. There are photos of photos, the large blown-up canvases of children tumbling together on a derelict playground, and shots of the decor, sparkling, dancing whitish-blue lights that look magical against the mirrored walls of the library.

"These are . . . magnificent. How did you make it look like this?" I'm practically speechless, and even as I reach the end of the slideshow and it starts over, I can't stop watching. He shrugs, a faint blush on his neck.

"Well, cameras don't invent beauty that's not there. They

just capture it at the right moment. This is what the night really looked like." He spins the laptop around to face him and begins to click. "These are the ones I want to use." He shows me.

There are six photos. Two of them are of me: one in profile, head to head with a female guest, giggling like girlfriends, my face in shadow and one with my arm linked through Henry's, my head resting on his shoulder. The rest are of Francesca, the event itself, the guests, the speaker. In the two photos of me, I can't see my features clearly; I'm in profile or turned, a vague angle, my face obscured. In one of the six photos, I can make out Molly and Gunther and my heart lurches, an acrid taste in my throat. I trace them with my index finger on the screen.

"Please, just . . . you can use the one of me and Henry. You can remove the one of me in profile." I point to the screen, my tongue thick. He cocks his head to the side, just as my cell phone trills. The display reads *Lydia* but I press decline.

"So, you knew that couple? They seemed to know you." His voice contains the forced nonchalance of someone fishing. He adds cream and sugar to his coffee and stirs it slowly, the spoon clattering against the white porcelain.

"Oh, I didn't know them. They claimed to know me from college or something, but . . ." I force a laugh. "College was a long time ago now, so who knows?" I lift one shoulder and purse my lips, waving my hand. All I can think is, *Please change the subject.*

"Oh yeah? Where'd you go to school?"

"UCSF." It pops out before I can think it through, because being close to thirty means college almost never comes up. I used to have the story down pat, but it's been awhile since I'd been asked, so the truth bubbled out like an uncorked spring. In an odd way, it's a relief to say it.

"Oh yeah? West coast girl!" He strokes his chin thought-fully and gives me a sideways grin. His teeth are straight and he has a kind, jovial smile. "So tell me, why are you so active in CARE? What made you choose that?" With slick movements, he clicks the recorder next to him and I eye it before speaking. "Ignore this. I have to, I have zero memory for this stuff. I want to write about you a bit, though, if you don't mind."

His interest intrigues me. Henry is always interested in me, in my hair or my clothing, how I hold myself, or how I present myself. What I've done or said at parties that needs mild correction later. What I've done with my day, my time. He's less interested, it seems, in my capricious ideas: my thoughts that flit here and there, unfocused. Aside from my activities at CARE, he rarely asks my opinion on anything.

I admit I don't always mind being under his thumb. There's a certain freedom in that, to not have to think about *things* in life, like what to eat for breakfast or dinner, or where or what to shop, how to dress. He likes to teach me how to be in his world. He flicks away my concerns that I've never been fully accepted among the upper echelon. He shakes his head dismissively when I point out how the women pair off, heads tilted together almost systematically, at his functions until I'm left standing in the center of the room, awkwardly alone.

But this is different. Cash seems genuinely interested in me, as a person, and the thrill I feel at that is almost embarrassing. It's not a romantic jolt, but not since Lydia have I had a friend, an honest friend, and truthfully, Lydia has been more of an acquaintance since I married Henry. *He's not a friend, though. This is all for an article.* The thrill escapes, *pfffffting* like air out of a balloon.

"I was adopted," I say, slowly and flatly, twirling the spoon between my fingers. I dance around this, the truth addled somewhere in the middle, stuck in some emotional desert I can no longer access. "My adoptive father died in a car accident when I was a baby. I never knew him. My adoptive mother died of ovarian cancer in 2009, my senior year of college. So, I sympathize with these kids. Some are orphans, some are foster kids whose parents are drug-addled. I haven't had parents in a while. So, I guess in a way, I get it. I had a birth mother who didn't want me either." I've never said this to anyone, and it feels dangerous to admit this much of my old life, a life I am no longer entitled to call mine. Lately I find myself belligerently wanting it back and, in small ways, throwing a stake in the ground. Even with the narrow escape of Friday night, the overall pervading fear has waned and in its place is a dried-up seed of resentment. A peaceful five years means that I am reckless with my safety. More than that, admitting my past in parts feels safe, like the vent on a pressure tank.

"Did you ever try to find her?"

"Who?"

"Your birth mother."

"Not seriously. I don't know why. I guess for many years Evelyn was all I ever needed. She was my best friend. We never had that silly high school hate thing going. Not that I tried to get away with much anyway, or that she'd let me. I just felt like looking for my birth mother would have been an insult to her. Or something."

"What about now?"

"Now?"

"Yes, since she's passed, why haven't you tried?"

I shifted in my seat, tucking my left leg under me. There were a hundred reasons. Finding Carolyn involved admitting on some level who I was before, either online or with a private investigator. Somehow, I had to use the name Hilary Lawlor to get there. To move on, to continue to live, I had been forced to cleave my life with a giant chasm that held Hilary on one side and Zoe on the other. There was no bridge back, not in my mind. I held a little fear that Mick or Jared and his group were still behind me, pursuing me or waiting for me to traverse that chasm again. It was as though once I crossed, once I became Zoe, Hilary ceased to exist. I didn't speak of her or think of her. I rarely recalled my past, instead choosing to pretend it hadn't existed, like I'd been born a full-grown adult named Zoe. Sometimes I fantasized that I'd fall ill and lose the memories altogether. Except for Evelyn. I still wanted her.

There were also the legal ramifications. I ran. I testified for a grand jury, but took off before Jared's trial. Jared was still convicted, partly because he'd branded all eleven of his girls. But I ran, despite subpoenas. I have no idea if anyone came after me, looked for me. In New York, among the shelters and the streets, I procured a driver's license and a phony birth certificate. They're surprisingly easy to come by if you ask the right questions. I looked like a drifter, unassuming and trustworthy. It cost me every cent I had at the time. But my identity wasn't mine, not legally, anyway. Still, I felt safer than if I'd let Detective Maslow do it for me.

"I guess I can't explain it. I technically could. I've been sort of lost lately." Lost in my thoughts, the words fell out of my mouth unbidden, and until I said it, I hadn't known it was true. Sometimes, things don't seem real until you verbalize them. I *had* been thinking about my mother, dreaming about her. The idea of looking for her again had seemed daunting and vague.

"I did a feature series once. Adoptive reunions. In Texas, seven, eight years ago," Cash said, leaning forward across the table. "I can help. Do you want me to help?"

"Are the society pages boring you?" I teased, poking the air in his direction with my spoon.

He sat back, crossing his arms. "Yes, God yes. Sometimes it's all I can do to stay awake." He scratched at the back of his neck, realizing his admission. "Not that your, uh, event wasn't spectacular. And I met you and you've been great, but . . ."

I laughed, letting him off the hook. "I get it. So many rich people, so little time?"

"I live in a studio in the East Village. I mean, the lean months can be a special form of torture."

I have a vision of my mother, Evelyn, dignified in her starched hotel uniform, adorably cinched at the waist, pirouetting in the kitchen, leaving for a night shift, while sixteen-year-old me licked peanut butter off a spoon. Evelyn worked as a housekeeper by day and a hotel maid by night or early morning, depending on her shift. Despite her patchwork jobs, we still struggled to make ends meet.

We'd laughed at our poverty then, called it "creative financing," collecting dented cans of creamed corn that we'd eat over toast. That changed when she got sick the first time, it no longer felt as adventurous. It felt precarious, dancing on the edge of a razor blade. There were real consequences to poverty, I learned.

I remember lean months.

A waitress appears, her heavy blue-lidded eyes darting back and forth between our single cups of coffee. I can see her calculating the tip and trying not to roll her eyes. Cash pays the tab, over my protest. "So let me help you." He bites his lip. He seems very into the idea.

"We'll see, okay? Write the story, see what you come up with. Will you send it to me before you run it?" I am concerned about the pictures. I realize the pictures combined with my admission of being from San Francisco could sink me. I haven't been this stupid in years. Not at least since that *New York* magazine feature photo, with me hiding in the corner, but still somehow with a maniacal rictus grin.

While I don't think I'm actively being pursued, the idea of hiding is long ingrained, the thought of going back claws at the back of my throat.

"Yeah, of course."

We stand to leave together. Out of the corner of my eye, I see his hand hovering lightly above my back, guiding me out. *Men and their shows of chivalry.* He opens the door for me and I step out into the busy sidewalk. The sun is gleaming and I squint, fishing around in my pocketbook for sunglasses.

"Call me when you have the article written. I really loved the photos, Cash. You're a talented photographer." I pause then because I'm being sincere and his smile is wide, a faint flush in his cheeks from the compliment. He walks with me to the corner, where I will go uptown and he will head downtown, to his office.

The white *walk* sign blinks and I step off the curb. The roar of an engine is the only sound I hear; the voices of the crowd are muted. I look up and freeze. A car is careening through the intersection, its headlights bouncing as the car hits a pothole. My feet are solid lead blocks, glued to the pavement. Suddenly, something hits me hard and I feel myself tumble through the air. I scream and close my eyes, my fingers losing their grip on my purse strap. When I open my eyes, Cash is breathing hard on the ground next to me, a sheen of sweat on his forehead, his eyes wildly scanning the intersection. The car—in retrospect it was a gray sedan, glinting in the sunlight—is nowhere around.

"It turned left!" Someone from the crowd points to the alley.

"Did you get a plate number?" Cash shouts back before scrambling up and running halfway down the street in the direction the car turned. He decidedly gives up, jogging back to me. I sit up. My shoulder burns where it hit the pavement.

"What the hell was that?" Someone says.

A slight Hispanic man is crossing the intersection, wiping his hands on his white apron. He's left his food cart across the street and his eyes are wild.

"That car, miss." He is breathless and nervous. "Are you

all right? He saved your life." He gestures toward Cash, who is preoccupied, looking up and down the street.

I nod and stand up, half-embarrassed, and force a laugh. "They must have been drunk."

"Ah, no miss. That was no drunk. He was parked, you see. Right there." He points to his peanut cart. "Across from me. For an hour or more. When you cross the street, he gun the engine."

"What do you mean? Like he was trying to hit us?" Cash stands, belligerent with his hands on his hips, ready for a fight with the unknown driver.

"Not you, sir, you headed the other way." He shrugged apologetically and pointed to me. "He was after her."

CHAPTER 5

The idea of going home to my apartment just to sit there holds no appeal. Cash hadn't wanted to leave me, but no one had a license plate number. A small crowd had gathered and someone patted me on the shoulder, meant as comfort, I suppose. There wasn't anything anyone could do and I had doubts that the car had really been after me. It seemed too random, too surreal. I figured it more likely that the driver had simply been careless or distracted, realized he was late, and in a panic ran a red light. I shooed Cash back to his office to write his piece. Reluctantly, he began his walk downtown but kept glancing back in my direction.

I walk uptown on Sixth Avenue, all twenty-two blocks, and stand uncertainly outside the glass and mirror front of La Fleur d'Elise. Even with the hike uptown my heart is still thundering from the near miss.

It's been awhile since I've been back—almost a year—and my cheeks flush. I picture Lydia in the back room, prepping and cutting, and Elisa in the front, relaying celebrity gossip through the propped-open industrial steel door. La Fleur is primarily an event florist. Designer to the stars.

Elisa has long held one of the top spots for floral design in the city.

I shake my hands at my sides and wriggle my shoulders to loosen them up. *This is a completely terrible idea.* But I have nowhere else to go. I have half a mind to just turn around and go home, or duck into a boutique, *anything.* I stare at the sea of taxis, a yellow tide, and my eyes glaze over. The decision is made for me.

"Well, well, look what the cat dragged in." Lydia is standing in the doorway, her arms folded over her chest and her feet crossed at the ankles. Something glitters on her eyebrow.

"Is that a new piercing?" I squint at her and give her a friendly smile. I hope it works.

"Is that Armani?" She juts her chin at me. I hold my hands up, palms out. Her black spiky hair is tipped with blue. Long, dangling earrings. Black leather and lace get-up. Possibly fishnet stockings under a long black gauze skirt. Red lipstick curled around blinding white teeth. We used to sit on that stoop and smoke cigarette after cigarette.

She steps back, holds open the door. Her head jerks toward the front room. I walk through the door, and she bumps me with her shoulder.

The shop is bursting with color and I'm nostalgic. The front shop, small and exclusive, is open by appointment only. Castoffs and leftover blooms are sold to small corporate banquets or private clientele.

"The library looked incredible the other night. Thank you." I dip my head, avert my eyes.

"Thank Javi, he did the designs, not me." She walks ahead of me, waves me back into the back room, which looks typically chaotic. "He's not here, though, although he'll be sorry he missed you."

Sorry like a hawk, I think.

Steel buckets of blooms littered with cuttings and flowers

that had been deemed "not quite perfect," although that to any passerby would look magnificent on the dining room table. I pick up a long-stem peach rose, fingering a single nicked and browning petal. There are more rejects than usual, which can only mean one thing.

"Wedding this weekend?" I gather a few velvety irises, their stamens a stark tiger orange against the deep purple backdrop.

"It's the Slattery wedding." Lydia is at the prep table clipping manically, her metal shears clattering on the stainless steel table. "We can't do too much until Wednesday but some of the heartier types can be prepped now."

I watched her splice stems on a bias with a knife, turn leaves back, and shape greenery. If I close my eyes I can imagine I still work here—Lydia and me side by side clipping and cutting with identically bandaged thumbs. I twirl my wedding band around my ring finger.

Landing the Slattery wedding is impressive. Mikael Slattery has been in the top half of the Ten Most Eligible Bachelors list for almost a decade. I'd seen him with a leggy brunette at receptions and parties with Henry. I forgot her name. *Natalie? Natasha?* Ah, Nadine something.

I resist the urge to touch one of the wayward blooms, position it back into place, suggest that the vibrant orange could be highlighted by peach, not yellow. These were the arguments of old Zoe and Lydia. We are new people, with a new friendship. If she'll have me back.

"So, where you been, Zo?" She gives me a smirk and the corner of her scarlet mouth tips up. "I called you."

"Yeah, I know." The event book is laying on the worktop and I flip through it. The pages are outlined with design ideas, colors, and specifications. I know in the front there is a bio of the bride and groom but I don't read it. "Where's Elisa?" I ask.

"She has a class this morning."

I glance at the clock. It is noon. Elisa teaches workshops at the New York School of Floral Design. A teaching day means she won't be back until after two. At least that's how it used to be. I reach out and cover Lydia's hand, which is tugging on a rose leaflet. Her knuckles feel rough under my palm. She falters and curses, dropping the stem; a thick drop of blood blooms on her thumb. An amateur mistake.

I rip off a paper towel and hand it to her. "Let's get lunch."

• • •

We walk the two blocks to Sam's, and Lydia tends to her thumb like it's a surgical incision. She inspects it and wraps it, squeezes it, unwraps it, pushes out a thick bead of blood. The café looks the same—warm browns and covered wall to wall in art. Bright frames, with shocks of color. Mosaic tables and iron chairs. The sounds of soft, jazzy saxophone float through the air. Sam is parked behind the counter. His prematurely gray hair has grown out, but he's wearing a T-shirt I actually recognize, despite how long it's been since I've been here.

"Zoe!" He jumps up with his arms out and I awkwardly hug him across the countertop, the cash register between us, pressed against my shoulder. "The usual?" He gives me a wink and I laugh and nod. I watch him add caramel and milk to a large cardboard cup. Lydia says something right as he flips on the froth machine. She motions to a table and we sit.

"Stop being mad at me," I say, too loudly, just as the whir of the cappuccino maker dies down. I can handle Lydia's moods, her temper tantrums, snarled comebacks, and caustic sarcasm, but her silence has always killed me. Lydia is gifted in silence—her stone walls stretch out, echoing and cold like a glacial plain.

Her face cracks a smile. She has laugh lines around her mouth that are new. "You always cave."

Sam brings us coffee and a plate of baked goods—baguettes and Brie, croissants with cranberry jelly. We butter in silence.

"I'm not mad at you. I miss you. Is that so bad?" She avoids eye contact. Lydia doesn't "do" sentimental. I don't know what to say. We've never been Hallmark-card friends.

"No. That's not bad. I miss you, too." I want to tell her everything. Molly and Gunther. The car. Cash. Henry. It floods my mouth, gathers right behind my teeth. I swallow.

"So what gives? Is this really the first time I've seen you in almost a year?" She pushes Brie and croissant into her mouth and I drop my baguette onto the plate, my appetite waning.

"No. I saw you," I squint my eyes and look up at the ceiling, "in January. At the Peterses' baby shower." I snap my fingers, triumphant.

She hangs her mouth open. "That was accidental. We did the arrangements. You were a guest. And it was awkward as hell."

"I didn't think it was awkward," I lie, then offer feebly, "You looked great. So did Javi. You all did."

"We used to live together, see each other every day. I get when you get married, you can't stay chained to me all the livelong day. But a year . . . I mean, come *on*. I've called you. I *still* call you."

"I know." I cross my legs and my knee hits the table. Coffee splotches on my wrist. "Besides, we've chatted. It's not like I've ignored you. We've just been . . . busy."

"Bullshit."

I bite my cheek to keep from smiling. In a world where every other person seems to have a hidden agenda or unfathomable motivations, I miss Lydia.

She doesn't wait for me to answer. "So what gives, why now?"

"I just need you back in my life. I'm sorry. Is that enough?"

She flicks her fingers, casting crumbs in my direction, and shrugs. "Probably. How's 'Enry 'Iggins?"

I ignore the jibe. "He's a lot . . . busier. I'm alone a lot. Do you think Elisa would let me, I don't know, volunteer once in a while?" I say the last part in a rush.

"Where? At the shop?" Her eyes grow wide, the diamond stud winking in her eyebrow.

"Yeah? Dumb idea, maybe." I fiddle with my fork, depressing my fingertip along the tines until it hurts.

"I'm sure she would. Are you okay?"

"I miss just being here. I miss the smell, the thrill of designing, you. I even miss *her* ridiculous demands."

"Two coffees, one hot, one cold. Seven napkins, please." Lydia's voice pitches an affected French accent that mimics Elisa's and we exchange smiles. "Why are you alone?"

"Because Henry's busy. He works seven days a week. Our apartment is huge. I feel like a marble in a jar. I need something to *do*. I feel useless."

"You have your charity, right?"

"Yeah, I do. The benefit was incredible." I smile at the memory and she clucks a sound of mocking approval. "But, I can't do it all the time. Every day."

"Will Henry let you?"

I try to pretend this is a ridiculous question. *Will he let me?* As though this is 1955. I roll my eyes. But I don't answer.

"Ha, you won't tell him." Her voice is flat. "Seriously, Zo? What kind of marriage is it where—"

"You act like he's abusive." I push my plate away and it clatters against the table. Lydia doesn't understand relationships, the give-and-take, she never has. I think of the parade of men, tall, short, thin, stocky. She didn't subscribe to any particular "type." She consumed men, devoured them, until she was their world. As soon as any of them ever asked anything of her—to change in any way, even if just to be around them more, maybe not work twelve to fourteen hours at a flower shop, because, let's face it, we weren't saving lives—she'd be gone. And if asked, she'd reduce them to nothing with a little sideways twitch of her nose, like they'd never existed. *Oh, Carl.* Eye roll. Simply because they wanted her too much. It was exhausting.

"No, I just think he likes to be in control."

I push down a flash of anger. "Lydia, stop. He's protective. He has a right to be. He's been traumatized by his past." I lower my voice. "He was married before but she died in a car accident."

She clamps her mouth shut in a thin line. She wants to ask details, I can tell, but she doesn't. Good thing, because I don't know any. He still has nightmares about it, kicking the sheets and shouting her name in his sleep. *Tara.*

Sam hovers near the cream and sugar counter, feet from our table. He fiddles with all the lids, stacking them one way, then the other, and when he can't seem to find a reason to be there any longer, he turns and heads back to the kitchen. The music volume drops to a barely audible level.

"We had so much fun in that crap apartment in Hoboken," I say. I remember the cramped quarters, only a hanging sheet separating our beds, a thin guise of privacy in anticipation of all the single activities that were sure to come. By the second week, we'd tied it back against the wall, tacked with kitchen twine and a pushpin. The apartment contained only a living room, big enough for a single plaid monstrosity of a couch that we dragged in from street pickup, and a kitchenette fit for a child.

"Hey, did you ever find Carolyn?" She cocks her head to the side, her eyes brightening. When I met Henry, I was immersed in the search. Lydia and I had scoured newspapers from San Francisco, Internet websites on adoption, even cold-called some long-lost aunt of Evelyn's. Lydia was a perfect companion, her lust for mystery and her creativity propelled me long after I might have given up. We never found anything. Lydia knows about my adoption, but not about Mick.

And only Mick knows what I did to Evelyn.

Then I got caught up with Henry and gave up. My earlier conversation with Cash echoes back to me. I shake my head. "I haven't looked again, isn't that weird? I sort of just forgot. I still think about it sometimes, but not enough to actually do anything about it."

I'm suddenly struck with the need to have a biological connection to someone, an unbreakable tether that might keep me from flying away in Henry's wind.

Two conversations about my mothers in one day is enough to cause panic.

Sam appears at my elbow, brandishing chocolates. We each take one. The candy coats my tongue, sweet and feathery. Decadent. He wisps away, leaving a trail of Polo in his wake.

"I can help you look."

I shrug and flit my fingers at her. She leans back and folds her arms across her chest.

"You're just so fucking different, now." She says this as though it isn't a matter of opinion and is also no big deal. "What is that, silk?" She touches the sleeve of my blouse with her pinkie. I yank my arm away, involuntarily. I hate being scrutinized, studied. I've lived so long feigning normality, invisibility, I forget how it is to be conspicuous. With Lydia, suddenly, I feel conspicuous—uncomfortable in my own silk blouse. "Your hair is all one color. And it's so damn long."

This is true. I've gotten compliments about my hair from strangers in public. The short, angled, punk bob I kept when Lydia and I lived together has grown into a thick chestnut mane that flows just to my shoulders. I don't say it's because Henry likes it to tickle his face when I slide on top of him.

"Let me help you look." She wouldn't be Lydia if she picked up subtle hints. The light from the window filters through her dyed blue hair, giving her a hazy azure glow. I shrug like this is no big deal, but my heart hammers a staccato rhythm against my rib cage. I shake my head. It's one thing to accept Cash's help, that's professional. It's another to reach out to Lydia, who still holds anger. With Cash, I could call it off at any moment, *Oh, never mind, it was a silly idea, ha ha.* Lydia wouldn't accept that, she'd push and dig, with her sharp eyes and capable hands, until she'd unearthed every sordid thing about my life, lay it bare for Henry to see. No matter what Lydia said, Henry was all I had left.

I glance at my watch. It is after two. Elisa will be back in the shop, angry about Lydia's absence, the *Closed* sign, the empty storefront. We pay the tab, I throw an extra ten on the table when Lydia isn't looking. I can't be sure that the motivation is entirely altruistic and flash back to Sam lingering near the table, his ears turned to our conversation. I did not dream up his curiosity. Was I saving face? *I might be under someone's thumb, but I have money now.*

The walk back to the shop is short and Lydia threads her arm through mine, bumping my hip as she walks.

"Can we do this again? Soon?" she asks, unusually timid.

"Will you talk to Elisa about my proposal? About coming back? Say, one day a week."

"It'll be like old times." Lydia flashes a red-and-white smile.

The shop is still empty, locked up and dark when we arrive, and Lydia sneaks in, flipping on the lights and propping the door open as though she'd never left. We hug, but quickly, an obligatory back pat and air kiss. Lydia and I are bonded in our discomfort with physical contact. I scurry down to the corner and hail a cab.

I'm halfway home before I even remember the careening car. I can't decide if I will tell Henry or not. It seems so silly, a careless driver, an inopportune *walk* sign. Not even worth bringing up, really. And besides he'll only worry.

He worries so much.

CHAPTER 6

Penny makes dinner after all—a finely sliced raw tuna over a bed of crispy radicchio and a loaf of crusty bread drizzled with garlic and olive oil. Henry likes light dinners because of his heavy lunches, surrounded by leather and mahogany, with cigars, steak, and a silky cabernet.

The table is set when I arrive home and I yell a greeting into the kitchen where I hear Penny humming something sensual and jazzy. I run upstairs to change into jeans and a soft button-down shirt. I pull my hair into a low, casual bun and make it back downstairs just as Henry arrives through the front door.

He gives me a brilliant smile, all teeth and crinkled eyes, and my breath hitches. His arms wrap around my middle and he kisses me, full on the mouth, his tongue running along my bottom lip until my knees go weak. He pulls out my bun and runs his fingers through my hair.

"Down," he murmurs, and I laugh. I step back with a teasing swish of my hips and pull my hair back. He shakes his head playfully. I take his hand and lead him into the kitchen where Penny is setting our plates. Mondays and Thursdays are for casual dining, ties undone, at the kitchen island. My afternoon with Lydia has given me new perspective, reminded me of what I'm blessed with. Our entire apartment would have fit in this gourmet kitchen.

"Perfect, Penny. I had steak at a lunch meeting and I was worried you'd make red meat."

"Henry, Mondays are never beef." She pats his hand and turns on her heel, busying herself at the sink. Her short gray hair is pulled into a tight bun and she's wearing jeans and a bulky sweater. She's borderline gaunt.

I used to think that "the help" would wear uniforms, or call us Sir or Ma'am. My assumptions come from Evelyn. She was "the help" for more than one household in the Bay Area. She'd take the BART from Richmond to Berkeley, and over to San Fran, a two-hour one-way trip in the morning hours. I sometimes try to imagine Evelyn here, in Penny's place, and the picture slides from my mind, slippery as wet spaghetti. She talked of her employers with such formality, with reverence, Mr. Mishka, Mrs. Tantor. She didn't just respect them, she *admired* them.

But Penny is different. She never feels like "help." Penny feels like a mother, quietly taking care of Henry and me and never asking anything in return. I've overheard her with Henry, shockingly casual, even joking. She mocks him, and he tolerates it. She's been with Henry's family since he was young, she knew his parents before they died, she knew his wife, she knows more about him than I do. She makes no bones about the fact that her loyalties lie with Henry. She isn't rude to me, but she's never overly friendly. I've caught her looking at me with a strange fascination, like a bug under a magnifying glass.

When we first started dating, I asked Henry about it. "Penny really seems to not like me much at all."

Henry's response was quiet, twirling pasta around his fork,

studying his plate. "She knows I pay her bills. If she doesn't get along with my new wife, it could ruin her lifestyle. She keeps her distance to protect herself, I'd guess."

"I wonder if she's in love with you?"

Henry laughed and dropped his fork. "In love with me? She's at least twenty years older than I am!"

"That means nothing," I protested. "You're ten years older than me."

"Her husband is terribly disabled, you know. From a fire, when I was a kid." His mouth bowed in a frown. "So tragic. She needs the money, Zoe."

And so I felt foolish. Stupid and petty and foolish.

Except sometimes she looks at us so oddly—as though she doesn't know who he is, like I am a specimen. She doesn't just look at me, she *studies* me. Then, when Henry and I are together, she barely glances my way at all. And once I came into the kitchen, just as I heard her saying *Henry, but it isn't right. It doesn't look proper.* And they had straightened up at the sight of me, Henry patting her shoulder and murmuring that they'd talk later. I knew she was talking about me, about my background, my mysterious past, rooted poverty.

But before I could protest or ask her, she'd appear at my elbow, my dry cleaning in hand, the bottle of expensive shampoo I was almost out of but hadn't yet ordered, our social invitations categorized.

"How was your day?" Henry is squeezing lemon over his salad, picking through the leaves with his fork.

"It was interesting." I can't decide how much to tell him. *Start with the worst.* "I was almost killed today."

Henry's fork clangs on the marble countertop and he stares at me with eyes rounded in fear and I realize how reckless I've been. How careless. *Tara.* Penny has whirled around and her mouth hangs open. *How cruel.* "Oh God, I'm sorry, that came out so awful."

Henry clears his throat. "What do you mean, *killed*?"

I place my hand on his arm, caress his wrist. "I'm sorry. I didn't think. . . . Well, I was crossing a street and a car ran a red light and almost hit me. A reporter from the *Post* saved my life." I use the moment to get in an introduction to Cash, as well. Not that meeting Cash for breakfast is off-limits or anything. Regardless of Lydia's attitude, Henry doesn't exert control. He's always exceedingly interested in how I spend my time, and he's protective. He means well.

"A reporter?" he repeats.

"I'm sorry, I shouldn't have been so blunt about it. I forgot about . . . well, Tara. I was thoughtless."

He wipes his lips, dabbing one side, then the other. After a moment, he sets his napkin down and pats my hand. "It's fine. Tara was part of my life, not yours. Tell me this again? A reporter? Saved your life?"

I relay the story and am able to work in Cash's name again. He leans over and kisses me and his lips taste like lemon and pepper.

"I'm glad you're safe. People are crazy drivers." His left hand rests on my thigh.

"How was your day?" I spear a slice of tuna and put it in my mouth. He's watching me, and I lick olive oil off my upper lip.

"Oh, the same as every day, I think."

Penny has her back to us and is storing the last of the dishes. She turns to face us, as usual speaking to Henry, not me. "Do you need anything else before I leave?" She casts her eyes downward. I wonder what would happen if I yelled, screamed, talked to her directly. Anything. I wonder where she goes, who she goes home to? Does her husband live with her? I imagine her in a house in Queens, an invalid husband sequestered to a bedroom, small and dingy, surrounded by fifteen cats, all named for Disney characters. *Captain Hook eats all the tuna.* She talks to them in her whispered, lilting voice, still young sounding, while they mewl and knead at her lap.

Henry doesn't flinch. "Penny, thank you. This is wonderful. Enjoy your evening."

Penny gives me a quick head nod and a good-bye, never *ever* saying my name—I'm not sure she's ever said it—and I hear the petite footsteps to the door. The latch clicks into place. I turn to face Henry and his eyes go dark and for a moment that seems to last hours, we just stare at each other.

"Who is this Cash?" Henry asks as he slides over, pushing his plate back. He tugs at my hand, pulls me against him and into his lap. I straddle him but pull away a notch. He only seems to want me, to be desperate like this, when he thinks he's being encroached upon.

"I saw Lydia today." I play with the buttons of his shirt, tapping them with my nail. I want to tell him about the flower shop, my idea of going back, how it could silence this suffocating notion that I'm not accomplishing anything. I'm going to be thirty years old and I don't have a career anymore. Or friends. Or anything else that other thirty-year-olds have.

He pulls my hand up and kisses my palm.

"I was thinking I could go back to the flower shop. One, two days a week. There's not enough to do with CARE to fill a whole week. I need to *do* something."

"You do," he agrees and kisses my neck, and then I realize he's being facetious. He means him.

"No. Henry, I'm serious." I lean back, away from him, but he smiles. A warm, open *come-on-in* smile. I love this Henry, the one who is undone, his face reminding me of a child's, full of hope and wanting. He slides his hands down to my waist and lifts me onto the marble countertop. His hands trace circles on my thighs and I feel my irritation fading, being replaced with a building want. This is what he does when I try to talk to him.

He tugs my blouse free and his hands inch up my rib cage. His touch is electric, every feather-light graze sends my skin zinging. He knows this and his lips curl up in a satisfied smile. But I am happiest when I'm the tormenter. He grips my shoulders and his head falls to my lap. When he lifts up again, he stares into my eyes, his hands cupping my cheeks so tight it borders on painful.

"I can't lose you, too." His voice rumbles, low and keening. He runs his thumb across my bottom lip. I bite it softly.

"Henry you're not going to lose me." I clear my throat.

"I know you want your freedom, to fly and do your own thing. I know I hold you back. I'm sorry. Just . . . have patience. Wait for me."

"Henry." I touch under his chin with my index finger. "You were with Tara when she died, right? Holding me back won't stop anything from happening to me. Do you realize that? We all have to live our lives."

"I never thought I'd love anyone again. I'm not a lovable man. I thought I had my one chance and it was over."

I slide off the counter onto his lap and face him. I kiss his cheeks, his closed eyes. "Nothing will happen to me." I can feel him through the thin fabric of his suit pants, hard and insistent, and I put my hand there, lightly scratching with my nails. His eyes flutter back.

I untangle myself and take his hand. "Let's go upstairs." We leave the dinner plates on the counter, the wine untouched. Almost like we were never there.

*   *   *

Later, our legs woven together, Henry's hand caresses my belly. His face is in my neck. His breathing is sporadic, sometimes regular and steady like he is sleeping, but then he startles and pulls me into him, like he can't get close enough. My stomach rumbles and I think of our salads, wilting on the island.

"I want pizza," I blurt out. He lifts his head sleepily.

"Pizza?"

"Yes. From a pizzeria."

We don't do that.

"Hmmm, okay. Order pizza, then." He wraps his leg around me, pinning me to the bed and pretends to doze. I struggle to push him off and giggle.

I extract myself and slide into one of Henry's workout T-shirts. He pushes himself up on his elbows and watches me, bending his head to glimpse the crescent of bottom peeking out from beneath the hem of his shirt. He gives me a low whistle and a quick pat on the bare skin. I wave him off.

From the bathroom, I order delivery. My chest is bursting with a skittered giddiness. I realize I hadn't finished telling him about my visit with Lydia. The afternoon feels so far away, like it happened to another person. I have a sudden stab of pity for her, with her scoffing superiority and preconceived notions about what makes a loving relationship, with no concept of the give-and-take. She would likely never feel full with love like this. She'd never allow herself to see the flaws of a man, to accept them, to bend herself in any way to accommodate them. She'd never realize it was a two-way street, the way the right man would bend to accommodate her, molding himself around her until they fit together, *just right.*

When the pizza comes, I pull on shorts to answer the door and then scamper back to the bedroom with paper towels. Henry sits up in bed, wrapping the sheets around his waist, and stares at me in wonder.

"I honestly think it's been twenty years since I ate pizza in bed." He pulls up a slice and takes a large bite, cheese dripping down his chin. I situate the box between us. I'm suddenly famished. We chew in silence. I realize I have no idea what time it is.

"So. About Lydia." I study the box in front of me, wondering what his response will be. He is sufficiently plied with pizza and sex, his legs in a loose *V*, our ankles crossed.

"The punk girl, right? I remember Lydia."

Was he not listening at all in the kitchen? I try not to be exasperated.

"I miss . . . having a girlfriend. I don't talk to her much anymore."

"Well, you have different ideas now. You're a rich woman, in a different world. She's not. It drives a wedge between a lot of people."

"It's more than that." I pull my ankle back and cross it under me, tugging at the hem of his T-shirt. I pick imaginary crumbs off the blankets.

"Oh?" He raises an eyebrow.

"Henry, do you like her?" I choose my words carefully, picking through the minefield that is a *delicate subject* with Henry. Again, I sense the closing door before its confirmed.

"I have no feelings about her whatsoever, Zoe." He sits up straighter, his face pulled in, becoming *Henry* again. "You can do as you like, with whomever you like." The kind of person who says things like *as you like* and *whomever* versus the guy who smacked my bare bottom twenty minutes ago. All these quick-changing people, like stage actors in a play.

"You've never seemed to approve." I put my pizza down and touch his hand. He looks at it blankly.

"I approve, Zoe. It's fine." He stands up, gathers the pizza box and the crumpled paper towels, and sweeps crumbs from the white comforter. He mumbles something that sounds like *crumbs in bed.*

I feel panicky; I'm losing him. I make a calculated decision.

"She reminded me of something I forgot about." I straighten the pillows, going for nonchalant. "When you and

I met, I had just started digging, trying to find Carolyn. I was striking out." He is staring at me, his eyes wide, his expression a marble wall. I rush on. "I wonder if you can help me now. You're rich, powerful, *connected*." Henry loves more than anything to be a hero, and a celebrated one. Nothing gets him going quite like *can you help me.*

I expect this to work, to be the bridge between us, to bring him back to bed, his ankles over mine, his face in my neck as he brainstorms about who he knows that could help locate her, and how we could do it. Who he could pay, *We'll hire the best PI I can find.* I genuinely believe this.

Instead, his mouth is set, his jaw working.

"Why am I not enough, Zoe?" His hands hang down by his sides, but his fists are clenching and unclenching.

"Oh, honey no, I just meant—"

"I *know* what you meant." He slaps the bed, hard, and I jump back. "In the course of one evening, you tell me you were almost killed, you've connected with an old friend— someone shady and who looks like a common criminal—and now you want to reach back into your past and find your birth mother, even though, by your own admission, your past is shrouded in secrecy and vague, and you have no living relatives. We've made a *goddamn* life, Zoe."

I'm stung by his words, his assessment of our evening and how drastically different it is from mine.

"Henry, I'm telling you this because I feel close to you! Please, just listen—"

"I said you can do anything you want to do. I mean that. But you are restless. You are not content in our life. With everything we have, you want more. You bring up this *Carolyn* every time I turn around. She's the woman who *left you.* I am the man who is here. And it will *never be enough.*" His eyes flash with anger and he spits the words at me.

"Henry! *NO!*" I shout, I can't help it. He's not even listening to me. This all seems ridiculous. He obviously doesn't understand what I'm talking about, what I'm asking.

"Don't you *dare raise your voice to me like that.*" He says it slowly, low and scary, and I shrink back. I've never been afraid of Henry before.

"Henry. I'm happy here. I will not be stagnant my whole life. You can't keep me in this marble box of an apartment." I speak slowly and clearly. I smart at his words, *the woman who left you,* but I won't tell him that.

We stand off facing each other, both of us in identical poses, his hands on his hips, for several minutes. His nostrils flare. The pizza is cloying, greasy and sickening.

"I just want to be enough for you, Zoe. This is my biggest fear—that I'm not." He drops his arms to his sides and turns his back to me. I cross the room and touch his bare back. His skin feels cold.

"You're enough for me." I touch my nose to his spine and inhale.

"I'm not. I won't be. You'll leave. I'll be alone."

"That's crazy." I wrap my arms around his waist. "I won't leave you simply because I find her. That's crazy. I don't even know if she'll want to know me."

"So this is Lydia, this is her idea. You've started mentioning Lydia and Carolyn at the same time. We've spent the last year in *this* world. It's different social circles, Zo. She'll drag you backward into her scene again."

"What? I have no mind of my own?" I pull him closer. "I love you."

He pats my hand, then pulls out of my embrace. He doesn't turn to look at me and instead sighs. "Now. You love me now."

"Henry, love isn't conditional on growth. If I make a new friend or find my birth mother, it doesn't mean I'll move on or outgrow you."

"You're an exotic bird, Zoe. You don't see that."

"This is crazy, Henry. I'll love you no matter what."

"I'm not ready, Zoe. I'm not ready for us to reach back into our pasts. We've been living in this bubble, living in the present. I've loved it. I spent the whole year before I met you completely living in the past. I can't look back. Not yet. Can you see that? Can you give me time?"

"Time." I repeat. The word seems senseless.

"Yes. Time. Let me figure it out. Then maybe I'll even help you. We can do it together. But I just need to be ready. There's a lot you don't know about me. I know that and it's my fault. I've kept myself from you, parts that I haven't been ready to access. It hasn't been fair, but . . ." he shrugs. "It is what it is."

"Okay." I nod slowly. I don't really understand but I know that real love is about sacrifice, understanding, giving when you just want to take. "I guess I can give you time." *Even though I have no idea what that means.*

He pulls me into a fierce hug, his arms around me like a vise. I can't be sure, but I think I feel tears on my hair. "I won't let you go. Not again."

CHAPTER 7

"You have a date?" In my hands I clutched a fistful of wilting anthurium, with their veined, leathery leaf-like petals, a masculine flower. Phallic, really, the stamen popping out like a penis.

"It's a corporate banquet." Lydia's eyes plead. "It's a big date. You'll be fine."

"Elisa hates me. She's going to hate this," I grumble, pouting, smoothing out the last of the bouquets. Elisa criticizes the way I change water buckets. I picture her smooth blonde-gray ponytail swinging as she shakes her head, her lined mouth bowed down, as she ticks off on slender fingers all the things I should have done differently in her clipped, efficient accent. Elisa is five feet tall and sixty years old and my hands shake at the thought.

Javi waits in the truck, honks twice impatiently.

"That's why you're not going to tell her." Lydia kisses my cheek and pats my head. Like I'm a dog. "You were going to go with me anyway. Now you're just . . . in charge."

"Elisa's going to flip shit and you know it. He better be worth it."

"He's not. If I'm not home by midnight, I've been roofied, okay?" She waggles her fingers at me and is out the door, the tinkle of the bell signaling her exit.

As he steers the van, Javi talks a blue streak, gossiping about Elisa, Paula (his partner-slash-girlfriend), even Lydia. I hmmm-mmm in all the right places, but eventually he gives up and we sit in silence in hot, beeping traffic. Lydia's right, it's just a corporate event, but I'm jittery and I wipe my palms on my jeans. I think of all the things I'm going to do wrong. I've been working at La Fleur d'Elise for almost three years now, and I still don't have my footing. My job feels precarious, at best. Charitable, at worst. Most, if not all, of my suggestions are met with an outward sigh. I'm still the new kid, the apprentice.

The dinner is small: twenty-five people in a restaurant called Brûlée in Tribeca. All I have to do is place centerpieces and a podium potted plant and leave. The arrangements are all ugly, corporate and masculine: the rounded globes of hydrangeas, the long tapered gladiolus. Literally, all cock and balls, against deep bloodred table settings. I can almost smell the self-congratulatory sweat.

I position the last table setting, only four in all, and one hand bouquet, presumably a gift. White, lilting, and feminine, I guess it's for someone's assistant.

I turn to leave and crash directly into someone coming through the door. A flurry of gift bags scatters on the floor, their contents spreading a remarkable distance, flinging under tables and chairs.

"Oh my God, I'm so sorry." I panic. This will be the thing that Elisa knows about, that she fires me for.

The man bends over, gathers up the flung silk scarves and pen boxes. His hair is shiny blond and when he looks up at me, he smiles, all teeth and dimples. My heart lurches.

"No worries. Nothing breakable. Help me rewrap?" He motions toward the long table where he stacks ten gift bags in various states of crumpled. I hesitate. Since I've been working at Elisa's, I've been around some very rich people. Florists are hired help, as invisible as janitors, maids, and interns. Clients may respect the designers, temporarily treat them as equals, but never the drivers. I'm merely the one delivering the masterpieces of the designer. In this case, Lydia.

The man studies the centerpieces. "Did you design these?"

I shake my head. I can almost feel Lydia elbow my side. If I'm the lead here, I'm the designer. I handle the criticism, take the praise.

He grins. "Good. They're god-awful. What are these, black flowers?"

"Um, bat orchids. Yes, black flowers." My tongue feels thick, unwieldy.

He reaches out, taps my arm. "Sit, help me. My assistant wrapped all these. I'm hopeless at wrapping things. You must be good at it?"

"Because I'm a woman?" I wrinkle my nose.

"Because you're in design?" he corrects, carefully. My neck flushes red.

He leans toward me, his long eyelashes lowered, dusting his cheeks. He smells spicy, full of oak and power and something musky, like the inside of a tree trunk. He passes me gift bags and I carefully wrap pens and silk scarves back into delicate tissue paper. Our fingers touch with each pen box, all ten, and then we're done. Too soon, it feels like.

I smooth my palms on my jeans and clap my hands together, too loudly, for some weird reason, as though he's a kindergartner. He gives me an odd look.

"Looks like I'll be leaving," I say.

He closes the space between us. "Stay. Be my date for this horrible, boring, boorish dinner. Where everyone will talk about who they've fucked and fucked over. You can tell me about bat orchids."

"I can't. Tonight? No. I don't have anything to wear. I have plans. I have a book to read. Just . . . no." I back up, feeling the wall behind me for the door. "You don't even know my name?" It comes out like a question, or possibly an invitation.

He laughs, a deep yet light sound. "I'm Henry Whittaker. What's your name?"

"Henry Whittaker? I know who you are." I swallow twice, the doorknob under my hand. Working with a high-end event florist means we know who's who in Manhattan. We gossip about the major traders and real estate moguls the way other millennials follow the Kardashians.

"I'm famous, then? Does that impress you?" He steps closer to me, his face cracked in a grin. He's joking, teasing me.

"No. You're a player. That doesn't impress me." I turn the handle and back through the door. "Have fun, though, really. I don't need to be added to the list of women you've . . . fucked or fucked over or whatever you said." I back through the banquet room door and into the main restaurant where wait staff are setting tables for dinner service. A few of them look up, startled. I rush through the dining room and from behind me, Henry calls, "Wait! I was kidding!"

I push through the doors and into the street, where Javi waits with the van, the bass thumping. I fling open the door and heave myself in the front seat. "Just drive."

I look back to see Henry standing in front of Brûlée, watching the van peel away, his hand raised in a jaunty wave.

●   ●   ●

Back at La Fleur d'Elise, I clean up. Putter, wash buckets, rinse bins, inventory foam bricks, wire, beads, dusting spray. I have nowhere to go. I could go home, rattle around the apartment, wait for Lydia and her terrible date. The worst that could happen is that she'd come home, draw the curtain between our beds, and engage in raucous sex. No, thanks.

The bell clangs out front and I dump the last bucket before wiping my hands on my apron and making my way out front. Henry Whittaker stands in the showroom, eyeing the refrigerator filled with arrangements. I stop and stare, unable to find the right words. The right tone. Haughty? Bitchy? Funny?

When he sees me, he smirks. "These are your plans?" He gently extends his hand, a large white box wrapped with a red bow.

"What is this?" I tilt my chin at him but I don't take the box.

"A book and a dress." He bows slightly. "Zoe Swanson."

I push my hair out of my eyes. "How did you . . . ?"

"I have connections."

I can't tell if he's serious. He sighs, sets the box on the counter, and pushes it with one finger in my direction. "Go on. Open it."

I do. On top of a pile of tissue paper, sits a book. I pick it up, turn it over in my hands.

"*Anna Karenina?*" I raise my eyebrows.

"What's not to love? Suburban unrest in nineteenth-century Russia?"

I set the book aside. It's old. I wonder, briefly, what edition. I wonder if he somehow knew it was my favorite, or if it was just a guess. A guess.

The dress underneath is heavy, beaded and eggplant. The book was a hit, the dress, a miss.

"Eggplant is my least favorite color," I tell him. Rude. Evelyn would be appalled.

"It's not eggplant. I prefer to think of it as bat orchid."

I can't help but laugh at this. Truly, men in general are fairly bad at banter. I've spent many a night tossing out jokes to good-looking dates, only to have them fall flat on the two-top table between us, with a puzzled smile. Henry is surprising.

He elaborates. "I heard once that there's no such thing as black flowers. That if you were to breed a true black, you'd make a million dollars. That all flowers are really deep shades of purple. Some might say . . . dark eggplant. Is that true?"

He steps closer to me, his chest inches from my face. He doesn't seem to care about personal space or social acceptability or my not-so-subtle back-off signals. He doesn't know how much I loathe the touch of strangers.

"That's true." I whisper. "But you already have a million." I've turned into that girl. The one who plays it cool then gives in, much too quickly. The coy temptress turns giggly. I straighten my shoulders, try to get it back.

"I do." He whispers back. "Come with me. Please?"

"I . . . I need to shower and do my hair, makeup. I live all the way in Hoboken," I protest weakly.

"Come to my apartment. I'll give you all the privacy in the world. I promise. I have a car."

"I . . . no. I can't." I smooth the back of my hair flat against my skull, a nervous tic.

"What do you want? What would make you come with me?"

His voice is so earnest and his eyes so pleading that I almost cave right there. I do cave, internally, it's over. Hook, line, sinker. My idea of dating is going home with the drummer of a band, tiptoeing past his roommate passed out on the sofa, and try to have quiet orgasms and, later, quieter escapes. I rarely proffer a phone number. I like this, my distant, detached life.

I slant my eyes at him, coquettish, for fun. "Convince me."

He laughs, his head tipped back until I can see the inside of his mouth, behind his teeth. "You want me to woo you, then?"

I place my hand on my forehead, a mock swoon. "Exactly. Woo me."

He leads me out into his car, which is waiting for my inevitable yes (I wonder if his driver has ever seen anyone say no). We drive to his apartment, which is appropriately spectacular, shiny and glossy with high ceilings and gleaming surfaces, modern furniture, tall windows, rooms as big as my entire apartment. I follow him to a guest room, complete with en suite bathroom. The shower I use would hold my entire bathroom. By the time I'm dressed and trussed and fluffed, I feel like Julia Roberts in *Pretty Woman,* minus the whole prostitution thing. An array of cosmetics, all new, waits for me to pick and choose. The whole setup leaves me baffled. Does he just keep all this, waiting for a woman? Is this his schtick? Then I figure, what do I care? I envision my dark apartment.

When I emerge into the hallway, he gasps. If there is a script for this movie, this moment in my life, it would have been written exactly as it played out. My heart hammers and my hands shake and I know in that instant, like the sappiest of romance movies, that this man will change my life.

At dinner, he is attentive. It's his dinner, I learn. He's the host. He barely pays attention to anyone else. *Do you need more water? More sorbet? Another glass of wine?* I laugh and wave him off. *You wanted me to woo you. So, I'm wooing you.* He hovers, this man, in his God-expensive suit and finely crafted leather shoes. His colleagues are curious, I imagine, about the defiant-looking girl with the pierced eyebrow and the spiky hair wearing an elegant dress. They are kind but dismissive. Henry doesn't tell them what I do for a living, that I'm practically hired help. His assistant is nice, in a self-serving way, as though he cast Henry as Daddy Warbucks and me as Annie, and maybe, just maybe, his good deed will make the paper. I catch his eye throughout the night, and he winks in a way I presume he means to be reassuring but does nothing to reassure me.

A woman in the group, blonde, coiffed, peaches-and-cream skin, simpers next to Henry. Her long red fingernails dance along his hairline as she shoots looks in my direction. He flirts back momentarily and then leans close to me, his breath curling around my ear: *Don't worry about Dianna. She's not nearly as attractive as she thinks she is.*

After dinner, there are speeches and some mingling, but Henry peppers me with questions, rarely leaving my side. A man has never been so goddamned interested in everything I have to say. We take his car home and he sits in the back with me but doesn't make a move. I can't tell if I'm impressed or disappointed.

He never flinches at my little run-down Hoboken neighborhood with the exposed fire escapes and barred windows. He walks me to the door with a chaste, gentle kiss on the lips, quick and soft as a feather.

His pursuit after that night is relentless. Hungry, primal. He can't stop thinking about me, he says. He whisks me away: Madrid, London, Los Angeles. I accompany him on business trips and each time he presents me with a new glittering gown. Strappy sandals. Five-carat diamond necklaces. Teardrop sapphire earrings. Everything he can offer, on display. The *Wheel of Fortune* with your host Henry Whittaker.

All this doggedness wears me out. I say this to him, "Henry, I can't be the woman you want me to be. Who will fit in your circles, go to your parties, be your arm candy. This is not a relationship that can *work*."

He says he's never loved anyone like this, so quickly, so intensely. He loves everything about me, he tells me. He comes to the flower shop sometimes, just to watch me work, late at night, working with a new bloom, willing new, thick stems to bend, not break. Trying to learn design, self-teaching, needing the elusive respect of Elisa. He takes home all my creations, successful or not, and sets them on his glass dining room table, prominently displayed at dinner parties. He calls me brilliant to his friends. Sometimes I think he's lost his mind. They surely think that, too.

Me with my hair spiked like, well, a bat orchid, and dyed just as black. With my facial piercings and my fishnet stockings and knee-high boots. With my too-short skirts and my dubious taste in music. My suspect circle of friends, acquaintances mostly, Lydia's friends. But most of them not so arrow straight, some who dabble in drugs. I've heard his colleagues say things, seen their looks. They smirk when they think I'm not looking—but I see it. I'm a dangerous hobby, an expensive yacht. I'm a midlife crisis. He's slumming and getting off on it. I see it, they see it. Henry doesn't. I tell him this and he just shakes his head.

"You don't know me. I've never followed a crowd in my life." So, he takes me. He takes all of it, never faltering. Absorbing Lydia's sarcasm and attitude, her jealousy, with a resonant laugh and twinkling blue eyes. That subtle dimple, that only appears when he's most amused. The way he pinches my chin. The way I can put on a show, all seductive kitten, and make him late for a meeting, a meeting he was running no less, just by using a whispered kiss of a voice. He rushes home, taking me in the hallway, unable to wait. He thought about it all day, he says.

I have no idea what to make of any of it. Slowly, I fall. I fall until I'm down at the bottom of the barrel so deep in love with those twinkling eyes and those dimples. I'm drunk on my own power and his power and his money and the world he holds, all for me. He offers it in one hand, without pretense, while holding his heart in the other. I want both, I take both. I let myself go, I stop pointing out that his friends and his colleagues laugh at me. I stop saying no. I stop protesting his indulgence, when he buys me clothing and shoes and jewelry. I stop looking for the catch. There doesn't seem to be one. So what do you do?

He rents out Brûlée, where we met, and fills it with flowers from Elisa's. In that back room, he gets down on one knee and delivers a speech that ends any doubt. He wants me for me, he claims. I don't believe it, but he repeats again and again: *You wanted me to woo you. So here I am.* It's all so hard to argue with. I say yes, crying and blubbering. Everyone wants to be loved for who they are, even if we keep our true selves locked up and hidden. It's a nice little fantasy to believe that the right person holds the key and all the things you do not say are just somehow, magically, known.

I justified it then: keeping Hilary a secret. I suppose I justify it now. It's been so long. I'm Zoe now, what does it matter? There are parts of my life I'd like to never think about again, even when it seems like all I do is actively avoid thinking about them. Evelyn, a barbaric burial. Rosie, abused, exploited. Those little pink nails, all those suburban moms, reaching for me, petting my hands. Wanting what I could offer, but never wanting me.

Then comes our wedding, small and private. His friends excluded, mostly because *I think* I'm not acceptable. He says no, insists it's a bad time of year. Everyone summers in the Hamptons. Our honeymoon. Lavish: a world tour. Two months, maybe longer. All love and sex and sharing ice cream, giggling, drinking champagne. My ship finally came in—at some point, Evelyn always said, everyone's does. We stroll the Gran Vía in Madrid, eat gelato, throw coins over our shoulders into the Trevi Fountain in Rome, spend hours in the modern art museum in Geneva. We spend months together, never tiring of each other. He hangs on my every word. Caters to my whims.

It's so easy to fall in love with Henry Whittaker: his easy smile, his lifestyle, his profligate praise and unabating interest, his strong, capable hands and the way they caress my body. He offers what I've been so desperate for: a root. He offers money, which I've never had; security, so long missing. He fills the gaps that Evelyn created when she left me alone at night in a tiny apartment, in a bad section of town, to go to work, or on a date, but either way, not there to soothe my fears, push the wet hair off my perspiring forehead at three a.m. when I'd heard gunshots or had yet another nightmare. He offers me love, a boundless amount of it, as though everything I say amuses him or entertains him and as though he understands *exactly* what I mean. We watch documentaries on National Geographic and I test him by saying ridiculous things like, *Do you think elephants are the communists of the animal kingdom?* He offers me recognition, where I'd often only felt isolation, trying on different identities: college girl, druggie, punk hipster. He offers me all this on a shiny, silver serving tray.

One might wonder, as I often did, what exactly could I offer Henry Whittaker?

CHAPTER 8

Lately, no matter what I am doing—going to CARE meetings, attending lunches—I find myself scanning the crowd for women who look like me: dark hair streaked naturally with mahogany and pale blue eyes the color of pool water. The sales clerk at Blush's Boutique has a lovely sprinkling of freckles across her cheeks, youthful for her age, in a recognizable pattern, and I study her until she shifts uncomfortably, averting her eyes and self-consciously patting her short, stiff hair back into place. Maybe she always called me *dear* for a reason.

I repeat *I am being ridiculous* like a mantra as I stomp around the apartment. But I can't help it. I'm restless and bored and can't shake the thoughts rattling around in my brain.

A large hall closet houses stacks of crates that contain remnants of our life before each other. I once asked Henry to show me his, his memories with Tara, his circle of friends—I saw once, quickly, some photos of beautiful people in tailored clothing on the back of a yacht, a picture-perfect ad for champagne or an investment firm. He always said *some other time*, with a casual shrug. The pictures were squirreled away. I've mostly given up.

In the back of this closet is my box. Singular. Pink-and-black striped, an old humongous hatbox holds all the remnants of my old self, and even my old-old self. I've been so many people I can barely keep track and this singular crazy-looking container is all I have to show for it. The top is dusty and I lift it, letting the bottom fall back onto my bed in protest. Inside is paperwork, old and new, yellowed and dog-eared. There isn't much, and most of it was kept for reasons I can't fathom. There's a cable bill from my old apartment with Lydia. Pictures of Lydia and me drinking martinis at clubs, hazy with smoke, laughing with men I don't recognize or remember. It's the spontaneity that calls me now. The idea of not knowing where my nights would take me, whose bed I would wake up in, when I would find my way home and how. That my life ever held so much easy adventure amazes me.

I have squirreled away an envelope that used to belong to Hilary. I was never supposed to keep it. I was advised to get rid of *everything* that could link me to my old identity by Detective Maslow, a kind but harried man with haphazard glasses and too long hair. He never looked like a violent crimes detective to me. He wasn't grizzled; he wasn't hard-boiled. He looked like an exhausted tax accountant.

In the beginning, his wife called once while I was in his office. I was under the impression she called often. At the time, I was terrified, living in a halfway house, no identity, no name to speak of. That murky middle time before I became Zoe. Hilary ceased to exist the moment I signed the affidavit, but deciding to become Zoe took some time. *We can protect you,* he said. I pressed my back against the chair—I remember it was leather, too rich for a city office, and cracked black—while Maslow sternly explained in detail all I would need to surrender, which was everything.

When he picked up the phone, he lowered his tone to a sniveling murmur with a series of *yes dears*. I realized Milton

Maslow didn't have the conviction to protect me. I wondered how many *me*s there were, how many men, women, children he had vowed to shield, sitting behind his desk, buried in the paperwork of forgotten identities. No thank you, very much. I'd manage on my own. I testified at the grand jury a mere ten days later. I packed in the middle of the night and I ran. I took the money they gave me, the money that was meant to start me off in witness protection, a mere thousand dollars. I bought a bus ticket with cash to New York, the only place I could think of where I could hide in plain sight. Plus it was as far away from California as a person could get. I left my dingy hotel room in the middle of the night and left Milton Maslow bumbling around in his office. I felt only a little bad, so I left him a note. *Thanks for everything. Bright lights, big city.* He could puzzle it out.

I pick up a thick manila envelope now and peel away the tape. I haven't looked inside it in at least five years. Inside is a single picture of Hilary, hair dyed with streaks of blonde, a big wide-open smile, a happy college girl. A California girl. I wonder who she would have become, if she hadn't become me? I can't deny it's complicated.

I sift through photos of Evelyn. Beautiful, nurturing, gentle. My memories of her are tinted pink and soft around the edges. Even the lean years. After she got sick and couldn't work and I wore jeans until my ankles stuck out. She thinned down to nothing, smaller than me, a child in an adult bed, but by then I'd turned eighteen. I studied her pictures. I'd saved three. One of her holding me as an infant, my father beaming behind her, the man who died before I could remember him, a slick road, a careening car, an ill-placed tree. I think. Hard to remember, I was so young when he died. All I have is Evelyn's voice telling whispered stories under the blankets with the lights off.

I was wanted, she said. I've never doubted it, which I

hear is a strange thing. I've read articles on the psychology of adoption and never connected with any of them. Evelyn's ovaries "dried up and plain stopped working," she told me, a predecessor to the ovarian cancer that would later take her life. But she'd twist her wrist with a tinkling laugh, "They call infertility a curse. Was the best thing that ever happened to us. We got you."

The second picture is Evelyn and me at the beach. I was maybe fourteen and we are hugging and smiling. I never went through that all too common phase, when teenagers hate their mothers. I could never imagine my life without her. Until, of course, I had to.

The third picture is after she got sick. Our last picture together, her head wrapped in one of her paisley scarves, her hair wispy fine underneath. She's grinning wildly into the camera, with her hands on my face. I'm not smiling, but studying her, like at any moment she might *poof* be gone, and I'd have only that moment to have memorized her face.

Evelyn lived her life in full force. She rejected all things mediocre, preferring only to spectacularly succeed or fail. She'd always said that she didn't quite do things right, but she didn't do them half-assed either, so when she failed, she did so *with enthusiasm.* Her advice to me, always, win or lose, do it enthusiastically.

I feel my eyes well up, and for the first time in a long time missing her fills me up, and I'm crying. I shove the pictures back in the envelope and ungracefully wipe my nose on my sleeve, which even *Henry's wife* can do when alone.

I thumb through the rest, quickly, until I find what I'm looking for. It's a yellowed copy of a birth certificate with the name of a hospital—Griffin Hospital, Derby, Connecticut—on the top. The father line is unsigned, a blank reminder that I belong to no one. The mother line, a haphazardly scrawled *Carolyn Seever.* The date is there, May 3, 1985. And my birth name is there. The first person I ever was before I became someone else. I run my finger along the raised letters. *Zoe Griffin*. Evelyn told me the nurses named me Zoe, after one of their favorite patients. Griffin came from the hospital name.

After my biological mother gave birth, she left me in the nursery. Sometimes I feel as though I am made up almost entirely of secrets, but the one that no other living soul knows is that I took my name back. Before there was Hilary, there was the baby Zoe, abandoned in a Connecticut hospital. After there was Hilary, there was a grown-up Zoe, living in an ivory tower. Sometimes I wonder how all three of us can possibly fit in this one body.

Haphazardly, I shove all the remaining papers back into the box and replace the lid. I hold on to the birth certificate and a folded-up memo from a defunct adoption agency that is fairly useless. The name on the birth certificate is a dead end, a false identity she'd left in a panic—I know this much from my last search effort.

I tip the box on its side and place it back in the corner, behind Henry's things. I see *Tara* scrawled in pen on the side of one of the crates and I can't help it, I lift the lid. I've seen it before, of course. But yet, I've never snooped. I don't know why I snoop now. Inside sits stacks of folders, insurance, trust account, taxes labeled with the year. I thumb through them quickly; it's all very dry. Underneath the folders is a frame and my heart skips. I've never seen a picture of her, isn't that odd? Not one single photo of Henry's wife, his precious *Tara*. I have no idea what she looks like, other than one drunken night when I had the nerve to ask Henry. He got this faraway look and murmured *beautiful*. I've been curious, and I grab it.

The photo is taken from behind; her head is turned. I can barely make out her profile. Her hair is loose in waves down her back, but covered with a wispy white veil. It is of their wedding day and the jealousy surges, this awful, clawing, clamping tightness in my throat. Her dress is fitted, she's impossibly thin, elegant in an ivory fishtail gown. I shove the frame back under the files. I back out of the closet, the bile in my throat. I push sideways the idea of being threatened by a swatch of bare spine and a mane of thick hair.

With the birth certificate and the adoption agency memo in one hand, I call Cash. He picks up before the phone even rings.

"Hi, it's Zoe. I was following up about the story? If you finished it?"

He pauses. "Yeah, mostly. I had a few other questions. Would you want to meet for lunch?"

I agree, but suggest a coffee shop closer to my apartment than his office. Neither one of us suggests the diner and the conversation is stilted. He asks if I'm okay.

I feign surprise. "I'm fine!" I say brightly. We agree to meet at noon. I check my watch and it's ten after ten.

I tuck paperwork into my purse, folded into a square small enough to fit in the pocket. I feel guilty, lying to Henry. Honestly, I'm not even sure what I'm doing yet. The lie feels good, fits like a well-made winter coat.

I step out into the sun and the air is brisk. It smells woodsy out, that faint promise of summer. I skip-step to the curb to hail a taxi and change my mind. I walk the six blocks and before I realize it, I turn west.

Henry works out every day at 11:30. Five miles on the treadmill, a hundred push-ups, a hundred sit-ups, exactly one hour, not including the shower. His gym is across the street from his office, and I stand in front of it, hopping from one foot to the other. I've never surprised him like this; Henry doesn't particularly care for surprises (his words, *I don't particularly care for surprises*).

Sometimes I think about the Henry who *wooed* me,

buoyant and boyish, and I remember that *he* liked surprises. I can't tell if I've been conned or if all relationships slow to the everyday, if marriages settle and become mundane at some point. To some extent, everyone puts on a show, their best foot forward, smiling at hobbies they hate, pretending to love football teams they couldn't care less about, or eating sushi and secretly spitting it into a napkin.

I hover in front of the door. I'm not even sure I can get in the building without a membership badge, which I don't have. He's never asked me to join him. I'm still trying to figure out why I'm here when a group of two men and two women barge through the doors, talking and laughing. I scoot behind them and let the mirrored doors close behind me.

The lobby is austere with mirrored walls, floors, ceilings, white and black countertops, and a single twenty-foot tree stretching up to the ceiling. I follow the group down the hall and skirt away before I reach the locker room. At the end of the hall is another entrance into one of the main gyms, and the last twenty feet of hallway is a one-way mirror, presumably for prospective clients to view the amenities without current members feeling put on display.

My mouth goes dry and I involuntarily place my hand against the wall, the heat from my fingertips leaving condensation prints against the cold glass. Henry is in there, his movements quick and smooth, his back muscles flexing with each up and down. Push-ups are last, he's close to done. If he makes a move toward the lobby or toward the locker room, I'll reveal myself as a pleasant surprise. Maybe blow Cash off and grab a middle of the week lunch with Henry.

He stands up and gulps water and I watch him lean in, whisper to a coltish blonde on the mat next to him. She throws her head back, as though he's said something hilarious, which I know could never be true because Henry is not funny. At least, not recently. But something about him is different to me: he's loose-jointed, almost swaggering, a hand poised cockily on one jutted hip. I lean forward until my nose is almost touching the glass. Henry cracks another joke and the blonde swats at his arm. He reaches out and pats her bottom, her round, perfect pink-spandexed bottom and hovers there, his fingers gently flexing on the rounded swell.

The heat flushes my face and I back away from the window. Men flirt, it's how it is. I still feel dizzy and I push the heel of my palm to my forehead.

With my head down, I scuttle through the lobby.

"Ma'am!" The receptionist calls but I flip my hand up in her direction and push out the front door. In the time I've been inside the club, cloud cover has rolled in, cloaking the sky in thick gray cotton. The cool breeze brings gooseflesh to my arms.

Henry wouldn't be unfaithful, I know that. Simple flirting, that's all it is. Men need their egos tended to, it's practically biological. I hush my panic with Henry's words. *He worships me.* Breathe in, breathe out. I wonder what he's said to her. He hasn't joked with me in a long time, or made me laugh like that. Like a protective reflex, my brain soothes me, hands me snapshots. Recent memories: Henry gently caressing my cheek at the benefit as we danced. His hands on my bare waist in bed, his low murmurs, *God, you're so beautiful.* These are not things men say and do to women they do not love. Passionately. *Passionately.* The word gets caught on my tongue.

I adjust my blouse and straighten my hair. I walk briskly, shaking loose the sick feeling in my stomach, the self-disgust. I've spied on my husband and been properly chastised. Dishonesty is rarely rewarding.

The coffee shop is two blocks away and when I blow in, bringing the newly cool air with me, Cash's head jerks up. He gives me a tentative smile as I slide into the chair across from him. We order two coffees.

"Hi Zoe. I wanted to call you. I, uh, wanted to see if you were okay? After the car thing?"

I shake my head and roll my eyes. I reach into my purse and pull out the folded paperwork. "I'm fine. Listen, I didn't really call you for the story. I want your help." I smooth out the creases in the birth certificate. "What do I do next?"

He picks it up in his thick fingers and flips it around, examining the watermark on the back.

"This is an original."

I shrug. That point is inconsequential to me.

"Well, they usually don't do that. They'll give out partials. Where'd you get this?"

I'm impatient. *Who cares?* "I don't know," I reply. "I just want to know what my next steps are. Where do I go next?"

He studies the memo. "You have a name, Zoe. *Carolyn Seever.*" His finger jabs into the paper.

"It's a fake name. It's worthless. I did all that legwork years ago. I just need to know what to do next."

"How do you know it's fake?"

"Because she doesn't exist. I even tracked down the receptionist from the agency and she confirmed her belief that she didn't leave her real name."

Cash looks out the window and runs his palm along his jawline. "Yeah, but think about it, when you give a fake name, especially under stress, you don't make something up out of the blue. This name," he says and taps the memo, "it means something. It could be the key."

"Okay, but if I didn't have the name? Then what?"

"Um, then you'd start by looking at all the babies born in that hospital on that day. Most likely if she gave birth in that hospital, she was local. I would start there. Most counties have a birth registry. It might give you the same name back, it might not. It would depend on where they pull their information."

"I don't know what that means."

"It means, let me help you."

"No."

"Why? I could do this in my sleep. You have more information than I've had to start with in the past. I could find her in a week, tops."

"Because, it's something I need to do myself."

"Why? That makes no sense, Zoe."

Because I'm not who you think I am. I'm not who anyone thinks I am.

"Just tell me what you would do," I insist. I tap my nails on my mug.

"It's so complicated. I'd do several things at once. I'd run all the births, like I said, then depending what returned, I'd study all the names and try to make a connection between the name the agency has and the names on the hospital lists. I'd expect a fake name at the hospital, too, unless she had insurance, which I doubt. I'd try to figure out the connection between the Connecticut hospital and the agency in California. I'd try to figure out why your adoptive mother ended up adopting a baby from Connecticut."

I feel overwhelmed. I want to toss the papers across the table and tell him to call me when he finds her. Instead, I gather everything, yanking the adoption memo from his hands, and shove it all back into my purse. Tears prick under my eyelids and I don't exactly know why.

"Oh, Zoe, come on. I'm sorry. You asked me!" Cash puts his hand on my arm and I pull it away. "Just stay for coffee, we can talk about the story. Don't go."

I hesitate, but stand up. "I'm sorry. I'll call you, okay?" When I turn to leave, I stumble over the chair and it crashes to the ground. I don't pick it up and hurry out the front door.

On the walk home, I feel so stupid. The entire day is eerily off-kilter, even the mood has changed again. The sky has darkened to a deep black and before I reach my apartment, fat drops of rain start to fall, a loud splattering sound that foreshadows an incoming downpour. I hurry past the doorman with only a brief wave.

I struggle with my card key, flipping it one way, then the other, before I can get the lock to disengage. I'm cursing at the door by the time I hear the release click. I push open the door and flick the hall light.

"Oh, my God," I say out loud, to no one.

The apartment is a disaster. End tables are upturned, drawers emptied on the carpet, broken glass everywhere. The brown velvet couch, with its intricately carved legs, has been violently ripped open, its cushions cut and the stuffing grotesquely exposed. I swallow the sick in the back of my throat.

Someone has come back for me.

CHAPTER 9

In the back of my closet is a soft-cornered shoe box and I'm relieved to see it's untouched. Underneath a pair of suede chocolate Mary Janes is a dog-eared business card with Detective Maslow's contact information. I dial the number and sit cross-legged on the bed.

When the other line picks up, I rush on, talking over the clipped, soft voice on the phone. "Hello, this is Zoe Whittaker. I mean, Swanson. Hilary Lawlor." And then I laugh because it sounds ridiculous.

"How can I help you?" The woman sounds like she's speaking through a tin can.

"I need to speak with Detective Maslow. It's an emergency."

"Are you in danger?"

"Not immediately, I don't think. My apartment has been broken into. But there's no one here now." My fingers are tapping on my knee; I can't seem to sit still.

"Hold, please." A hold line clicks on and I hear classical music, which strikes me as ironic. Anyone calling this line is dealing with a possible life-or-death situation. *Here, have some Chopin.* "Detective Maslow, you said?"

"Yes."

"Detective Maslow retired close to three years ago. Do you have a case number?"

"I do." I relay the seventeen-digit number back to her, written in Maslow's careful script on the back of the business card. Maslow. With his painfully thin frame and jutting cheekbones, but honest smile and appraising eyes.

She murmurs the numbers back to me and puts me on hold again. Pachelbel this time. I pace the length of the bed, sit, stand up again, walk the hallway, all while being careful to avoid the toppled boxes spilling from the closet.

"Ms. Lawlor?" She clicks back on the line. "What exactly are you looking for?"

"I need to know if Michael Flannery or Jared Pritchett is out on parole?"

There is silence and clacking while she types. "Ms. Lawlor? I don't see these names in here. What do you want this information for?"

"Five years ago, I testified against them in a grand jury. Then I was kidnapped and brutally beaten for information, which I did not have. Then I ran away, forgoing witness protection. Now, my apartment is broken into. Can you see why I might be concerned that one of these men are paroled?"

"I understand. I will work on sorting this out. I'll contact Maslow. In the meantime, I encourage you to contact your local police department regarding your break-in."

"That's it?" The abandonment feels like a heavy boulder on my breastbone and I can't breathe.

"Call us back after you talk to the police. Make sure to get the report number."

"The report number." I repeat dumbly. "Okay."

We hang up and I sink down onto the floor. I stare at the paper in my hand and know I won't call back. It was a risk in the first place. Then I panic, wondering if they'll trace my call. If Maslow will come out of retirement to find his missing witness. I stole their money. It's laughable, no one cares anymore. It occurs to me that I could probably find out what happened to Jared or Mick myself.

I call Henry. I don't call him at work often because he generally calls me several times a day. I'm surprised when he doesn't pick up. I get voicemail at his office and cell phone. I pick up the phone and stare at the numbers, trying to think of who else I can call. I think of Lydia and her *'Enry 'Iggins*.

There is no one.

· · ·

Our building has six doormen who rotate shifts, and I like all of them. Then again, it is their job to be liked by the occupants of the building. Today, Trey is on duty and I sigh with relief. Trey is youngish, with smooth coffee skin and a smile to swoon over, but he has the build of a bouncer at a rough nightclub. I would have felt a lot less safe with Peter, who I'm guessing is around eighty and looks like a strong wind might be the thing that kills him.

"Our apartment was broken into," I say, panicky, in Trey's direction and he looks at me disbelieving. I dial 9-1-1. I relay all my information and the woman on the line promises a police car in five minutes. I hear the quick *blirrrp* in less than two.

Two uniformed officers approach the revolving door. They appraise the building with raised eyebrows and whispers. I can't imagine they've ever covered a reported break-in here. I watch them scan the gold elevators, the inlaid mosaic tile. Their shoes squeak on the floor of the silent lobby. Trey wrinkles his nose with concern. A break-in on his watch may cost him his job. I lightly tap his arm and shake my head.

"Hi, I'm Zoe Whittaker." I extend my hand to the officer standing slightly in front, an athletic woman of about forty. Her dark hair is slicked back into a severe bun and her eyes are heavily rimmed with blue eyeliner. "Hi Ms. Whittaker. I'm Officer Yates and this is Officer Bernard."

The man standing behind her steps forward and we shake hands. I give them a quick rundown of what I found.

Officer Yates turns down the volume on her belt-clipped radio. "We need to ensure that no one is still upstairs, okay? Please stay here." She motions for Bernard to follow her and they both walk efficiently to the bank of elevators and punch the *up* button.

I turn to Trey, who is pacing along the bank of mailboxes. "Don't worry. This is not your fault."

"I've been here since seven a.m., Ms. Whittaker. I have not seen anyone suspicious or anyone I didn't know come in or leave."

I nod. "It's okay. It will be okay. I'm sure they'll want to talk to you. You might want to call Mr. Price." Mr. Price is the manager of the building.

Five minutes later, Yates returns alone. "The apartment is empty. Whoever did this seems long gone. Would you two mind coming down to the station and answering some questions?"

I nod, but Trey hesitates. "I'll need to call my supervisor and get a replacement before I can leave."

Yates nods and motions me outside and into the squad car. She opens the front door and I'm surprised. She gives me a wide smile, the edges of her mouth forming deep creases in her tanned cheeks. She has cartoonishly big features all competing for space: wide lips, large nose, thick lashes. "The backseat is for criminals," she explains, with a quick grin. I relax and I adjust the sleeves of my shirt, pulling it away from the dampness underneath my arms and on my back, above my bra strap. My mouth is dry.

"What about Officer Bernard?" My voice cracks and I clear my throat as I climb in the front seat. I pick imaginary lint off my linen pants and smooth the crease with my thumb.

"He's waiting for the forensics crew. We'll take some prints and we'll need either you or your husband to establish what's been taken."

"Oh, I have to try Henry again," I say dumbly, but when I call I am again sent to voicemail. I leave yet another message.

Yates chatters the entire four blocks to the station and, despite being in a squad car, I'm oddly relaxed. At the station, she pulls into a small underground garage that seems to house only marked police cars and leads me up a concrete walkway, dimly lit by sickly fluorescent bulbs, the walls painted a greenish-yellow. I can hear a low buzzing, the intermittent zap of a bug catcher. Inside, the station is a veritable hub of activity, police officers zipping this way and that, and I follow her to an interview room. On the way, she deftly grabs two Styrofoam cups of coffee and a handful of creamer and sugar packets. She gives the door a quick kick closed and indicates for me to sit with a jut of her chin. Her movements are quick and efficient. She places a burnt-smelling coffee in front of me and I thank her, knowing I won't drink it.

She opens a folder and clicks a pen, at the same time hitting record on a digital recorder. She studies me with open interest; her eyes are two different colors, one brown one yellow-gold.

"This should be quick, I think," she reassures me. "What time did you arrive home?"

"About one, I think."

"How long were you gone?"

"I'd left the house around ten thirty." I blow across the top of the black coffee, just for something to do.

"Okay, that's a good, narrow time frame." She writes something down in a notebook and chews a thumbnail. "Then what happened?"

I tell her about doing a quick inventory and returning to the lobby to call 9-1-1.

"Your husband is Henry Whittaker?" She gives a low whistle. I nod. I never know what to say when people are impressed by Henry, by virtue of who he is or what he has. *Thank you?* That seems proprietary, like I earned something. It might be easier if I was a guy, I could nod knowingly, maybe wiggle my eyebrows Groucho-style or lightly punch them on the arm. Women don't have a female version of "dude speak." Maybe I mistakenly imagine all men as over-grown teenage boys.

"Have you been able to get in touch with your husband?" Yates asks.

I shake my head. "Um, no. I tried. Twice."

"Okay, this is pretty much it. You can hang out here until we clear your place. It'll be another hour or so." She squares the folder in front of her and half-stands up, clicking stop on the recorder.

"Um, I have one thing. I feel like it's important." I take a deep breath and wipe my palm on the table top. I jostle the Styrofoam cup and coffee spills onto the table. Yates says nothing, but sits back down and opens her file. She clicks the recorder back on and waves her fingertips in my direction. *Go on.*

"I'm . . . God, I haven't told another person this, ever. In 2009, I testified against two men, Michael Flannery and Jared Pritchett, in a human-trafficking case in San Francisco. I was threatened and kidnapped. I left San Francisco, changed my name, and started over here. Could they have found me? Come back for me?"

Yates stares at me, unflinching. I know she's a New York City cop and has heard and seen it all. I still imagine she wasn't expecting *this* from a routine break-in.

"It's possible. Let's not jump to conclusions." Kindly, she

touches my hand. She has a long scar that runs along her jawline and I wonder what it's from. She holds my gaze and reaches over, hitting the off button on the recorder again.

"This." She runs her hand along her scar, turning her head slightly to the left so I can see it, glinting and silvery in the bright light. "Isn't from the job. It's from a man. A man who owned me and beat me, within inches of death until I ran away. I had to hide, too, for a while. Then, fuck it, I became a cop. I was the oldest one at the police academy."

"Where is he now?" I play with a small lock of hair, twirling it between my index and middle fingers and as I wait for her answer, I pull. Hard. My eyes tear.

"He's locked up now. Couldn't get him for what he did to me, but I got him for what he did to the next girl. Almost killed her. I have guilt about that."

I nod again. I feel tongue-tied around this weathered woman who wears all her scars on the outside. I'm jealous of her many physical reminders, the ones that tell the world she's a warrior. Sometimes, I forget who I am. I have one thin pink line on my right wrist to remind me.

She pushes away the file and folds her hands. Her nails are manicured bright red. She catches my stare and fans her fingers out for me to see. "I'm Not Really a Waitress."

I shake my head, confused.

"That's the name of the color. It's a . . . reminder." She winks at me. She takes one of those red manicured hands and touches my arm. "Tell me."

I know she's not talking about nail polish. I tell her. I tell her about San Francisco and Mick, and I find myself loosening, spilling long locked-up details. Jared twisting my arm behind my back, that glint of the gun in his coat. Things I thought I'd forgotten. The smell of Mick's aftershave, mingling with the tang of sweat. The sharp sting of betrayal from Mick, how I'd thought he was shady, a borderline abuser, but never really evil, until later, then I knew. I wondered how close Evelyn came to his circles, how involved he'd been when he'd known her. I said all this, and more, rambling and disordered. She nodded like she was following.

I told her how later, two men—Jared's lackeys, I assume— broke into Evelyn's apartment and, pressing a gun against the small of my back, threw me in a white utility van, the back stripped and separated from the front with a stainless steel cage. They cut my clothes off, tied my wrists and calves together with electrical cable. I tell her how they wound duct tape around my middle anchoring my wrists to my back. I tried to knee the larger of the two between the legs, and he brought his boot down on my forehead, quick and shockingly forceful.

I tell her how sometime around the three-day mark, near as I can figure, the smaller guy came back in the middle of the night, alone. He'd asked me, where are the girls? And no matter how I pleaded, he wouldn't believe I didn't know. I don't know how he thought that I had the resources to hide anyone. I was barely getting by. He was a bottom-feeder, scared and hung out to dry. I had shrugged. I was gagged. My seeming indifference enraged him and he pushed a gun against my temple, screaming in my face, *Tell me where the fuck they're hiding! I know she talked to you. You helped her.* But I couldn't. Before he got out, he kicked my foot so hard, he snapped my left ankle, clean in half. I could see the white knob of bone pushing out against my skin.

I studied the inside of the van, favoring my right side so my left ankle was supported. In the corner lay a child's white sock, the kind trimmed with white lace. A sock for church, or preschool graduation. Maybe Easter Sunday or Christmas Day. I was able to flip it over with the toe of my shoe, exposing a quarter-size bloodstain. I was tortured by images of a little girl, blonde and freckled. Pink-ribboned pigtails. Covered in blood.

When I began to lose my grip, my sanity sliding through my fingertips, I began to dream I was little again, going to church with Evelyn and her lady friends, bright lipstick and large hats. Sunday best. Lacey socks. Bloody feet. I'd wake up screaming.

I tell her how they left me there for five days—a time I couldn't discern and would learn later. They might have left me there forever, to rot in the back of an unidentified vehicle parked outside an abandoned construction site. Except I had figured out how to kick the metal floor in the right way to make a racket. Initially, I kicked for hours. Then later, I faded in and out of consciousness, waiting for the right moment, listening for a noise, straining my eyes against the crack in the van door, searching for any faint light. I heard the muted *whirp* of the siren before I saw the quick glint of headlights, and I hit my right heel against the gas tank, banging hollow and empty, again and again. My left ankle, flopping lifelessly. I don't remember it hurting. The headlights beaming in after they'd crowbarred the van doors open—that hurt. The noise, the sirens that came later, the ambulance, and inexplicably a fire truck—that hurt. My body did not. My body felt blissfully numb.

The whole time I talk, I rub the thin, pink scar on my wrist, from where the cable ties tore into my skin. I had seven stitches there to hold the flesh back together. It's barely visible. Lately, I find myself running the pad of my finger along the edge, a reminder of where I've ended up and maybe what I don't deserve.

I tell the entire story, which is something I've never done before. Not to Detective Maslow, not to the lawyers, or the cops, or later to a psychologist I saw a total of three times. Everyone knows bits and pieces of the story but no one has ever heard me tell it, all at once in a rush. I say it all, quickly but flatly, dispassionate, almost like it happened to someone else.

Which is true, when you think about it. It happened to Hilary.

CHAPTER 10

Yates promises that she'll be in touch and drops me off in front of my building. She touches my hand once, a tactile *thank you* and *don't worry* all at the same time, her crimson fingernails flittering.

I stand on the sidewalk, studying my apartment building with Hilary's eyes. The opulence, the gold and brass. Fear pricks at the back of my scalp and I scan up and down the street, expecting to see Mick or Jared Pritchett leaning languidly against the black stone of the building. Picking his teeth. Grinning like a Cheshire cat. *You're dead now, chatty girl.* His scarred face glinting in the afternoon sun. My brain is flinging memories at me, long buried. The curled snake around Mick's bicep. His nails, cut square and rimmed with black, fingers *tap tap tap* on his knees, his foot bobbing.

I haven't relived the kidnapping in years, maybe ever. I buried it, deep and inaccessible. Now, on the streets, the lights seem too bright, the cars seem too loud. I can't catch my breath and I feel shaky and weak. I think of Henry's face if I told him, how his eyebrows would protrude downward, his mouth slightly open in disbelief.

Peter is at the door, hunched over and white-haired. He gives me a sympathetic pat on the back. It seems everyone needs to touch me today, but in that quick funeral parlor way—taps and pats.

"There's a man inside the lobby waiting for you." He wheezes. My heart lurches into my throat and sticks there. He turns his head to the side. "He says he's from the *New York Post*? Might want to write about the break-in? Seems funny."

Cash. I blow out a breath and shake my fists loose. I need to get a grip. I hesitate in the vestibule and check my phone. No Henry.

Cash is hunched over, elbows resting on his knees on the plush sofa in the lobby, fiddling with his cell phone. At the click of my heels on the marble floor, he looks up and gives me a half wave.

"How do you know where I live?" I halt about ten feet from him and eye him suspiciously.

He half stands, fumbling with something on the sofa next to him and it falls to the floor between us. It's my wallet. He snatches it up, almost guiltily.

"You, uh, left this. When you ran out this morning." He extends his hand and rushes on. "I tried to call you a few times."

"I ignored them. I . . . I didn't recognize the number. It's been a . . . hectic day." I take the wallet and feel a stab of sympathy. He looks flustered and awkward, and he shoves one beefy fist in his pocket.

"So I also had an idea. About our conversation this morning?" His eyes slide over to Peter.

I hesitate. I don't want to discuss my adoption in the lobby. The apartment is still torn apart, likely streaked with fingerprint powder by now. I'm overwhelmed. At least Cash is a friend. Sort of. I sigh and motion him to follow me. We ride the elevator in silence and I'm self-conscious of the apartment. The flaunting wealth never bothered me before, but now as I slide the card across the top, I view the apartment through Cash's eyes. The custom designed flooring and rich paint hues, large, European antique furniture, fourteen-foot ceilings. The ransacked belongings.

I clear my throat, hang my coat in the hall closet.

"Holy shit! You've been robbed!" He pulls out his cell phone. "Here, I'll call 9-1-1—"

"No!" I wave my hand. "The apartment was broken into this morning. That's where I was all day. I'm sorry. I feel so . . . disconnected or something. I should have mentioned it in the elevator." I *do* feel disconnected. My reactions are out of whack.

I study the living room. The credenza has been emptied, its contents littering the carpet like a flea market. I bend down, pick up a pair of pewter candlesticks, and place them back in the cabinet I think they came from. It's such a small gesture, like taking a chip out of a block of ice. I shrug.

"Are you okay?" he asks, raising one arm to pat me and I involuntarily step back.

"I'm okay, let's sit in the kitchen. There was nothing done there." He follows me and takes a seat on the kitchen island. It's been so long since I've had a friend, I feel like I've lost the skill. If he was Lydia, would I cry? Would I ramble about being insecure and violated and scared? Would I tell him about Mick? I can't remember how to need someone. A year is a long time to be so emotionally self-reliant. I feel tired.

I open the fridge and pull out two water bottles. On second thought, I pull out a bottle of pinot grigio and uncork it. I tilt a wineglass in Cash's direction and he shakes his head no.

"Thanks for the water, though." He takes a long time to unscrew the cap and take a sip. I down my glass of wine and feel the heat behind my breastbone. My back relaxes almost immediately, that taut string between my shoulder blades, and the release tingle travels down my arms and into my fingertips. I flex my hands. I pour the second glass and take a deep swig. It's cold and acidic. Cash doesn't fill the silence, which I like. Neither does Henry. *Where the fuck is Henry?* And suddenly, I'm filled with anger. It's bubbling up, fighting its way up my esophagus against the river of wine, and before I know it, I'm crying. The kind of crying where you can't see and you can't stop. It's embarrassing, and I know that, but I can't do anything about it. I'm just so tired of always trying to "do something about it." The release feels good, if not vulnerable.

Cash half stands and I wave him down, blubbering and gasping like a fish out of water. I pull a paper towel off the roll and blow my nose in it, ungracefully. The whole outburst can't last more than a minute. When I'm done, I feel better. Cash looks worried.

"Honestly, Zoe, you don't seem okay."

"God, Cash, I can't explain it. I have *no one*. Not one person to call. To talk to. My ex–best friend thinks I'm pathetic. I have no family. My husband has chosen today of all days to be MIA. Do you have someone? Do you have people?"

He nods, slowly. "I have friends, yeah. My mom lives in Jersey. I have seven brothers and sisters."

"Seven! I can't even fucking imagine that!" I slam my hand down on the counter. Cash smiles. Dropping the f-bomb while wearing Chanel linen pants feels good.

"It was crazy growing up. We were all shoved in a three-bedroom duplex in Jersey City. I couldn't hear myself think half the time."

"I'm so tired of hearing myself think."

"That's why you want to find your biological mother?" Cash peels the label off his water bottle. He's a fidgeter, it makes me feel at ease, all his outward discomfort.

"Yeah, I guess? I just can't take this. I have no roots in the world. At all. It's disconcerting."

"You have Henry." He rolls the label around his thick index finger and avoids my eyes.

"Do you see Henry?" I throw it out there, even though I know it's irrational. But honestly, where the hell is the man? It would be nice to have another person to call.

"Zoe. I have to tell you. In that feature I wrote? Very rarely did the biological parents remain in the picture. In most cases, they had already moved on. They had new lives, new families."

"I know all that." I dismiss it, although I'm not entirely sure that I *do* know all that. "I can't explain it. I have no roots. I just want a root. I feel . . . untethered. If I just floated away, who would notice?" I don't mention that I've already done it once before, floated clear across the country and no one cared. Except maybe now, maybe now someone cares and they care enough to try to kill me. Or scare me. I'm still unsure, and the wine revolts in my stomach.

"Okay, well, I was thinking. Probably 60 percent of all domestic adoptions are in-state. But you said you were raised in California. Your birth certificate is from Connecticut. Of those 40 percent out of state, I'd guess that more than half of them were because the adoptive mother knew the biological mother. A cousin, or a sister, or something. So, those are decent odds. I'd start there. Try to find a link between your adoptive mother and the name on that memo."

The birth certificate and memo are shoved in my purse. The room is taking on a soft blur, the wine doing its job, and I feel hot and lazy and tired. So incredibly tired. I sink down onto one of the stools at the island and rest my temple on my hand. I want to sleep. I think about the living room with the ruined sofa and overturned end tables and I want to sleep for days. Which might be fine. Penny can clean up the mess.

The one thing about having no one is that no one expects anything from you.

"Will you help me?" I ask him, pathetically, running my index finger along the lip of the glass. It hums.

"I said I would help you. Give me all the information you have. I'll help you."

I reach over, clumsily grab at my purse, and hand him the crinkled paperwork. "Evelyn Lawlor. My adoptive mother's name was Evelyn Lawlor." Then, even softer, "I miss her." I've passed the point of loosening and am starting to feel unraveled, like no moment after this one will be the same. Like I won't be able to go back now and be the Zoe I used to be. Which makes me laugh, a gurgling, wet sound in the back of my throat. *Who is the Zoe I used to be?*

"Zoe, what the hell is going on?" Henry's voice booms above my thoughts, echoing in the austere kitchen. Cash and I both visibly jump.

Everything snaps to sharp focus. Henry stands in the kitchen doorway, his hands on his hips, his chin jutting. Out of the corner of my eye, I see Cash shove the paperwork into his back pocket. Cash's eyes go from Henry, to the bottle of wine, to me.

"Who the fuck are you?" Henry demands. "Did you do this to our home?"

"Henry! No! This is Cash Murray from the *New York Post*. He did the article on CARE. I met him this morning to go over the article and I left my wallet at the coffee shop. He returned it."

"Drinking wine with my wife?" Henry crosses the kitchen and swipes the half-empty bottle away, holding it away from me, like a snappy parent.

"Henry. Stop. You're embarrassing me. I was the only one drinking. See?" I point to the single wineglass. "I was rattled from the break-in."

"I'm sorry, Zoe, Mr. Whittaker, I should probably go." Cash stands up, wiping his hands on his jeans. Henry gives him the once-over, with a raised eyebrow and a small smile. I love how Cash calls him *Mr. Whittaker*.

Then, it's like a switch. Henry smiles. Cash hesitates, his mouth flickering up to return the smile, but dubiously. Henry crosses the room in two long lopes and extends his hand. Cash shakes it.

"I'm sorry, Cash, was it? Listen, please accept my apology. I've been rattled, my home is torn apart, my wife is drinking wine with a man I've never met, I've had a hellish day—" His smile widens and I wonder if his face will crack, split wide open. His eyes are steely in a way that maybe only I notice.

It fleetingly crosses my mind that *I've* had a much more "hellish day" than Henry, and I remember the way his hand cupped Pink Spandex. The hand that is now snaking possessively around my neck and across my shoulders, his fingertips massaging into my collarbone. It also occurs to me that he has yet to ask if I'm okay.

"I understand. I should go, anyway. I'm sorry that we had to meet under such unfortunate circumstances. It's nice to meet you, Mr. Whittaker."

"Please call me Henry. Let me walk you out." He claps a hand on Cash's shoulder and steers him toward the front door. "Were you at the CARE benefit, then? I'm sorry, there were so many people there that night." Their voices fade into the living room, then the hallway, until I can't hear them anymore. I marvel at Henry's *smoothness,* his voice is warm butter, but I shiver. I hear the front door latch open and shut and seconds later Henry appears in the doorway. His tie is still closely knotted and I think about how other men would pull it loose, unbutton that top button, sink into a chair, and get wrinkled. Henry never gets wrinkled. Even his boxers are starched.

"Are you sleeping with him?" His face is dark, his eyes look black in the fading kitchen light.

"What?" The question throws me off guard. "No. Are you sleeping with a girl at the gym?"

He advances toward me, his fists clenching and unclenching. He reaches up, his warm hands pushing hard against my shoulders. "Don't play games, Zoe. What is going on?"

I'm tired. "Nothing, Henry. Nothing is going on." I break free of his grasp and hold his gaze, backing up against the sink. Trying for casual.

"Cash is just a reporter?"

"Yes."

"Is he the reporter who saved your life? With the car?"

"Yes."

"What was he doing here?"

"Trying to get more information about CARE. He's building it into a full feature." The lie is effortless. If nothing else, hiding has made me slippery, adept at lying and quick on my feet. Sometimes it unsettles me, but today I am thankful. As the words leave my mouth, I realize I've just made the decision not to tell Henry about finding my mother. It is unplanned.

Henry scrutinizes me, his eyes narrow. "Does it occur to you that Cash was there when you almost got run over by a car. And he was here today, when the apartment was broken into. Does this strike you as odd?"

"No. It doesn't," I snap. He says nothing back.

We're locked in a staring contest, he and I. He's not asked me about my "girl at the gym" comment, and I can't figure out why.

His shoulders slump and he cocks his head. "Zo, please. Let's stop attacking each other. I'm sorry for being out of touch today. Are you okay? How did all this happen? You didn't see anyone, did you?"

He reaches over and thumbs my cheek. His hand feels warm, inviting. I close my eyes, try to forget the spandex girl, his rage at seeing Cash, his reaction to me, his almost-palpable hatred. I want to forget it, but I can't.

"Henry, you haven't even asked until *right now* if I'm okay. Where the hell have you been?"

"I'm sorry, Zoe." He pulls me into an embrace and I breathe in his fresh-laundry, lemony Henry-ness and I remember that I love him. "I've been in a lockdown meeting, no one in, no one out. Those things are brutal. We were in there for almost four hours."

I look at the clock. It is close to four. It was *possible*. With very tight timing. I don't know what to think.

"Can you call Penny? See if she can get a crew in here to clean up? I can't do this, Henry." I can do it, of course. When I lived in Hoboken I cleaned a rich couple's house every week. I'm not opposed to housework—in some cases, I revel in it. I just don't want to. Let Henry spend his money, it comes so easily to him. I wonder if Henry knows I used to be a housekeeper. I wonder if he remembers Evelyn was basically a version of Penny. I can't remember what I've told him.

"Of course. Of course. God, what if you had come home early?" He pulls me against his chest. "This is the second time in a week I could have lost you."

"I'm sure that's overstating it." I turn my face to the side and return his hug, one-armed. Halfhearted.

"Let's go away. We can ride to Pennsylvania tomorrow. Get out of town, I'll call in to my meetings tomorrow. We'll open up the country house."

The country house. Henry's four-bedroom "cabin" in the small town of Fishing Lake, Pennsylvania. It's a family home, owned by his parents and passed down. He grew up there, I think. I've only been there once, one fleeting weekend, in mosquito-laden July. All I remember is oppressive heat.

"Henry, I don't know. Officer Yates might find something or need something . . ."

"Then we'll come back. It's only an hour and a half. Zoe, I'm worried about you. First the car, now this. I want to keep you safe."

All I hear is *I want to keep you.*

I could fight him. I could. I would win. Henry doesn't forbid me from anything ever. But I think back to what I'd said to Cash. *I feel untethered.* Because the truth is, the only person I have in the world is Henry. He is my root.

Slowly, I nod. "I'll go pack."

CHAPTER 11

The city recedes behind a curtain of fog while Henry's fingers tap the steering wheel to the Rolling Stones. His arms are bare in a navy blue polo shirt tucked in to khaki shorts. He whistles along with the radio and every few minutes glances over and gives me a smile.

This is the Henry I fall in love with, again and again. He is relaxed, in his arrowroot Henry way. His blond hair is "vacation" messy. The day is warm for April and smells of summer, wet pavement, and popcorn, like a state fair. We have the windows cracked and I am happy. Well, I am mostly happy. I have the previous evening's fight in my mind and I can't turn it over. I keep thinking about Henry's hands pushing down on my shoulders, his cold glare at Cash. His quick about-face.

I tried to say something later, in bed, telling him he worried me. He curled against my back murmuring apologies. His hands snaked up my midsection to cup my breast and I shrugged him off, blaming fatigue from the day. He pulled me against him until I felt like I could suffocate, his breath wet on my neck, my ear, and whispered "poor baby" again and again. I fell asleep, a deep dreamless coma, while he was still awake.

Now in the car, his fingers tapping to the radio, his lips moving to the words, basking in the glow of his carefreeness, I close my eyes and breathe. The day is overcast and gray, and in front of us is open New Jersey countryside, rolling green hills and yellow wheat fields.

"Penny will be taking care of the apartment," Henry says mildly, as though all Penny had to do is water the plants.

In the light of day, my fear about Jared being the burglar seems melodramatic, even silly. I gaze out the window, analyzing this. I've had two strange occurrences in less than a week. The car, which may or may not have been intended for me at all. A speeding car running through an intersection toward a crowd of people didn't imply any intent, when you think about it. The crowd around me was maybe seven other people, including Cash. Who's to say that one of them wasn't the target, if in fact it was deliberate at all? I cling to the careless driver/late for an appointment theory. The break-in seemed a clear signal until Henry drew up a list of missing items, including several expensive diamonds and several thousand dollars in cash. The safe had been impenetrable, but given the scratch marks around the dial and latch, it wasn't for lack of trying.

The police found no sign of forced entry. The investigation is ongoing, they tell me, but they say precious little. They asked if anyone had a key to the apartment and Henry said no until I jostled him with my elbow, hissing *Penny* under my breath. He corrected himself, "Oh yes, Penny does. She's harmless, though." Trey swore he'd been watching the door, had taken no breaks within the time frame, and to his knowledge, there were no visitors to tenants. Henry grumbled at this, rolling his eyes. "Of course someone got in *somehow*. But he's saying what he needs to say to protect his job."

But now, sitting in the driver's seat, his left knee bopping to the softly playing radio, he looks ten years younger. I can't figure out why we don't do this more often. The house sits vacant for months at a time. Henry has gone up a few times in the past year, hunting, he says. *Alone?* I'd asked him once. I always pictured hunting retreats to be for groups of men. Men unlike Henry, with burly beards and large bellies. Men who drink Miller Lite and wear camouflage, fingers orange with cheese ball crumbs. Henry laughed at me. "There are lots of kinds of hunting, that's for deer."

"Well, what do you hunt?" I pressed. I mean, it was incredible that I didn't already know.

"Rabbits. Pheasant. Sometimes fox."

"Fox? I thought that was with the dogs and the horses and only done in nineteenth-century England?" I pictured bugles and plaid vests.

"No, you can hunt foxes without dogs and horses, Zoe. That's the sport. The basic hunting uses a fox whistle."

"So you have guns? At the cabin?" I felt incredibly dumb.

"Yes, Zoe, I have guns." He rolled his eyes at me and rubbed his forehead. He hated my *interview mode,* firing questions at him like a journalist. "Besides, in Fishing Lake, everyone hunts."

"What do you do with a fox? Can you eat it?" I wondered if Penny had cooked us fox one night, pink gamey slices laid glistening over a bed of radicchio. I shuddered.

"You can't eat fox meat. I sell the pelt sometimes."

"You what?" I waved my hand. "Never mind."

New Jersey fades effortlessly into Pennsylvania and we drive through a small town on an isolated road until even the houses dwindle down to one or two per mile. At the top of an isolated hill, looking down onto the farmland below, sits Henry's country house. It's hardly a cabin. A stone farmhouse set a quarter mile back from the road, shrouded by enormous pines. Henry has his own forest.

He empties the trunk, dragging two Rimowa suitcases behind him on the gravel driveway. I follow him inside the house, which smells like wood and must. He runs around, opening all the windows, the breeze lifting the curtains, bringing with it the scent of lilacs. The living room is sparsely decorated, wide plank floors and brightly colored woven rugs, canvas sofas and original local artwork. Simple but expensive. Surfaces gleam and windows shine. I want to ask if Penny has been here, but I don't.

I follow him up the wooden steps to our room. Through the screened windows I can hear birds and the soft distant whirr of a lawn mower, but not one car. I get up and cross the room, part the white, gauzy curtains. As far as I can see, it's green and brown rolling hills. My city heart pumps for action, for movement. In the distance, all I can see is the soft sway of soy and wheat. I exhale and try to relax, but all I feel is edgy and unsettled.

"Are you relaxed?" Henry wraps his arms around my waist from behind, his voice a low rumble in my ear. I nod in half agreement. "For dinner, we'll get something from the store down the road. Venison or duck?"

I shrug, I don't have any preference. Henry is energized by the sweet, lilting breeze. He bounces on the balls of his feet. His hands rub across my back, between my shoulder blades and work their way down.

I inch myself out of his grasp and give him a too bright smile. I owe him this. I feel guilty for not accepting this house, this countryside escape, as the gift he means it to be. Of everything he can offer me, I should be grateful, but I'm not. I'm edgy and unsettled and I watch Henry's arm flexing under his shirt and try to take deep quiet breaths. Henry's need to paint last night with a rosy brush and make it all perfect is suffocating.

"I think I'm going for a walk."

"A walk?" His mouth opens and closes, like a fish around a hook.

"Isn't that what country folk do? They walk. And knit? Something like that," I murmur with a flick of my wrist. I'm being deliberately dismissive and his eyes cloud with confusion. Before he can stop me, I wave gaily and head down the steps, my feet clattering on the wood.

Outside, I should be able to breathe again, but I can't. My lungs feel like they are going to burst. I'd be the first person to suffocate in open air, choked to death by the stench of cow manure.

I remember our very first fight, after our wedding, when Henry started to change from suitor to husband, that elastic period when my head was still spinning. We'd been to a party, they all blended together but this one was for a colleague's retirement. They had sickly sweet cocktails with a deceptive amount of alcohol and I drank until the room spun. The night blurred together until I couldn't be sure in retrospect what was sequential. I got caught in a conversation with a man and a woman, the woman, blonde and beautiful in a short black silk dress, her hair carelessly piled up in a sexy bun, her makeup an ad for "barely there." I felt overdressed and overly made up, in my sequined green gown and crystal heels. She laughed and touched my shoulder, called me a member of Henry's Harem, unaware that we were married, despite the large rings—plural—on my finger. With a thick tongue, I kept trying to insert my status, *my husband, have you seen him?* Henry had disappeared for hours, lost in the throng.

She linked arms with me, her name was Cynthia, she'd said, and guided me to the bathroom. While I listened to her tell me, mean and incisive, through the stall divider all the ways I would never be one of them, I pressed my cheek against the cold marble of the stall door. She left me in the bathroom, where I vomited up the rest of the cocktails.

Later I found the man we'd been talking to, his name was Reid, Henry's junior assistant. Baby-faced and kind, he was a sucker for mascara-streaked faces. He got me water, helped me look for Henry.

He found Henry smoking a cigar at the bar, the center of a circle of men I hadn't met. Henry gave me a chilly smile and didn't invite me in, didn't pull me into the group, introduce me. He left me on the outside and, with calm precision, he turned his back. That was the first time I'd seen what being on the outside of Henry's circles could do. Every cruel word that Cynthia had uttered through that stall door had been rubber-stamped by Henry himself.

I left alone. Took a cab back to our apartment and fell asleep on the couch. Henry came home, turned on every light in the place. I tried to tell him about Cynthia. About how I looked for him for what felt like hours and he waited, very still, for me to finish. Then he smiled. "The next time you want to spend the night flirting with a man half my age, you won't be welcome back here."

The next day, we flew to Musha Cay. A suitcase full of clothes I'd never seen before, complete with string bikinis and linen skirts. Tropical drinks and expansive, private beaches. Nude sunbathing. Long days on white, gleaming yachts full of people I didn't know. It took four days for me to forget the blackness of his eyes. Four days of tropical bouquets and fresh island fruit delivered in bed. Four days for the heat of his mouth on my body to replace the chill of his smile, as he showed me the life he would give me. All for the small price of forgiveness.

The "corner" store is a mile away and the walk feels good—it slows my thumping heart.

When I push open the door to the store, a bell tinkles overhead. The cashier is round and in her late thirties, perched on a backless stool, reading a year-old *People* magazine. At the sound of the bell, she drops the magazine and gives me a motherly smile.

"Well, hello!"

"Hi." I'm not used to friendliness; it feels invasive. "I'm looking for venison steaks."

"Oh, sure! Are you new in town?"

"My husband has a vacation house up on the hill. We're from Manhattan."

"Oh. The city." She says it like it's a filthy word, *a cuss word*. "I'm Trisha. I've owned the shop ever since my brother, Butch, died, oh's about ten years ago now. He had a bad heart, got it from his daddy." She flips up the Formica countertop and shimmies behind me to the deli counter. "Funny, right, that he was called Butch? That was his name long before he became a butcher. Now it's just me, sometimes Sheena, she's my cousin, but mostly it's me. I'm a cashier, a butcher, a cook, and a housekeeper. I don't do too bad, though, ya think?" I shake my head, taken aback by the sheer number of words she's been able to get out in such a short amount of time. Her voice is sweet, bubbling over the *house* in *housekeeper*. She dons an apron and a pair of gloves and hustles into the back room. The heavy wooden door swings shut behind her. When she reappears, she's holding two purple-red, thick slabs on brown butcher paper and her eyes are gleaming.

"Don't they look beautiful?" She means it, too, and this baffles me. I'm not the kind of person who would ever describe raw meat as beautiful. I nod and try to look impressed. She wraps it up, ties it with string, and weighs it.

I like Trisha. I mean, honestly, you can't help but like Trisha.

She brings the steaks to the counter. "Do you need anything else? Some salad? Greens?"

"Do you have wine?" I ask hopefully. I have no idea what Henry keeps in his house.

"We can't sell it, darling, but I'm never without it." She

holds up a finger and scurries into the rear room, through that swinging wooden door again. When she returns she's holding a bottle of rosé, with a plain white label *Table Red.* Henry will die, he's actually going to die. She must see my face because her cheeks flush, round and pink, and she falters. "Oh, I know it's not what you're used to but—"

"No, it's completely fine. I will love it. Who doesn't love rosé?" I give her a wide, friendly smile. "You know, I do need more than just steaks. What else should I make for dinner?"

She busies herself behind the deli counter, rationing out couscous salad and some simple grilled vegetables: mushrooms, peppers, and onions. My mouth waters.

"I think you have the makings of a wonderfully romantic meal for two." Her apple-cheeked smile is back, *resilient Trisha.* You can tell she bounces. "Where's your house, darlin'?"

I tell her. Her eyes light up.

"I know that place! I walk there every day, usually 'bout six or so. Gotta lose these last twenty pounds. God, my baby is thirteen and you'd think I would have done something about it by now."

I nod, averting my eyes from her sloping breasts and full belly. She rubs one chubby hand over her midsection and stands up straight. She rings me up. "Twenty-three ninety-two."

"This would cost double in the city," I say with a sly wink. She taps my hand.

"You're funny." She writes something in a journal next to the cash register, her bright pink nails clicking against the metal spiral binding. On impulse, I want to invite her to eat with us. Henry would kill me; he likes neither impulse nor dinner guests.

I open my wallet to pay the tab, and the heat crawls up the back of my neck, flushing my face. My credit card is gone.

• • •

"That reporter, he returned your wallet, yes?"

We have finished eating, one remaining small sliver of venison on a ceramic platter between us. The pine farmhouse table is littered with supper castoffs: half-empty wine and whiskey glasses, crumpled linen napkins. The dining room is dimly lit by flickering tapers and I am sleepy drunk. I have all but forgotten the missing credit card and I blink twice instead of answering him.

When I arrived home Henry called the bank immediately, shrugging it off with only a nebulous murmur of admonishment. When he hung up, he rubbed my back, between my shoulder blades. "You probably just left it at the diner. I'll leave you cash." He patted my head. Instead of being grateful, I swatted Henry's hand away. It was all so patronizing.

It's a blessing and a curse, having someone like Henry. On one hand, I could sit and drink a glass of wine, let him sweep in on his white horse, wave his giant hands, and fix it all with his booming voice. Take his cash, tuck it into the satin folds of my purse with a demure smile, as though I were a kept woman. On the other hand, lately, I'm tired of simply letting things happen.

"Cash? Yes, he brought it back." I cross and uncross my legs.

"Interesting." Henry taps his fork against his plate, a quiet *ting* in the silent room. The silence up here, hovering on the top of this mountain, kills me.

"You think he took it?" I'm incredulous. That had never crossed my mind.

Henry shrugs. "I'd have no idea, Zoe. We don't know the man."

"Well, I know him a little. He doesn't seem like a thief. He's a reporter."

"Ah yes, an honorable bunch." He pulls his mouth down into an ironic frown that also seems almost like a grin. "It's just something to think about, that's all. That man, he's around a lot when all these . . . things seem to be happening."

The bottle of table red has worked a number on me. I've drunk the bottle alone while Henry nursed a glass of Pomerol he brought up from the cellar. Henry leans back in his chair, his lips lifted at the corners. His hair uncharacteristically mussed, flopping down over one eye. He looks boyish. Henry never looks boyish.

He holds up one finger, like he's forgotten something. He pushes himself up and comes around to my side of the table. He perches one leg up, smoothly sliding my dinner plate to the side. From his pants pocket, he retrieves a small velvet box and sets it gently in front of me with a wry smile. On top of the box sits a small card, no envelope. I flip it open.

As you are woman, so be lovely:
As you are lovely, so be various,
Merciful as constant, constant as various.
So be mine, as I yours for ever.

"Henry." I can't stop the smile, it's all so unlike him. "Poetry? Did you write this?"

"Of course not. It's part of a Robert Graves poem. I've always loved it."

He touches his finger to his lips, his thumb poised under his chin, and gives me a look of reflection. I open the lid and nestled inside the pink velvet folds is a bracelet. The chain is intricately braided yellow and white gold and it sparkles in the candlelight. At first blush, I think it is a charm bracelet, which seems uncharacteristically trendy of Henry, and I give him a questioning look. The chain threads through three beads. I unclasp the hooks on either end and delicately hold the jewelry in my palm.

"It's pretty," I say, feeling like I probably don't understand the significance. I'm not lying, it *is* pretty. It's just not Henry's style: too simple, too trendy. It's more *my* style. Then again, Henry is often thoughtful in ways I am not.

I study the beads. The first one is engraved with a small, squat tree, its branches reaching up and wrapping around the gold. The etching is delicate and fine, and the detail takes my breath away. The second bead is carved with a simple flower, what looks to be a gladiolus. The third bead contains a set of wings, each feather intricately scored.

"Very beautiful." I nod my head, as though I understand it.

Henry watches me with amusement, his eyes crinkling at the corners. "Oh stop. I'm not fooled. I can read you, you know."

"Well then explain it." I laugh.

He fastens the bracelet around my wrist, his hair tickles my cheek. "I had these made. The tree is because you give me roots. I want to do the same for you. The tree is actually a bonsai. The Japanese believe that when left in nature the bonsai grows wild and unruly and ugly. That only when carefully cultivated by people is it beautiful."

"Am I the bonsai?" I have always felt like Henry's pet project, to some extent Lydia wasn't far off. I've been groomed to fit into his life, among his friends and colleagues.

He laughs and kisses my nose. "I am the bonsai, Zoe. Without you, I am an angry, singly driven man. A man with one purpose. I become one of those loveless rich men. I become Krable."

I lean back and study Henry as he speaks. It's surprising how well vulnerability suits him. It's the sexiest thing he's ever worn.

"Go on." I tilt my head.

"The wings are easier to explain." He touches the bead on the end, his thumb massages my palm. "I'm sorry. I have no desire to hold you back. I fell in love with your grit. These past few months I've been afraid of losing you. I've clipped you too much and I'm sorry."

"We're both . . . damaged." I run my index fingernail over the veins in the top of his hand, his smooth large-knuckled hands. I love his hands.

He clears his throat and holds the center bead between his thumb and index finger, his hands cool on my wrist. "The middle bead is a gladiolus."

"The flower of infatuation." My voice hitches.

"Yes, technically 'love at first sight.' Which is us, don't you think?" He stands up, tugs on my hands until I stand with him. "It's also a symbol of character and strength. It reminded me of you." He steps back, rubs his forehead and gives me a sideways smile.

"It's beautiful, Henry." Which is clichéd and stupid but I'm speechless.

"I want you to go back to the flower shop. I'm saying it's okay." He tugs on my hand, leading me away from the table, through the living room, and up the wood steps. I follow him, swaying slightly, tilting my wrist in the moonlit living room to get a closer look at the bracelet. I can't believe he'd thought of all that, and I have no idea when he'd had it made. It means more to me than all the diamonds and rubies in our safe.

Without warning, the want creeps up on me. I gently push on the small of his back, down the hall and into our bedroom, where I shove him, wanton and drunk, onto the bed. We pull at each other's clothes, and I am laughing. The room spins, and the next morning when I try to remember the moment, all I can see is Henry's smile, the love reflected in his blue eyes, and the overwhelming feeling that, here in this secluded country, despite all his flaws and our imperfections, where I know not another soul, I am home.

CHAPTER 12

On Saturday, I'm up at six, brewing coffee in a stainless steel percolator, standing at the gas stove, watching coffee gurgle and spit into the glass top. I can't sleep. In our penthouse apartment, we hear very little street noise, so I can't figure out the difference. But I had lain in bed, my leg jittering, shifting one way, then the other, before I finally snuck out and downstairs.

Arms snake around my middle and I jump. "You scared me." I smile, my head tipped down, and Henry plants a feather kiss on the back of my neck.

"Ah, sorry," he whispers in the dark kitchen. "Don't be mad, but I have to drive back for a few hours."

"Today?" I step forward, putting distance between us.

"I'm sorry. It's going to be overcast, but not rainy. You could hike out back, there are trails. They're not all ours, but no one cares. Just don't get killed by a hunter."

"What season is it?" I wonder.

He rubs his jaw. "Spring turkey maybe? I'm not sure. I generally hunt in the fall. Spring is too busy with work."

I don't understand Henry's work or his hunting. It's completely possible, likely even, that I don't understand Henry. I pour us two cups of coffee in pottery mugs, but as I turn to retrieve the cream and sugar (for mine only, Henry drinks his coffee black), Henry's eyebrows pucker, his mouth twisting apologetically.

"You have to go now," I say, flat as stone, and sigh. I pick up his mug and pour the coffee into the carafe. He drops a kiss on my lips and lingers there, his hand pressed between my shoulder blades.

"Don't pout. I'll be back right after lunch. I just have to address some unexpected . . . issues."

"Issues with what?" I'm curious now. What are the issues on a Saturday if you work on Wall Street?

"Zoe, do you know how boring my job is?"

"No, tell me. Put me back to sleep, and I'll sleep till you come back."

He laughs and the sound swallows me. I love it and miss it all at once. "Okay, fine. So Japan's market is not actually closed on Saturday, and we have a security issue with the agency bonds."

"Okay, okay. I feel like you just made all that up. Go." I give his arm a gentle shove and he laughs again. I think it's possible that this house, this town, has let out a new Henry, like he's been unzipped. I picture him stepping out of his own skin, clapping his hands together, looking around. *Okay, what do we do first? Fish? Hunt? Hike?*

He kisses his fingertips and touches them to the crown of my head and I hear his shoes clack on the hardwood floor and the door click shut, and *just like that* I'm alone. I'm not necessarily afraid, but I have a pit settled right under my breastbone. I'm at loose ends. It's hard to have a whole day in front of you and nothing to put in it, nothing to pencil in, no phone calls to make. I have this feeling often but generally I can fill my time by going out, taking in Manhattan. In New

York, you're never bored. I look at the clock above the sink. Six-thirty.

I part the curtains. *Out* leads to a forest in the back and a copse of trees in the front, then a quarter mile away, a road. I take my mug and from the back of the easy chair in the living room, I grab a sweater that I assume must be Henry's but I don't recognize it. It's heavy and cable knit, its sleeves are long, with big wooden buttons. I wrap it around myself tightly and open the back door.

The deck is wide and spans the back of the house, looking out to a sea of black and green. In the corner is a single rocker, made of rough-hewn logs, a deliberate attempt to look woodsy. I curl into it, bring my knees to my chest and cup my coffee. It's cold for April, I doubt today will be a day for exploring the outdoors. It smells like wet pine.

I'm reminded of Lake Tahoe. Evelyn had nabbed a cabin once, a gift from a friend. She had a million gifts from friends. She didn't have any money, but always said she had a lot of friends, and some of those friends had money. She'd come home with steaks that she'd gotten as a gift, or wine she "found." All trinkets that people gave her, she claimed. She'd explain it away with a wave of her hand, and a soft tinkling laugh. *You can get anything you want if you're nice to people. People like to do things for people, it's so easy to be kind.* She dragged me to Tahoe, where the rich vacation, she'd said. *We'll be queens for a week!* My seventeen-year-old heart had nearly broken at the idea of a week without television and very little phone communication. I dragged my feet, I huffed and puffed, *whatever*-ing my way through half the trip. Sneaking calls to friends when Evelyn wasn't looking.

Evelyn never faltered, her grin bright, coral lipstick smudged on her two front teeth when she smiled, which was all the time. It's easy to glorify the dead and say things like that: Oh, they glowed, they were always happy. With Evelyn, it was true. Any attitude I threw at her that week, it's like she caught it all with Jergens-soft hands and never stumbled.

She unmoored the boat, a ramshackle rowboat that I insisted would sink (*So what,* she'd scoffed. *We can swim, right?*) and paddled us out into the middle of the lake with one oar, one side, then the other. Her cheeks had grown bright red and I thought she might pass out. I'd rolled my eyes and took the paddle from her, *Don't die, Ev.* And her arms had looked so thin. It was the first time I'd realized she'd grown so incredibly tiny.

"God, Evelyn, you're a stick. Eat a sandwich or something." I knew I was being mean, but it would be so embarrassing to have an anorexic mother, like one of the fainting cheerleaders at school. She leaned over the side of the boat and swatted a handful of water at me. I took the oar and with a sweeping motion, drenched her. She laughed, but it sounded like it came from inside a barrel.

She looked away and when she looked back, she bared her teeth. "Do I have lipstick?" For the first time, she didn't. We'd made it back to the cabin, where we blasted Billie Holiday and simmered vodka sauce, and she let me drink wine until the edges of the room blurred. She got me to talk about boys, or who I thought were men at the time. *Don't be afraid of sex. Be afraid of love, but not sex. Love can swallow you whole, consume you, change you, but sex? Sex is just for a night.* And I had no idea what she meant.

Later, I heard her on the phone in her room. I stood in the hallway of that cabin and I swore she was crying. I pushed against her bedroom door but couldn't hear the words.

She was sick then, and it was only after she'd died that I realized she'd known it.

A thought nags at me, one I'd asked Mick, filled with hate and anger. If she had so many friends, where were they? When she died, where'd they go? No one called. No one offered to pay for a simple cremation. I'd stayed in her apartment for weeks after her death, that foggy milky time before I ran, but never once did the phone ring unless a bill collector was on the other end. I search my memory for who Evelyn said was the cabin's rightful owner and come up empty.

The sky has lightened to a dove gray and the rain mists all around, not falling in drops from the sky, but like it's raining from the bottom up. My coffee cup is empty and I'm cold. I venture inside and look at the clock. It's not even nine. I wander upstairs halfheartedly, to find my book buried under sweaters and jeans in my overnight bag. All the doors in the hall are closed and I nudge open the one next to our bedroom. The bed in the center is made simply and a hand-stitched brightly colored patchwork quilt adorns the bed. The pillows are made from old jeans pockets and the walls are adorned with red wooden stars, an upmarket Americana theme. I am sure of two things: Penny decorated this room, not Henry. And nothing has changed since Tara died. Upon closer inspection, the bureau top contains bottles of women's perfume, turned yellow in the sun. The nightstand holds a mystery book with page 137 folded down at the corner. There are blue peep-toe bedroom slippers (Chanel makes bedroom slippers?) peeking out from under the bed. She could have been here yesterday. Then there is the dawning realization that there's not the slightest layer of dust on anything. It's not as though this room has been closed off, never to be entered again. Someone cleans this room. Rearranges the perfume bottles, *just so*. Moves the slippers to vacuum, and replaces them so that their toes line up perfectly underneath the dust ruffle.

My arms are pricked with gooseflesh. I back out of the room and close the door, my hand paused over the doorknob. I am at once anxious to leave and glued to the spot. My desire to know more about the woman Henry was married to battles some unknown restraining force. I try to pinpoint it and can't, but suspect I fear measuring up. It's hard enough to keep pace with an ex-wife when the relationship was permitted to slide downward on its own. But I suspect Tara was ripped from Henry's arms at the peak of his adoration, and yet I still bumble along somewhere in the middle. It's a hard thing to know, that you're second.

I leave the room and turn to examine the other two rooms. The door at the end of the hall is Henry's office. The door between what I've so quickly come to think of as *Tara's room* and his office is padlocked. Padlocked? I halfheartedly give the doorknob a good jimmy but unsurprisingly, it doesn't move. I do the same to Henry's office and am startled to realize that that door doesn't open either. It's been locked from the inside.

My phone buzzes from inside my pocket and a text from Cash blinks. *Give me a call ASAP. I sent you an email.* I check my service and see that there's no data—only one unsteady bar of network service. When I open the web browser, the loading circle spins around and around. I jam my phone back in my pocket. *Stupid in-the-middle-of-nowhere-land.* The house doesn't have wireless but I vaguely remember Henry assuring me his office computer had Internet access. I jimmy the handle again for good measure. I pull my phone back out and dial Henry. It rings four times and goes to voicemail. *Henry, it's me. Where's the key to your office door and why is it locked? I want to use the Internet. Call me back.*

There's only one reason that Cash would be calling me, and it has to do with my birth mother. I'm sure he's found something, and my heart pounds. I clatter down the steps and dig through the kitchen drawers until I unearth a screwdriver.

Back upstairs, I stick the screwdriver through the old-fashioned keyhole and wiggle it around until I feel it catch the lock. It takes me a few minutes but after the third try, the mechanism clicks backward and the handle gives. I pause, with my hand on the door. I've never been in Henry's office before, and now I'm doing this without his permission.

The office smells of the one leather chair, with a faint overtone of sawdust. Henry's desk is a simple Quaker-style table with a single middle drawer—so unlike his offices at home and work, which boast rich mahogany and more drawers and cabinets than he could possibly fill. The house was his family's, and I wonder if this was his father's office. Later, I'll ask him, when he's properly plied with whiskey. He's said very little about his parents and I scan the room for signs of them. Nothing.

I pull out the chair and sit, hitting the power button on the computer. The desktop is a surprisingly old Mac, nothing at all like the sleek silver laptops Henry carts around, always the newest, smallest model. I briefly wonder if the office is even his. I wonder what Tara did for a living.

I'm surprised but grateful that the computer doesn't prompt me for a password to log on. I click the Internet icon and it takes a minute, but it chugs to my email site. I call Cash back.

"Hi, it's me. I'm at a computer, what's up?" I'm breathless and I realize my fingers are shaking.

"Hey, hold on." He covers the phone and I hear voices and then scratching like he's got the phone in his pocket. After a minute or so, he comes back. "Okay. Did you check your email?"

"Yeah, it's open."

"I sent you a link. Click on it."

I do and it brings me to a genealogy-tracing website with Evelyn at the top of the page. Her picture knocks the wind out of me. Her smile is bright. She looks *so young*. I don't realize I'm crying until a tear hits my forearm. I sniff.

"Are you okay?" Cash asks. I realize I've been quiet too long.

"I'm fine. But what is this? How do they have her picture?"

"She must have made a profile. When was this picture from?"

I study it and realize that based on her weight, she was probably already sick, maybe in her first remission. "Maybe six or seven years ago? She was already sick."

"Okay, scroll down until you see the name Janice Reeves." He's clicking in the background. I do what he says. "Do you see the names under her?"

"Gail, Belinda, Caroline," I say out loud. Then again, "Caroline."

"It's a hunch, not a fact yet. I wanted your feedback." He talks quickly, the words piling out in a rush.

"But the name on the birth certificate is Carolyn. With a *y*. And the last name is . . . Seever."

"Remember how I said no one makes up a truly fake name?"

I can't breathe. "Cash . . . is this really her? Were they cousins?"

"I don't know. There's no picture. You have to create a profile to get a picture. But Zoe, I sent you another link."

I click back to my email and click on the second link. I don't prepare myself, I don't think about it, I just click. And when the page opens, the room tilts.

"Oh my God, Cash." It's a Facebook page, a woman staring defiantly into the camera, with a twisted mouth, a coy smile, daring the world. Her eyes are twinkling, that pale, translucent blue that I recognize. Her hair is dark and unruly in spots, glossy in others, and I bet she has a hell of a time finding good product for it. Her nose is straight with an identifiable ridge and her left eyebrow shoots up noticeably higher than her right.

Like mine. It's all like mine. It's my face. Aged twenty years.

"It's her. You've found her."

. . .

For the rest of the day, I keep going back to the office and staring at the computer, at that picture. That sassy, smart-aleck face, the expression I recognize but maybe haven't seen in a long time. I have the vague recollection of making *that exact face* for a picture during a night out with Lydia. In the bathroom mirror, I try to imitate it, pulling my mouth to the side, arching my already asymmetrical eyebrow. Back in the office, I download the picture and email it to myself.

I stretch and look around the room. On the far wall there are built-in bookcases, floor to ceiling with books: old, new, hardcover, paperback, thrillers, and mysteries; Ruth Rendell, Dennis Lehane, Ross Macdonald, Arthur Conan Doyle. I run my finger along the shelving and wonder if they, too, are Tara's. The eye-level shelf holds knickknacks and picture frames, and I realize with a start that there's a simple, black frame that holds a picture of me.

I'm sitting on a rock, overlooking a stream, wearing a violet shirt and a pair of khaki shorts. I remember that day, the hike at Breakneck Ridge. It was a strenuous hike, and I was panting by the top, hot and out of breath, out of shape. A breeze was lifting my hair while Henry snapped pictures with his Canon at the summit. I remember him finding the spot for the photo, off the main trail, to a sketchy side path, overgrown and treacherous. Claiming he wanted pictures of me for his offices, at work and in our apartment, something he could look at. I protested, pushing my bangs off my forehead, my hands on my flaming cheeks. It was September, the leaves still green, the air still humid.

I remember him helping me down from the steep rock, the way he pushed me against the closest tree without saying a word, pawing at my clothes, wanting me, his hands everywhere, his mouth hot and gasping. I remember the way the bark scratched my bare back as he thrust, only twice, before he fell against me, his body limp and panting. I remember being surprised by the need, the sharp, tangible desperation, as he whispered "I'm sorry" into my hair.

I had teased him about it later, and he growled at me, "It's only because you're so goddamn beautiful." He'd pulled me against him so I could feel how he was still ready, and he softly bit my neck.

I take the picture over to the desk and hold it up next to the picture on the computer. If not for the age difference, we could be twins.

CHAPTER 13

I'm still staring at the computer when my phone rings in my hand. I jump and answer it without looking, assuming it is Cash. Instead, it is Henry.

"Who did you think it was?" he asks, ruffled, after my distracted *Oh*.

"No one! I thought it was you. I'm sorry, I'm on the internet. Hey, why was your office door locked?" My tone is accusatory and I silently chastise myself. *Catch more flies with honey*, an Evelyn favorite.

"Oh, was it? Habit, I guess. I sometimes rent out the house and I lock some of the doors. I don't need people going through everything. The key is in the kitchen on the key hook. It's an old skeleton key." He clears his throat.

"Okay. I jimmied it open. If you don't want people in there, you should get a padlock. Like the other room."

There is a beat of silence. "That room has old client files."

"Okay."

"Anyway, I'm on my way back. I'll be there in a half hour or so. Dinner?"

"Sure." I check the clock on the wall. Somehow, it is four

o'clock. I've literally killed a whole day staring at a picture. My head pulses and I realize I haven't eaten anything. "Is there a restaurant in this town?"

Henry laughs. "This town is 90 percent Italian. There's the best homemade Italian food you've ever had, inside or outside of the city." Vacation Henry is back.

I laugh with him. "Then . . . hurry home," I say coyly, and we hang up.

I can't stop staring at her. I blow the picture up and use the scroll bars to move across her face. Her right eye is slightly larger than the other. A thin scar slivers her forehead, close to her hairline. Her ears are double pierced, but she only has earrings in one set of holes. With each new discovery, I race to the bathroom and examine my face. *I have a tether.*

My head hurts and I'm tired of thinking about Caroline, of analyzing her. On a whim, I navigate to Google and type in the first line of the poem on the card from Henry. *As you are woman, so be lovely.*

"Pygmalion to Galatea," by Robert Graves. *Pygmalion.* The Greek sculptor who fell in love with his statue. Henry is typically not overly literate nor self-reflective. Poetry and fiction are time wasters, and self-reflection is a hallmark of self-doubt.

I'm still sitting at the computer when I hear his car pull in the driveway. I shut it down quickly and stand up. The blood rushes to my head and my vision swims.

We meet in the hallway and we both laugh.

"Hi."

"Hi." He dips me back a bit and kisses me hungrily on the lips. I kiss him back, but distractedly. I haven't had time to think about what to tell Henry, if anything. He'd hinted at wanting some distance between Cash and me. I'm hesitant to tell him that he helped me find Caroline, especially considering his reaction at my wanting to find her in the first place.

I need to handle it delicately, so I push it all away, bury it in my mind.

It's too easy to get caught up in Henry's buoyancy. His hair is tousled from the drive, like he's had the car window open. His face shines from the misty air, his cheeks puffed and pink.

"Go get dressed." He pats my bottom and gives me a wink. I skip-step into the bedroom and pull open my suitcase.

"Oh, I brought something for you." He's holding out a hanger and a bag. I unwrap a simple straight sheath dress, black with tiny silver faux-buttons up the back.

"Where did you get this?" I ask him, eyebrows raised.

He shrugs and gives me a lopsided smile. "I bought it a while ago, but I've just been looking for the right occasion to give it to you. We'll be hopelessly overdressed."

"Better over than under," I say, another Evelyn-ism. Evelyn, who would wear her Sunday best to the grocery store, just for fun, complete with hat. *You only live once, you know. And who knows, maybe someone will think we're really somebodies.*

I slip on the dress and it fits like a glove. Henry always knows my exact size, even if it fluctuates due to brand. When I turn around to face him, he hands me a pair of simple black sling-backs, an impeccable complement to the dress. I cock my head to the side.

"What, are you surprised?" He shakes his head, a curved smile playing on his lips.

"Always." I snatch the shoes and slide them on, wiggling my toes. I bounce back and forth on the balls of my feet: The day has energized me, filled me with nervous anticipation. I've sworn not to think of her, but I find myself wondering what she'd make of me. Of this whole scene, this rich, powerful husband of mine who buys me clothes in the perfect size, in a style he likes, even though I hadn't stopped to ask myself if I liked it.

I give a twirl in the mirror and decide that I do. I wouldn't have picked it, but then again, some of my favorite pieces come from Henry's mind. The man knows how to dress a woman.

Feeling daring, and unlike myself, I whistle at him. He turns and, with a quick movement, I shimmy out of my panties and toss them on the bed. He lifts a brow, his mouth bowed down in surprise.

"Well, now. Dinner should be interesting."

• • •

The restaurant is small: one waitress and ten tables, only four are filled. The room is dark, lit by flickering candles and twinkling white lights that are absorbed by the maroon tablecloths draped over two-top round tables. Everyone knows one another, on a familial level, the Sartinis, the Petruccis, the Tomasis, they descend on us newcomers like a flock of seagulls. Fishing Lake used to be a textile town, Henry explains. Two mills flanked the small community, attracting hundreds of Italian immigrants in the early 1900s. When they both closed, in the early seventies, the population divided: one half bedroom community commuters with long drives into the city, and the other half descendants keeping up the remaining tourist industry. A small restaurant, a bakery, a corner store, a rental management company.

"My father was the former," he tells me. "A lawyer, commuting into New York." I hold my breath. He hardly mentions his parents. I know they are dead. Henry has mentioned a car accident. I tried to relate, my own father died in a car accident, I said at the time, but he'd brushed me off.

"Mr. Whittaker was a wonderful man," stage-whispers a man from the table next to us. He is small, his shoulders hunched into the table. His hands are large and his knuckles misshapen. He claws a fork that shakes over his plate of ziti. "My boy got in trouble, that boy was always in trouble. Mr.

Whittaker saved his hide plenty of times." His eyes twinkle and he nods at Henry. "But he knew how it was to have a troublemaker son." He shakes his index finger at Henry. Henry smiles at the man.

"Were you a troublemaker?" I tease, coyly. Henry smiles and rolls his eyes in the man's direction.

"That's Mr. Zappetti. His mind," Henry says and taps his temple with his middle finger. The man shakes his hand in Henry's direction and laughs.

"You kids." The man turns to me. "My son, he's a good citizen now, just like your Henry. The wild boys. They run wild."

Henry is pulled into another conversation. The men, they want his advice on their investments, the women compliment my dress and *ooh* and *ahh* when I tell them Henry bought it as a surprise. They cluck and raise their eyebrows when I order white wine *(What's wrong with the red?)* and when I remind them which house is Henry's, Mrs. Zullo, a tiny gray tuft of a woman, nods knowingly and clicks her tongue.

"That's the old Vizzini place." She raps the table with her knuckles and all the tables around us say *ohhhhhh* in unison. "That old *strega*. She died in that place, you know."

Her husband elbows her. "*Vita mia*, hush now, that was forty years ago."

I look over at Henry, who is forty years old, and wonder when they moved there. Where did he live before? So much to learn about my husband, so much I don't know. It's odd, I realize, to have this much blank space in a marriage, this broad of a canvas to fill in. Maybe. I don't know, this is my first one. His foot touches mine under the table.

Mrs. Sartini, as round and wobbly as Mrs. Zullo is small, shakes her finger at us. "Mrs. Vizzini, she died of a broken heart. Left by a man at fifty. *Zitella!*"

The crowd breaks up laughing. I don't know what *zitella* means, but even Henry tips his head back in belly laughter.

I can't stop checking my phone. For what, I'm not sure. Another email from Cash? Another picture of her? The clock creeps toward nine and one by one, the tables empty with bids of *good-night* and *nice meeting you,* and too-friendly cheek kisses, until Henry and I are finally alone. His fingers tickle my thigh and I shift away.

"What did you do today?" His eyelids are drooping, sleepy-drunk, and he has a dopey smile on his face.

"Not so fast. You were a troublemaker?" I prod, tapping his toe with mine.

He waves his hand, annoyed. "Mr. Zappetti is a storyteller. No, I was not a troublemaker. I was a kid. I think we soaped his windows one Halloween." I cover my mouth with my hand. "Hey, it's tough to entertain yourself in this town," he protests, his eyes shining.

"Tell me what you did today," he says, again, smiling. My mind goes white. I hesitate, my hand fluttering above my wineglass.

All at once, I remember Caroline, her arched eyebrow, her dark wild hair, her mischievous eyes. Then, *Aren't I enough?* I can't do it. I can't kill the evening, break this spell. I picture his smile fading, his posture straightening, how he would adjust his collar or clear his throat. He'd say something so *Henry* like, *I thought we discussed this before, Zoe* or *You found your birth mother . . . on Facebook?* As though it were laughable and it would be diminished. Instantly reduced in the way that only Henry can, with a flick of his wrist or a twist of his lips. Then we'd sit in silence. I'd clear my throat and he'd throw back the rest of his wine and we'd leave. No, no, no. Henry looks so happy and free, his shoulders loose and the furrow between his eyebrows is smoothed.

"Not much," I say, deflecting. "I read a book by Ruth Rendell. A mystery novel. Have you read her?" I twirl a fork between my fingers. I'm fishing.

Henry scratches his chin and looks up at the ceiling. "I don't think so."

"Really? You have one of her books on the nightstand in the other bedroom," I say and raise one eyebrow, an expression I excel at.

"Oh well," he says flippantly, "that was Tara's room. She read voraciously."

"Oh? The guest room was Tara's bedroom?" I'm not exactly feigning surprise—I hadn't expected him to be so blunt about it.

"She would sleep there sometimes. I worked late, she liked to go to bed early. I suppose it sounds odd now. It seemed so normal at the time."

I picture a *Brady Bunch* relationship: chaste kisses on the cheek, while he brought her chamomile tea and McVitie's biscuits. Pats on the cheek. Making love in the dark, missionary style.

"No, I think it's fine. I just had no idea." I take a deep breath, the words stuck on my tongue. "Henry, I don't know anything about her."

He leans back in his chair. "She was very different than you. Very timid, a bit scared of the world. You wonder why I don't know what to do with you." He laughs and I relax back in my seat.

"Do you keep that room hers?" I cock my head to the side and study his face. He averts his eyes, squinting at a grapevine wreath on the far wall.

"Not intentionally, Zoe. I don't come here much anymore. Do you know that we used to spend every weekend here?" He shakes his head and chooses his words carefully. "It's hard to come back sometimes."

"You still love her." I feel stupid even as I say it. It's so obvious, but I'm not even sure if there's anything wrong with it. Why wouldn't he? She never gave him a reason not to, except for the simple fact that she's gone. His love for me, then, is by default.

I've broken the spell anyway, and for the wrong thing.

"It's complicated," he sighs. "It's not like a divorce. I didn't have any control over the end of my marriage." He rests his cheek against the *L* of his thumb and forefinger and studies me. "Is that hard for you?"

"Not usually. But we've been married nearly a year and we've never had this conversation. That's hard for me." This was the kind of talk that we should have had a million times, drinking wine, wrapped in blankets on a cold winter night. The kind of close, furtive confidences of lovers, whispered kisses and shared breath.

"The room is not a shrine to Tara. I guess I'm lazy. I rent this house out, just a few times a year in the summer and again in the fall to hunters." His eyes flick across my face.

"You've never been called lazy in your life," I joke. Half-joke. The room is fuzzy and I feel coquettish, preening, looking up at Henry from under my eyelashes.

"You call me out, Zoe. I never knew how much I would love that. I've certainly never had it before."

For something to do, I pour another glass of wine. I realize I've drunk almost the whole bottle of white alone, and I slosh more than a sip full down the side of the goblet and onto the tablecloth, which I then rub with the pad of my thumb.

"It's not a shrine," he repeats. "It's just easier. I have a new life. I'm remarried. Sometimes, it's like I've lived twice. I wonder if she ever existed at all. That room is physical proof, that's all. I don't think about it, I don't go in there. Do you want me to change it? I will." He blows out a breath and it tumbles across the table, warm and sweet. "I'm not preserving it. It's just that I haven't changed it, that's all. Do you see the difference?" He seems desperate for me to understand now, his hands splayed out across the tablecloth, and I feel a stab of guilt.

"Why is it so goddamn spotless?" I laugh, my voice slurring on the word *spotless* so it sounds like *spa-aaaas*. He pretends not to notice.

"I had it cleaned last weekend. I had the whole house cleaned. Penny does all the rooms before I come out."

"Penny?" I sit up straight. For some reason, this fact gets under my skin and sits there like a fat, well-fed tick. He had Penny clean the house last weekend? He'd made the trip seem spontaneous, a reaction to the break-in.

"Sure. Who else?" He tops off my glass with the last of the bottle.

"But you made it seem like this was a last-minute trip," I protest weakly. I can't find the right words.

"What does that matter? I was thinking about surprising you. Is that a crime? Then the break-in happened and it seemed like an opportunity. Jesus, Zoe, are you always so exacting?"

"I don't know what that means." My stomach roils.

"I just mean, you need to know every little thought and if it doesn't align with the script in your head, I'm the bad guy."

"You're not the bad guy." I push away from the table, roughly, and the table wobbles. "You're not a bad guy."

I mumble something about the bathroom. I concentrate very hard, walking in a straight line, with my head up, as though I'm perfectly fine. I find the ladies' room in the dark, back corner of the restaurant. Inside I lean against the door, the room spinning and whipping around me. I feel along the wall and flip the light switch. Without warning my stomach heaves and I retch into the toilet. The tile floor is cold on my legs and I remember that I'm naked under my dress. I feel my face flame red. God, did I think I was twenty years old? I'm just a second wife living someone's second life, at thirty.

I wipe my bottom lip with the back of my hand and push

myself up to standing. The room has stopped spinning and I smooth the front of my dress down with my hands. I feel better. At least like I could walk across the room. I wash up and rinse my mouth. I slowly make my way back to the table.

"Are you all right?" Henry leans forward and takes my hand.

"I drank too much," I say, plainly.

Henry smiles, teasing me. "Let's get you home."

I lean on Henry and he leads me out. I remember saying earlier that it would be good for us to walk. The spring air is cold on my arms and the night is black and quiet, the kind of quiet that seems to absorb sound. Our footsteps are silent. I occasionally laugh and it sounds muted, like coughing into a pillow.

I concentrate on walking straight as to not give away my level of drunkenness. I'm reminded of the countless nights stumbling home, my arm linked through Lydia's as we leaned on each other. We'd whisper and giggle and bump hips as we walked, her hair in my face smelling of cherry candy and cigarettes.

I lean close to Henry and wrap my hands around his arm. His bicep bumps and flexes under his cotton shirt. I nuzzle his neck and he smells like the ocean, fresh and salty.

At home, I peel my dress off and lie on the bed, the fan moving the air across my skin. Henry runs the bath, the pipes creaking and groaning under the floor. The water rushes up the wall, all around me, until it sounds like it's coming from inside my head. He calls my name from the bathroom.

"I'll be right there," I whisper, and then I giggle because I know I'm lying. I wave in his direction, the diamond on my left hand catching the dim light and throwing prisms on the wall. I fan my fingers in front of me and study the ring, a solitary glittering stone, the size of a marble.

If I squint my eyes, it looks like there are two of them.

CHAPTER 14

Washington Square Park, desolate and gray in the winter months, is lush with life come April. Aging beatniks loaf on the grass, retirees challenge children to a competitive game of chess, mothers sit on park benches with their e-readers, rocking baby carriages with one foot. NYU students take to the park in droves, studying the human condition for psychology, sociology, and film classes. The park bursts with budding cherry trees and barely contained hope.

It is Monday. *Vacation Henry* is back to *Work Henry*, buttoned up and pressed, heavy on the starch. I'm back to reality. My credit card is still not functional and Henry has promised to call the bank. He's left me a hundred dollars in cash on the counter for daily expenses, which feels both extravagant and oppressive. I could surely ask him for more, I reason. But for what?

I've called Yates twice, who tells me nothing. She sighs into the phone, a *tap tap tap* of her acrylic nails on a keyboard coming through the line. She talks a good game. Tells me all the things they've done, but that everything is inconclusive. Penny has an alibi, and besides, what on earth could her motive be? The hazard pay? Henry wasn't a fan of that joke. Henry has changed the apartment locks; we are safely sequestered in our tower again. I should feel more relieved than I do.

Away from Fishing Lake, with nothing else to think about the burglary being "inconclusive and all," the idea of finding Caroline has trumped all else. Cash sits on a bench, in the middle to discourage company, and is heavily involved in a paperback. His forehead is ridged in concentration, his heavy bottom lip protruding out, curling back against his chin as he works at a hangnail on his thumb with his teeth. I peek at the cover before he sees me. *As I Lay Dying.* When he sees me, he stashes the book under his left thigh and scoots over, patting the boards next to him. I sit, my purse primly on my lap, a good foot between us.

"Faulkner?" I can't help but tease. He shrugs.

"You're so surprised? Because why? My muscular physique?" His eyebrows waggle Groucho style and I laugh. He's flirting with me. I sit up straight and he clears his throat, holding out a manila file folder in my direction. "So. Because you dragged me *all the way to the Village*, for some unknown godforsaken reason, I brought you this." He hands me the folder and I open it.

"You live in the village," I remind him with a smirk.

A picture of Caroline Reeves glosses under my fingertips. She is making another playful face into the camera, her lip curled in mock anger, her eyes twinkling, her mouth curved up in a half-smile, a pronounced double *V* on the bridge of her wrinkled nose. Someone else's hand rests on her shoulder. In the background glitters a Ferris wheel.

Underneath the picture are two typed pages of information. She has a family. She lives in Danbury, Connecticut. I do the math: She had me when she was seventeen. A fresh stab of rejection lands right under my sternum. I'd expected, somehow, my birth mother to still be wallowing in her thirty-year-old decision, pale and gaunt with greasy hair and a listless expression. But she's not; she's moved on and, judging by her fun-loving online presence, quite happily.

Cash rubs his knees with his palms and looks around. His posture inches forward like he's going to get up.

"Wait," I say. I open my mouth to ask how he got all this information, but instead I hear myself say, "Will you come with me?"

"Where?" He looks startled.

I shrug, knowing it's a bad idea. I think of driving alone and my stomach clenches. Truthfully, I'm so sick of *going alone*.

"Yeah, of course, Zoe. I'll go with you." His voice softens and I give him a small smile. If Cash goes with me, the narrow window I have to tell Henry about Caroline closes, and I know that, but Henry would never go. By making the decision to invite Cash, I'm inadvertently making the decision to leave Henry out. My brain reasons this out, almost subconsciously. The justification follows just as fast: *Henry will have to work. Henry will be busy. Henry won't want to go.*

"When?" My brain is three steps behind my mouth.

"You should call her first." Cash looks startled that I haven't thought of that before and I feel my cheeks flush. He checks his watch, I'm sure he thinks surreptitiously, but he scoots forward, restive, crossing and uncrossing his ankle over his knee.

"Okay." I squint at her photo again, the sun glinting off the high gloss. "I'll call her today."

"Zoe, I don't know how to say this, but you seem like someone who can handle things. She might . . . not want to see you. It happens a *lot*. Just be prepared for that. But if she agrees to see you, give me a call. I'll go with you. I've done it before."

"You have?"

"Yeah, a few times. People don't like to do this alone and sometimes I was the only person in their lives who knew. From that series, remember?"

"Like me," I say softly, and that stab of guilt is back like a hot poker, reminding me that I'm a liar. I'm lying to my husband. I mouth the words to myself to see how they feel, but it's not so bad. Technically, I've always lied to him.

I stand, abruptly, and a few pages slide out of the manila folder. Cash bends to pick them up.

"I'll call you, okay?"

"Oh! Zoe, wait." He holds out a folded up newspaper. "It ran today. It's a good spread. Take a look, give me a call. We'll talk."

I stare at the newspaper and it takes me a minute to figure it out. *CARE.* The event seems aged and distant. I shove it clumsily under the file in my arms and force a smile.

"I'll call you, okay?" I say it again, turn and rush through the crowd. The sun suddenly seems too bright, a glaring, carnival spotlight. A man on a unicycle swerves in and out of park benches, tipping his hat for money. I glance over my shoulder and Cash is heading east, his hands in his pockets, his head tipped back, black hair glinting, as he looks at the treetops. For what, I don't know.

Before I can lose my nerve, I pull out my cell phone, flip the folder open with one hand, locate her current phone number. I dial.

"Hello." An impatient female voice picks up and I clear my throat.

"Hi, is this Caroline?"

There is a whoosh like she's rubbed the pad of her thumb over the mouthpiece.

"That depends, are you selling me something?"

"No."

"Then, sure, I'm Caroline." Her voice is tired, worn thin like we're talking into two tin cans and a string. I open and close my mouth, stuck on what to say next. I feel like that children's book with the bird, asking the bulldozer, *Are you my mother?*

"Hi. My name is Zoe Whittaker. Um, do you know Evelyn Lawlor?"

"Who is this again?" She's sharp now, like broken glass.

"I'm Evelyn's daughter. Well, her adopted daughter." I stop then because the next logical thing to say is *I'm* your *daughter,* but I can't actually say that because it sounds too hokey. Like an awful movie. So I stand there in silence and watch the park. The unicycle man is chasing a screaming towheaded boy who clings to his mother's skirt. An oversize yellow helium balloon drunkenly weaves up toward the clouds. Two men are arguing in what sounds like Polish over a chess board.

"What is your name again?" Her voice has dropped to a whisper.

"Zoe Whittaker."

One of the men stands up and pounds the board with his fist. He turns and stalks off, his partner leans back in his chair, a satisfied grin on his face. We make eye contact. *"Wygram, eh?"* He points to his chest and shrugs his shoulders.

I realize that Caroline hasn't spoken.

"Hello?" I say.

"I'm here."

"Would you meet with me? I'd come to you." I feel like I'm ambushing her, but I'm panicky, I can feel my only tether slipping through my fingers like that goddamn yellow balloon. I look up and it's a speck now, so high I can barely see it.

"Can I think about it? I'll call you back in an hour." She hangs up. No good-bye, just *click*, gone. I stare at the phone in my hand. The Chess Man gives me a good-natured shrug and ambles away.

I wander back to the benches. I don't want to go home. The park seems as good a place as any. I'm nowhere near Henry's office building or our apartment.

When Henry and I were dating he brought me here, to Washington Square Park, on a day like this. It was warmer, maybe May. The mosquitoes had settled into New York that year like overstayed houseguests. He spread a blanket, some quilted monstrosity he nabbed from Fishing Lake. We opened it out on the grass, under the trees that dipped low to the ground, shrouding us, and we kissed. *In public.* That amazes me now, Henry kissing in public is like saying *gentle grizzly bear.* There's no fitting mental image.

I wore a navy blue dress he'd bought me, brandishing it as though it were from the Queen Mum herself. It cinched at the waist with a wide belt and an A-line skirt and reminded me of something I'd seen in an old *Life* magazine, a black-and-white ad for cream deodorant: *Are you really lovely to love?* Henry's eyes crinkled at the corners when he smiled. I was drunk on his love, his hands, the line of muscle from his neck down to his shoulder blade, the small scar above his eyebrow, the freckle in the hollow of his ear. I wanted to memorize him.

We'd only been dating a short time, and yet by all accounts, I was becoming a contender for a Fascinating Person (capital *F* capital *P*), one of a few women who were taming the wild beasts that were New York City's most eligible men.

"I'm going to marry you, Zoe Swanson," he'd whispered as his fingers danced up my thigh.

"Are you now? Will you at least ask me?" I teased, biting at his bottom lip.

"I'd never give you the chance to say no."

"Oh, bless my stars." I toyed with his hair, my voice

a thick syrupy accent. "Who would ever say no to *Henry Whittaker*?"

"My first wife. She said no. Twice, actually."

I sat up, pushing his hand off my leg. "Your what?"

"I was married before. You didn't know?" Henry had a way of phrasing things, just so, to delicately pass off blame. As though I should have been able to glean this information out of his inky, black silence. Blood from a stone.

"No. I'm pretty sure I'd remember that." I pulled my knees up to my chest and hugged them. "What happened? Is there an ex–Mrs. Whittaker, slowly funneling all your money?" A thought occurred to me. "Oh my God, Henry, is there a Henry Jr.? I can't be a stepmother. I mean, I guess I *could* be, but I don't know how to be—"

He pulled my arms away from my knees and kissed my palms one at a time. His lips were soft, slightly greasy like hour-old ChapStick. "There's no Henry Jr. My wife . . . she died. In a car accident. Three years ago."

Henry lived in the abrupt.

"What? How? What was her name? Oh God, Henry, that's terrible!" My heart had thudded in my chest.

"Her name was Tara. We were driving home from a dinner. The next thing I know we're at the hospital and the doctors are talking about life support and feeding tubes and that was it. It was over and twenty-four hours later, I was a widower. Married one minute, the next . . . not. It's so strange how life can happen that way."

"What happened?"

"Oh, details. I'll tell you one day." He kissed me full on the mouth, his breath coming in huffs, his hands gripping my waist as though he were drowning. *He needs me now,* I'd thought at the time. Still think. Sometimes.

But then, he never did tell me. I've broached the subject on any number of occasions. It's the wrong time. Later. I'm tired. The excuses are endless. I have, periodically, pushed the issue. His stalwart chin, sticking out as he shakes his head, disappointed.

My phone vibrates in my hand. I somehow manage to answer it without breathing.

"Can you come Friday? I'll give you an hour."

CHAPTER 15

I leave Washington Square and hop on the F train at the West Fourth Street station. The subway is mostly empty because it is two o'clock on a Monday. In April, people walk. They've been confined to subways and cabs for four months, so come spring the sidewalks flood with people: no distance is too long. A lone violinist hunkers down in front of the subway door, his bow crying a haunting melody that I don't recognize, the upturned baseball hat at his feet is empty. When the brakes squeal at Twenty-Third Street, I bend down and fold two dollars behind the brim. He gives me a watery smile and returns to his swaying.

Once I emerge on street level, I join the throng of moving people and walk north for five blocks until I reach Manhattan's flower district. The street is filled with tall green trees, grass, even a large, tilting palm, potted in thick black plastic, its fronds cupping the hood of a Lincoln Town Car. The jungle street, we always called it. The macadam is wet from the misters, the damp pavement and lush greens providing a unique perfume. The early morning rush has dissipated, leaving only the workers, the warehouse movers, designers, shop owners, and a few passers-through.

I hesitate outside the door, just long enough for Javi to spot me and whistle. His fishnet shirt is pulled tight against his bulging chest and he's paired it with white cutoffs and a pair of nude patent leather high heels. He slinks like a cat and, when he smiles, I can almost see the canary, caught and fluttering between his pointed teeth. I roll my eyes and straighten my back. Some ribbing will come.

"Well, well. I hardly recognize you, *guapa*." He *tsks* at me and then calls over his shoulder, "Elisa! Eliiiiisa!"

When she appears in the doorway, she's wiping her hands on a black work towel that is clipped to her waist. Her blonde hair is streaked with white and secured with an oversize blue bow. She hovers in the doorway, framed by protruding pink orchids and purple lisianthus. A sixty-year-old Alice in Wonderland. She steps aside and motions me into the shop.

"Zoe. Lydia said you'd come. I didn't believe her." Elisa has one tone. Clipped. Her diction always seemed slightly Eastern European to me, but years ago, she had family come to visit from Texas and Lydia swore they'd said she'd grown up there.

"Elisa," I breathe out. I'm in her world now. This woman, who had on occasion reduced me to tears because the hydrangeas were not precisely the blue she'd "had in mind." An image comes to mind of late nights in the warehouse, pulling leaves and bleeding as she towers over me, clucking with soft disapproval.

She straightens to her full five feet, her childlike hands patting down her pockets like she's forgotten something. Soft, thin lines pucker around delicately painted petal-pink lips. A pair of butterfly glasses balances on the bridge of her nose.

"Are you back to work?"

"Not today." I don't feel as confident as I pretend but she nods, conceding. It's the first time I can ever remember controlling the conversation. "Today is a . . . visit of sorts. Is Lydia in?"

"She is. We are starting to prepare for the Krable wedding." She twirls a headless stem in her fingers, studying me. I shift my purse from one shoulder to the other and pretend to study the industrial shelving lining the walls. It's new.

Krable? I cock my head to the side. "Norman?"

"His daughter, Sophie."

I didn't know he had a daughter. Come to think of it, he likely has several, and possibly some he doesn't even know about.

She grins, all Cheshire cat. "I am surprised you are not invited." She clucks and just like that, I'm reduced again. An outsider for life, an observer of certain circles, not a participant. Elisa with her award-winning designs and sought-after events. Henry with his charisma, a fat checkbook, and fluid pen.

The Saturday after Henry proposed, I had fled to the shop at six a.m., breathless and heady, in the clothes I'd worn the day before, my hair matted and bed-tousled, smelling of Henry's cologne and the warm, soft, slight musk of sex.

"I'm engaged!" I flashed my hand in front of Lydia's face and Javi snatched my finger, turning it one way then the other, whistling at the size of the diamond. We all squealed and jumped up and down, because of *Henry Whittaker*.

"Zoe Whittaker is the most elegant name I've ever heard." Javi jutted out a hip and glided around the shop, twirling a make-believe train in his hand. "You gotta act the part now, bitch. You are *not* cut out for grace like that. Look at your face. I see three holes, not including that big-ass mouth. What is that fine man thinking?" He pointed his long, filed nails at my eyebrow ring, my lip ring, and my nose stud, and held up three fingers.

Lydia threw a bucket of clippings at him. "Shut up, Javi. You're just jealous."

"Who is jealous of whom?" Elisa stood between the shop and the warehouse, her sleeves rolled up.

"Henry asked Zoe to marry him," Lydia supplied, and there was a beat of silence.

"Henry . . . *Whittaker.*" Elisa shifted a bucket of blooms from one hip to the other. "Engaged?"

"New York's most eligible bachelor is no longer," Lydia singsonged.

Elisa onced me over, head to toe, and then crooked her finger. "Come with me." She pointed at Lydia and Javi. "You two, stay."

I had followed her into the warehouse, a wide-open seemingly endless bay of stainless steel and concrete used to assemble millions of dollars' worth of arrangements a year. Elisa plunked the bucket onto one of the long tables and turned to face me.

"Your courtship was what? A month?"

"Almost four." I had five inches on Elisa and I used them. My chin hovered around her forehead.

"That is nothing. You know nothing about each other. Henry is . . . a complicated man, Zoe. I don't know him well, but I've known him for a few years now. He wants a wife, he's made no bones about that."

"He loves me." I had meant it to sound strong but it dribbled out, like weak spittle.

"You have talent. You have a future here. Do you know that?" Her voice was soft, but stern. Her eyes, over the brim of her glasses, flared.

"I'm not going anywhere, Elisa."

"You say that now. Henry's wife will not work as someone he, himself, could hire. These people, they don't operate like that."

"You have Nolan." Elisa's partner for the past thirty years was wealthy, in real estate. Prior to Henry, dating him, *loving him,* I'd never tried to attract men from these circles. Too high profile, too public. Henry, with long, strong hands, veined and powerful, molded me into someone new. Like putty.

"Nolan is not in the same league as the likes of Henry Whittaker. Believe me. You've been to their parties, their benefits, their galas. It's a pretend world, Zoe. All diamond and glitter facade." She moved closer to me, her breath hot on my face, her fingers wrapped around my bicep. "Made of glass and just as fragile."

"I love it here. Okay?" I'd shaken my arm out of her grasp and she'd stepped back, shaking her head.

"Don't lose you." She stared at me, her eyes slits above the top of her glasses.

Who was that, exactly? She'd patted her hair back into place and huffed to the back of the room.

Henry and I married three months later. Shortly after that, I'd quit to travel the world, believing that the choices I was making had no repercussions, that my leaving would affect no one but me.

Now, Elisa is poised in front of me, a reminder that she is forever right. I am back to grovel for my position. Javi bounces back and forth on the balls of his feet in barely contained joy, his head bouncing back and forth between us, like he's about to witness a fight. She points him to the back room and inside the small shop front, points to a chair. "Sit." Javi shuffles through the metal double doors, and I'd bet my wedding ring he's hovering, ear pressed to the crack between them.

The storefront is barely a store. It doesn't serve to walkins, just by appointment only. It contains a desk and a large glass-front cooler. You can order small bouquets, exotic arrangements, mostly castoffs. If you know Elisa, she'll make you anything. If you don't, she'll turn the door sign.

She busies herself pulling together blooms by color, as they arrive to the warehouse bundled by type and color. "You haven't been gone so long." Creamy peach roses mingle with apricot tulips, and I close my eyes, taking a deep breath. "I have no qualms with welcoming you back, Zoe. You've always shown huge promise as a designer. You have an impeccable eye for incorporating modern trends with classic looks."

I nod. I've never gotten a compliment like this from Elisa. Ever, ever. Wait until I tell Lydia, if she still even cares. I can't believe I had to wait until I was no longer working there to hear it.

I can hear Javi singing, his Barry White voice echoing off the concrete walls. I hear other voices, employees I no longer recognize, hired to process, leaving the design work to Elisa and Lydia. I know from experience that they've been at it since the wee hours of the morning. Weeks of large events, celebrity weddings, city galas, and once a mayoral ball: the days start at three a.m.

"What I'd like to know," Elisa continues in her even, flat voice, "is why now? Why will Henry let you come back now? Will you just up and leave again when he says so?"

"Henry never asked me to quit. That was my idea," I interject. It's a true statement. We'd been traveling, sometimes weeks at a time, Paris, Rome, Madrid. Henry wanted to show me the world, and it was impossible to keep a schedule. Was I supposed to just tell him no? Madrid can wait—we have the Bankers' Ball!

I had *done things*. I heard "Ave Maria" performed by a hundred-member a capella choir, in the Pantheon. I'd met the pope, shaken his wizened hand, his eyes kind behind papery, lash-less eyelids. Yes, I'd given up my little job in a fancy flower shop. No, I no longer dyed my hair fuchsia and purple. Were people not allowed to grow?

"People change, Elisa. I'm young. I had an opportunity

to *do something* with my life. Outside of this city. When we came back, I decided to use my newfound money for something good and got involved in CARE. I'm *allowed* to do these things. Not you, or Henry, can change that."

Elisa pulls out a large bundle of yellow roses and, mumbling to herself, she throws them in the large, green plastic trash bucket.

"Is it *your* life, Zoe? All I ask is that you make sure of that." She waves me away, back toward the warehouse, where I can hear a boom box blasting "Respect." I hold up my hand, palm out, tired of her cryptic morality messages.

The warehouse is overwhelmed with color, an overabundance of light pink. I spot Lydia in the corner, instructing a small dark-haired woman on what to look for in a bloom. The girl is nodding and fidgeting with her apron string. Lydia sees me and flashes me a grin, nodding in Javi's direction. I shake my head. She motions to the girl, who nods and continues to strip leaves, slicing the stems on a bias with a sharp knife. She stops every few minutes to examine her thumb. I look at my own thumb, the skin still tough and lined with the fine, delicate scars. I run my index finger over the pad and feel the healed incisions. When I flip my hands over, palms down, the skin on the top is newly smooth and creamy, groomed by manicures and coddled with expensive lotions.

"I don't think it's even possible to cut my skin anymore. It has to be made of leather by now." Lydia stands in front of me, her eyes bright and blinking, her mouth curved in a genuine smile. Gone are the double entendres and chilly pretenses from last week. She radiates warmth.

I remember why I'm there. "Can we talk somewhere *he's* not?" I jerk my head in Javi's direction. He's giving me the stink-eye from across the room, whispering to one of the warehouse runners behind his hand, laughing in my direction. "What is his deal?"

Lydia shrugs and rolls her eyes. "You know Javi. He's just a pain in the ass. He thinks you abandoned us. He's wrapped his own insecurities around you, thinks that you think you're better than us."

"I did come back. I have come back to say hi. I was *on a trip*. For *months*. What the hell, Lyd?"

She leads me to a corner in the front of the warehouse and gives me a metal folding chair. We both sit so our knees are touching. Her foot bobs and I know she wants a cigarette, but when Elisa lurks around, you can't just simply take a smoke break. I remember the drill, you wait for an errand you can conveniently volunteer for, otherwise Elisa's eyes dart around like an eagle, performing a constant head count. "Come on, you know him. He's got a stick up his ass. He thinks you're a Richie Rich now, all judgy of his wardrobe. That you're too good for his scene. I don't know why—"

I cut her off because I can't keep it in anymore. "I found her. Lydia, I found my mother." I reach out and grab her shoulders without even realizing it and she looks startled.

"Wait. What?"

"I found my birth mother. She agreed to see me Friday. I got Cash, this reporter I've weirdly become friends with, to take me. Can you come with us?" I throw it out there, reckless and unplanned. I suddenly want a guard wall of friends.

"I can't. It's Cissy's birthday." Cissy is Lydia's mom. A freckled, blonde version of Lydia, their faces identical. When I met her, in the kitchen of Lydia's childhood home in Woodbridge, New Jersey, surrounded by rooster decorations and rustic signs painted with things like *Fresh Eggs* and *Home of the Free * Because of the Brave,* she'd just baked a pie. She wiped her hands on an apple apron and handed me a homemade chocolate chip cookie from a mooing cow cookie jar. Lydia always took umbrage with her childhood: It had been too happy to retain any sort of street cred, despite her piercings and tattoos. Cissy never batted an eyelash at her punk daughter, her full, fleshy arms wobbling as she hugged both of us at once, as though I was somehow included, too. She smelled like Jean Naté.

"Tell her. See if she cares." I persist because now that I've told her, now that I've let Lydia in again, I want to share everything with her. I've been friendship starved, and now I want the all-you-can-eat, twenty-four hour buffet.

"Gawd, she'll want to come." Lydia curls her lip. "I can't. We're going out to dinner. Probably to the Golden Corral or something." She can hardly stand the provinciality. She pulls my hand up to her face and studies my French manicure. "You'll cut these, you know." Little more than a year before, my nails were clipped down to the beds, raggedy and hang-nailed.

"I know. I'm ready for it. I want to come back. I want to *be* back."

"And Henry says?"

"He's fine with it. He wants me to be happy."

"Will he let you come back every day?" She arches one penciled eyebrow at me, toeing my shin with a black, original Chuck Taylor.

"That's a trick question. I don't *want* to come back every day." I'm pretty sure that's true. I stand up, abruptly, dusting imaginary crumbs off my slacks. I'm pretty sure Lydia has never worn *slacks* in her life. But still, *As you are woman, so be lovely* darts across my mind.

"Are you leaving?" The snotty tone is back, with an unspoken *I told ya so.*

"Yeah. I want to be home for Henry." I say this defiantly, daring her to make a snotty comment.

Instead she stands and gives me a hug. "Good luck Friday. Call me as soon as you leave. I'll be waiting by the phone."

I rest my cheek on her pointed shoulder, the tulle of

her shirt scratching my skin, and breathe in her Lydia-ness. Patchouli and some kind of herbal hair spray. I forgot about having someone to call "as soon as you were done." Henry could schedule a call down to the minute, but I could never call him "as soon as I left" anything. That was a girlfriend's station, someone to dial as you were leaving a doctor's office to tell her the sun spot was nothing, or send a picture of a new haircut, or text as soon as you got the job with lots of exclamations and smiley faces. The back of my brain skitters on the thought that maybe Caroline could be this person. I know what Cash said, and it has merit. But who's to say we couldn't be friends?

I promise to call and give a quick flitted finger wave in Elisa's direction, who raises her chin and sniffs back at me, which is as good as I was likely to get. I didn't bother going back into the warehouse, preferring instead to duck out unnoticed.

"See ya in a year!" Javi's deep echo follows me out, chased by a chittering of laughter, echoing off the steel walls of the warehouse.

CHAPTER 16

The spread is not only above the fold, but spans two full pages in the Living section. Cash managed to hunt down and interview the board president of CARE, and true to his word the piece is entirely devoted to the charity. The event itself, a small subset of the entire article, was brilliantly tacked on at the beginning and the end to keep it in both the Living and Entertainment pages. He highlighted the organization's purpose, our triumphs, where we're lacking, what we specifically need funding for—our scholarship program, propelled by Amanda Natese—and some of the other success stories. I've been working on developing a program to improve book distribution in the city's public schools, but I haven't given it much thought in the past few days. Admittedly, the whole Caroline thing has taken up residence in my brain, edging out all else.

I smooth the crease of the page flat with my index finger and wipe the ink on a dish towel. I'm perched at the kitchen island, waiting for Henry. The apartment is restored, the break-in erased with a deft hand, the fingerprint powder scrubbed clean. The slashed sofa has been replaced—it's not an exact replica, but a shade darker, a bit rounder and puffier. I wonder if there were surreptitious conversations about the sofa: *I'd like it to be just the exact same size. Can it be slightly larger? It's only slightly.* Does she beg? Does she plead for Henry to accept her suggestions? Who holds the power between them? I can't figure it out. Does Henry keep these conversations away from me purposefully? If I asked him, he'd say no. That he just has them at work. They're minutiae, he'd say. Pat my hand.

Penny has left a tapas plate of Brie and olives to rest on the counter, and the apartment is heavy with the aroma of braised lamb. I pinch an olive and pop it in my mouth. Because it is Wednesday, Henry will have had a light lunch, takeout from the catered delivery service at the office. Wednesdays are beef and lamb days. My stomach rumbles and I lick my thumb and turn the page.

There is one photograph of me. The camera is behind me and I am talking to Sophia Restan, a B-list celebrity who was famous in the nineties for her antics as a spoiled heiress but who has become active in and supportive of the city's charities. She attends almost all the CARE benefits with a different guest, someone with a large checkbook and the desire to impress his date. Our heads are bent together and we're both smiling, but my features are barely distinguishable in profile. I nod slowly and exhale. It's a good piece, focusing on the influence of the cause and how it has helped thousands of "system kids" graduate from high school, trade school, and sometimes *college.* The college graduates always come back.

I hear the elevator doors swoosh open in the hallway. Henry comes through the front door, dusting off the sleeves of his suit, his mouth tipped in a half-grimace.

"Hi!" I stand in his path, raised on my toes to kiss him, and he blinks twice like he's forgotten who I am. He then leans forward and kisses me, distracted. Perfunctory.

"This goddamn city drives me crazy. I can't go two blocks without walking under scaffolding and getting covered in sawdust."

I study his suit and see nothing. I shake my head with a little smile, just to see how easy it will be to break his mood. He stops and smiles back at me. "I'm a grump. I'm sorry. I've spent most of the day arguing."

I tug on his hand. "Come. Look at this." In the kitchen, we pick at cheese and I fan the paper out in front of him. He reads it, nodding thoughtfully, his fingers tapping gently against the countertop. The bottom half of the second page is devoted to the event, and as his eyes travel down the page, his fingers stop tapping and he frowns.

"What?"

"I don't know, Zoe, this guy, whatshisname?"

"Cash." I square my shoulders.

"He seems very interested in you."

I snatch the paper from his hand. "What are you talking about? This was *my* event. Of course I'm featured heavily."

"A lot of quotes from you, that's all. I have a feeling you were a big influence in the entire write-up. Maybe he talked to other people, but all of this about the scholarships and the schoolbooks? These are things I've heard *you* mention."

"Well, he did talk to me. That should be fine. The story is what's important." I can feel my hackles rising, my chin jutting out.

"And this picture? It's practically a seventies smoking ad. You're all curves and seduction."

"You can't even see my face."

"Exactly. Just your bare back, a glimmer of shoulder, long sexy hair, and a hint of a smile in profile."

I can feel my mood plummeting. "It's not like that, Henry. This is what I wanted." I shake the paper at him. "This is a *good* thing. Why is it always like this with you? You're so afraid to be happy, you automatically jump to the negative. Just be happy for me."

"I'm happy for you. It's a decent article, as far as newspapers these days go. Reporting isn't what it used to be." He shrugs. The oven timer goes off and I toss the newspaper back onto the countertop and stalk to the kitchen. I hear him snap the pages back open.

In the kitchen, I remove the lamb, prep the plates, the china clattering off marble, the silverware tinny, making as big a racket as I can. Henry hates plate clanging.

We'll sit in the dining room with our lamb and salad and pesto orzo, prepared by Penny but served by me. I've complained a few times that I can't handle being served dinner, Penny hovering like a skitzy bird over our chairs, ostensibly to see if we need anything but, to my mind, just plain old-fashioned eavesdropping. I can't handle her light feather touches to Henry's shoulder, and yet her eyes dart around when I speak to her, as though she's channeling an apparition. She squints in my direction, though not so much at me. Though she is never outright rude, I need to feel comfortable dining in my own home.

I carry the plates to the dining room, where Henry has brought the paper with him. He jangles ice in a whiskey glass as he studies the print over the top of his reading glasses. I can't help but think that he looks sexy, even when I'm exasperated with him.

"Who did you argue with today?" I set his plate in front of him, lightly scratching his neck, expecting him to do what he usually does when he's unreasonable or childish, which is offer me an impish smile and some vague overreaching flattery, but he does none of those things.

"How many times did you meet with this man, Zoe?"

I sit carefully, in the chair to Henry's right, concentrating on unfolding the napkin in my lap. Half of me flares up: how dare he ask, how dare he *care?* I'm free to talk to whomever I'd like, this is hardly the fifties.

"Three." I spear a piece of lamb, the tender meat falls apart, a perfect doneness. Sometimes I'd like her to, just once, burn a meal. Overestimate the cooking time. It hasn't happened yet.

"Yet, you've said nothing. I ask you about your daily activities. You've remained vague. Why?"

I tip my wineglass and swallow it all down at once, like a nervous freshman at a fraternity party. "Not purposefully. They've all been brief. I'm sure whatever else I did that day was more interesting."

"Your *entire* day is interesting to me, Zoe. You know that. Why would you lie? Why would you cover it up?"

"I'm not covering it up, Henry. This whole conversation is ridiculous. We met three times in public places, discussed the charity, my involvement, that's it. Enough of this."

I stand, planning to get another glass of wine.

"Sit," he commands in his boardroom voice, the one no one dares defy. I ease myself back down in my chair.

As you are woman, so be lovely. And obedient?

"I can't tolerate the lying. Even by omission. If it was no big deal, then why not tell me?" He scans the paper, pointing one buffed, manicured nail to a sentence. *Zoe Whittaker is personally attached to the cause of helping orphans and those left to fend for themselves, because she relates to the isolation.* "You've been personal with this man. This is an intimate conversation." Stab at the paper again, this time at the picture. "*This* is an intimate photograph."

I see the picture through Henry's eyes, the long curve of my spine, a sly, sexy smile, one delicately arched eyebrow, my hand floats near my ear, where I have just tucked a lock of hair. I sigh heavily. Stupid is what it is. "Henry, I will not have this conversation—"

"This man has feelings for you. If you were not aware of it, you wouldn't have lied to me."

"I never lied to you!" I protest sharply. "I just wasn't willing to be monitored."

"Bullshit." His voice is loud now and he stands up, his palms bracing against the table. "You have feelings for him, too? That lowlife barely reporter, who makes $30,000 a year and lives in a one-room apartment in the East Village? Where all the hippies and the druggies hang out?"

I gape up at him. I never told Henry where Cash lived.

"I know everything about him, Zoe. He's involved in my life now. I need to know these things, do you think I'm haphazard? Do you think I can afford to just let people in? I will not let my life, my wife, be compromised in that way." He's practically yelling, even his hair has taken on an unusually disheveled appearance.

"Henry, are you insane?" I spit.

He leans close to me, his eyes flashing, small dots of white spittle have foamed the corners of his mouth. "Zoe, do *not* question me about this. I will know what you are doing. I will know who you are spending time with. I will know—"

My heart races. I've never seen Henry angry, not like this. Cold, calculating, yes. Not this wild rage. My hands shake and I mentally swing between wanting to fire back at him and calming him down. "Henry, I can't live like this! Under your rules, your roof, your thumb, your—"

He's so quick, I hear the glass shatter before I realize what he's done. The smell of whiskey stings my nostrils and pierces the back of my throat. The wall behind me drips brown amber liquid.

His voice is low, hard and barely controlled. "Then get out." He spins around, and is gone.

• • •

I don't *get out*. Where would I go? Lydia's? I could hear the *I told you so* out the side of her mouth, lips twisted in a smirk. Or worse, if she reacted with pity, like I was seeking refuge at some kind of abused women's shelter. No. In the end, I stay in the apartment. Henry's office door is closed and I wonder if that's where he'll sleep. The room has a long, black leather sofa and once or twice when he's been working late, he has slept in there. Never out of anger, that would be a first. Isn't sleeping on the couch a sitcom staple? Pillows flying down the stairs and a hapless, balding, middle-aged man scrambling to catch them: *Linda, please, I'll take out the garbage.* These are normal, married people things. Truthfully, I have no idea what normal, married couples are like, outside of movies and television. I've never witnessed it.

I think of Evelyn, precancer, with her thick, dark hair, red string bikini, and cutoff jean shorts in the driver's seat of a borrowed black convertible, blasting Bruce Springsteen all the way down the Pacific Coast Highway to Capitola Beach. She'd spread blankets, twist and heave a heavy umbrella into the ground, and sit, smoking cigarettes and humming softly under her breath while I dug holes in the sand.

"We need a radio, bud, don't you think?" I loved *bud*. She never called me darling or sweetie. She and I were pals, united against the world. I was twelve, edging into teenage angst while reaching back to my mom, my *bud*, with one hand. "I'll find us one."

I shrugged because I was collecting baby crabs, their soft, gray bodies scuttling up the sides of the yellow bucket and sliding back into the mush at the bottom. The wind picked up, my hair whipping around like sandy cattails, slapping at my eyes. I eyed the girl on the blanket next to us, her hair pulled back taut against her head and held in place with a hair band. Evelyn never had a hair band with her in her life, I was pretty sure. She wasn't a "Band-Aid in every pocketbook" kind of mother.

Evelyn screamed when the umbrella uprooted and skipped dangerously across the sand, toward the ocean. Beachgoers shouted, pointed, and ducked, but no one jumped up. She stood helplessly and watched our only beach umbrella pinwheel away. She flopped back onto the blanket and gave me a dazzling smile, all sparkling teeth, and shrugged, like it didn't matter. Like we could just buy another one, which of course, I knew we couldn't. I squinted down the beach, but the umbrella was gone. I went back to my digging, scooting down toward the wet sand, but she never called me back.

When I wandered back up to the blanket, a man sat next to Evelyn, his chest tan and shiny, his dark hair slick.

"Bud, look! This nice man here brought our umbrella back!" She rubbed his bicep.

"Hi, Hilary. Your mom was just talking about you. I'm Michael, but people call me Mick."

"Not Mike?" There was a Michael in Mrs. Hoppit's sixth-grade class, but everyone called him Mike.

"Nope. Mick. It's Irish."

He didn't look Irish. Mick hung around all day, anchoring the umbrella deep into the sand, and I was relieved we wouldn't have to buy another one. I hated buying stuff with Evelyn. She'd walk it to the counter, hesitate until the cashier huffed, and she'd put it back. It was embarrassing.

Back in our apartment, Evelyn made dinner and Mick stayed. When I woke up the next day, he was perched at the breakfast table while Evelyn hummed over a pan of fried eggs. When I got home from school, he was reclined on the couch, reading Evelyn's newspaper that I was never supposed to touch because it was her *only luxury*. His dirty sneakers rested on the armrest. *Hey bud,* he said, and I said nothing because we were not buds.

He stayed for quite a while, his big hands around her shoulders as we watched baseball at night instead of our usual

Golden Girls reruns. I tried to protest but Evelyn smiled and patted my knee, and kissed Mick's cheek. He stayed through Evelyn's birthday, which was in October, and right up to Halloween. I had wanted to be a hippie but Evelyn forgot to make me a costume so I was a scarecrow again, my outfit from the year before recycled. The jeans with the hay hems were too small, so we just left them unbuttoned.

When Evelyn and I came back from trick-or-treating, Mick wasn't there. The next morning, he wasn't at the breakfast table, or hogging the bathroom, filling it with steam and stink, and Evelyn's face was red and her eyes were half-closed. I knew she'd been crying.

Then a week later, he still hadn't come back and I was flopped in her room, watching her get ready for work after school. She stood facing her closet wearing just her bra, her hands resting delicately on her hip bones as her foot tapped impatiently. She was searching for her uniform, a starchy maroon-and-white thing. One of her jobs at the time was as a hotel maid working early mornings.

"What's that?" I pointed to her arm, yellow speckled dots, four of them in a row, like thumbprints in icing.

She looked, casually, and ran her index finger over the smooth vanilla skin of her bicep and shrugged. "Oh I must have bumped into something." But she turned away from me and put on her uniform real quick after that.

Only later, when I was a teenager, she'd tell me how hard it was to *find a good man.* I'd remember Mick and think, *he was not a good man.* Sometimes he'd come back, then disappear for long stretches, leaving her to cry alone in her room, long into the nights. I'd asked her once if my father was a good man. She'd laughed, always, that tinkling soft giggle. *Only the best.*

I swore I'd never be like her, the preening, making it all *just so,* promising this time would be different. I hated to see her weak, could hardly stand it.

Once I started college, I'd catalogue the boys I met: *Good Men* and *Not Good Men.* Sometimes it was easy to tell the difference, the *Not Good Men* would drink and paw at me, pulling on my jean shorts in dark corners of fraternity parties. If Evelyn had met Henry before she died, she would have clapped her small hands together and sighed. *Oh! You found one!* Evelyn was easily charmed, and Henry's favorite pastime was being charming.

I think of Henry now and his gentle smile, his eyes crinkled in the corners as he humors me. The way only I can make him laugh. The way he checks up on me, worries about me, frets and fusses like a finicky cat. His soft, careful hands on my body, his mouth on mine. The way he gives me the last piece of lobster always. How he brings me gifts, small trinkets, flowers, a key chain, because he *just can't stop thinking about me.*

He's nearly perfect. But is he good?

CHAPTER 17

I lurk near a potted plant, my hair tucked back into a baseball cap that I found in the bottom of our closet, dusty and faded. I've never seen it on Henry. The gym buzzes with people entering one door in business suits with briefcases and attaches, exiting through another in spandex and Lycra, as though on a conveyor belt. I hover behind the one-way mirrored wall. I can see in, no one can see out. I scan the lobby. I'm semiprotected but nowhere near invisible. I have maybe five minutes. To see what? Hard to say.

Henry jogs on the treadmill, his cooldown pace, and on the machine next to him, the pink-spandexed blonde keeps pace as they laugh. He's gesturing with his hands, and he throws his arms wide for the punch line. The blonde tosses her head back laughing and then stumbles, grabs at the safety bar. A sharp pain stabs my center and I grit my teeth. They both slow and step off, Henry towels the back of his neck and watches her while she pulls up one leg, then the other in a postworkout stretch.

I know this is crazy. I'm spying on my husband. I've become a suburban cliché, minus the twenty pounds of baby weight and minivan. His behavior has been so erratic and this woman, his hand on her behind, against a backdrop of pink Lycra, has become a mental picture my mind hands me at inopportune moments.

Henry and I have always talked about partnership, working together to make things work. He's always said he'd never divorce. That divorced rich men are inevitably poor men. That any marriage can be fixed, that love fluctuates. His viewpoint, while coldly practical, was one of the reasons I married him so quickly. A four-month courtship, a simple but elegant wedding, an expensive dinner party, and voilà, a cemented spot in high society. Henry with his beautiful, charming wife. Me with my handsome, rich husband. *Illusions are dangerous*, said Evelyn. Yet, I have no illusions about marriage. No expectations of handsome princes and white horses and happily ever afters. Evelyn never believed in happily ever afters, warning against falling in love with an idea over a person. *Ideas are infallible, people are not. Don't confuse the two.* She was an optimist, but never naïve. There's a difference, she'd say.

So here I sit, next to a remarkably lifelike ficus tree, wondering if I've done just that. Is this an affair, or a harmless way to pass a grueling workout?

He walks by her and flicks her hair, like he's a third grader at recess. It's the playfulness that's so foreign.

"Zoe?"

I spin around, my heart in my throat. Reid Pinkman stands in front of me with his head cocked. I hardly recognize him outside Henry's office. Reid is younger than me, in his late twenties, ambitious and single and often lightly flirtatious. Henry is his mentor and fawns over him. I'm always slightly embarrassed around Reid, ever since the night before Musha Cay, when Henry was cruel and Reid witnessed it. He's never brought it up, thankfully.

"Hi, Reid!" I say brightly, giving him a dazzling smile. "What are you doing here?"

It's ironic, given my circumstances, that I don't actually enjoy inventing lies on the spot. My mind races and my heart thunders in my ears.

"I'm . . . surprising Henry. Well, I was going to, but I just got an urgent call from a friend and I have to run."

I glance back through the one-way glass and Henry has the gym towel tossed over his shoulder and he and Blonde Spandex are walking toward the door, but slowly. She touches his arm and he leans down to hear something she says.

Reid follows my gaze and nods. "Ah. Okay, then will I see you tonight?"

My head snaps back to Reid. "Wait. What's tonight?"

Reid looks toward Henry, who has stopped walking. Henry and the woman are now involved in deep, serious conversation, and Henry rakes a hand through his hair. The blonde crosses her arms over her chest and juts her chin out and I'm struck with the thought that you don't typically get mad at someone you barely know. Anger is an intimate emotion.

"The firm's celebration for Nippon. The Japanese steel account? Henry didn't tell you?"

"I'm sure he did. I probably forgot." I pull the hat off and shove it in my purse. "Do me a favor, Reid. Don't tell Henry I was here, okay?"

"Sure thing." He touches my arm and says hopefully, "See you tonight?"

"Yep, see you tonight."

I rush into the revolving door just as Henry and the blonde come through the door into the lobby. They are stopped by Reid and I use the opportunity to scuttle through one revolution before I'm spit out onto the sidewalk. Around the corner, I lean against the stone building, under the concrete plaque with the number 58 on it, and take deep breaths. Who is the blonde? Does Reid know her? This is Reid's gym, too. If Henry was having an affair, Reid would most likely know about it. I have to figure out a way to get to tonight's event. I wonder if I can call Henry's secretary and ask where it is.

My skin buzzes hot. It's a warm day, for April, probably pushing eighty degrees, and my shirt sticks to my back. On a whim, I pull out my phone.

Lunch? I text.

Starving, Cash texts back.

• • •

We arrange to meet in ten minutes at a Black and Bean, a coffee shop a block away. I know we need to talk to make plans for tomorrow, *tomorrow!,* and my stomach flips. I haven't talked to him since Monday in the park, when he agreed to go to Caroline's with me. I still haven't told Henry about Caroline. After last night and this morning, I'm not sure I will.

My mind swims with unmade decisions and doubt. My ears ring with the sound of broken glass, shattering on the wall behind me, crunching under my shoes. The stench of whiskey, the air permeated with violence.

I might be overreacting. He didn't throw the glass *at me.* He threw it at the wall. Is that different?

Women have girlfriends for this very reason: to bounce their irrationalities off each other. I long for Lydia, the way we used to be. Nonjudgmental and totally accepting. She once slept with two different men in the same night, and when she'd confessed it, the next day, lying in our side-by-side beds, with the late afternoon sun filtering through the smoky haze of our bedroom, I remember sitting straight up in bed, my mouth hanging open. Her choices were not my choices, and all I'd ever said was, *Who was better?* And we howled with laughter. As far as I could tell, she never stopped to question herself when she passed judgment on me. It hardly seemed fair.

When we'd met, I'd been staying at a homeless shelter, wearing third- and fourthhand suits to job interviews that I was neither qualified for nor eligible to work, having not had a valid identification, a college education, or a permanent address. I wandered, exhausted, into La Fleur d'Elise and sat helplessly on a chair, clutching the help wanted ads from the Treasure Hunt.

"What the hell is wrong with you?" The girl had snapped her gum in my direction. "Also your clothes look like shit. When did you last go shopping? Nineteen ninety-two?"

"Do you always greet people this way?" I sat up straight, studying her pink-and-purple-tipped hair, the large curling tattoo on her wispy upper arm, her bloodred lipstick.

"Most of the time. Do you always wear suits to interview for custodial positions?"

"Custodial? I thought it said florist assistant."

"You're basically pushing a broom, sister. Do you think you can handle that?" She studied the paper in front of her over a pair of electric blue glasses. I realized, with a start, that the lenses were fake, and suppressed a smile. I nodded and she handed me a broom.

"That's it? I'm hired?"

She snatched the broom out of my reach. "Unless you don't want the job . . . "

"I want it."

"Good. Now, what are you doing tonight?"

"Tonight?" I blinked at her, wide-eyed. The shelter had a curfew.

"Yes. Tonight. You need to see the inside of a mall, stat."

"There are malls in Manhattan?"

"There are, but we're going to Joisey." She shrugged. "I live in Hoboken. There are malls there. You can stay with me."

"You just met me." I gave her a slitted-eye stare. A few months distanced from all that had happened in San Francisco, I was unaccustomed to common courtesy, downright wary of kindness.

"Call me crazy. Or nice. Or lonely." She shrugged and unwrapped a Dum Dum. She stuck out her hand, a ring on every finger. "I'm Lydia."

"Are you new to the city?" I asked her, thinking of her *or lonely.*

She furrowed her eyebrows. "No. But everyone is lonely. Right?"

She was arrestingly vulnerable, even while she was cutting you. You could just see people blink, unsure if she was putting them on. She linked her arm through mine. "I have a feeling about you."

I miss her. I miss her laughter, her unique bitchy-nice. I miss having a friend.

• • •

In the coffee shop, I wait for Cash, restless and fidgety. With a start, I realize then that I didn't get my call from Henry at nine o'clock. There had been no envelope of cash on the counter this morning, no note. No *I'm sorry,* nothing. I wonder if he's called the credit card company. These little money envelopes feel like a leash that he can take away at any time and I'm left powerless. My face flushes at the thought. What would I have thought of an allowance five years ago? It would have been an extravagance.

I text Henry's cell. *Are you okay? I'm sorry about our fight. Love you.* I avoid saying I'm sorry for any specific thing, because I'm not sure that I am. But I struggle with being ignored. Everyone has fights, this I know. But our relationship feels cracked down the middle.

Cash slides into the seat across from me with two paper

cups and a tray of sandwiches and I quickly tuck my phone into my purse, depressing the ringer down button.

"Can you ever pick a place with mugs, please?" He flashes me a grin and I make a face at him.

"Are you really too good for paper cups?" I peel off the plastic lid and let the curling steam escape.

"Hey, just because I scrape to make rent doesn't mean I don't enjoy the finer things in life." He gently pushes a turkey sandwich in my direction.

I smile and busy myself spreading mustard on the roll. "Are you still up for helping me? Tomorrow?"

"I am. What's your idea for a game plan?"

"Well, I can rent a car. I just want a navigator. I have no idea where I'm going. I have no idea what to expect when I get there." The turkey suddenly looks limp and slimy. Oh, God. Tomorrow I'll meet my *mother*. It feels so weird to think about, to say, because my whole life, my mother has been Evelyn, although I haven't called her Mom since I was fifteen. The word *mother* gets twisted around on my tongue, snagged in its own connotations. Who is more my mother? Caroline, who birthed me and left me? Or Evelyn, who rescued me and raised me? Who bought me my first bra, taught me about love and sex, and later, death. Why are the words *mother* and *love* synonymous?

"Expect the best, prepare for the worst?"

"Ha. That's a Henry-ism." I almost laugh.

"He's a smart man." We sit in silence for a moment while Cash chews. He dabs his mouth with a napkin and wipes a splotch of mayonnaise off the table. "Have you told him?"

I shake my head, averting my eyes. I don't want to talk to Cash about Henry. I'm not naïve, you don't talk to another man about your marriage. "No. Not yet. I will. He's been stressed about work lately. If it amounts to anything, I'll tell him."

"What do you expect?"

"I don't know. Probably nothing?" I feel the lie slip around my mouth.

He nods and presses his forefinger into the tines of the fork. "It's okay to want something, Zoe. I knew a man, back in Texas, dying of AIDS. He had no one, not one single person in the world who cared about him. His friends didn't know how to handle a sick guy, and this was in the late nineties. Anyway, he read my article and he called me. Wanted to find his mother. Not his father, just his mother. He was raised by his father, a real son of a bitch. Anyway, it took me a few months, and I was racing the clock with this guy. Finally, I found her. I had concrete proof that it was her, there was no doubt in my mind. There still isn't. Anyway, I called her, explain the whole situation. I tell her that her *son*, her flesh and blood, is dying in hospice care, not fifty miles from her house. Her response? She denies the whole thing. Says she never had a son, to never call her again, and hangs up on me. I kept calling for days. She never picked up the phone. He died a week later."

I push away the tray. "Why did you tell me this story?"

Cash taps the fork twice on the table. "I don't know. I guess it's the one that stuck with me the most. The way you can deny your own child that way."

"Right. You're not helping."

He laughs. "I'm sorry. I have a bunch of wonderful reunion stories, too. Do you want me to tell you those?"

"No, it's okay. I'm fine. I guess my goal is just to have a connection, that's all. Just to know it's there. Somewhere in the world, someone knows I exist." That sounds overly dramatic and I shake my head. "Let's talk about the plan. I'll call the car service today and rent a car."

"Don't bother. I have a car."

"You live in Manhattan and have a car? On a reporter's salary?" I tease and pick at a potato chip.

"I'm secretly rich. But I find all my money repels the ladies." He smirks at me. "No, seriously, it's a used Honda. I
park it in my mother's garage. She lives in Queens. We can
take the subway to her house and pick it up in the morning."

Cash pulls out his phone and maps the route. We'll meet
at eight at the train station, and I wonder for a brief second
what I'll do when Henry calls at nine. If he calls. When Cash
checks his watch and announces that his long lunch is over,
I quell a stab of disappointment. With a quick tap on my
hand and a "See ya tomorrow," he's gone and I'm left at the
table alone.

I think of the apartment, the shattered glass on the dining
room floor that I haven't yet bothered to clean up, and I feel
rooted to my seat. I picture Penny finding the sticky mess,
wondering about its meaning. Calling Henry, compassion in
her voice, *Are things okay?* I rummage through my purse for
my phone, which is blinking with a waiting text from Henry.
*Are you at home? I'm sorry about our fight. I've been hopelessly
stressed about work. I want you in my life more than anything
else. I forgot all about the celebration tonight, I've been so distracted. I love you. Please say you'll go with me. It's formal. I've
sent something to the apartment. Call me when you get it. I'll
pick you up.*

The long message is a stark difference from Henry's usual
short and to the point texts. I feel my heart, like fluttering
wings in my chest, and close my eyes. I look at the time
stamp, when did he send it? 12:05, right as he would be leaving the gym. I shove the image of the blonde out of my mind
and feel a rush of love for him. We're not perfect, we may not
even be good, *right now*. But there's hope there, and I know
there's love. I can see it in the way he looks at me, and I flash
back to his face, captivated, in the flickering candlelight of
the Italian restaurant as he detailed the history of the town.
Every woman should have a man who looks at her like that,

like she's the only one in the room. Was that really only a few days ago?

I sent you something. I stand up so quickly that my knee hits the table, and I shove my phone back inside my purse. I hurry through the crowded café, jostling elbows and bumping into tables. On the way, I toss the paper cup in the trash. I have my head bent down and I'm so lost in thought that when I push open the front door, I crash right into Molly McKay.

CHAPTER 18

"Hilary!" Her voice is shrill, with the urgency of a reporter covering a tabloid story, and it takes me a second to make sense of her. She keeps going. "I know it's you."

"Did you follow me here?"

"Just talk to me, please. Why are you doing this? You were my best friend, you know." She leans toward me, her pink lipsticked mouth twisted into a grimace, but her eyes are imploring, clouded with hurt. I have no doubt that she believes that to be true. I tended to follow her around, I was a hanger-on, which was Molly's favorite kind of friend. Probably why I felt such kinship with Mick. "I can't just let it go. Why do you keep running away? What happened to you?"

"I—I have no idea who you are or what you're talking about, but please, leave me alone." I start to turn, but she grabs my bare arm, twisting it slightly, and jabs a bright pink manicured finger into my elbow.

"Right there. You had twenty-two stitches, right there, and I sat in the ER all night with you. You fell off a horse. You liked the ranch hand, what was his name? Oh yeah,

Harlan. He checked up on you, later, and we all thought for sure you'd get together, but you didn't. *Because he was actually married.* But I'm the only one who knows that, because I came back the next day, mind you, from staying at Gunther's, and he was still there, at six in the morning. You can't pretend you don't know me."

Her clear blue eyes never waver. I'm not even sure she blinks. Molly was never a shrinking violet, but I'd never known her to have this kind of verve.

As careless as I've been, I can't shrug off Detective Maslow's words. He'd cautioned about ever going back to San Francisco. *We caught Jared and the others, the ringleaders. There are still powerful men in hiding. We'll never catch them all.* I think of Mick, languishing in prison, for he was always an underling. The real terror was Jared. And possibly others: nameless, faceless threats.

I think of my ransacked apartment. I think of the driver careening through the intersection. All the things I don't know for sure. Then, I think of how Molly, if I relented, even for a second, would surely call anyone she kept in touch with. The idea of it, the story alone, was just too juicy. I imagine the news floating out over the airwaves, through the Midwest, back to San Francisco. I imagine the idea of it finding Mick, or worse, Jared. *Hilary Lawlor, the bitch who put you in jail, is in New York.*

"I'm sorry, but I have no idea who you are. Please, leave me alone." I wrench my arm out of her taloned grip.

"Fine. If you want to be that way, you can pretend all you want, but Gunther and I, we live here now. It's not *that* big of a city. You took yourself away, like I didn't even matter." Her round bubbly face hardens at the dismissal. "We'll see you around, Hilary." Her voice comes out like a hiss, and on the *Hilary,* her lip curls. It's the anger that surprises me. I expected confusion, even sadness. She sees it as a rejection and her cheeks mottle. She gives me a small, slight smile and I inhale quickly.

I recognize the look, the covert determination, hollow and self-serving. Our sophomore year, Molly had turned in what she thought was an A paper and had gotten a B. She stared at that paper with this same face, the same dappled cheeks, red and wind-burned, the same hardened black beaded eyes. Three days later, I heard a rumor: The professor was trading grades for sex. Unsubstantiated rumors. He was suspended for three days for "investigative purposes," after which he was reinstated. No permanently marred record. No *real* damage. That was the terrifying part, really. I could never prove it was Molly, but I would have bet our whole apartment on it. When I'd asked her, her lips turned up in the slightest smile. She raised her eyebrows and murmured *I'm not surprised, really.* That's when I knew.

I turn and rush away, fighting against the lunchtime crowd, away from that smile. I wipe a sheen of sweat from my forehead and pull my hair back, off my neck. She's not going to let this go; who would? It's a crazy story. I imagine her friendless while Gunther is at his new office all day, out to happy hour at night with coworkers. I picture her bored, roaming her apartment, not unlike the way I roam mine but without CARE to distract her, performing Internet searches, staking out my building, tracking me down. It could become a hobby to someone. The idea of it squeezes my heart.

I duck into a souvenir store, covered floor to ceiling with hats and T-shirts, prepaid cell phones, and miniature Statues of Liberty.

"Can I help you?" I spin around and the man stands two feet away, crowding me, and I jump back.

"No, I . . . I'm fine. I just needed the air." The door is open but the shop is air-conditioned. I pretend to peruse postcards before adjusting my shirt and exiting back out into the street.

I take a deep breath and scan the street. No Molly. I head home. I don't look back.

* * *

There is a box on the dining room table with a single long-stemmed red rose resting on top and a note.

> *Zoe, I'm sorry about our fight. I've been under stress at work. Please understand, last night was all my fault. There's a party tonight to celebrate our partnership with Nippon. Wear this, be ready at 6, and I'll pick you up. I love you. You are the light of my life.*

I set the rose down on the table and place the note next to it. Pause, take a breath. I don't know if this is real, if Reid told Henry he saw me at the gym and this is a placating measure. Was the blonde the real date, the first date? Am I the backup plan?

Slowly, I lift the lid off the square box. I unwrap the tissue paper inside and pull out the gown. It's a calf length, sleek, silk cocktail dress, in a deep plum. The neckline plunges, more provocative than anything I'd select, and it is trimmed in crystals. I feel my breath catch. It's gorgeous. A hanger lies diagonally in the box, and I slip it under the spaghetti straps and hang it up in the doorway.

I scan the kitchen: The glass has been cleaned up, like last night never happened. I suppose I should feel at least unsettled by the fact that my home has been righted in my absence, like a pencil eraser over the sketch of last night's fight. Sometimes it's as though people move around me, thin and wispy like ghosts, quietly arranging my life to Henry's convenience. Penny. Reid.

"I'm sorry to intrude. I didn't know you were going to be home."

I drop the box I'm holding and let out a quick staccato

scream. "Penny. Jesus Christ, you scared the living daylights out of me."

"I'm sorry, I heard you out here. I was cleaning the bedrooms." She gives a quick flick of her head toward the hall. "Dusting."

We don't have many one-on-one encounters like this. She frequently comes and goes, conveniently, when I'm out of the house. Too frequently to be coincidence, but not in any way that could be questioned. I tend to believe Henry tells her my daily schedule. She fidgets, a duster in her hands, a white button-down shirt tucked into jeans, bare feet pushed into Birkenstocks. Her toenails are painted a surprising red, her feet a healthy tan. She shifts her weight and checks the time on the stove.

"Penny, do you like me?" I don't mean to ask the question, but I'm a tad fed up from my day, tired of sidestepping people and issues, and trying to do the right thing for everyone else. I'm tired of roadblocks I can't see, hidden agendas I can't fathom.

Her head snaps back and her eyes meet mine. "I don't know you, Mrs. Whittaker."

"You can call me Zoe. You call Henry, Henry."

"I've known Henry since . . . well, for a long time." She steps backward, like she's going to leave the room. I can feel the impending dismissal.

"How long?" I bend down to pick up the box and turn it over in my hands.

"How long what?"

"How long have you known Henry?" I press.

"A long time. I've never counted." She glances nervously over her shoulder and then becomes intensely interested in the duster in her hand, turning it over one way, then the other. Her fingernails match her toenails.

"You knew his parents. You knew him as a child?"

"I . . . did, yes." She backs up toward the doorway, pushing her gray bangs off her brow with her forearm. She has deep-set lines around her mouth, crow's feet at her eyes. I try to remember how old Henry has said she is, but then I realize he hasn't. I'm guessing sixty-five. Maybe even seventy.

"Tell me about him. Tell me anything. He says nothing about his upbringing. Very little about his life before me." I take a step forward, closing the gap between us, desperation comes off my skin like a stench. I don't care.

Her voice is a whisper. "He . . . was an unusual little boy. So curious. Brilliant really." Her voice trails off and she looks away. When she looks back, she squares her shoulders and levels her gaze. "None of this is my place, Mrs. Whittaker."

"Penny, I—"

"I should get back to it. I'll be leaving very soon." She turns and scurries from the room. I actually consider following her. Pestering her with questions, forcing her to talk to me. I toss the box back down onto the dining room table, frustrated, and head to my bedroom after grabbing the dress from the doorway.

I clip the hanger carefully on the back of the door and lie faceup on the bed. It's a beautiful dress and I wonder where he bought it or when. My eyes feel heavy and I drift to sleep. I dream of college in San Francisco, of Molly McKay in an eggplant evening gown, and Birkenstocks.

• • •

The car arrives at 5:57 p.m. and I smile to myself. It's so Henry. I smooth the front of my dress. I'm wearing the charm bracelet, the bonsai, the gladiolus, the wings. It's an olive branch. Henry gets out, holding his hand up, palm out to the driver, indicating that he'll escort me. He stops in front of me and his eyes are bright, his hair tousled. We don't say anything for a minute, then both speak at once. He laughs and motions for me to talk.

"There's nothing between Cash and me," I blurt out. He pulls me against him, his lips on my hair.

"I know. I know that. I'm sorry. Let's just not talk about it. I overreacted." His hands graze down my spine, his fingertips hot on my skin. He pulls away and gestures toward the car, his hand resting on the small of my back. He touches the bracelet on my wrist as I climb inside, and says, "Ah, Zoe."

"Have you called the credit card company?" I inquire, as though I just thought of it. Innocent.

"Yes. They're sending a new one, but these things take time, Zoe." He pats my arm. "Do you need more money? Is that an issue?"

"No. I'm fine. I don't even use it all, really, not all the time. I just wish I didn't have to be so . . . dependent. Or something . . ." I falter then, not sure of how to proceed. He's studying me.

"Whatever you need, Zoe, just ask. I'll do anything, you know that." He squeezes my hand and kisses my temple, at my hairline.

We ride in silence but he grasps my hand, running his thumb along my fingertips. I think of the CARE benefit, the last time we were in the car like this together, made-up and sparkly. I had felt so loved then, a mere two and a half weeks ago. Now, I can't stop thinking of the girl from the gym. The mental image of his hand, cupped around that bright pink backdrop, the pert little swell.

"Henry, would you ever be unfaithful?" I stare at our fingers intertwined.

"Why would you ask that? No. Never." His answer is quick, definitive. He flashes me a smile. "Peter's wife will be there tonight. Remember her?"

I nod. Peter Young, the only person I've ever met that Henry may have called a boss, with his prematurely white hair, straight Chiclet teeth, and deeply lined cheeks. I vaguely remember his wife Muriel, small and dainty in her fifties but with sharp, restless eyes and an infectious laugh.

We pull up in front of Heiwa, a trendy Japanese restaurant, a mere four blocks from Henry's office skirting the line between Tribeca and Soho, depending on who's asking. Henry leads me inside, giving my hand a quick squeeze. We're led to a private dining room where twenty people mill around, in cocktail dresses and glittering jewelry. I've met most of them. Henry's colleagues are both wary of outsiders and welcoming once you're one of them. I probably have one foot in each camp at this point.

I spot Muriel Young from across the room, deep in conversation with Reid Pinkman, and I make my way to them. Reid gives me a wide smile and a kiss on each cheek, hovering just a second longer than necessary, his cheek cool and smooth against mine. He's dressed in a navy blue suit with a slim, trendy fit and yellow tie. I look around for his date and see none.

"Zoe." Muriel gives me a quick, cool hug. "It's been a while since I've seen you, dear. How are you?"

I give a blithe answer, something utterly unsubstantial. She nods and returns to her conversation with Reid. They're talking about Nippon, the partnership, and my mind wanders. How does Muriel know so much about Peter's business deals? Henry acts as though he's a federal agent.

". . . and when Henry goes there, he should be able to see exactly what Peter's so concerned about."

"Right, I can't say that I blame him—"

"Wait," I interrupt. "When Henry goes where? When?"

"Japan. Tomorrow?" Both Muriel and Reid look at me like I've lost my mind.

"Oh, right. Sorry. I forgot." I recover quickly and my mind spins. When was he going to tell me? For how long? I scan the crowd but I don't see him.

Reid plucks a glass of red wine off a nearby waiter's tray and hands it to me. He then taps my elbow and gives a quick *I'll-be-right-back* hand motion. I nod, dumbly. Muriel studies me, spinning the stem of her wineglass in her hand.

"You didn't know, did you?" She cocks her head to the side. I pause. I'm so accustomed to self-sufficiency that it feels uncomfortable to relent, even with this small an admission.

"No. I didn't know." I search the restaurant again and still don't see him. "He's been distracted. It's okay. For how long?"

"A week." She gives me a comforting smile. "Henry is a tough man, Zoe. I've known him for a long time. I never thought he'd recover from Tara."

"How so?"

"Oh," she waves her hand around, her bracelets clattering together. She smiles guiltily and lowered her voice. "He was a mess for a while. Determined to find out who was driving the car. That sort of thing. He seemed to all but forget about it after he met you. You're very different."

The wine warms my cheeks. "Did you know her well?" I tilt my head back and take the last swig, the red burning the back of my throat.

Muriel gives me a surprised look. "No, I never met her."

"Really? Why not?" The back of my mouth goes dry.

She leans in, taps my shoulder once. "Tara was agoraphobic, dear. No one ever met her."

．　．　．

Muriel moves on, circulates among the crowd. Eventually, I find Henry and hover next to him but somehow get pushed outside the circle. He doesn't make any gestures to include me, and I border on being ignored.

As the night wears on, I grow more and more angry. Why did he invite me? If he's leaving tomorrow, why not enjoy the night together? Why not *tell me you're leaving tomorrow?*

Finally, I grip his elbow and drag him away. "You're going to Japan. You never told me that."

"Relax, Zoe." His tone is dismissive and his eyes narrow. "I was going to tell you tonight."

"Muriel Young even knows. Reid Pinkman knows. I look like a fool."

"You're being overdramatic. You don't look like anything. Everyone knows how busy I am." He shakes loose from my grip and holds up his fingers to a waiter, indicating another drink. He turns back to me, his eyes dark. "Besides, I thought you'd know already. You're so cozy with Reid these days."

"What does that mean?" I snap.

"Oh, I'm sure you know." So Reid told Henry I was at the gym.

At that moment, Peter Young taps the microphone and asks everyone to sit for dinner. Henry places his hand on the small of my back, to guide me.

We file into two sides of a straight, long table. It's a larger crowd than I originally thought, about thirty people. Henry sits to my left and I expect him to pull my chair out but he turns to the man next to him, ignoring me. I've never seen Henry act so impolitely; he opens doors for women and carries grocery bags for little old ladies on the street. Reid sits on my right.

"No date tonight?" I raise my eyebrows and take a sip of water. Henry's back is inches from my face, an obstinate wall.

"Not tonight." Reid has what is known as boyish charm. Round, pink cheeks, shiny like a newborn's bottom, and long, curling eyelashes so dark he looks like he's wearing makeup. I've seen women (girls, really) actually swoon from his smile. In this day and age of smartphones, he still keeps a little black book.

Reid is one of those people you meet and instantly know you could be friends. Almost everyone feels this way about him. If you shake his hand, your mind spins with all the future memories you could have, all the mischief you could make. You could almost envision him, a grown adult, egging suburban houses and peeling away in his yellow Porsche. People get confused, *Have we met before, maybe when we were young?*

Even now, as he talks, I find myself thinking back to the Cynthia night. The night before Musha Cay. The night he helped me, rescued me. I almost laugh at my own dramatizing. *Rescue me.*

"I need to find a wife. I'm almost forty, you know." He unfolds a napkin and takes a swig from his whiskey glass.

"No. I thought you were in your late twenties. Younger than me." I'm honestly surprised.

"I'm an old man. Not in spirit, like your Henry. He's an old soul. But I'm not getting younger. Know of any single women who are looking for a husband?" He rests his chin on his palm and faces me, his apple cheeks red from the alcohol.

"In New York City?" I raise my eyebrows. "Are you kidding? We must have the highest available woman per capita ratio in the country. Wear a sandwich board and stand on the street."

He snorts, a quick huff of air through his nose, and shakes his head. "Find me someone. I need a smart woman, independent. No plastic surgery. No fascination with measuring their thigh gap."

"What in the world is a thigh gap?" I blink, twice. I'm not sure I want to know. The concerns of half my gender baffle me. In Henry's world, there is no shortage of beautiful, wealthy women who behave like teenagers with limitless bank accounts.

"See? Don't you have any friends who are like you? Conscious of the world? Grateful? That's our problem. No one is fucking grateful anymore. Look at you, with CARE. You're grateful. I bet you were poor growing up, right?"

I shift in my chair. At that moment, the sashimi is placed in front of me, beautiful with its brightly colored fish and green vegetables, and a swirl of scarlet miso on the square, white plate.

"You don't have to answer that. Don't you have friends? I need to find someone like you." He slurs the *like* and the *you* together. At that moment, I realize that Henry has turned around and is paying close attention to our conversation. I meet his gaze and his eyes narrow. He snaps open his napkin in one quick wrist motion and gives a short shake of his head, staring stonily ahead to some point on the far wall. I imagine it's one of Henry's most marketable skills: the stonewall. His face smooths out, perfectly unlined, like chiseled marble. A *David* statue of my husband and just as cool to the touch. While anger heats most people up, buzzes them and makes them hyper, it has the opposite effect on Henry. He becomes cold and still, his flesh hardens. A corpse taken straight from the morgue refrigerator.

Reid blathers next to me, his words skipping and sliding into each other, oblivious to the undercurrent between Henry and me. I lean to my left, nudge Henry with my elbow, press my fingertips into his quadriceps, he doesn't flinch.

The sashimi plates are replaced by dinner plates, large and gleaming with impossibly small portions. Four courses come and go, with Henry smiling at Muriel across the table and Reid chattering to anyone who will listen. At dinner's conclusion, while everyone is drinking dessert wine and sherry, Henry stands, his hand on my elbow, and with a wide apologetic smile ushers me to the waiting car.

In the car, the radio plays classical music at low volume, like Henry always instructs the driver to do. The city street passes silently by, life on mute.

"Say something, please." I run my fingernail along the window edge, inexplicably damp with condensation.

"I don't want to worry about my wife and other men. I'll say that." His hands are clasped across his knees, his back rigid. The ball joint of his jaw trembles underneath his skin.

"Is this about Cash or Reid?" I feel my shoulders droop. I'm so tired of this conversation, for no reason. I want to bring up the blonde but I can't. It's a big new door and the room behind it is filled with unknowable variables. I'm so tired. "I've never given you any reason to worry. That's your own doing."

"Zoe."

In the apartment, he says nothing and goes right to his office. The door closes with a heavy click, a hushed echo in the marble hallway. I go to bed, knowing, acknowledging for the first time, that we are in trouble. Our life, not what I expect or want, but just the way it is. I realize that tomorrow Henry is leaving for Japan and I don't know for sure when he's coming home. It occurs to me that maybe he won't be. That our marriage will be over.

I spin the charm bracelet around my wrist. Such a unique, creative gift, so out of character for Henry. Just last weekend, he'd been windblown and free. Loving. Writing poetry, or at least copying poetry. And now, back in the city we call home, he's this other man again. Cold. Calculating.

I feel the bed move underneath me. The blankets pull back and Henry's hand, soft as silk across my skin. He pulls me against him and my stomach swoops with relief. We've always done this, we've always made up, made love, nothing has ever been permanent. I was silly to think otherwise. His breath flutters, hot in my ear.

Before I know it, his hands push up my nightgown and he's on top of me, in me, hard and pressing, his wet gasps against my collarbone come quick and his hand grips my hip as he grunts, once, twice. It's over in a minute. He pants quietly next to me, his palm smooths my hair off my forehead.

In the dark, he stands up, the moonlight reflecting off a sheen of sweat on his skin and I realize that he is naked. That he came to me for one purpose and I've served it. He's leaving. He pauses in the doorway, his hand resting on the doorknob, a thin, white line of light reflected down his back and leg. His face is turned and in the half-light, his mouth opens and closes, like he wants to say something, and still, stupidly, my heart catches on the unspoken maybe.

"I'll see you in a week, Zoe."

CHAPTER 19

The Japan trip has eased some of the pressure. I could not have reasonably told Henry about Caroline if we were a) barely speaking and b) he was out of the country. Maybe. Who knows? I've decided not to care. The weather has suddenly gotten hot, in the eighties, and today, it's all anyone can talk about. Cash's neighbor, the gas station attendant, even Cash himself. I'm meeting my mother for the first time and all I can think about is whether she will look as much like me as her picture? Will she have the oddball habit of tugging on her ear when she's nervous? Will she bite her thumbnail cuticle? And yet, all I seem to be conversing about is temperature and humidity. *They say tomorrow is supposed to be even worse!* Even as I hear myself say the words, I can't fathom anything about tomorrow.

We take the subway to Queens and walk to his mother's house from the station. His childhood home is a square clapboard, smooshed in on the sides like someone had taken it between their palms. The street is lined with similar structures, variations of dinginess, and yet there are flowers in the window boxes (some are plastic) and well-worn but not tattered American flags hanging from the flagpoles—the kind that stand tall, not the suburban idea of a flagpole that hangs jauntily from the porch post, usually draped with a nylon slip of fabric silk-screened with a smiling cat, *Have a Mawr-velous Day!* The lawns are shorn, bare in some spots, but maintained.

His mother's house is empty. She's working, he says, a doctor's office receptionist, and I nod. Cash waves his hand around and mutters something about the neighborhood, how it used to be better. It's the way the middle class always feel around the rich: apologetic. I'm used to the excuses, the explanations. Truthfully, there's no appropriate response. My money is not mine. We are the same, Cash and I. But to say that denies the privilege that comes with Henry's influence. Instead, I nod and smile. We climb in Cash's late-model Honda and head onto I-87 North.

The city recedes and Cash turns on the radio to a Top 40 station that plays music I've never heard. I think about how that's possible, that I'm thirty years old and I'm not familiar with contemporary pop music. Lydia would be appalled. Our apartment in Hoboken was never quiet, always bursting with underground punk, hard-core rock, and then sometimes just blasting the latest Pink song. Lydia lived her life in music. Loud, harsh, thrumming beats for Saturdays and soft jazz for Sunday hangovers. The past year of my life has been outlined in shades of silence.

"What will you say?" Cash turns the volume down on the radio.

"I have no idea." I shrug.

"What do you want from her? A mother?" He avoids my gaze and taps the steering wheel to a softly thumping beat.

"No," I'm quick to reply. Maybe. "Do you know what it's like to have no one?"

"You have Henry."

"Henry's not around. He's in Japan. I didn't even know he was going."

"You were the model couple at the benefit."

The benefit seems like ages ago. We *were* the model couple then, what was that—two and a half weeks ago? I remember his hands flitting across my shoulders, fastening the solitaire diamond, and then hovering there, reluctant to let go. Everything has gone downhill since the benefit. Molly McKay and Gunther Rowe. Henry's erratic behavior, his violence and mood swings. I can't reconcile this man with the Henry in my memory. But now, removed from Henry and Lydia without the pressure to be one person or the other, the transformation is a bit clearer. The day Henry gently suggested that a nose stud was juvenile. *You're too beautiful for these teenager endeavors. Like you're thirteen and trying to piss off your mother.* I took it out because I was twenty-seven and felt immediately silly. It was impulsive anyway, Lydia's influence, my newly short hair spiked magenta. Piercings. Attempts to hide, but at the same time discover who I would become, with Lydia's help whether she knew why or not. That night, I popped it out, tucking it under the sapphire necklace he'd given me as a replacement in my jewelry box.

Or maybe it was how he'd taken my short, spiky lock of hair between his thumb and forefinger: *This is such a beautiful color, is it natural? I bet it would be knockout if you let it grow.* Subtle comments here and there about my clothing, how they reflected my spirit but *not my intelligence.*

And then came the waves of gifts, cashmere, silk, Versace, and Donna Karan. Thick, draping fabrics. I'd stand in the closet and hold the softest silk to my cheek, like a child's security blanket. Fabrics I didn't even know existed, much less thought I could own, their colors vibrant and buttery rich. Suddenly, my thrift store plaid skirts and lace tops felt pop-bubblegum. Cheap. Evelyn used to say that *it takes a lifetime to grow into the person you'll become.* As I stood in the closet, facing all this glorious elegance, she all but whispered in my ear.

Then, gradually, I started wearing Henry's clothes to the flower shop. Then I wore them all the time. Eventually I bagged up all my old stuff and gave it to Penny to donate to Goodwill until the last of me was gone. At the time, I didn't feel sad; the parts of me that were old, torn, ratted, and worn were being shucked away in plastic bags. The best parts of my life were yet to come. Hemingway once said that bankruptcy happens "Gradually and then suddenly." Maybe that's how I became Henry's wife.

"You're not the same person," Lydia scoffed one day as we processed, sliding the stems through our fingers, slicing the bottoms on a bias with our knives, shearing off leaves.

"No one is ever the same person. Stagnant people are boring." I was defensive.

"So you're saying I'm stagnant? I'm boring?" She stopped cutting and stared at me, her nostrils flared, an angry horse about to charge.

"No. I'm saying I was bored. With me." I plunked a gangly zinnia into the nearest stainless water bucket.

"But what you're really saying is that you're bored with *us.*" Javi stood behind Lydia, his hands resting on his hips. "Will you come to Paula's show later?" Javi asked the question with a sarcastic sneer. Paula, Javi's partner, played bass in a punk band in the basement of a bar on Tuesday nights. Except that night, Henry had opera tickets. I raised my eyebrows and opened my mouth, unable to verbalize the rejection. "Yeah. We didn't think so." He turned and stomped off.

I shrugged in Lydia's direction, like *What's his problem?*

She twisted her mouth. "I'm with him here, Zo. You're too . . . something for us." She clicked the knife closed and tossed it, clattering, on the stainless steel table.

That night, Henry comforted me, assured me that yes, I had changed a bit, but yes, that was okay. "This is what life is about, Zoe. No one stays the same person forever." At the time, I snorted through tears. Truly, how many people can one person be?

Now as I sit here in Cash's hot car, the windows down, the warm eighty-degree air rushing my cheeks, I can't help but wonder, am I yet again destined to become someone else? It seems impossible that I will arrive home tonight the same Zoe that left the apartment this morning.

Cash steers the car off the highway and through an elaborate maze of suburban streets. The sign on the side of the road reads *Welcome to Danbury*. It seems like a nice place to live: tree-lined cul-de-sacs, backyards with wooden play gyms, winding driveways with glossy SUVs or black BMWs. He makes a sudden left, sliding the Honda behind a navy blue Audi. The clock on the dash reads 10:55. "We're here."

. . .

I stand just behind a palm fiber doormat printed with a glass of red wine and the words *Welcome! I hope you brought wine!* in a jaunty sideways script. The porch holds two rocking chairs, but they're for show, not function, as evidenced by the thick layer of dust and pollen that coat their seats. The house is large and looming, a mix of sunny yellow siding and brick facade. The gardens are sculpted out of arborvitae and impeccably round topiaries.

The door swings open before I ring the bell. Caroline blinks twice at me, as though I were a FedEx man without a package.

"Who's in the car?" She squints toward the driveway.

"I, um, had a friend bring me, but he thinks maybe we should talk alone." I shift my weight from one foot to the other and hitch my purse higher on my shoulder. I use the opportunity to study her face: clear, with only the barest hint of crow's feet at her eyes. It's possible that we look the same age.

She opens the door a crack and motions me in. The foyer is grand, thirty feet high, with an imposing chandelier. She closes the door quickly and quietly behind me.

"We can sit in here." She brushes past me and I follow her into a sitting room. The windows are floor to ceiling and the room is flooded with light. The carpet is white, the furniture is white. I squint.

She sits to face me and we study each other curiously. She's slighter than I am, almost waif-like, and dressed in jeans and an oversize long-sleeved T-shirt. Her hair is long, just as lustrous and thick as my own but pulled back into a low ponytail at the nape of her neck. We have the same watery, cerulean eyes, the same long but slightly too large nose. The same thin, curved upper lip, but pouty lower lip.

"We have to be brief. I have . . . an appointment." Her eyes flick to the clock on the far wall and back to me. She picks at imaginary lint on her jeans. "You kept your name. I didn't think Evelyn did that?"

"She didn't. She named me Hilary. I changed it to Zoe when I moved east."

She looks startled. "Why?"

"Um . . . it seemed easier somehow. Than taking a third name, I guess. I was escaping my past life. It's a long story." I scan the room, white and glass and sleek black art. It's all so cold.

"Zoe. Are you in trouble now?" Her expression is so intense, I almost want to laugh.

"In trouble? No." I wipe my upper lip delicately with my index finger. "I'm married. To Henry Whittaker, do you know him?"

She shakes her head. "Should I? Is he famous?"

"In some circles." The conversation is so inane, so civil,

like I'm chatting casually with a bank teller. I run out of
words then, and the silence seems to take over the room. I'm
not sure what to do with my purse. I sit it on my lap but feel
very prim, so I move it to the side and tuck it between me and
the white leather arm of the sofa. Inside, I can see my phone
has a waiting text message, from Cash. It pops on the locked
display. *Everything okay?*

"Zoe. What do you want from me?"

My head snaps up. Why does everyone keep asking me
that? Cash, Lydia, now Caroline. "To know, I guess. A friendship at best. A meeting to remember, at worst. I guess I'm
having a bit of an identity crisis." I'm surprised by the truth in
that, considering I hadn't thought it exactly that way before.

She leans forward, places her hand on my arm. We have
the same hands, long thin fingers, with short nail beds. "We
can't have a relationship, Zoe. I'm going to tell you a story, not
to hurt you or to scare you off, but because it's the truth and
I've come to terms with it. Would you like a glass of water?"

I nod my head and she stands up to get it. With her out of
the room, I peek into the adjoining room, a stark contrast to
the sterility of the one I'm in. It's richly decorated with warm
shades of brown, and there are children's toys and books
scattered on the floor. One of the couch cushions has been
unmoored and lies cockeyed on the floor.

"I don't have any lemon . . ." She bustles in, handing me
a glass and perches on the edge of the white leather chair,
opposite the couch I'm sitting on. She smooths out her jeans
with the palms of her hands. She has the posture of a dancer,
straight and confident. "So, the story. Well, when I was seventeen, I fell in love with a boy named Trout Fishman. Not
his real name, of course, his real name was Troy. But everyone
called him Trout. Get it? Fishman?"

I nodded in the way one does when they've just learned
their father was named Trout Fishman.

"Well, he was in a band, played the drums and had a chin dimple. There's something about a chin dimple, right?" When I don't answer, she gives a little cough and continues, "We met the usual way, and dated. I loved him, probably more than he loved me, but I think that's typical in high school. He was a good kid, stayed out of trouble. Until he got his girlfriend knocked up."

She pauses and for a split second, it occurs to me that he's out there somewhere. Another link, another tether. Someone else to find.

"There was the usual drama at first. Our parents cried, the kids at school whispered. But I hadn't been the first girl to get in trouble and Lord knows I wouldn't be the last. Our parents talked of helping us, so we could finish high school, maybe even go to community college. Trout took electrician classes at the vo-tech school. We were *excited*. But not always. One night, we fought. I was riddled with insecurity, thought I was holding him back. I was a burden. I was seven months pregnant and hormonal. He left, slamming the door behind him and went to blow off steam with his friends. He ended up at some druggie's house, a guy we didn't talk to in school because he was going nowhere. But then again, I was a teen pregnancy statistic so who was I to judge? This guy gave him a handful of quaaludes and told him it would erase all his cares. To a seventeen-year-old kid, staring at fatherhood and dealing with a hormonal girlfriend, with no job? He couldn't have said anything more perfect. Trout took the whole handful at once. They laughed, thought he'd be stumbling around bumping into walls, they weren't really known to kill you back then. It was the eighties. But Trout had a weak heart, as it turned out. He just couldn't handle a street drug. He had a heart attack that night. Fell into a coma and died a week later."

And just like that, the idea of a father slips away. The shock must have registered on my face because she pauses to drink a sip of water, licks her dry lips, and gazes off into a corner. Off in the distance, in the kitchen, I assume, a phone rings. Once, twice, and then goes to voicemail. She doesn't even acknowledge it.

When she finally continues, her voice is flat. "I was heartbroken. Naturally I suppose, the way a pregnant teenage girl would be. My parents were at a loss with what to do with me. I dropped out of school, wouldn't leave my room. Labor was a nightmare. I was just so angry, I've never known such anger, even now. Can you understand that?"

I nod, although I can't. I've never been pregnant, never borne a child. The love a mother must feel for a child is ephemeral to me, out of reach. An idea, unattached to any real, rooted emotion.

"After I had you, I got involved with drugs then, myself. Which, admittedly makes no sense. I was a different person. You said you were running from your life? That's what I was doing. I didn't change my name, but I ran away. Bobbed around the country. Didn't hold a job, got arrested a bunch of times. Was addicted to heroin. Went to rehab, found God like I'm supposed to, met Ronald one day at church."

"Ronald?"

"Oh. My husband. He's at work. An accountant. We have a son, Benjamin. He's at Ronald's mother's house right now. I didn't want him here, for . . . this." She waves her hand between us, like *this* is something horrid. I'm her first, failed attempt at motherhood. The anger slices under my rib cage, sharp and unexpected. "Ronald doesn't know everything about my past. He knows I was in rehab, but he doesn't know how bad it was. How I was homeless, how I was destitute. He doesn't know I've already been a mother. Can you see?"

She keeps asking me to *understand* and to *see*. Perhaps I should be more lenient, less judgmental, comfort her. But I can't. I should be tolerant, our stories are shockingly parallel.

I imagine nodding sympathetically, maybe touching her arm, *I understand,* with a soft cluck of my tongue and maybe that would be the key. She'd invite me back, we'd have coffee, I'd learn that after all these years all she needed was an outlet and now here I am. Conveniently. I'll become somewhat of an accidental friend, a hidden secret, almost arcane. The vision is romantic, like a love affair.

Her liquid blue eyes implore mine, mirror images of each other, to simply go away. She rambles on, as if talking to herself. "I've already done this once and that was enough. I'm done, okay? There are only so many times a person can explain herself."

I interrupt her. "So who was Evelyn, then? To you?"

"Evelyn? Oh, she was my mother's cousin. They spoke once in a while before you were born, but I was such a wreck afterward, my mother didn't know what to do. She heard Evelyn and her husband, God I can't even remember his name, Tom, was it?" She taps her fingernail on the edge of the table, thinking. I don't fill in his name, partially because I don't want to divert the conversation. His name was Tim, a tall shadowy man I barely remember. Dark hair, Old Spice. She shakes her head. "Well, whatever. My mother had heard they wanted to adopt. I don't know how or under what context. One of the bad nights, right before I ran away, Mother called her. Begged her. Evelyn didn't want to at first, she said it could get messy with family. She wanted a baby to love, all her own. Not to lose, later, you understand. I guess that had happened before, an adoption fell through. We had to promise to never seek you out. That Evelyn would tell you on her own, when she felt the time was right."

I appreciate this simple kindness. For all her chilly demeanor, she doesn't have to give it to me, the reassurance that Evelyn's hesitancy came from love, not rejection. She is, above all else, self-aware then.

She sits up straight, pulls her arms against her midsection, protective. "How is she, your mother?"

"She's dead." My voice is flat and I close my eyes. "You didn't know?"

Her face freezes, her eyes go wide. "No. We . . . well the whole family sort of fell apart later. After my mom died. There was talk of a reunion at one point . . ."

The genealogy website. Growing up, I remember asking Evelyn about family. Other people had cousins, big Fourth of July barbecues and vacations, dramatic fights and people to call when your car broke down or you needed to borrow a hundred dollars. This is what I saw on television. At the time, she'd touched her eyebrow, shook her head. *We have only each other, bud.* I wonder now, had *she* wanted it that way? To protect me? Or to keep me?

Caroline leaned forward, her breath hot on my cheek. Her eyes studying my face, so close we could touch. But we didn't. "Listen," she said. "No one wanted to hurt either of you. It all happened so fast, and I was barely functioning. But you have to understand. Mother thought if she knew, she'd back out. She didn't know there were two. That she wouldn't want you both. I know it wasn't the best thing to do, but you have to *understand*—"

My heart picks up speed. Two? "Both?"

Her hand flies to her mouth and between those long delicate fingers I hear, "I thought you knew. I thought that was how you found me. She knows about you. I just assumed she sent you."

"Who? Who sent me? Who is she?" My mouth keeps asking questions my brain already knows the answers to.

"I had twins, Zoe. You have a sister."

CHAPTER 20

"I don't understand," I say. "You've met her? Where is she?" I whip my head around, like she's going to magically appear in the living room. My hands are shaking and a pulse throbs in my neck.

"I think she lives in Brooklyn with her parents. She was here, oh maybe three or four years ago? She knows about you. I told her, but she had already known. Her adoptive parents . . ." Caroline splays her hands outward and lets me fill in the missing information. *Evelyn didn't know everything.* Why?

She takes a deep breath and stands up. "Her name is Joan, but hold on, I'll get you all her information." She scuttles out of the room on the balls of her feet, nervous. She's had control of the conversation up to this point, and now she's anxious. Impatient. She returns not more than a minute later holding an index card. She pauses in front of me, running her fingernail over the words, before she hands it over. "We didn't keep in touch. It's all the information I have."

Her eyes are huge against her pale face. She's beautiful, my mother. I look like her but in small ways. In person, our differences are obvious. I'm a cartoonish version of her, I'm drawn with a Magic Marker, deep confident lines. She's sketched with an artist's touch: feathery strokes and skittish shadows.

"She's like me, nervous. I take medication, do you? Is that genetic? It was interesting, her mannerisms are so much like mine. You . . . not as much." She studies me and I duck my head, studying the index card, the words sliding around as my vision blurs.

My sister's name and address in Brooklyn are scribbled with disjointed handwriting, slanting one way then the other. *Joan Bascio.* I look up at Caroline questioningly.

"You can keep that. I copied it." She looks over at the chair, like she can't decide if she should sit or if the conversation is over, and she ends up half-hovering over me, stooped and nervous, like a Bryant Park pigeon.

"If Evelyn had known, she would have taken us both," I say confidently. "Why didn't she know?" Evelyn was the most maternal person I'd ever met. Her need to nurture was a constant presence in my childhood, every twisted ankle tended to as though she were a wartime nurse. Every cut and scrape thoroughly scoured with alcohol. Despite being woefully unprepared and hopelessly scattered, she'd make up for her lack of preparedness in fret time alone. Her concern was never limited to me. Any lone wolf, lost child, homeless puppy. She was a natural adopter of all misplaced things.

When I was sixteen, I broke my wrist, just a hairline fracture. I'd been helping her clean the faculty office buildings at Berkeley after school, one of her many patchwork jobs. We'd take the train down from Richmond to the UC campus, moving in and out of the administration building, quiet as mice. I'd stood on a chair, trying to dust a light fixture hanging from a conference room ceiling. When I fell, she screamed louder than I did.

In the emergency room, I alternated between reading and daydreaming, trying to distract myself from the pain. Evelyn was quiet, mostly concerned with the bill, her mind running constant stream of co-pays and deductibles against account balances and paychecks. She processed numbers like a ticker tape. A young girl, about my age, paced along the far wall. Hours later, with my arm set and casted in a thick, white plaster, I emerged through the big double doors back into the lobby and the girl was still there. She sat on the floor, her back pushed up against the wall, mascara streaks down her face. Evelyn squared her jaw, marched right over to her, and after a short, whispered conversation, brought the girl over. *This is Rachel and she's coming home with us for dinner.* She said it so matter-of-factly, neither Rachel nor I dared argue, despite the fact Evelyn and I had eaten hot dogs and baked beans three nights running. *Eat what?* I didn't have the gall to ask. We ate whatever meat Evelyn could find, white and mysterious in the freezer, chopped up with canned vegetables, and then she drove Rachel home. When she returned, her eyes were red-rimmed from crying, but she never explained why. When I pressed her, she just hugged me and called us lucky. *This, mystery meat surprise and all. We're lucky.*

The idea that Evelyn could know about another baby and reject her? Impossible.

"She had no idea there were two babies. She wouldn't have taken you. She *couldn't* afford both of you, there was no way. If she would have known, she would have backed out." She runs her palm along her forehead, as though massaging a headache. "It sounds awful now, I know. At the time, it was just . . . survival. The whole thing was a mess, but I was in too bad a place to care. Mother found someone else interested in adoption and she took your sister. It was all done privately, through an agency." She finally sits on the edge of the chair, crossing her legs, all knobby knees and pencil calves. "Mother kept tabs on both of you for a long time. Then Joan came to see me."

The implication is obvious: *Caroline* did not keep tabs on us.

"So everyone knew I had a sister but Evelyn and me? She knows. You knew. We're the only ones who didn't know?" I set my water down on the glass-top end table with force.

"Well, you can't understand unless you're in the situation. Then later, I just think Joan wanted to find you in her own time. Or maybe she tried and couldn't?"

Yes, that made sense. Hilary Lawlor became Zoe Swanson, then Whittaker. An amateur sleuth might lose that link.

"But you didn't try? To help her, I mean?"

"She didn't ask. I gave her what I knew, which wasn't much." She presses the pad of her thumb along the arm of the chair, avoiding my gaze.

I say nothing.

"Zoe, there's something you should know." She reaches around me, parting the window curtain and for a second I can smell her shampoo, her shower soap. She's so close I could lean over and kiss her cheek. "I shouldn't tell you this but someone called me." Her voice is low. "I think it was a man, it was hard to tell. But someone is watching me, or maybe you." She touched me then, her hand cold on my shoulder. "He threatened me. He said to leave you alone."

"Who was it? Who called you?" I'm so confused.

She holds her hands out, palms up, and shakes her head. *I don't know.* "I have a child. He's six. I'm forty-six. He wasn't supposed to be able to be born. I tried for years, to no avail, and honestly believed I was being punished for what I did. To you. To your sister. For my abandonment, my selfishness."

I become fixated on her words: *I have a child.* My mind snaps back at her, sarcastically. *No, you have three children.* But then again, I don't think of her as my mother, so why would she think of me as her child? Because, *because*, shouldn't you always remember your children? I never had the luxury of forgetting a woman I've never met, a vague figure of a mother, mostly invented or derived from old, yellowed Polaroids of Evelyn's old friends that I found in her closet. I flipped through them like I was shuffling cards, greedily pawing, until the women's faces were smudged with tiny fingerprints. I always wondered if one of them was my *real* mother. I could never bring myself to ask.

Caroline had easily forgotten us. The evidence is right here: *I have a child.*

I realize then, her darting eyes, her fidgeting, her reluctance to talk to me. She was *afraid.* But also maybe, just maybe, relieved. The decision was made for her, who can blame her now?

I stand up. "But you did. You did talk to me. Why?" I swallow. Out of nowhere, I want to cry, I feel the bite in the back of my throat.

"I owe you. I owe . . . Evelyn, I guess? Joan? I'm sorry, whether you believe that or not." She rocks back on her heels.

"I have to go." I think of Cash in the car. The faceless, nameless man who threatened Caroline. Later, the way she'd surely be watching out her curtains all night. I hitch my purse high on my shoulder and it swings back, knocking over the half-full water glass. Water edges down the sides of the table, and on the floor, creeping toward the rich, leathery sofa. I suppress the urge to apologize. Caroline's eyes dart from me, to the puddle, and back, and I know she is struggling over which is a larger disaster.

She stands woodenly in the living room, eyes closed. "Zoe," she says softly.

I stand there expectantly, stupidly still hoping for something, a hug, an apology, a gesture of kindness. Friendship.

"Don't ever come back."

. . .

I climb into the passenger side and slam the door. Cash had reclined his seat and is startled awake. He shakes the sleep from his eyes.

"Already? What happened?" He adjusts the backrest upright.

"She was threatened." I blurt. He cocks his head, confused. I take the card with Joan's information and flash it in front of his face. "Also, I have a sister."

If he's shocked, it doesn't register on his face. He just nods.

"Did you know?" I demand.

He shakes his head. "No, Zoe. I swear. I had no idea." He turns the key in the ignition and backs slowly out of the driveway. He keeps his eyes forward, trained on the road. "What happened with Caroline?"

"She's a bitch." I say it forcefully, partly because I'm tugging on the seat belt and it finally breaks loose, but the curse slips out easily and it feels *good*. Even as I say it, I know it's not completely true. It occurs to me then—even without the threatening phone call, would the outcome have been any different? She didn't stay in touch with Joan. "She has a new life. I don't fit in—you were right. Is that what you want to hear?" I huff and sit back, crossing my ankles.

"No. Zoe, I'd hoped I was wrong. You know that, right? What did she say?" He shifts uncomfortably as he puts the car in drive.

"Cash, she got a phone call. Someone *threatened her* if she talked to me." We're stopped at an intersection and he turns to look at me, his mouth hanging open.

"What? Who called her?"

"I have no idea." I shrug. "Here's the weird part. My sister, Joan? She knows I exist. She found my mother, *our mother*, three years ago! Evelyn had no idea that Joan even existed. The whole thing is fucked up."

"I'll admit that's odd." He rubs his chin. "Will you look for her? Joan?"

"I don't have to look for her. Carolyn gave me her address." I wave the card in front of him again, blocking his view of the road. He swats it away.

"So what do you want to do now?"

I think about it for a minute. "Honestly? I want to find Joan. I want to meet her."

"Right now?" He gives me a sideways smile. My anger is like an ocean swell, forceful and overwhelming one minute, receding to calm the next. I watch as we turn the corner, off Caroline's street, and her house fades from view. I feel a small prick of fear: Who called her? Then a crazy idea; could she be lying?

"Yeah. Would that be awful? To just show up?" I wonder out loud.

"Maybe. I think you should call first."

I let that sit, thinking about what I care more about. My sister's comfort level or my increasingly desperate need to see her. We drive in silence, merge onto I-84 W, and just like that—my mother is gone. Whatever tether I've had is dissolved and I poke at this feeling, repeat the words in my mind. I explore it, the way your tongue finds a hole in your mouth where a tooth once was. I can't decide if I care. A small part of me worries for her, that whispered threat, for her and her little boy and her accountant husband.

"Thanks for coming with me. This has to be so boring for you." I avoid his gaze by staring at the trees that whiz past the passenger side window.

"Are you kidding? I've said this before, but what I cover daily? It's nothing that gets your blood pumping. This is interesting, Zoe. Reminds me of my Texas days." He taps the steering wheel. "Who called Caroline? Why would anyone threaten her?"

THE VANISHING YEAR 213

I think of the break-in. The careening car. The overwhelming feeling that I'm on some kind of runaway train. That my whole life—the penthouse apartment, the perfect marriage, the money and security—is about to come crashing down around me. I've been too complacent, which never goes unpunished. It's all been too lucky, too happenstance. Something is going on, buzzing just under the surface, and I can't figure it out.

"Do you wonder why she hasn't called you?" he asks, evenly.

"Who, Joan? She must have her reasons," I say a tad snappily, trying to figure out what those reasons might be. "Maybe *she* has a family, or a crappy relationship, or in general, a busy life. Maybe she's an ad executive, or she works nights trying to make ends meet. Who knows? There could be a thousand reasons. People typically believe they have all the time in the world to accomplish things. There are a lot of theoretical 'somedays.'"

"That's true." He raises his eyebrow in my direction.

"You don't believe it," I say, but he just shrugs.

"Who called Caroline?" He comes back to that. My head pounds; I'm so tired. Joan and Caroline and some whispered threatening phone call. It's all too much.

I study his profile—his long, straight nose, his clear intelligent green eyes with a compassionate twinkle, his skin, rough and uneven, presumably from too many days in the hot Texas sun investigating the newest political scandal.

"I know nothing about you," I say, realizing that it's true.

"You've never asked," Cash says with a sideways smile and a quick flicker of a glance. I feel my cheeks flush. He's right; I haven't.

"Our friendship started because you were writing a story on *me*. It's not really conducive to a two-way conversation." I'm justifying myself. Our friendship, if you can call it that, has been shamefully focused on me.

He laughs. "Touché. So, ask away. I'll answer."

"How did you end up back on the East Coast?"

He shifts in his seat and cocks his head. "Go right for the hard stuff, eh?"

"Is it? I thought that was a softball." I smile.

"Yeah, well, ah, you didn't know. So I was engaged. Her name was Mary. We met at an Astros game, actually Game Five of the NLCS in 2005." He coughs and shifts in the driver's seat. "I was sitting behind her, and we were all standing and jumping around because Berkman had just hit a home run. And some jerk knocked into me, spilling my beer all down her back. She turned around and took one look at me, holding an empty beer cup, and threw her daiquiri in my face. Who drinks a daiquiri at a baseball game? I think I said that. I bought her another one as a peace offering." As he tells the story, he gets a funny, faraway look and I think of all the ways Cash has held himself at arm's length. Although I'm married, I feel certain it wouldn't be different if I wasn't.

"I've never been to a baseball game."

"Never? You've lived in New York for how long and you've never gone to a Mets or Yankees game? That's, like, un-American."

"I know. I guess, just it wasn't Lydia's thing, and it's certainly not Henry's thing. I think his firm has had events at Yankee Stadium, but we haven't gone." I flick my fingertips in his direction. "I didn't mean to hijack the conversation. Keep going. This Mary, she liked your daiquiri, then?"

"Oh, sure. Who wouldn't?" He winks at me, and I laugh. "So, I got to plead my case, that it wasn't my fault, ruffians and all that. She believed me, I guess. I saw her later at a bar outside the stadium and bought her another daiquiri. We met for dinner the following Saturday. She was . . ."

I give Cash his reverent moment. *Beautiful? Amazing? Luminous?*

"Bat-shit crazy. That's what she was. She was a lawyer, an attack dog in the courtroom. She got an offer from a New York law firm after killing them in an insurance case. She drove a hard bargain and walked away a partner and a rich woman. I followed her here. I was a journalist. There had to be a ton of work in New York, right? I was working freelance but she didn't think I had a lot of ambition and suggested the *Post* as a way to be more structured with my life. *A real job,* she called it."

"Huh," is all I can think to say.

"Yeah. Huh. But I did. And we had a spacious high-rise on Fifth Avenue, overlooking Central Park. She worked long hours, so I started working long hours. I proposed to her, to fix it, which is just about the dumbest thing a person can do. She said yes, because, well, I don't know why. I surprised her at work one night to find her screwing one of the partners in her office. Wouldn't you lock the door?" He offers a quick glance over. "I'd lock the door. I mean, c'mon."

"Ouch."

He sighed. "So I moved out and haven't spoken to her since. Oh!" He snaps his fingers like he just remembered something. "That's a lie. I covered a wedding a few years ago, and she was there as a guest. With him. She *married* that guy. She was all tucked and lifted, her face was a thick cake of makeup. She was like an ice sculpture of Mary. When I said I still worked at the *Post,* she laughed."

"What did you say?" I ask, incredulous.

"I asked her if she still fucked her husband in her office. He was standing right there and by the look on his face, I could tell *that* answer was no."

I laughed. "So you're not still hung up on her?"

He's quiet for a moment. "No, not hung up on her. She was the only woman I was ever engaged to, so sometimes I wonder. Plus, she was such a loose cannon. I find myself sabotaging relationships with other women, that's all. They're all so normal. Am I self-destructive? My mother thinks so."

"Maybe a little bit." It feels so nice to swing the camera around and focus on someone else's problems.

"Well, self-destruction seems to be something we have in common." He turns the radio on, but to a low volume. Something classical. More surprises. "How did *you* end up on the East Coast?"

The question is tangled up in *the things I cannot say.* I think of how to be honest, truthful, and not give away all my secrets. For me, the basest act is also the most admissible. *Evelyn.*

"I was in college. I was in a bad place." I trace swirl patterns with my fingertip on the cold windowpane. "My adoptive mother, Evelyn . . . she died. I was depressed and too poor to take care of her so I . . . ran away."

"She was sick?"

"She had cancer." I try to avoid saying it, that big looming pit of blackness in the corner of my mind. The one that I skirt around with euphemisms and niceties like *common burial* and *state-funded*, when I really mean abandoned. Unloved. "So New York was an escape for me. I saw an opening at La Fleur d'Elise and started working there as a glorified custodian. I worked on design at night. Then . . . I met Henry." My voice drops on the *Henry.* "The thing is, I left my mother." I square my shoulders and stare at Cash's profile, willing him to pass judgment. I see nothing, not a flicker of understanding, even. "In the morgue. I couldn't afford to bury her. I left her."

I see comprehension dawning in his eyes. He reaches out, touches my hand. "Are you that same person?"

"No. I was a mess then, running from myself. From other people. I'm only a slightly more put together mess now." I pat my running nose with a napkin I find in the glovebox.

"Have you tried to go back? Find out . . . what the county

did? I can do that for you. You could have a memorial. Have closure."

"No. I can't." I shake my head vehemently. "They did a state-funded burial. That's what they give to people who are abandoned. The only people who are abandoned in death are those who die unloved. I . . ." I can't finish my sentence. I can't even finish the thought, except I push. My brain pushes past the whooshing in my ears and the whir of the tires on the road and the awareness of my body and I think the thought I've avoided since I left San Francisco five years ago. "The last thing I ever did to Evelyn was tell her that she was unloved."

The words themselves don't feel so terrible out there, clunked out on the console between us. Cash covers my hand with his, and his eyes are so filled with compassion that I think I might break, right there in that shitty car on I-84. I gaze out onto the interstate in front of us, a large, flat expanse of nothingness with no cars and no people. It's all so lonely.

I depress the window button and feel the warm air hit my face. I take some deep breaths. I've said the worst things about myself to someone who seems to care about me and I'm still here. My hands are trembling and I shove them under my thighs, my diamond digging into my skin.

Cash reaches over, taps my shoulder. "Okay?"

I nod awkwardly. I feel like someone who has impulsively confessed something horrible on a crashing plane that ends up righting itself only minutes later. I cough. "Yeah. I want to find out information on Joan. How can I do that?"

"Do you have a computer?" he asks. I give him a *duh* look and he laughs. "If you give me fifteen minutes and decent Wi-Fi, I can find out pretty much anything."

I shrug. "Okay, let's go. But I'm taking advantage of Henry being gone and ordering Chinese for dinner. He generally considers all takeout to be the lowest form of food, barely edible."

"Well, that's a real shame. I happen to *love* chicken and broccoli."

. . .

We order takeout and sit on a blanket on the living room floor, surrounded by foil and cardboard containers, the sauce oozing out of the corners. I eat until I could burst and we chat about the city, being transplants, and what things were hardest to get used to.

"The speed of everything," Cash said without thinking. "Everyone walks fast, the subways are fast, the taxis are fast. And yet, it can still take an hour to cross a one-mile island. Why? It used to be frustrating. About eighteen months here, I stopped trying to figure it out."

"Yes! For me, the hardest part was the massive amounts of people. I come from a city but San Francisco has nothing on New York in terms of sheer number of bodies. But no one looks at each other. In California, people are *nice.*" I pour us both a glass of wine in the supplied paper cups. "I met Lydia and it got easier. I had a ready-made band of misfits."

"Well, it was easier for me at first, then lonely later. I have friends now, guys at the paper or from the gym."

"What about girlfriends now?" I blurt.

He shrugs and leans back against the easy chair behind him. "I do okay." He rubs his hand across his jaw and gives me a sideways grin. I briefly think of Henry—he would die if he saw us eating in here. The rug cost $5,000. To cover the silence, I reach into the greasy bag and pull out a fortune cookie. I crack it open, the crumbs dusting down to my legs, on to the blanket. I pull out the little folded rectangle of paper. "'In case of fire, keep calm, pay bill, and run,'" I read. "What does that even mean?"

"I like how they tell you to pay the bill first, though." He stretches his legs out and grabs a cookie. "Here's one. 'It never pays to kick a skunk.' Honestly, these are the weirdest fortune cookies I've ever seen."

"Kick a skunk? Oh my God, that's ridiculous. Okay, here's one." I unfold another little paper and drop it. We both reach for it and his hand accidentally grabs mine. I pull it away. "'The greatest risk is not taking one.'"

We both ponder that one. Cash smiles. "I guess we should get a move on our search for Joan, then?"

I laugh as he pulls the last cookie from the bag, cracks it open, and unfolds the fortune. His smile falters.

"What? Read it."

"Ah, Zoe. 'You are extraordinarily beautiful.'"

"What?" The flush creeps up my neck and my cheeks grow warm. I clutch the collar of my shirt.

"That's what it says, look." He hands it to me. He's right. *You are extraordinarily beautiful.* My pulse thumps under my thumb. I feel it then, his crush on me. We don't know each other enough for it to be any more than that but I've been abusing his friendship, pretending the undercurrent wasn't there. Why else does a man go to such lengths for a woman, driving her a hundred miles in one day?

"Cash, I—"

"Did you hear that?" Cash whispers. He holds up his hand, and then I do hear it. A single bang coming from the kitchen fire exit. All penthouses in New York must have a secondary exit—it's part of the fire code. The door back there is locked with a key, not a card the way the front door is, and it's rarely used. The only key that I know of is in the kitchen drawer.

I stand up, all wine-fueled courage, and tiptoe toward the kitchen. The room is dark and light filters in from underneath the emergency door. The light in that hallway is bluish fluorescent and gives the kitchen an eerie glow. I scoot along the cabinets, my back against the countertop. Underneath the door, I can make out the shadow of two feet. I can't breathe, my heart pounds. *We have got to get out of here.*

I'm staring at the door, my feet rooted to the marble floor in terror, when the door handle jiggles.

I back up and crash into one of the metal kitchen stools. The door handle stops moving.

"Henry. Is that you?" I yell at the door, my words dribble out much weaker than I intended. Cash grabs my arm. I hadn't even heard him come into the kitchen.

"Zoe, we should get out of here." He's pulling me out through the front door and into the elevator. The service stairs are on the opposite end of the floor. Whoever was back there could cross the building and surprise us on another floor. Difficult and unlikely, but possible. The elevator door closes and we start to move down.

"Why would he come in the back? Does he do that?"

I bend over at the waist, trying to catch my breath. My legs feel like Jell-O from the adrenaline. "He never has before. It's not Henry. Henry's in Japan by now."

I stand upright and dial Henry's number. He picks up after one ring.

"Zoe? What's the matter?"

I inhale, not expecting him to answer. I sag against the back wall of the elevator as the numbers light up: ten, nine, eight . . . "Henry? Someone is in our apartment. I don't know who." My voice comes out like a squeak.

Four . . . three . . . two . . . L . . . "Zoe? Are you okay? I'm in L.A. Should I come home?"

I don't know what to say. He shouts into the phone, "Can you hear me? I'm coming home, okay?" I can barely hear him over the blood rushing in my ears.

The elevator doors slide open.

CHAPTER 21

The lobby is empty with the exception of Walter, the night doorman.

"Call the police, Walter," I'm out of breath and spin in one direction, then the other, to find where the service stairs come out. I think of my apartment a week ago, a leveled wreck, all our belongings strewn across the floors and furniture. I think of the car. The whispered threat to Caroline. I realize with a sudden thud that none of this is accidental. It's all a deliberate attempt to send me a message.

"Are you okay, Mrs. Whittaker?" His brows crease and he reaches a hand out for the telephone. I shake my head.

"I can't stay here. Someone tried to break into my apartment. Just call them." I run across the lobby, through the revolving doors, and into the street. The April air is still cool at night, despite the daytime heat wave, and the streets of New York are never quiet. Horns honk. People talk, shout, sing. There is always music. It's a comfort, this never abating circus.

"Where to?" Cash huffs behind me, as breathless as I am. I jog west on Hubert Street, make a quick right on to Collister.

Cash follows me, waiting to hear my grand plan. I have no grand plan. Stay alive, that's my plan.

My mind is racing, what could anyone possibly want with me at this point? Revenge? The last time they came after me, they wanted to know where Rosie was. They thought I would tell them if they pushed me enough. This felt different, more final, less desperate. There was only one reason anyone would come back for me: revenge, pure and simple. There were only two people who would want that: Jared Pritchett and Mick Flannery.

I stopped in an alley to catch my breath.

"I don't have a plan," I say to Cash by way of explanation. "I don't really have any place to go, but I have to call people. Officer Yates."

"Let's go to my apartment. We can call everyone there."

I think of the floor picnic and the half-empty glasses of wine. What will Penny think when she finds that in the morning? Penny.

"I need to call Penny." Then I realize that Cash has no idea who Penny is. "Okay, your apartment, let's go."

I follow him into the subway station at Canal Street. On the train, I scan up and down looking for anyone suspicious. Jared Pritchett is just a shadowy figure in my mind. Mick's thick blond hair five years later could even be thinning by now. The zigzag purple scar on his cheek that curled along his hairline from where he'd almost lost an ear in prison. I can't recall how I know that story. I was fourteen when he was away the first time for about a year. DUI, Evelyn had said. *Not his first.* His absence both freeing and hollow, the refrigerator devoid of beer, the ashtrays wiped clean and stacked in the kitchen cabinet, waiting for his inevitable return, thirteen months later. One day he was gone, the apartment sunny and cool, and the next he was back, the air thick with sweat. He wasn't mean, not always. But his breath smelled like Sen-Sen, those red-and-gold packets stacked like playing cards under the quartz ashtray at the kitchen table, the curling smoke while he and Evelyn played gin rummy, her high-pitched giggle as the nights wore on. They were mostly happy, until they weren't. I suppose that's true for most everyone.

The R train stops at Union Square and we exit without incident. No Jared. No Mick. No one is following us. I'm back to checking over my shoulder again, the way I used to, looking for men with guns. The streets are strangely deserted. We walk the four avenue blocks to Cash's apartment. Cash lives in a walk-up, a skinny flimsy building with no doorman. I eye the window, which looks easy to break, and the dead bolt, which looks barely operational.

He ducks his head, shyly, as we enter, and holds his arm out, by way of a tour. His apartment is sparse but small and clean, and his kitchen is an efficiency. The tile linoleum and white steel stove scream fifties, complete with Formica-topped table and red vinyl stools. The living room houses one small plaid love seat and a faux wood entertainment center that even has the back cut out and magnetic doors. A sheet divides the bedroom area from the living room. I can see the whole apartment from the vantage point right inside the door, which could fit in Henry's master bathroom.

"It's so cozy." I mean that as a compliment, but I can tell by his face that he receives it as an insult.

"That's what nice people say when they mean *small*." He smirks.

"No! Genuinely. Most days I could lose my mind in Henry's apartment." It's the first time I've ever said it that way, Henry's apartment. It's always been *our* apartment.

I fish my cell phone out of my purse and pull out a kitchen chair. The first phone call I make is to Officer Yates.

"Zoe." Her voice is all business. "Glad you called, girl. Listen, I found something you should—"

"Officer Yates, a man tried to break in my apartment to-night. Again. He came up the service steps into the kitchen. I ran, but the doorman called the police. Can you go?"

"What? Where are you?"

I sigh. I'm so tired. I relay the events of the evening, in more detail and slower. I don't tell her about Caroline or the phone call and I can't decide if I should. It seems excessive, a distraction from everything else that's happened. I can tell her when I see her, which I'm sure I will. She *hmmm-mmm*'s and *uh-huh*'s as I talk—I think she's taking notes. I hear the clicking of her long fingernails on computer keys. She promises she's on her way, and I hear the swoosh of her windbreaker as I imagine her getting up from her chair, motioning to her partner to come with her. The phone disconnects.

I dial Henry.

"Zoe where are you what's going on?" he answers, in one sentence, one breath.

I close my eyes. Perhaps, then, he still cares. But do I? It's so hard to know. I tell him about the latest break-in, the man at the service door.

"There are things I haven't told you. I know why all this is happening. There are things you don't know." It comes out of my mouth in a jumble of facts. "I testified against some terrible men in California. My testimony put them away for a long time—I can tell you more when you come home. I'm not relaying the entire story now, but I think one or both of them is out of prison and has found me. Someone is trying to scare me. The break-in at the apartment must be connected and same with that car. Remember, a week ago? It's all just a hunch." I don't tell him about Caroline. About the phone call.

"I don't even understand what you're saying. Where are you now?"

I'm silent for a moment. "Lydia's."

The lie slips out easily, before I have time to think about it. It just seems easier, I justify, than having him worry the entire time he's on the plane about an affair that's not actually going to happen.

"Are you coming home or going to Japan?" I ask, hopefully. I tap my fingers against my cheek, a nervous gesture I'd seen Evelyn do a million times.

"I'm in L.A. right now for a layover, but I'm coming home. My plane boards in . . ." he's silent for a minute, "ten minutes. I'll be home in six hours. It's a red-eye." A chuckle comes through the line, soft and insistent. Familiar. "Zoe, I've never taken a red-eye in my life."

"Well, I'm honored." We're both quiet then.

"Zoe, I've been so stupid. Willfully ignorant of your past. Ignoring my past. Thinking we can live in this bubble where neither of us has baggage. It's just . . . not real. We'll fix this, okay? Together?"

I press the phone tighter against my face, wanting to feel his breath against my cheek, feel his whisper in my ear. My stomach swoops like a roller coaster. I want this love, the one he promises me when we're apart. The love we try to reclaim again and again, chasing it like dandelion seeds. I want *that* love.

A voice blares through the phone, announcing that it's time to board. Henry says a hasty good-bye. I wait until I'm certain he's gone and say "Henry" one more time into the mouthpiece. There's no answer. I miss dial tones.

I lay the phone down on the table and wait for Cash to come out of the shower. I tiptoe to the kitchen window and peek out through the gingham curtains. Cash's building sits in the middle of Fourteenth Street, between First and Second Avenues. Underneath a storefront awning, front lit by a streetlamp, stands a man, smoking a cigarette, a dark baseball cap pulled low over his eyes.

I let the curtain fall and edge away from the window. I'm officially back to looking over my shoulder, eyeing every dubious character, doubting every stranger's smile. Suspicion fits me like a glove. Truth be told, I've missed it.

Yates calls back and our conversation is brief. They didn't find anyone. Just like last time, it's all inconclusive and I can hear a thin edge of skepticism in everyone's voice. Yates. Henry. Except Cash. Yates asks if I can come in tomorrow for an official interview? The apartment is secured, someone is watching it. Am I safe? I tell her I am and we hang up. I eye the window again.

"Are you okay?" Cash leans against the kitchen doorway, his hands in his pockets.

"I'm fine. Just tired." I smile weakly.

"Ah. Follow me."

Cash lends me his bed and sleeps on the love seat, despite my protest that I'm shorter and would be more comfortable. He hands me two neatly folded blankets, and we stand awkwardly, the dividing sheet in Cash's thick fist. His face is a mask I can't read.

"Do you have a gun?" I ask. I'm wondering about the door again, if someone could find me here. If the man in the baseball cap is actually a threat.

"No, I don't. But I have a baseball bat." He smiles, too flippant for the situation.

"If they come, they'll have guns." I hold the blankets against my chest, nervously twisting my wedding ring.

"I'll keep watch. Don't worry, okay? You need to sleep." He nudges me toward the bed. His room is soft. Worn woods, a weathered rag rug, and a yellow incandescent light give the room a cabin-like feel despite the street noise. I can hear him rustling around, mere feet away, nothing but the sheet to divide us.

The wall opposite the bed is exposed brick, each painted

a different color, and the overall picture is a rudimentary sun in shades of orange and reds. It seems much too feminine for him to have done himself. The rays are curled around each brick, vinelike and intricate.

I make up the bed and climb inside. I fall asleep in my clothes, staring at that sun, wishing for all the world that it gave off some warmth.

• • •

I sleep in fits and starts, shooting up straight every half hour, at every car that starts, every door that slams, never sure if the noise is real or imagined. My dreams are vivid and violent. Evelyn carrying babies in a tattered dress, like a zombie. Caroline running from a burning building. Henry, shot and bleeding on the floor of Cash's apartment. At five, I realize I'm famished and wander out to the kitchen. I find Cash's kitchen cabinets and refrigerator well stocked with coffee, eggs, bread. I work quietly, using only the stove light so as to not wake Cash, who snores like an old steam engine from the love seat.

While I work, I examine my options. I can't stay here with Cash. I could probably call Lydia, but I can't shake her *I-told-you-so* face when I tell her Henry went to Japan. I can't stomach the idea of painting a rosy picture of my marriage, either. No, better to just leave it alone for now. Cash, with his unassuming open-ended questions, is easier.

Henry will come home today and I check my phone, wondering why he hasn't called. He should have landed. When the sun rises, I plan to go to the police station, meet with Officer Yates, figure out what is going on. I resign myself to the fact that today is the last day I will fully live under the guise of Zoe Whittaker. Hilary Lawlor has been an apparition in my mind for five years, existing only subconsciously. The jig is up. Henry will know my past, my drug use. Evelyn. Some of it I can keep hidden, certainly the details are mine to spare.

My throat closes up with shame at the mental snapshots: stealing pills. Those shiny, glistening moms, so perfect it hurt. Those giant thousand-dollar wobbling prams. Legs piled like matchsticks in the backseat of a car. Me, drunk on whiskey, falling in the street while Mick and someone else held me up. Evelyn, abandoned in a morgue cooler. That I left my mother's body to rot. I've never listed it all out, not even to myself. My sins are smaller, less significant, and more manageable if they remain in their individual compartments.

Henry won't understand any of it. He's never been poor. Desperate. Lost. Henry, above all else, has always been consistently, unflinchingly *found*. Certain. Linear.

I think of Joan then, my sister tucked in her childhood bed, only about ten miles away. If I truly believe I am in danger, that someone has come back for me, then so is she. We're twins, the same faces, mere miles apart. It's a reach, but it worries me. I can't help but feel a small thrill, that soon I will meet her. Then a stab of fear that my life will smear into hers, that whoever is after me will somehow find her first. Because I know now, there is someone, some nameless, faceless person who is watching me. Coming for me. I have no idea what they want, all I can do is wait.

I can't fix Evelyn. I can't go back and make right what I've done. I left her, first to die, then to rot. The woman who loved me, raised me. I could never right those two wrongs.

I think of Caroline with a sweet baby boy. Six years old, with sticky hands, gap teeth, and shaggy hair. She is a mother now, a real one this time, with responsibilities, playdates and schedules, kindergarten, and T-ball. Whoever called Caroline is watching me. I can't shake the feeling that I'm being monitored. They could find Joan. It's possible. Technology has made everything so incredibly possible. The world is smaller than it's ever been.

I calculate the distance between Cash's apartment in the

Village and Bay Ridge, Brooklyn. It's not far. Twenty-five minutes by cab, maybe? My heart picks up speed.

Cash wanders into the kitchen at seven, as I'm sipping my third cup of black coffee. My eyes feel tacky behind the lids, sore and scratching.

"So, today, will you call your sister?" He opens his mouth wide, half yawning, half stretching.

"More than that—I'm going there." I run my fingertip along the lip of the coffee cup.

He covers his surprise. "Really? When?"

"As soon as this coffee kicks in."

"Why?"

"I haven't been entirely truthful with you." I stand up, blow out a breath, sit back down. "When I lived in California, I got mixed up in some really terrible things. I was a mess. I did drugs, I even sold drugs."

"I can't tell you how this blows my mind." Cash smiles. He stands up and retrieves a plate of cinnamon rolls from the refrigerator and motions for me to take one.

"You don't seem shocked?" I tuck one foot under my leg, touch the icing with my index finger. It comes away white and sticky.

"Zoe, a *lot* of people do drugs, sell drugs, clean up their lives. Change their lives. It's really not that shocking."

I turn this over, the idea that maybe the life I've been desperate to bury under layers of silk Chanel isn't as awful as I'd thought.

"I'm a different person, sometimes I think maybe that person didn't exist, or at least I wish she didn't. She wasn't a particularly *good* person, I don't think."

"You're too critical. Young people do stupid things. It's the basis for every coming-of-age romantic comedy I've ever seen. It's the plot of most novels. The basis for a zillion rock songs."

I say nothing. Being forgiven for my choices has never

been an option. I pull a piece of gooey iced roll apart and pop it in my mouth. It melts on my tongue, perfectly flaky and sweet. "Holy shit, did you make this?"

"Give me a break," he says, his mouth twisted in a smirk. "My father was a baker. I learned from the best."

"It's amazing." I pull another piece and chase it with a swig of hot coffee. Sitting here, in this cozy kitchen in the dim light of morning, I feel comfortable. Accepted. "Anyway, I wasn't done. I ratted out what ended up being a high-profile sex-trafficking ring. I testified in a grand jury and was . . . threatened. Nearly killed because of it. *That's* why I ran. Changed my name, left everything behind. Left Evelyn." The words slide out almost easily, these words that I haven't said to anyone in five years. It's surprising. Cash has a stillness about him that begets confessions, like the bulk of his body can absorb shocking words, pulling them away from the source the way a tributary shunts water. It's why I told him about Evelyn in the first place, back in the car.

"You think they're back? These men who . . . threatened you?" Cash asks softly.

"I really do. I know it sounds crazy and I can't prove it. Officer Yates was looking into it after the first break-in. I called the old detective from the case but he's retired and the case is old and things get lost." I shrug. "But now, I'm certain of it. The careening car, the missing credit card, my ransacked apartment, and the break-in last night. It's all too coincidental. I can't shake this feeling. And all when I'm finding Caroline, too. Then she gets this threatening phone call?"

"What do you mean?"

"I don't know!" I push my palm flat and hard against the tabletop. "I can't explain it. I just feel like this is all connected somehow. I have to call Yates back today. I have to find my sister. Maybe warn Caroline. This is all on me. I've brought these people to their doorsteps. Maybe."

"Zoe, you're being way too hard on yourself. Do you hear you? None of this is your fault. Everyone has a past. In some ways, everyone runs from them. Maybe not literally." He gives me a gentle grin. "What could they want from you after all this time? Do you think they want revenge?"

"I'm not sure, but it's scaring me. I feel like I could jump out of my skin." I rub my arms, trying to get warm. I stand up and fill his coffee cup, absently.

"I could get used to this. What's your fee?" Cash laughs.

"Oh, you can't afford me," I joke lightly, then wince at the perceived truth in that. I shake my hands loose. "Did you paint the sun in your room?"

"Um, my little sister did. She said I needed some light in my life." He scratches his cheek and leans back in his chair.

"Some light?"

"Oh, that came out more melodramatic than I wanted. It was right after Mary. I was in a permanent bad mood most days." He smiles and sips his coffee, raising his eyebrows. "Hey, this is good!"

We sip in silence until he breaks it. "Do you want me to come with you?"

I think about it. "No, I don't think so. I think I can take a cab there."

"If you're right, and you're a target, should you be alone?"

"What will you do?" I tease. "Carry your baseball bat around?"

"Point taken." He raises his cup to me. "Call me right after, okay? I'll be worried."

"And curious. You *are* a reporter." I give him a sly smile.

"I admit. I'll be curious. But more than that, *I'll be worried*."

"Sure, sure. But first," I wipe my palms on my jeans, "I need to call Yates."

• • •

"I don't know, Zoe." Yates's voice huffs through the line, soft and kind, but doubtful. "It seems like a stretch. Everything you're chalking up to one person could all be coincidence, or even yawing bad luck."

"Did you look up Michael Flannery? Jared Pritchett? Remember what they did to me?" My voice hitches higher and higher and I can feel the screech in my neck, my throat. I take two deep breaths. I'm just pissed, I want to be believed. I want *someone* to say I'm not overreacting. Someone to say it makes sense, they'll look into it, help me. That I'm not crazy. "Are you sure there was no one at the apartment?"

She sighs into the phone, a defeated heavy, empty sound. "There was no one there. No one saw anything, no one heard anything."

"Can you dust for prints?" My thoughts spin, seeking something to latch on to.

"We didn't, Zoe." I hear the din of the office die down and I wonder if she's taken the phone into an interview room for privacy. I'm now a call that warrants privacy. "First of all, prints are only good enough if we have someone to compare them to. That hallway has seen the building staff, repairmen, yourself, Henry. There was no evidence at that door that there was even an attempted break-in—"

"Because we ran!" I protest. Cash peeks out from the living room and mouths, *Okay?* I wave him away. "Cash was there, he'll give a statement."

"I know, Zoe. I believe you, I do. But look, it's a resource problem. You say a man was outside your door. He didn't do anything, didn't take anything, we have no evidence that he was there. We can't send techs out to dust for prints and process them through the lab when there are *real* crimes being committed all over Manhattan. Can you see that?"

"I'm being pursued. I know it." I dig my nails into the soft denim on my thighs until I feel the sharp tang of pain.

"Zoe, I wanted to tell you this last night, but then you called me and the attempted break-in took precedence." Her voice lowers a register until I can barely understand her. "I looked up Michael Flannery. I don't know how to say this, but I couldn't find any record of him in the system."

"What?" Her words make no sense, this looming untenable feeling, like I'm about to be harpooned and left as chum for circling sharks.

"Your guy, Mick." She coughs nervously into the phone. "Zoe, he doesn't exist."

• • •

I cross Fourteenth Street and hail a cab. I pull the index card out of my purse and huff the address across the divider to the cabbie. The East River is in front of me, wide and almost dark green in late morning sun. Within minutes, the cab is crossing the Brooklyn Bridge, speeding through those iconic double stone arches, surrounded by ramrod cables so thick and straight that if I squint my eyes, they look like prison bars. I think of the mysterious Mick, so elusive now, so present in my mind. Yates said she could find no record of him: in prison, in the system, now or ever. He wasn't living in San Francisco. She couldn't find a man with that name and approximate age anywhere in the United States. He was a ghost. A phantom.

Phantoms can slip in and out of your life with ease. Nothing she said was a comfort. If anything, the fear had worked its way down into my heart and my stomach flipped and gurgled. I still felt the connection between the strange events of the past two weeks, as real and tangible as though they were tied together with metal cables. But even Cash seemed skeptical. How do you convince someone of an unlikely truth, even if you know it down deep in your bones? You don't.

Mick was always less of a concern than Jared, with his

shock of black hair, his black eyes, pale skin, the bulging scar that ran from his forehead to his chin. The smell of his breath, hot and sour on my face. The feel of his hands on my arm, twisting, twisting behind my back. Rosie's pink, shining lip glistening with the word JAREd in black ink. A man who will brand a teenage girl will think nothing of tracking down the woman who put him in jail, only to kill her. Terrify her, then kill her. Mick was never a ringleader. He was a user, of both people and drugs. He was lost, like me. Did Jared kill Mick, and now he's after me?

Bay Ridge, a neighborhood in Brooklyn, sits in the loop between Gowanus and Shore Parkway, punctuated at the bottom with the Verrazano-Narrows Bridge, like a happy exclamation point. *Exit here!*

I wonder how long she's lived here, if she commutes to Manhattan. If so, have we been to the same stores, the same hair salons? What would have happened if we'd seen each other? Would we have gotten the same haircut, switched places, like a Hayley Mills movie? I would be Sharon, she could be Susan. I imagine biting my nails to match hers, exchanging wardrobes.

Although we've lived mere miles apart, it might as well be a thousand. New Yorkers are shockingly local—if it's not available within a three-block radius, it simply no longer exists. We like to walk everywhere, even subway rides are inconvenient. I once overheard a man in a coffee shop refer to his girlfriend as a "long-distance relationship" because she lived on the Upper East Side and he lived in the Village. There were just too many train connections. You can forget anyone who commutes in from Jersey. Brooklyn and Manhattan are like different states.

The cab pulls on to Seventy-Seventh Street and parks in front of a tan-painted Cape Cod, almost gingerbread-like, with a brick facade and a cemented-over front yard. It looks well cared for, surrounded by a black iron fence. I pay the cabbie and climb out, taking a deep breath at the gate.

The hedges are neatly trimmed, and the window boxes have bright, bursting flowers. Too bright for April, pinks and yellows, daisies and spring mums, it's much too early for so much bloom. In front of me, looking solemn and kind with her arms outstretched in welcome, stands a concrete bathtub Mary. She's beautiful, ensconced in a periwinkle shrine, two clamshelled cherubs at her feet. I look up and down the street—more houses with too bright flowers, more Madonna statues. The flowers, I realize too slowly, are silk.

I ring the bell and from inside calls a voice, "Hang on!" A woman opens the door. Big hair, dark skin, long nails, probably sixtyish. She visibly pales and yells into the house without taking her eyes off me. "Bernie? Bernie! You betta come here!"

She opens the door for me, wide so I can pass her, without waiting for me to speak. I scoot past her awkwardly. The front hallway is red deep-pile carpet, with a tin-covered radiator acting as a hall table. The whole house smells like meat loaf. Until this moment, I never knew I wanted to live in a house that smelled like meat loaf.

A man ambles in, sweaty and red-faced, the sort of man who people might call jolly. He sports a yellow-white ribbed tank top, tucked into plaid belted shorts. He pushes his thinning hair back and blinks at me.

"Hi, um, my name is Zoe, and I'm—"

"I know who you are." She cuts me off and wanders into the living room, sinking into a chair. "Damn near gave me a heart attack, you did. But I know who you are."

Bernie stares at me, his fat little fingers keep pushing that one strip of hair against his red scalp, again and again. He peers at me, blinking, with giant gray, watery eyes. "Goddamn, you look just like her."

"I'm Joan's twin? I'm looking for Joan?" My statements

come out like questions. A fan whirls overhead, and I can hear somewhere in the kitchen the distant calls of a baseball game on television.

"Patrice, did you invite her to sit down? Get a drink of water?" Bernie tears his eyes away from mine for a second and glares at his wife. She shakes her head.

"I didn't do anything, Bern. I can hardly think. You want a glass of water, or something dear? I just made *pizzelles*. They were for Lorraine's baby shower but my God, that recipe makes so much . . ." She ambles into the kitchen and Bernie and I are left alone.

He coughs once. "I know I'm staring at you, I just can't help it. You look so much like my little girl. We've known about you, and talked for years about maybe looking you up, but Pat's had a hard time and we weren't sure, you probably had a family, who knows?"

Patrice comes back, extending a glass plate of golden snowflake cookies, dusted with powdered sugar, and she shimmies into a chair opposite mine. They both study me, and I shift uncomfortably, reaching for a cookie. They're light, flaky, and sweet, and I close my eyes. For a moment, I want this. These people, with their buttery cookies and their quiet homemade dinner in front of the Mets game and their family baby shower and church bake sales. I feel gypped.

"Honey, what can we do for you?" Patrice reaches out, her long nails tapping my knee. Every finger has a gold ring on it.

"I'm, um, looking for Joan. Is she here?" They haven't made one move to get her. Yet, Caroline was clear that she lived here, with her parents.

Bernie and Patrice exchange glances and she takes my hand in hers.

"Honey, I don't know how to tell you this." Patrice does a quick sign of the cross. "But our Joanie died three years ago."

CHAPTER 22

The room is hot, stifling, and the clock over the mantel starts its song. Three o'clock.

"She's dead?" I repeat. There's a wad of *pizzelle* stuck in the back of my throat and I start to cough. Patrice hands me my water glass and I gulp it, gratefully, wiping a drip from my chin.

"She was killed in a hit-and-run. She was a pedestrian and . . ." Bernie's voice peters out while his mouth keeps moving. He gives a little shrug, like *it happens*. "It's New York," he finally finishes.

"She didn't even live here anymore." Patrice stamps her foot, suddenly bitter, her painted toenails flash inside peep-toe bedroom slippers. "She was married, moved to Manhattan, hardly ever came back."

Bernie pats the couch next to him and Patrice stands up, relocates. He leans into her and closes his eyes, his lips move almost as though in prayer. Patrice wipes fat tears from under her eyes with her thumb.

"I'm sorry, honey, we do pretty good most days. It's been three years after all. I never go a day without thinking of her, but I don't cry so much anymore. But you. You're a shock. Just how you look, your mannerisms. It's all our Joanie."

"Can you tell me about her?" I don't know what I'm looking for, but I can't leave yet.

"She was a kind person, that's what everyone at her service said. That she was the kindest person they'd ever met. She'd help anyone. Small animals, children. She gave money to the homeless, always. Anyone with a hat or a bucket or a coffee can. It didn't matter what they were doing, she didn't care."

"'They're not begging, they're busking.' She always said that." Bernie rocks back on his haunches, his big hands covering his bare knees. He laughs. "I thought it was so naïve."

"She worked at the library. She had friends. She had a life, not a big one, but a life nonetheless." Patrice waves her finger at me, her mouth twisted in anger. "Then she meets Mr. Fabulous at some library charity event and *poof!* She's gone. Eloped! Not even a Catholic wedding for her mama. Some big fancy honeymoon in Paris. Paris! She'd always wanted to go to Italy."

"Patrice." Bernie shrugs. "She fell in love. Happens to all of us," he nods over at Patrice with a wry smile, "at one time or another."

"Then where'd she go, eh?" She leans in, rests an elbow on her knee. "When she died, we hadn't talked to her in almost a year. She was mad at me." She straightens her collar. "I didn't want her to move away. Her life was here."

"She grew up, you know. That's what kids do." Bernie rolled his eyes in Patrice's direction and she sat back, *harrumph,* against the couch cushion.

"I just wanted her to keep her life. She wanted a new, big fancy life. She didn't have to stop speaking to me." She turns and levels her gaze at me. "That's my regret. We weren't on speaking terms."

"When she died, we didn't know she was in the city. She

died in Midtown. Midtown! Who goes to Midtown? What was she doing, seeing a show?" Bernie shakes his head. "And she was alone. Her husband didn't even know she was here. No one knew why. It was the damnedest thing."

"Out of character, too. We've never been able to figure it out. She was a little anxious, you know?" Patrice tilts her chin at me, like I should know this. Like maybe I was anxious, too. "She took medication but it was getting better. She was coming out of her shell. We thought marriage would be good for her, at first. Even in high school, she was a homebody." She shakes her head. "It's my one regret, in my whole life."

"Patrice." Bernie's tone is pained.

Patrice stands up, the sofa cushion inflates with a sigh. She waves her hand behind her, in my general direction, a motion of apology, and sways out of the room. I hear her heavy footsteps on the carpeted stairs.

Bernie lets out a large belly sigh, mops his brow with a handkerchief from his pocket. "I'm sorry. We're mostly okay. You're just so . . ." He examines my face like the words are written there. "Unexpected." He stands up and looks at me sadly. "We were old parents. I regret that. We tried for years to have babies, almost a decade. Had a lot of miscarriages, no one could tell us why. It wrecked Patrice. Wrecked her. Joanie was our saving grace, it seemed. We maybe protected her too much because of it."

I thought of Evelyn and nodded.

"You should go, honey. Listen, leave your number. I'll have Pat call you when she gets her strength back." He stands up, the couch permanently molded into the shapes of their bodies. I pictured them there, night after night, in a darkened living room with nothing but a flickering television to cover the silence.

I scribble my cell phone number on the back of an old

lottery ticket that he gives me. He takes it and sets it on the television stand, which is just an old wooden box television with a flat gray screen. He walks me to the door, pats me awkwardly on the back.

He holds up one wide, pink hand. *Hold on a moment,* and ambles down the hall. A moment later, he comes back.

"Here, you can keep this. We have tons of them." He hands me a small, laminated card. The front has a picture of Joanie, in front of a library, a short floral dress, a smile filled with endless summers and infinite possibilities. It could have been me. The back of the card has a prayer.

"That's her college graduation." His hand shakes, a violent tremor, and he shoves it in his pocket. "She went to Queens College. Library science major. You know the trip was an hour and a half one way? Three transfers. Does that sound like someone with anxiety to you?"

I shake my head.

"You understand. It's hard." His eyes are watery gray, without any distinct color, and up close his neck wobbles.

"I know. I'm sorry. I didn't mean to spring this on you. I didn't know about Joanie."

He coughs, thick and mucousy from the back of his throat. Then he says something surprisingly empathetic. "You've lost someone, too. You just didn't know it."

I don't tell him I've lost a lot of people I didn't know about in the past few days. I reach up and kiss his cheek and leave him there, patting his jowl.

• • •

Once outside I call a car service. I stand on the corner, a half a block away from the Bascio residence. Someone keeps parting the curtains in the front window of the closest house. I half expect a police car to show up because I'm a *suspicious person.* I text Cash while I'm waiting. *Joanie is dead. Joan Bascio. Find out all you can. She was married. Find out who.*

Before I can think it through, I dial Lydia. She picks up on a half ring, her voice high and echoing, like in an airplane hangar. "Zoe?" There is a loud commotion behind her, a crash followed by a deep voice, almost in a yell.

"I'm here, are you okay? What's wrong?" My heart picks up speed.

"We've been vandalized. Everything is ruined." There's a loud rustle, like she's turned her face away from the speaker, the scrape of her chin against the mouthpiece.

"What?" I wait a beat but there's silence, then talking. "Lyd. Where are you?"

"The shop. I have to go, we have to call the police. I'll call you back."

"Is everyone okay?" I ask, panicked, my brain sifting through everything that's happened and settling, with a heavy, foggy dread, on the idea that I'm involved. This has everything to do with me. It's all connected.

"I think so," she replies.

"I'm in Brooklyn." Apropos of nothing. "It'll take me a few. I'll be there as soon as I can." My brain is white hot. My hands shake as I hang up and dial Cash. I tell him about the shop. "Come with me?" I hate to ask him another favor.

He doesn't hesitate. "I'll meet you there."

• • •

I meet Cash outside La Fleur d'Elise and survey the damage from the street. The storefront windows are smashed in, the glass splintered inward toward a single point, as though hit with a heavy object. I step over the pieces in the doorway. Inside, the exposed bulbs in the ceiling are broken, shards of glass screwed into fixtures are all that remain. The glass counter has been crushed, the refrigerator door hangs off its hinges, the arrangements inside have been ripped apart and flower heads scattered around the floor, which is wet with large puddles. The water buckets have all been upended.

"Two weddings' worth of inventory, gone," Elisa laments as I come through the door. She stands up when she sees me and crosses the room. Her spindly arms fold around me in a limp, defeated hug. Javi works the broom in the corner pushing all the glass and floral carcasses to a sopping pile in the center of the room and then looks at it impotently, like *now what?*

Lydia hovers in the doorway, a drooping amaryllis dangling between her fingers.

The counter in front, next to the register, is heavy, stainless steel. Meant to be a table for last-minute arrangements and trimming, if necessary. It's more functional than aesthetic. The top is etched with a thinly carved message. A message that is meant for me, I feel it in my bones, heavy and leaded. I run my fingers over the metal.

JAREd

The ugly word is scrawled with a dull straightedge. Words carved into metal are violent by nature, the message is practically irrelevant. The letters themselves are sinister, the way magazine clippings pasted on paper are indicative of ransom notes.

But this, this note is meant for me. In a way Lydia or Javi or Elisa could never know. The small *d* hovers slightly lower than the rest of his name. It's the brand, inside Rosie's mouth, that deliberate small *d* clinging to the corner of the *E*.

The blood rushes to my head. I feel at once hot and sick, a sheen of sweat coats my arms and I feel it down my spine below my bra strap, one single drip of fluid tracing lazily down my backbone. I sway and from what sounds like the inside of a tunnel, Cash yells, "Catch her!" but I don't remember anything else.

CHAPTER 23

The first person I see when I open my eyes is Officer Yates, her rounded dark eyes, long lashes, bright lipstick. My first thought is, *Why am I sleeping at the shop?* Elisa peers over Yates's shoulder, her face a mask of concern mixed with something else. Anger? Latent impatience at the very least.

I forget, then remember, seemingly at the same time. "How long was I out?" I sit up but feel sick and sink into the velvet-covered pink office chair that has been brought over just for me.

"No more than a minute." Cash is on one knee next to the chair, leaning close. The smell of his aftershave turns my stomach.

"I just got here," Yates offers. Elisa brings me water and I can't help but enjoy it, just a little. Elisa, waiting on me. Elisa, who once sent me to Duane Reade to buy a pencil sharpener. Twice. Because it's apparently possible to buy the wrong kind. Yates stands up and motions everyone back, long nails flickering. "Give her some space, okay? Let me talk to her."

They disperse. Javi pouts with his broom, pushing it insolently into corners. Elisa pretends to flip through paperwork.

Yates pats my hand while I ask her about the man at the back door. She has a report from the night before she wants me to sign.

"I'm sorry we can't do more, there's just nothing to investigate." She raises her eyebrows, and all I see is doubt.

Cash overhears and chimes in, "I was there. I saw the same thing Zoe did. There was someone at that back door. The door handle jiggled."

"I believe you." She pats Cash on the shoulder, placating. It's just no use. The word *resources* bounces around in my mind.

"What about Jared Pritchett? Did you look him up?" I press my left palm onto hers, so our hands make a sandwich, and close my eyes. A chill goes up my spine, like the trill of a xylophone. "Mick Flannery exists. This is all connected. Do you believe me now?"

"I do. I did before, but this helps." She waves her arm around the mess and smiles a little, unexpectedly, flashing a nicotine-stained incisor at me. "I have ideas though. Give me time, okay. I believe you, I do. I looked up your testimony. This was some heavy shit, girl. Those kinds of crime rings are not run by one or two people. It's usually more like thirty. Fifty. This?" She motions toward the counter, the mess. "This is revenge, pure simple. To terrify you."

"Then what? Kill me?" My mind flashes back to the stripped-down van. That bloodstain. That child's lacy sock. My stomach roils.

"Zoe, there are officers stationed at your apartment. We'll protect you."

"I need to call Henry." My tongue feels coated in sawdust.

"Do you have a place to go?"

I look at Elisa. Javi. Lydia. They all blink at me, silent. Then, Lydia nods her head, just once.

"Yes."

"That won't be necessary." Henry stands in the doorway of the shop, his hands on his hips. At the sight of him, my chest pops with relief. He looks like hell, his hair is disheveled, his face is red on one side, like he's been sleeping on it. I push up off the chair and I'm across the room in seconds. I stand in front of him, unsure, until he pulls me against his chest, which feels foreign and familiar at the same time.

"You're here. How? I didn't even have time to call you."

"Zoe, I tried to call you, about ten times. You tell me someone is chasing you and then I hear nothing back. Except you stayed at Lydia's." He surveys the room and sees Elisa, and gives her a nod of recognition.

Lydia opens her mouth to protest and then closes it, shakes her head, keeping the secret. I half thought she'd blurt it out, right there: *Zoe didn't stay with me.* Despite our gulf, she keeps it.

Yates pulls me away from Henry and I realize the refrigerator still hums in the corner, spitting out cold air through the broken glass. My arms gooseflesh. "Zoe, listen to me. I need you to be careful, do you understand me? You can't go back to your apartment. We'll put you under surveillance. Come to the station."

"Yes," I say automatically.

"Not an option. I'm getting her out of here." Henry crosses his arms over his chest. This is his Henry pose, the one I've seen at parties; where most men relax, hold a drink, let their arms drape around a woman's shoulders, Henry stands like he is keeping guard. He, himself, is a counterargument. *His hand on Pink Spandex.* His eyes flick to Cash, cold and dismissive. His expression, tight eyebrows, slightly turned chin, say, *We have things to discuss.* I wonder then if he will bring an agenda. He turns to Yates. "Is she done?"

Yates nods. "Technically, yes. For now. I think it's best that you stay at a hotel. Somewhere in the city."

"Yes. I understand that." Henry holds his arm out, toward me. I know he's thinking of Fishing Lake. My mind spins.

"She needs to stay close by, Mr. Whittaker." Yates's voice is stern, in a way I've never heard another person talk to him. "This is an active investigation. We need to be able to get a hold of Zoe."

"Yes, Officer, I understand that. I have a house about an hour away." He's resolute and Yates pushes her mouth together, her arms on her hips, her starched blue uniform gapping in the chest. Her broad shoulders rival Henry's and she looks at him, just as determined.

"I'd advise to keep her here," she demands. I've never seen anything like it.

"Henry, the house won't be safe," I interject, playing peacekeeper.

"It's all right, darling. I've got security coming. I just need to arrange it." He holds up a hand in Yates's direction and mollifies, "Just find this Jared person. I want this bastard caught." He herds me into the street, swooped and protective, so I don't even have time to say good-bye to Lydia, Javi, and Elisa, or thank you to Cash. He ushers me into the back of a car and we're in the street headed downtown before I can think.

What could possibly be the connection between Caroline, Joan, and Jared? What happened to Mick, how does he fit into all of this? I trace back Evelyn's relationship with Mick in my mind. Their meeting at the beach. His seemingly random disappearances. What is his connection to Caroline? I try to connect these dots, but pain pulses a quick beat behind my eyes.

Henry pats my hand the whole car ride, as though it's a pet. I want to tell him to stop, but I can't find the words. The sun hangs low in the sky, slung between buildings, orange and bright. Within minutes, we're in the Lincoln Tunnel, speeding to safety. Henry the Hero. I check my phone to make sure it's on. Waiting, waiting. As we speed through the tunnel, the side lights flickering past the window remind me of a searchlight, seeking out lost, drifting ships. *Seeking, seeking something.* I touch my finger to the glass.

CHAPTER 24

By the time we get to the house, evening has fallen, quiet and thick. The sky is blue-gray, clouds covering the stars, and in the country, so much emptier than twilight in the city. Henry lets us in and the air smells freshly laundered, clean and safe. The innocence of dryer sheets.

The kitchen contains a cold spread: cheese and hummus, fresh vegetables so crisp I find myself looking around for Penny, who couldn't have left more than moments ago. There's no one, of course. It wasn't that long ago that I found this sort of convenient arrangement of our lives to be charming, like a party card trick. A sleight of hand here, a simple misdirection there, and *Voilà, here's your dinner.* Now, it crawls under my skin and festers there, like a chigger, and the whole thing makes me itch.

Henry makes me tea, chamomile, lightly sweetened with honey that he insists on serving me in bed, against my protest. It's barely eight o'clock for God's sake. My head feels so heavy and I want to do nothing but sleep.

"You must be exhausted. Please, let me take care of you." He pulls the covers up to my lap, fluffs my pillows. His hair is flopping down on his forehead and he's changed into a dark oxford shirt and khaki shorts. He looks relaxed, nurturing, his eyebrows pulled together in concern. He keeps kissing me, my forehead, my hands, my cheeks. *As you are woman, so be lovely.*

He brings me a hot washcloth for my headache. He brushes my hair, kneads my back, his thumbs working the tender muscles between my shoulder blades. I let him. His hands guide me back down to the bed, lying on my back, and his fingers work the buttons on my blouse. I close my eyes and let him remove my clothes until the breeze blows in, chilling my skin where he's kissed it. His fingers trace circles around my belly, my thighs, my breasts, and I let him. They find me open and wet between my legs and I let him.

I feel loosely disconnected, lubricated at the joints, floating above the bed, watching now-naked Henry make love to me, slow, insistent, loving. His face flickers in the light of a candle I don't remember lighting, and it embodies one word: *rapture.*

I don't come. I feel numb and weightless, like I've had too much to drink. Or like I've taken something. A thought pops in my head but flitters out before I can catch it. Henry shudders and bucks, his soft yelps in my ear remind me of a caged puppy, and he whispers things I can't quite hear.

Except one. *My most precious thing.* He says it again and again until I fall asleep, hard, like falling off a cliff.

• • •

I dream of Evelyn, her teeth bared, red and bloody. She screeches, *What have you done?* She comes at me, hands clawed out to attack my neck, my throat. I can feel her nails on my neck, my collarbone, scratching, and she shrieks like a banshee, her hair wild. Her hatred is so real, so palpable, that I wake up wrapped in sheets soaked with sweat. Henry isn't in bed.

It's two a.m. I roam the house and find him sitting in the kitchen, sipping bourbon. He leads me back upstairs, changes the sheets, and tucks me in. I sink into the freshly made bed. I'm quite sure I can't handle even one more little thing. Henry's quiet care is such a relief. He brings me orange juice, *For strength,* he whispers, and I drink it gratefully, chugging it in large, heaving gulps.

"Have you heard from Yates?" I ask. "Did they find him? Can we go home?"

He shakes his head and I flop back against the pillows, exhausted. I'm asleep in no time, a thick, wool sleep, heavy and dense. The kind where when you wake up, you don't know if it's morning or night and the numbers on the clock swim around, bumping into each other.

I don't have any dreams.

• • •

I wake sometime later, could have been hours, could have been days. I'm feverish and chattering. Henry, bedside, tucks thick, patterned quilts around me, murmuring about germs and summer colds. Fluffing pillows, clucking and puttering around the room, like a nursemaid. Picking random objects up and moving them for no other reason than to have something to do.

I push myself up on my elbows, watching him. "Have they found him?"

Henry shakes his head. "Just worry about getting better." He kisses my forehead, his hand cupping the back of my neck. He brings me more tea, toast, and Penny's buttery, flaky scones. I wonder when she made them and feel a sharp beat of unexplained hatred. I leave them all on the tray untouched. On the nightstand, he sets down a tall tumbler of orange juice. "You have to stay hydrated or you'll only get more sick."

I chug it down and fall back to sleep, the kind of thick

sleep you fall in and out of quickly, dreamless. He wakes me every few hours to drink, until I shove the glass away. I can't remember Henry ever taking care of me sick. Prior to today, I wouldn't have imagined it.

"I can't drink any more orange juice. Henry, I think we need to go back to the city."

"We will. We will. As soon as I know it's safe." He pushes my hair off my forehead, which is slick with sweat.

"Yates should have called by now. Did she call?" I try to get out of bed, but my vision swims. I have a fever and I thunk back onto the bed.

"It's the flu. Your fever was up to 104." Henry speaks in hushed tones, like we're in hospice. "I've called the doctor and had something delivered. It's an antiviral. It will help but it might make you vomit." He's asking my permission in the way Henry asks permission, which is to not ask at all. He's *telling* me permission. He brings me two small pale pink tablets and a large glass of water. I chug them down.

I pull the blankets in against my face. I imagine the sheet getting sucked into my mouth, cutting off my oxygen. I hear Henry's footsteps on the floor, the quiet creak of the door, and only when I'm sure I'm alone, do I drift off to sleep.

When I wake up, the bedside table holds a full glass of juice and a note. *Be back soon, Henry.* On the chaise longue he'd laid out my clothes, a gentle nudge to get up. Get dressed. A purple T-shirt and a pair of white shorts, like maybe today we would just go hiking. *Hiking.*

I dump the juice in the toilet and get dressed under self-protest. I have to fight every movement to not crawl back under the blankets. I'm so cold. But underneath some layer of hopelessness flames primal anger, a spark off a flint. Everyone seems content to just let Jared come to me. Yates seemed blasé about it, Henry was no help. If no one is going to help me, I'm going to have to help myself.

If I could reach Cash, he'd surely do some investigating. I need help. Joanie's death, Caroline's threat, Jared, the vanishing Mick, it's all related somehow, I just can't find the link. Every single thing is connected, my whole body vibrates, that's how confident I am. I'm right, that Jared and Mick and Joanie's death are connected, that it's somehow my fault. That I killed my sister. I have a sudden thought: If I find the missing Mick, I can unravel this whole thing.

I make my way downstairs to the kitchen, looking for my phone. My blood is pumping now, thumping through my veins in a steady rhythm. *Find Mick. Find Mick.* A drumbeat of redemption with a touch of revenge. I still feel foggy and weak from the fever and my stomach turns with nausea from the antivirals, but the anger perches right under my skin and could easily fan to full flame.

I search the kitchen, the sitting room, and the sunroom, pulling out drawers and cabinets along the way. No phone. I head back upstairs and sift through the drawers in our dressers, suitcases, pants pockets. No phone.

It was right on the bedside table when I fell asleep, I was sure of it. It has to be somewhere. I have an idea: Henry's office.

In Henry's office I yank open desk drawers and flip through files. In the closet, I find file boxes and dig through them, finding nothing notable, save for a small padlock key that I slip in my pocket.

On the bookshelf my eyes settle on the picture of me in the woods, that day on a picnic. I realize I'm wearing the same shirt I have on. I pick up the picture and study it, and my hand goes to my collar, feeling along the ribbed edge of the crew neck. I touch the shirt in the picture, a smooth hem in a deep *V.* A hint of cleavage, a shadowy swell of breast.

It's not the same shirt.

I only have one, purchased as a gift from my darling husband, in a color I've never liked. I study the picture closer. The same uneven eyebrows, the slight widow's peak at my hairline, my dark hair newly grown, shiny and soft to my shoulders. The mole at my left ear. *My left ear.* My hand flies to my face, gently tapping the mole near my *right* ear.

The woman in the picture is not me.

CHAPTER 25

I fish the key out of my pocket and slide it into the padlock. The locked room. The room filled with files and personal effects that Henry wanted protected when he rented the place out. The room I've never seen.

With the picture tucked under my arm, I turn the key and the lock pops open. It takes me a minute to dislodge the latch, and the door gives with a stutter catch. The room is pitch-black, and it's only three o'clock in the afternoon. I realize there are room-darkening shades on the windows. I flip on the light.

On the far wall, file boxes are stacked five across, four high, identical and unlabeled. The wall on the left contains large crates. The wall on the right is covered by a large sheet.

The room smells musty, unused. I pull the picture out and examine it again, tilting it one way then the other in the light. There are subtle differences: she has a chipped front tooth, barely noticeable. She has a red, slivery scar across her collarbone. Had I not been looking for something, I wouldn't have seen it. My hands shake.

I pull down the top box, anchor it on the floor and lift the lid. Files. I flip through them. *Tara taxes. Tara student loans 2007.* I pull down the next box. More files. Then the next. Until all the boxes are scattered around me. What am I looking for? I don't know. There's only one explanation for the picture, I just need proof. *Bingo. Wedding pictures.* I flip open the album and fan the pages. Tara in an ivory fishtail gown, her hair pulled back in a chignon, smiling a smile I recognize as my own, the same smile I've given to Henry. A secret smile. A lover's smile. Lips half-parted, turned up on one side.

I turn the pages with my thumb, one after the other. A wedding with no guests. A lavish dinner spread, a glistening plate of scallops, Tara's mouth opened goofily to eat one. I hate scallops.

Through my husband's old wedding photos, I learn that my dead sister liked seafood.

A first dance, an intimate restaurant, a single violinist. *Oh Joanie, why were you so isolated from the world?* Did she have friends? Did her parents want to come? Where was this wedding? I examine the pages, twice front to back then back to front. Looking for clues, but finding nothing. She looked so happy, so gloriously, no-strings-attached happy. The way dogs and toddlers are happy. With abandon.

I set the book down. Move to the large crates and unfold the flaps. Inside, neatly folded, are clothes. Piles of slacks, blouses, dresses. Fabric so fine, you wanted to bury your face in it. I look at the labels. Versace. Donna Karan. Silk, velvet, cashmere, varying shades of purple.

I think of all the clothing he's given me, eggplant, violet, lavender. A color I abhorred my whole life. *Tara's* favorite color. He didn't buy me new clothes, he gave me her clothes. My mouth tastes like copper and I suck air through my teeth. I can't catch my breath. I've been nothing more than a fucking Barbie doll.

I stand up, cross the room, and rip the sheet off the wall.

Underneath, a hundred little pictures flutter. A corkboard, mounted to the wall, is pinned with pictures, articles, scribbled notes, sheets of loose leaf, random pieces of paper. One side of the board is labeled *Tara* in thick Magic Marker, the other side is labeled *Hilary*. The blood thunders in my ears.

Pictures of me at the flower shop. Lace skirts and fishnet stockings and combat boots as I arrived at work, or stiletto heels as I left for the night. Lydia and me laughing, holding our sides, sharing a cigarette.

The pictures of Tara are wide-ranging. Early shots show her with long flowing hair, younger, freer, with pink cheeks and loose, open smiles. Later, she is guarded, as though she was holding a secret, thin lipped and a bashful look away. More enigmatic. In some cases, all the more beautiful. Her eyes are darker, hooded.

I tug down a newspaper article, pulling the paper through the pushpin and ripping the top.

September 5, 2011: A woman, 25, was killed in a hit-and-run at the corner of 32nd and 6th. The victim is identified as Tara Joan Whittaker . . .

I smooth the article out with my hand, leaving ink smudges across the paper. There it is. Confirmation. Proof. Tara and Joanie were the same person. I lurch forward, grab a box with both hands, and heave. I feel like I'm going to be sick, the nausea rolls through me. I put the box aside.

Tacked to the board is a thick, ecru card. I pull it down and examine it. The front simply says *Hal*. Inside, eerily familiar handwriting loops around a just as familiar poetic verse:

As you are woman, so be lovely:
As you are lovely, so be various,

Merciful as constant, constant as various.
So be mine, as I yours for ever.

I turn the card over. On the back is another verse:

Lovely I am, merciful I shall prove:
Woman I am, constant as various,
Not marble-hearted but your own true love.
Give me an equal kiss, as I kiss you.

A laugh-sob gets caught in my throat. This was Tara, subtly telling Henry, *I know you.* I see through you. He'd never gotten it, of course. For all Henry's intellectual prowess, I should have known he would never indulge in something as frivolous as poetry. My sister, with her mystery novels, her introversion, and her crippling agoraphobia . . . she may have been timid, but she would never be mistaken for stupid. *Not marble-hearted but your own true love.* Galatea telling Pygmalion that she is more than his creation; she's her own living, breathing soul. *Give me an equal kiss.* Is Henry capable of considering a woman his equal? Clever girl.

There's a picture pinned, Tara and Henry in front of the Eiffel Tower, and I flip it over. *TJ and Hal. Honeymoon 2008.* She's wearing a black dress with a large silver rose pinned to the collar. Black-and-white-striped skirt. I recognize it. I wore it in France, right down to the brooch. My mouth tastes like pennies and my hands shake.

All these pictures, her wide, happy smiles. Free of anxiety. Certainly, outside in public. In crowds. Not agoraphobic then, all dated 2008, 2009. A few from 2010. Nothing from 2011. Like she'd simply disappeared in the year between 2010 and 2011. Even if she'd struggled with anxiety, as Mrs. Bascio suggested, she wasn't home-bound. She was functioning. *Oh, Joanie, what did he do to you?* I feel it then, the pressure of what being *Henry Whittaker's wife* would eventually do to me, and it's as heavy as a house, perched right on my chest.

I pull down the other articles on my side of the corkboard. Small, typeset blotter notes from the trial. Witnesses and defendants. Jared Pritchett and Michael Flannery. It's right there in black and white.

It suddenly occurs to me that I'm in danger. In what way, exactly, I'm not certain. I cannot be found in this room. I push my hand against my forehead. I need to leave this place. How? I pin the articles back to the board, restack the boxes, close up the crates. I take one last look around at this . . . shrine. It's been right under my nose the whole time, like he'd wanted me to find it. I feel the sob catch in my chest. My whole life is a lie. This whole room is a lie.

I back out of the door, slam the padlock back together, and rush to Henry's office. I slide the keys back into the box in his closet, and I hope I remember the right one. I realize I left the picture in his secret room. No time.

I race to the front door. I need to leave. Call for help. Something. I try to imagine explaining all this to Yates. She'll lock me up, straightjacket and all.

I realize I have no car. *Thinkthinkthinkthink.* I'll walk to the corner store. And then what? Call who? Is there even an "Information" to call anymore? I think of Trisha, with her chipmunk cheek grin and her shiny, excited eyes. I imagine clawing at her to call the police, gasping and panicked. It'd be the most exciting thing to happen in Fishing Lake since the Italian witch lived up the hill.

I turn the handle on the front door and pull. It's locked. I flip the dead bolt, try again. Locked. The door doesn't budge. My heart is starting to pound. Bad things are going to happen, I can feel it. The panic crawls up my spine and wraps around my neck and I can feel the back of my head starting to sweat, big fat drops dripping down my neck. My life, unraveling at my feet, and I'm left stumbling and tripping over the threads. I turn the dead bolt and the door lock and give a swift tug. Nothing moves. The fear rises up, choking and tearing at my throat until I can't breathe and I cough a sob against my forearm.

The door is locked from the outside. I'm locked in. I rest my forehead against the glass and take deep breaths, trying to calm down. Windows. That's all. Windows. You can't really lock a person in a whole house. I don't care if I have to rappel the wall. The claustrophobia is setting in fast and I can't catch my breath. In. Out. In. Out.

"Going somewhere?"

I whip around and there stands Henry, tall, familiar-looking Henry, with his vacation smile and tousled hair, a soft, fraternity boy curl falling down onto his forehead. His head cocked to the side, his eyes marblelike, little rat beads of eyes. I push my back up against the door, the knob digging into the small of my back.

In his left hand, he's holding a gun.

CHAPTER 26

He leads me gently to the bedroom, his soft, manicured hand resting on my elbow, almost caring, if it weren't for the hard metal of the muzzle pressed up against my spine. He urges me onto the bed and I resist with a look, and he sighs.

"You've always been obstinate." He shakes his head with a small smile the way I imagine mothers react to strong-willed four-year-olds, like my resistance is infantile. Cute. My tongue tastes like sulfur. He jabs the gun farther into my skin, pulling my arm behind me and giving it a solid twist. "Get on the bed, Zoe. I could kill you right now. Who would care anyway? It's not like you have anyone." He says it off-the-cuff, chillingly calculating.

He shoves me face-first onto the bed and grabs my left wrist; in one smooth motion he handcuffs me to the iron headboard. He pulls on my arm, checking to make sure it will hold.

"So Joanie is Tara." No point in beating around the bush. My heart thumps in my throat, but my head remains clear, maybe for the first time in weeks. "Then who am I? To you?"

His back is to me, and he's fiddling with something on the dresser. He turns then, holding a filled syringe.

"You're my replacement. Do the math, Zoe. When did Tara die?"

My mind spins on dates and facts that up to this point I'd only been peripherally aware of. *Three years ago.* I swallow hard but say nothing.

He doesn't wait for me to answer. "And when did your Jared get out of prison?"

I have no idea. I shake my head.

He gives me a pitying look. "Tara was so much smarter than you. It's a shame really, for so many reasons." Sigh. "I'll give you a hint. It's three years ago."

My stomach seizes and I feel the sweat on my upper lip. I lick the corners of my mouth, but my tongue is as dry as sandpaper.

"Is that why they're back now?" My voice is a rasp.

"What people? The people you screwed over back when you were living a disgusting life? Selling drugs on playgrounds?" Henry chuckles softly and shakes his head, tapping the bubbles out of the syringe. "No one is 'back now.' I found Jared and killed him. Two years ago, because the police were incompetent and I realized it was you he wanted. He didn't know Tara existed. Biggest mistake of his life, I'd say." His mouth twisted once, a sideways kiss. "Mick died of a drug overdose in witness protection. Years ago."

"Witness protection?" This is why there was no Mick. "Wait, you killed Jared?" I stare at him. This man, this elegant, manicured man, my husband, who likes lamb only on Wednesdays and thinks that cabernet should never be drunk with pasta because they are both too heavy. He is a murderer. It's inconceivable.

"Don't be so shocked, Zoe. He's not the first, he's not the last. No one will miss him either. Just like they won't miss you." He flicks the syringe once more with his finger and walks slowly toward the bed. I inch backward. "It actually wasn't even hard. He's not that smart."

"But . . . but if there is no Jared, and Mick is dead, *you* were doing these things? The vandalism, the break-in?" My voice hitches to a screech.

Technically, I am the reason my sister is dead. Technically, Jared killed her. But only because he thought *she* was *me.* My life, my choices, my mistakes. A simple case of mistaken identity, that's what set this ball in motion. Jared was coming back for me, a revenge plot for bringing down his house of cards. Henry only continued what Jared started, after, of course, he killed him.

"Do you think I got to where I am by chance, Zoe? That my money, my life, my position is all a happy accident? Truthfully, you've tired me out."

"I don't know what that means." I hiss it out between my teeth, kicking my foot in his direction.

"Tara used to just sit in the house and read. You? You're out of control, running all over Manhattan, following me to the gym." I must look shocked at this because he half-laughs. "I know every move you make. Your phone, the apartment. With technology, it's so easy now. GPS. Cameras the size of thumbnails. How do you think I found you at Elisa's? I know all about your dates with that little reporter, even the little sleepover—*that you lied about.* Every keystroke on the computer has been recorded. Everything you've done since you've lived in my home, Zoe."

"Who's the girl at the gym?" I spit.

He shrugs. "She's nobody." He means it, too. She is nobody to him.

"Caroline? The phone call? That was you, too?" I try to sit up, but my arm flails, shackled above my head and I can't get purchase on the bed.

He stands over me, with a faint icy smile. "You're just so out of control all the time, Zoe. You don't listen to me. You don't need me, not the way Tara needed me. Tara was sweet, compliant. She needed me. You are defiant. Unlovable. You're just so fucking unlovable." His voice is low and the words pierce my heart. He could be right. "You're indifferent to me, Zoe. I can't have that. It was different before, with your blissful ignorance. But you had to push, seek her out. Find Caroline. Then your sister. You ruined everything, not me. You're never content." His hand grips my knee and I open my eyes. He slides the needle into my thigh and depresses the plunger.

I gasp. "What are you doing, Henry?"

"You didn't just owe me a wife, Zoe. You owed me Tara. Do you see now?" His face is inches away from mine and I can see all the pores in his skin. His breathing comes in quick rasps. He fades from view and the room wavers and spins.

• • •

When I wake up, the room is dark. The clock on the dresser blinks two a.m. I sit up and my arm shoots through with pain. It is numb and buzzing cold. In the dark, I hear the rustle of sheets next to me. *Henry.*

"I can't feel my arm," I mumble groggily and Henry flicks on the light. I realize I've been dressed in a white silk nightgown and robe that isn't mine. It looks like a bridal negligee. I can't lift my arms, my legs. I need to get out of here. Henry, clad in pajama bottoms and a T-shirt, holds a small key. Deftly, he lifts my arm, pinning it against the wall, while he unlocks the handcuffs and switches them. In the brief second the handcuffs are off, I make a clumsy attempt to flail, softly fobbing him in the cheek. He slaps me. Hard. My face beats a steady hot pain, and my eyes water.

"Do it again, Zoe, and I'll kill you right now," he spits at me. Then his expression sags, my sleepiness softening the edges of his face.

I try to focus my eyes on Henry, who is splitting and coming back together, again and again. It reminds me of watching Evelyn's old television when she worked nights: scrambled soft-core porn channels, a flash of skin here or there, maybe a blinking Technicolor breast. I close my eyes, yellow spots and flashes of color.

When I open my eyes again, Henry is standing in front of me, naked, erect, cupping his penis. His hands move and slide up my thighs. I turn my face away and he pulls me back by my chin. I realize that I'm naked under the negligee and I kick my feet. I struggle to sit up.

"No," I mumble. The drugs are wearing off, I think. The "No" sounds clearer to me but I can't tell.

"Settle, my love." Sometime in the last few minutes, he's lit candles, turned off the lights. He lies on top of me, kissing my neck, and I push against his chest. "Goddamn it, Zoe. Just for once, be compliant." He stands up, hastily, embarrassed, slapping at his thigh, at his flaccid failure. "This has never happened before." He's both apologetic and accusing; his eyes shine with hatred and he hovers over me until I think he might hit me, his fist clenched, knuckles white. I set my jaw, prepare for the punch, and close my eyes.

He turns away and dons his pajama bottoms. When he turns back, he's holding a syringe. A quick pinch in my other thigh and my vision swims.

• • •

He brings me trays of food, and I become fixated on the clock each time I'm awake. 6:27 a.m. 4:13 p.m. 5:42 a.m. I try to track the days, but I keep losing count and have to start over. I give up trying to remember and with my free hand, press my thumbnail into the skin along my hip bone until it comes away tinged pink with blood. One half-moon for each day. Or what I think is a day, sometimes it's hard to remember if it was a.m. or p.m. when I woke last, and therefore has it been a day or twelve hours? I can pass my index finger over the healing lines, feel the scabs, and count. Sometimes, when I bolt awake, panicked and gasping, I feel for these small incisions. *Six, I've been here six days.* Then *eight.* Then *ten.*

I think he dresses me in Tara's clothes, black cocktail dresses and silk pantsuits. Where would an agoraphobic wear pantsuits?

He walks me to the bathroom, two, maybe three times a day, handcuffed with the steel tip of the gun in my back and then plank-walks me back to bed. Then, he props me up, feeds me crackers and juice. Talks to me, tells me about his day. His words float around, echoing as though he's in an airplane hangar. If I say *what* too many times, he gets angry. I wonder what he wants with me? Will I just be here forever? His replacement *Tara*, chained to the bed like an animal?

Will I die here?

Will anyone miss me?

Does anyone care?

A shot to the leg. I barely feel it.

* * *

I've started getting sick. Throwing up, hot green bile on the bed, which makes Henry furiously angry.

"What will you do with me?" I ask him, weakly, a long string of spit trailing from my mouth. I'm lying on my side, my face sweating. Whatever he's injecting me with, it's too much. My body has started to reject it. It's making me nauseated and weak. I will die here, in this isolated house in clothes that are not mine.

He's toweling up my filth and he smiles, a clever, Henry-ish smile. "Yates called me, said she's been trying to call you. I said you'd left me. You were staying at a hotel in the city and I didn't know which one. She said she had news on Mick, so I'm guessing she's discovered his death. A shockingly good detective for a woman. He was living under a different name.

WITSEC, you know?" He says all this conversationally, as he works at a stubborn sticky spot on the bare mattress. "After you left town, he turned state's witness, brought down the whole organization. He did a very small amount of prison time, then went into witness protection. I figured it out easily enough, but then again, I'm fairly well connected. The feds, they don't talk much to the police."

My head feels heavy and I let it sink down to my arm, my face wet with tears, sweat. Maybe spit. I am starting to stink.

"But what will you do with me?" I ask again, dumbly, not knowing if he'd even answered the question or not.

"We have three months until hunting season. See, you'll come back to me then. Realize your mistake, how much you've missed me. You're all alone in the world, Zoe, you have no one. You only have me. You leave your hotel, come back here. To beg for my forgiveness. You try to find me in the woods behind the house, as a surprise." His voice has lowered to a whisper, his finger caressing my cheek. "I'll think I've hit a deer. It's tragic, really."

"Henry, people will look for me. Officer Yates, Lydia, Cash. Someone will wonder. You can't get away with this."

"Tara never thought I was stupid, Zoe. But you, you question me at every turn. Honestly, it's so infuriating." He says this conversationally. "I asked Yates to pass it along to Cash and Lydia. We had a rather heated conversation about your past. Your secrets. I told her everything, your drug pushing. Evelyn. You are not the person everyone thinks you are." He purrs in my ear. "You just want to be left alone. You're afraid. You've run away again." He walks over to the dresser, picks up a wad of cash, waves it in my face. "You've even taken some of my money."

I had shared different pieces of my story with different people, but no one knew the whole thing. Cash knew the most, he wouldn't be deterred. But, *but,* he would go to

Yates first. After her talk with Henry, she'd assume I'd stolen Henry's money and skipped town.

Henry lies on the bed, curled into me, his breath hot and wet on my neck and I want to kick him away but I can't make my legs cooperate. *Three months. He's going to keep me here for three months.*

I'll die first.

. . .

I wake up covered in urine. I smell it before I feel it. Henry is ripping the sheets from underneath me and I tumble against my cuffed wrist, shearing the skin until the blood runs down my arm, which enrages him even more. He is angry, yelling words I can't understand. The sheets come away piss yellow and red. He rips off my underpants and nightgown, feels along my hip, those crusty ridges. He asks me, *What the fuck is this?* I answer him, *It's my clock.* I don't think it through; it just comes out and not even coherent. I can't even be sure of what I say, it sounds garbled. All he hears is *clock.*

He marches to the dresser. Rips the clock cord out of the wall and slams the door behind him. With my free hand, I feel along my naked hip. *Twelve days. I've been here twelve days.*

. . .

I think he leaves the house during the day. I force myself awake, hear the door slam, the car slide down the driveway. I scream for as long as I can. I imagine Trisha from the market down the road in a little pink warm-up suit, shiny and metallic looking, a bright purple sweatband, new sneakers, trekking past the house, on a power walk trying *for the last time* to lose the baby weight. I scream for Trisha. I scream until my voice gives out and I am weak, hoarse. I scream all day. Or at least what I think is all day. I scream until Henry comes home.

. . .

Sunup, sundown, faint lights through the curtains, switch arms, a sponge bath. His hands roam my naked body but he can't keep it up, so he gives up. More foreign clothing: track suits and gym clothes, baggy and falling off, I'm wasting away. I'd rather just starve to death. That will come faster than three months, surely.

"I got you a present."

A smaller syringe, a faint yellow liquid.

"It won't make you sick." He smiles. This is my present. A drug that will kill me slower. I need to do something.

"Henry, wait. Hal." I recall the name on the back of the picture. *Hal and TJ.* My voice is thick, molasses coated, stuck like tar on my tongue. I feel the edge of my dress, a summer garden dress, fit for bridal and baby showers, sweet-smelling perfume, and flutes of champagne. *Pizzelles. Where did that come from?* I remember my sister's picture, smiling in front of the library on her college graduation day. A flower dress.

"What?" He stands at the foot of the bed, his fingers tapping against my bare foot impatiently. I struggle to sit up. Between doses, I retain a shocking amount of lucidity. Like the drug doesn't so much seep from my system as much as it dumps out, the fog lifting like a heavy stage curtain.

"Hal," I repeat.

"Don't call me that." His eyes narrow, his wrist, holding the syringe, flicks.

"Why? Isn't it what you want?" I inch forward, suddenly sure-footed. Steady. I reach out, the handcuff pulling against my skin like a vise and I touch his arm. It's warm under my fingertips and I close my eyes, remembering when, not that long ago, I would have made this gesture sincerely. Loving. The flat bones in his wrist are unyielding. He meets my gaze and falters. "Let me try."

I see him consider this. I see him think about me, in *her* clothes, reading Ruth Rendell and Sherlock Holmes in peep toe bedroom slippers and calling him *Hal*, picnics in the woods, patiently waiting in our towering apartment for him to arrive home, excited to see him, jumping up, wrapping my legs around his waist. A lifetime of missionary positions and dinners determined by what Henry ate for lunch, or what day of the week it is. Me, being content with this. Obedient. Compliant. He wavers. I see it in the way the syringe wobbles in his hand.

"Hal." I say it again, but softer, coy, and I avert my gaze. Demure. How I would act if I were truly submissive, try to channel this *twin intuition* I've seen on *Oprah*. Even think, for a crazy second, if she can see me or hear me, *Give me a goddamn sign, Joanie. What would you do?* "What if I could do this, we could be happy, couldn't we? We were once, right? Remember, the day in the woods? The picnic, I wore that purple shirt? We made love against the tree?"

I take a chance here, remembering the force at which he pushed me against that tree, the bark gouging into the soft skin on my back. I think back through our marriage. All the moments of the highest intensity, sweetest romance: Paris, the rooftop. Washington Square Park. Were they all repeat performances? His attempt to revive Tara, relive his past? I'd venture yes, by the way his eyes cloud and narrow and he's studying me, torn between his logic and his base-level desires. His face softens, loses an edge.

He shakes his head, says nothing. I continue, "Paris? Our honeymoon?" And here, he breaks a bit, I can see it. His eyes widen and his jaw slacks. Henry is a rational man, but he *wants this.* Most people forgo logic when faced with something impossible that they viscerally want. "Let's go to Paris. Again. You and me. We'll relive it. Again. This time for real. Hal and TJ," I choke out, lower my voice, dip my chin to my chest, and whisper, "You can help me, Hal. Show me. How to act, I mean. All I've ever wanted is for you to take care of me." I realize with a sickening jolt that it's actually true.

He doesn't speak, he simply backs out of the room, his hand clutched tight around the syringe, his knuckles and his face an identical shade of white. He doesn't agree. Yet. But he will.

At the very least, I'm here, still chained, but clearheaded. All I have to do is wait.

• • •

"Hal. Hal." I shake him, gently. It's midnight, or later, I can't tell. "I have to go." He mumbles something against the pillow.

He hasn't drugged me in a whole twenty-four hours. He avoids me, and this is either very good or very bad. He's considering my offer. He hasn't talked to me, but I chatter at him, rattling off every little thing I can think of that I saw in his boxes, on his corkboard. I talk about our wedding, my plate of scallops, the ornate centerpieces, how it was all *just for us*, which was the most romantic thing I'd ever seen. I pretend to swoon and I'm girly. Excited, even. We could reenact it. Renew our vows, in Paris! He pretends to ignore me.

It's brass tacks time, I blather about whatever comes to mind, about all the things I might have said, if I had been myself, but completely and totally under his thumb, meek and in love with him. It's not even hard, like my brain has blocked out the mental images that should come naturally. *Remember that day on the boat?* I vaguely remember a boat, I don't even know if Tara was on it. He has yet to speak. I'm becoming one person in his mind, I can feel it in the way he looks at me when I say certain things and he's not sure: *Tara or Zoe?* Or rather, even if he *knows* that we can't possibly be the same person, he sees the possibility exist for the first time. That I could pretend this, and stay. That maybe if I did that, became his preferred reality, we could be happy the way he and Tara were happy.

I see him doubt his own sanity. But sometimes, I see the way he draws a breath, quick and sharp, and I know my wildly flung guesses are occasionally hitting bull's-eyes. I just have to throw out enough of them.

I nudge him with my unchained hand. "Hal. Please. I don't want to wet the bed again. Remember how mad you were?" I try not to remind him of *Zoe*, only *Tara*. I try to morph into her, but biology trumps psychology. I have to go to the bathroom.

He staggers up, grabs a key off the dresser, and without a word, unlocks me. He studies me as I use the toilet, and I even find myself wondering if Tara would do this, this way. I wash my hands. He clears his throat in the doorway, the bathroom low lit with the vanity bulb.

On the vanity sits a wide, flat candle. I slather the soap between my fingers and stare at it. It has three wicks. Five pounds? Maybe two? I don't have a plan, I just have the vague formation of a plan.

I dry my hands completely—I don't want them wet slick. I glance at Henry, who is studying the handcuff key. Waiting in his boxer shorts. He glances back toward the bedroom.

I pick the candle up, over my head, and bring it down, fast and hard, right on Henry's forehead. The edge hits the bridge of his nose and blood explodes everywhere.

I think he screams. I don't wait to see if he's conscious or knocked out.

I just run.

. . .

I'm out the front door and pounding across the lawn. The woods slap at my arms, my legs, my stomach. My stomach is bare. I'm in Henry's T-shirt and women's underpants that are falling down my hips. The branches scratch my face, but

I run. I'm faster than Henry, who runs his five miles a day. I'm weak and small now, winded, out of breath, but I'm still fast. I cut a zigzag, off the path, and run in what feels like circles and the rocks dig at my heels. I'm barefoot and when I look down, my legs and my feet are bleeding. My hands are covered in blood that might be mine or Henry's.

I can't tell if he's behind me. I can't hear anything over the huff of my breath. My lungs burn and my stomach aches, a cramp pulling at my hip. I step on a rock, and I feel it break the skin, right in the bottom of my foot at the arch. I don't scream, I don't stop.

In the distance there's a light. A soft beacon. A house. A tiny clapboard Cape Cod, a night-light shining in the window. I don't know if it's empty or if everyone is sleeping. I risk a look behind me, nothing but inky blackness. I stumble up the porch and fall, hitting my face on the step. Pain shoots up my nose and when I put my hand over it, it comes away bloody. More blood. God, so much blood.

I pound on the door and finally, I scream. "Help me! Please open the door! God, open the door!" I'm crying, the snot and the blood and the tears all mixing together in my mouth and it tastes like salt and metal. I pound harder, "Please answer the door, please please please please."

The door flings open. Bare, red painted toenails, gray hair pulled back in a bun, her mouth open in an *O*, small and petite, her eyes wide with terror.

Penny. She pulls me inside, dead-bolts the door.

"Call the police," I say, blubbering, still crying. She wipes my face, my hands with a towel and can't stop murmuring *Oh my God, Oh my God.* When she picks up the landline, it's dead. Her cell phone has no service. "We have to leave. He's coming after us."

"Who?" she whispers, her face chalky.

"Henry. He's trying to kill me. Just please, we have to

go. Get your car." I pull at her sleeve, her arm. Panicked and wild, checking out the front window. He won't announce his arrival. He'll be armed. I say all this.

"I can't leave, Zoe. Frank is upstairs." Her face is horrified.

"Who's Frank?"

"He's my husband. He's quadriplegic. I can't leave him. Take my keys, go. Get help." Her eyes dart from the front porch and back, to the stairs and back. I take the keys from her. "I have a gun," she says.

Right as she says this, the front window cracks—spiderwebs, the glass implodes, and instinctively I duck down. I hear Penny scamper behind me, across the hardwood floor and into the kitchen. She leaves me here. Henry stands on the porch, framed by the hole in the glass.

"You think I'm stupid, Zoe."

"Henry, you can't fix this now. You can't kill us all. Just put the gun down." I'm calm now, I'm not crying. I can't do anything else. This will be how it all ends, with Henry and a gun and me in my underwear pretending to be my dead twin sister. This is how I will die.

The crack behind me barely registers before Henry falls, thrown backward, his toes pointed up almost comically before settling back down to the earth. I smell the gunpowder and the blood before I see anything.

Penny stands, framed in the doorway between the living room and the kitchen, holding a shotgun up on her shoulder. *A hunter. Everyone hunts.* When it falls to her side, her face looks blank, unlined and white with shock. She trembles. On the porch, Henry's leg twitches, just once, like one of his dying deer.

"Now. Zoe. Go get help, now."

CHAPTER 27

A steady *beep beep* pulls me from sleep, heavy and dragging. I want to sleep, I'm so tired. The dark is comforting, a warm electric blanket that I want to burrow under, but instead, my eyes twitch under bright lights.

Someone stage-whispers, "She's waking up! Hurry!" There is a commotion, a rustling of arms and legs, and I blink. A face appears. A nurse. Round and pink, the kind of no-nonsense demeanor others might call plucky. She chatters on, telling me it's Tuesday, that I slept through Monday. I want to speak but there is an oxygen mask over my mouth. I tug at it, my arms are connected to tubes and wires, the *whoosh-hiss* and muffled bleating of hospital sounds. Machines for monitoring heartbeats and blood pressure. I wonder what the side effects of my drug use will be.

She moves the bed to sitting position and takes the mask off my face. She asks me questions I know the answers to—my name, my age—and she bubbles up, *Oh, you've passed!*

I look around the room, which is empty, save for a chair at the foot of the bed. Cash is leaning forward, watching, waiting. When I meet his eyes, he smiles grandly and waves his arms around like a game show host: *Look at all this!* I smile weakly back.

"Why are you here?" The question comes out unintentionally rude and I flush.

He shrugs. "I was frantic, I can't even tell you, Zoe. I knew something was wrong when you wouldn't take my calls, answer any of my texts. I called Yates. We'd been looking for you."

"How long was I . . ." I don't know how to finish the sentence. Missing?

"Ah. Two weeks."

Two weeks. It's unfathomable. I close my eyes, *white negligee, Henry's hands*. My eyes fly open and I grip the nurse's arm.

"I need a rape kit," I rasp, urgently.

She leans forward, smelling like lavender. "It's been done, sweetheart. It was negative."

Thank God. I fall back against the pillow.

"Henry is dead," I whisper. It's not a question. I think of his leg, Penny with that gun.

"Yes," Cash says softly, almost reverently.

"Penny saved me," I murmur.

"Yes," Cash agrees.

"I want to see her. Can I see her?" I struggle to sit up, pinned down by the needles and the tubes. *A little pinch.* My forehead sweats. I want to cry, I'm so relieved.

"I'll find her. You can't go anywhere. Yates is on her way."

"God, two weeks." It's all I can think of to say.

"We were going crazy, Zoe. Yates couldn't find you, Henry said you left him. It wasn't until I uncovered who Joanie was married to that Yates agreed to fill out a missing persons report. She was this close to applying for a search warrant. I thought he was going to kill you."

"You knew? That Joanie was Tara?" I'm incredulous.

"We just put it all together yesterday. I had Yates convinced that something terrible had happened. Remember when you texted me? You asked me to look into who Joanie married?"

I nodded.

"That was the ticket. You knew it, didn't you? Deep down?"

I shake my head. "I don't know what I knew. I didn't think she was married to Henry. I couldn't shake the feeling that it was all connected. I had no idea how, though."

I'm just so tired. All I want to do is sleep.

The doctor comes in and Cash gracefully waits in the hall. I'm pushed and prodded, latex gloves examine my mouth, my throat, my eyes. My vitals are monitored, oxygen, heart rate, blood pressure, muscle function.

The doctor pulls a chair up to the bed, tents his fingers under his chin, asks me if I have any questions. I don't. Then he talks. Through him, I learn all the things that Henry did to me. He'd kept me barely conscious for more than fifteen days on a mixture of Dilaudid and Benadryl, a narcotic injection. They'd found oxycodone and hydrocodone in my blood, as well as a drug called midazolam, a highly potent sedation drug primarily used for its amnesic properties. I wasn't likely to recover many memories from my two-week ordeal at Fishing Lake.

How did Henry get all these drugs? Don't hospitals control *this kind of thing?* I am angry, demanding, slapping the hospital mattress with my palm.

The doctor is kind and apologetic. Men with money, it seems, can obtain almost anything they'd like. I, of all people, know how easy it can be to find narcotics on the street. I shudder to think of the drugs in my veins, cut with God knows what. I think of Henry's collection of prescription pain medication. Henry, who knew my history, my past.

My only external injuries are the stitches in my foot from

running through the woods, and my left wrist where Henry's handcuffs sheared the skin. I have matching scars now, thin lines on the top of each wrist, a physical reminder of what I've been through. Literal scratches on the surface, I suspect.

Yates follows closely on the heels of the doctor and takes her place by my bedside. She tells me about their investigation, a formality because of Henry's death. They are trying to trace the root of the drugs.

As much as Yates can figure, Henry solved the crime of Tara's murder when the police could not. He admitted as much to me. He tracked me down, planning to kill me out of revenge. But the idea that he could have Tara back, a stand-in who looked just like her, was too tantalizing. Who cared if we were different people? He could simply turn me into her. He'd nearly succeeded. I remember his relentless pursuit, his almost overwhelming attraction. I question myself, really. Only someone desperate for love wouldn't recognize the insincerity in it. He'd proposed after four months. He'd never felt love for me. Obsession? Yes. Hatred and blame? Yes. But love? Yates thinks a man like Henry is incapable of love. Sometimes I still dream of his hands. I wake up, disgusted with myself.

A few days later, Yates brings a criminal psychologist to the hospital who can explain Henry. He is a behemoth of a man, folded into one of the hospital chairs, dwarfing it like a piece of dollhouse furniture. He tugs on his beard as he talks, his thick fingers combing the edges of the wiry hair, and I watch, fascinated.

"It doesn't make sense to me that Henry would go through all the pains of trying to run me over. Break into his own house. For what? It makes no sense," I protest, helpless and weak, sinking back onto the pile of pillows behind me.

"It makes perfect sense." Dr. Reginold taps a pen against his notepad. "All your talk about finding Caroline, this pushed him over the edge. Did you ever walk an unruly dog, Ms. Whittaker?"

"I'm sorry?"

"When you walk a dog that isn't trained, it wanders. The longer the leash, the more erratic it becomes, sniffing here, crossing in front of you, tripping you up, darting after cars. But when reined in, it'll walk straight and with purpose. It can still be unruly on a short leash, but it won't. It's psychological. A short leash sends a message."

"I'm the dog, here?" I am numb, tired.

"Yes, unfortunately, you are. I'm sorry." He coughs briefly, then recovers. "To him, you were spinning out of control. If he could rein you in, he could resume the role of protector. He knew your past, why not just simply use it? If you're scared for your life, you're not gallivanting the countryside looking for your biological mother. If you find her, there's a good chance his secret comes out. It was all distraction. And then, when you rebelled, there was rage. Do you understand why?"

I shake my head no.

"Sociopaths are coldly, almost blindly, logical. He'd never think twice about plowing down an intersection full of people if it accomplishes his goal. They care about one thing and one thing only: their objective. Their agenda. His goal was to replace his beloved Tara."

"Was he capable of love?"

"Tara was his obsession. Someone well below his station in life, whom he could easily manipulate. Someone happy to be isolated. Or at least compliant."

Tara was so compliant. You are defiant. Unlovable. I wonder if my sister knew she was being manipulated and remember her poem to Henry. A subtle, coded thumbed-nose gesture, almost assertive in the knowledge that he wouldn't get it. Could it have been her first step in breaking free? Maybe.

"So, it was all an attempt to control me, keeping me under his thumb."

Dr. Reginold nods. "There is endless psychological research on evil people. But in my experience, the average sociopath has no idea they are wrong. They're born this way, not made."

As for Mick, Henry wasn't lying. There was another trial, one I hadn't known about, where Mick testified against Jared Pritchett and then later implicated men several rungs higher than Jared in both drug and sex trafficking, in exchange for a lesser sentence. He never went to prison. Jared was out in five years, thanks to overcrowding laws and some kind of a deal. The reason Jared tracked me down and inadvertently killed Tara is unclear. Revenge of some kind. They're looking into it. *Following all leads,* I'm assured. Jared killed Tara, Henry killed him, I killed Henry. There was a circle of life feel to the whole thing but it left an acrid burn in the back of my throat if I thought about it.

Mick, on the other hand, never had a knack for catching the right break, always a half beat behind, lagging in the wake of the wave. That he'd eventually succumbed to drugs didn't surprise me. That he ended up testifying against Jared did.

There is still one remaining mystery. Tara had been living in New York City with a controlling man who refused to call her by the name her family had used her whole life: Joanie. He called it low class. Blue collar. (I could see him saying this with a slightly curled lip, a subtle roll of his eyes, that dismissive wrist flick.) Tara had been borderline agoraphobic, unable to work, ridden with such anxiety that she had to take a myriad of medications just to control it. Or at least she thought she did. I suspect Henry simply liked his women medicated.

In Henry's room, they found a bottle of Dexedrine, a medication for treating hyperactivity disorder known to cause paralyzing anxiety in patients who did not have ADD. The prescription was for forty pills. There were seven left.

Yates tracked down Maslow, and he filled in a few blanks. Tara had found him, through the public records, six months or so before she was killed. According to Maslow, Tara called him, begged him for information on Hilary Lawlor. He refused, but the call always nagged at him. Truthfully, he said, *I* always nagged at him. *My* story. Everything that had happened and how it all went down. He hated how I left town, didn't trust him to do his job. He lost sleep wondering if I'd survived. He checked up on Jared and Mick. As long as they were in their rightful places, he left well enough alone.

He was retired as it was, gave sunset sail tours off the coast of North Carolina. When he was invited to a wedding in the city, he called Tara back, agreed to meet her. He could never shake that call, he'd said. Not that he knew a whole helluva lot, but he was drawn to her because of me.

He said he nearly fell over when he met her at a diner, she looked so much like me he thought she *was* me. He told her what little he knew about me. My name was likely Zoe—I'd told him that before I left. I was headed east, as far away from San Francisco as possible. He still had my note. *Bright lights, big city.* He suspected New York, but didn't have a lot to go on to back it up. As much as I can figure, shortly after that, the feature in *New York* magazine ran with that silly group shot at La Fleur d'Elise. It would have been a lot of luck, I suppose, but a sister might recognize a sister, no matter how small the face.

The idea that Joan was there that day looking for me wakes me up at night, panicked and profoundly sad. I brought all of this to her. Me. All of this was my fault.

Likely, Jared had been watching me for a while, waiting for the right time to make his move. By sheer chance, he'd followed through on the wrong sister. She was killed only a half dozen blocks up from the flower shop where I was working that day. She was alone, contrary to Henry's story. He hadn't been with his wife, going out to dinner, married one minute, the next not. It was all a ruse, a ploy, specifically tailored for me. It's all a theory, and mine alone, so Yates tells me.

It all seems so serendipitous, except whatever the exact horrible opposite of serendipity is. I actually went so far as to look it up once: *zemblanity*. That's the word. Coined by William Boyd, it means "unpleasant unsurprise," which doesn't seem quite terrible enough. I caused my sister's death, and the whole resulting chain reaction led to Henry's almost two-year-long psychotic break and his eventual death. There were buckets and tracks and pulley systems in place, but I was the moving piece that set it all off.

Sometimes I imagine an alternate universe. The idea that I could have stumbled on her by chance, fetching Elisa a ribbon the exact color cornflower blue as the latest batch of hydrangeas. *No not that one, try again, that shop uptown?* Maybe we'd order the same thing at the coffee shop. *Extra whipped cream, extra caramel.* She'd be so happy she finally found me, I'd be shocked she existed at all. I imagine showing her Elisa's and my apartment with Lydia. I imagine a friendship with her, someone I can be myself with, whoever that may be. I imagine I'd never married Henry at all. It's a nice little fantasy and I allow myself the indulgence.

Then sometimes, very late at night, I have to nip the bud of happiness that threatens to bloom at the idea that anyone was looking for me at all. I realize it makes no sense. In the daytime, I'm gutted by the whole thing. *My fault,* I wail to therapists and doctors. I'm not acting. I feel these things. But at night, alone, sometimes my mind wanders. My sister, wanting to meet *me,* scouring the city, her anxiety-ridden heart hammering at all the noise and the traffic and the subway. She braved that for *me.* For a second, if I let it, my heart swells a bit at this. This whole time, I'd had a tether, some invisible thread linking me to someone else.

I just never knew it.

· · ·

"Zoe."

I blink my eyes open, startled awake. I'd been dreaming, but it flits away faster than I can catch it. Penny stands at the foot of my bed, her purse hugged tightly across her middle. Her eyes twitch from the window to the door and back to my bed. I struggle to sit up.

"Penny." My mouth is dry and cottony. She moves to my bedside and refills my water cup. The pitcher wobbles in her hand. "Thank you."

The chair scrapes the tile floor as she pulls it closer to the bedside. "Will you be all right?" she half whispers. "I'm sorry."

"You saved my life." I stare at her face, willing her gaze to settle, just for a moment. She fidgets, her hands smoothing her pants, rifling through her purse. I reach out, touch her hand, and for a second, she stills. "Did you know I was there? At that house?"

She shakes her head, vehement. "No. No, Zoe, I didn't. He fired me. It's . . . all my fault he got away with all of this." She takes a gulp of air, like a half-sob.

"You've known." Of course she has. I hadn't thought of it until this very moment, but Penny knew Tara. Joanie. The shock of seeing me, for the first time, then. A flood of half-overheard conversations rush back. *Henry, but it isn't right. It doesn't look proper.* The way she couldn't look at me, never said my name. "How much did you know? That we were twins?"

She nods slowly, for once, leveling her gaze. She clears her throat. When she speaks, for the first time, her voice is clear and steady. "Frank and I lived in that cabin behind the Whittakers' property." The surprise must register on my face because she halts, and coughs, a resonant, wet sound from deep within her chest. "Henry grew up at Fishing Lake. They bought it from the Vizzinis. Frank and I worked for the Whittakers for years."

I knew much of this, that Penny worked for Henry's family. That the Fishing Lake house was Henry's parents'. I close my eyes, smooth my eyebrows with my index finger. I wave my hand around for her to continue.

"In the back, at the edge of the property, used to sit a guest house. Much like the one you saw. It was almost an apartment, really. I tended the Whittakers' house, affairs, bills, and social calendar, and Frank was an accountant at Mr. Whittaker's law firm. Mrs. Whittaker was in advertising. They were nice people. They just had one very troubled teenaged son." She rummages in her purse, pulls out a tissue, and dabs her eyes.

I remember then: a fire. And I know what's coming before she says it.

She shakes her head. "I saw the smoke from the upstairs bedroom. I came running down the lane, Frank was in the house. He'd been sick with shingles. By the time I got to our walk, Henry was there, just sitting on a rock, watching it burn. I screamed at him. Told him Frank was in there, that he was trapped, but it was like he didn't even hear me. Or didn't care. He just watched it burn, mesmerized." Plump tears fall down her cheeks, one after the other, and she blots them as they drip off her chin while she speaks. "By the time Frank knew there was a fire, he'd tried to come down the stairs. They collapsed underneath him. His spinal cord was severed." She pauses, pours herself a drink of water from my pitcher into a fresh Styrofoam cup. "The Whittakers were traumatized. They took Henry to every psychologist in the tristate area. They were good people. They kept me on until they died. Could never apologize enough, never pay for enough. Rebuilt a house for us, bigger, on another patch of property, farther down the trail, the one you found. Said we could live the rest of our days there, rent free. Henry wasn't allowed back there as a teenager."

"How did they die?" I set my cup down on the nightstand, shocked to realize that I don't know. God, there was so much I didn't know. I can almost see Henry, the flame alight in his eyes. I imagine his barely there smile. I recognize it.

"A car accident. Some kind of brake malfunction. I've always wondered . . ." Out in the hall, an alarm sounds, and a clatter of orderlies and nurses rush by with a gurney. We both turn our heads to watch. When it returns to silence, she continues, "Then there was Tara and as an adult, he always claimed that fire was an accident, and he was in shock. But I . . . I saw his face that day. He was gleeful. All that light, reflected in his eyes, it was like Christmas to him." Her voice hardens, takes a sharp edge. "Well, anyway, he was charming as an adult. He brought me back. Apologized again and again. Paid me more than I had any right to take for what work he gave me." She studied the tile floor. "I needed the money. Frank's disability benefits were dwindling. All we had was social security. And then Henry got married, and Tara was so wonderful, so quiet, polite, respectful. A delight. And then she died and he comes home three years later with you. Zoe, believe me," she says, and leans forward, pulling my hand into hers, her palms cold and her nails digging into my wrists. "I didn't mean for any of this to happen. I tried to ask him about it. He told me to mind my own business. I told him that it just wasn't right, that you didn't know. He said he was going to tell you, but he was in love with you and thought you'd leave him. That he deceived you. He swore he just stumbled on you one day, that you had done the flowers for a company event."

I nodded. "That's true. But, he set it up that way. He found me, knew it was all . . ." my voice cracks, "a lie."

"He said he was captivated by you, by your spirit. He can

be very convincing. Could be, I mean." Her mouth twists, and I see this for what it is. A confessional. Penny feels guilt for accepting me at face value. For not questioning it. I remembered overheard conversations, Penny's voice. *It just doesn't look proper, Henry.* Oh God.

"How didn't you know I was there? Didn't you come back?" I press, needing all the puzzle pieces with newfound urgency.

She shook her head. "He fired me. He was unraveling, I think. He called me a liability. The last day I worked for him is the day he brought you back to Fishing Lake. He asked me to clean the house, set up a spread. I did that. He said you were sick, that you'd been threatened. I begged him to tell you who he was, who your sister was. He screamed at me to mind my own business. Told me to go home. So I did." She folds up her tear-dampened tissue into a neat little square and tucks it back into the pocket of her purse. "I did come back once. It was evening. He was sitting on the back deck, drinking a glass of brandy. He said you'd left him. Gone back to the city, stolen some of his money. You were furious about Tara. He blamed me. He was angry as hell." She shakes her head, a quick snap like a self-admonishment. "I'm afraid of my own shadow most days. Henry Whittaker scared the living daylights out of me."

I touch her hand. "I forgive you, Penny. And I'm forever thankful."

She stands up, waves her hand in my direction, and turns to leave. At the door, she pauses and turns back.

"I have nightmares about that fire. Do you know, a week prior to that, I had caught him cutting off the tail of one of the neighbor's farm cats with a hacksaw? I told his mother." She retrieves the tissue from her purse, blots her chin and cheeks. "I always thought that fire . . . was retribution. Frank is paralyzed because I snitched on Henry."

"Oh, Penny," I say, softly.

"I was scared, Zoe." She stands in the doorway, backlit by the bright hall lights, looking diminutive. A hunched rounded figure. "I spent years looking over my shoulder. I considered telling you about Tara myself. But I always stopped to wonder, what would he have done to me?"

EPILOGUE

SIX MONTHS LATER

It was Lydia's idea. In fact, she made all the calls, talked to all the right people. I come home from the CARE office one day, she's running circles around me like an excited puppy. She grabs my hand, leads me into the living room, and sits me down on the couch, her hands flat on my shoulders.

"Please don't be mad, okay?"

We've moved in together, a different apartment in Hoboken, bigger, more luxurious. Warm and rich colors, browns and oranges. Decorating it has been a form of therapy.

I'm a rich woman now. New York is an intestate succession state, which means that because Henry died without an updated will, as his current wife, I inherited everything: all his liquid assets, his apartments, his stocks and bonds. I'm sure he never counted on that. His will was hopelessly outdated, still named Tara as his sole heir.

"I won't be mad." This is all so unlike Lydia, who generally has one lukewarm mood, forever perfecting her bored face. She's giddy, pushing her palms against her knees, starting and stopping sentences until I finally say, "Oh God, just say it!" out of frustration.

"I found Evelyn." She takes a deep breath, her hands grasping mine. "The state pays to cremate unclaimed bodies but the funeral homes don't always do anything with the remains, in case anyone ever wants them."

I shake my head, nothing about that made sense. I remember that spastic little estate lawyer and his tiny closet office. He said they disposed of her ashes. "What? You're crazy, Lydia. Evelyn died more than five years ago . . . Anyway, they said that wasn't true. Most funeral homes' policy is a few weeks. I talked to a lawyer at the time . . ."

"It doesn't matter. I talked to the funeral home director. He said he has metal boxes in his basement from the seventies. They can't bring themselves to dispose of them, although they have every legal right to do so. He said most funeral homes have a basement full of ashes. Which is so sad, when you think about it. But Zoe," her eyes were shining, bright blue, "they have one labeled Evelyn Lawlor."

My heart stops, time itself stops. The idea that I could go back, fix the worst thing I ever did . . . I can't even wrap my head around it. "There has to be a mistake. I don't even know what funeral home she was sent to."

"I just called every funeral parlor in the Bay area. It wasn't that difficult. I think it was maybe the eleventh one I called?" She scrunches up her face, eyes to the ceiling in thought, then shrugs. "It doesn't matter, the point is, she's there." She extends a piece of notebook paper with a name, address, and telephone number. *Howey Funeral Service*. I stare at it. I could have a memorial for Evelyn. My mom. The only one I've ever known. I could think about her without this hollow, empty feeling in my stomach.

"Would you come with me?" I ask softly.

"Of course." Lydia hugs me, her metal bangle bracelets

clattering against the back of my neck. My hair is short again. Some kind of emotional protest. Truthfully, I miss the length.

I've become someone else yet again, although Dr. Thorpe—my psychologist—agrees this is what should happen. I can never be my pre-Henry self, but Henry has changed who I would have become. She assures me that this is what life is: a sum of experiences. That I cannot grieve for the woman who may have existed had Henry not come into my life. Or rather, if I had not let him in. She assures me that I will be whole again, that a person cannot simply vanish because of one traumatic year. I'm convinced I have. She assures me that I will heal. And that is, for now, enough.

I am not without my scars: I have wretched nightmares, night terrors really, where I'm asleep but am wandering the house, screaming, terrified, sweating, until Lydia finds me trying to cut off imaginary plastic handcuffs with pinking shears from the kitchen. I'd be terrified to live alone.

I went to the dentist not that long ago and had a panic attack at the sight of the Novocain needle. Yes, there are remnants. Dr. Thorpe, whom I see three, sometimes four times a week, says I have post-traumatic stress disorder, which is often medically treated with antidepressants. Since I won't take any medication, we use a combination of hypnosis and cognitive therapy, and I do think it's helping. It's hard to say. I don't make a move lately without consulting Dr. Thorpe, caught once again in this limbo between the person I was, and the person I might be should I ever find my way back to her.

Most of my sessions revolve around two topics: Evelyn and Henry. I have guilt about Evelyn, of course. My issues with Henry are layered and complex. Sometimes, in the early morning space between sleep and consciousness, I miss him. I miss his vacation hair and his large, capable hands. I miss the way he took charge, dealt with complications for me: money and finances, bank issues, insurance. I'm grieving for the

Henry I thought I knew. I'm grieving for the caretaker I've lost. Then I alternate between self-loathing and frustration.

When I tell her about Evelyn, she clucks her tongue once and says, "Zoe, I think that'd be lovely." Dr. Thorpe is the kind of person who uses the word "lovely" freely, usually in combination with the word *simply.* She's also the kind of person who wears *slacks* and *blouses.* Her burgundy acrylic nails tap rhythmically on her notebook. Her teeth are capped and her gold hoop earrings glimmer as she shakes her head.

"Do you think the plane will be hard?" I ask her. If she says yes, I'll have a panic attack. The people. Ironically, I have a hard time with crowds. I see Henry's face, or Jared's, and sometimes I shake so bad I can't see, my teeth clatter and my vision swims.

"Do *you* think the plane will be hard?" She drums her pen against her watch, a subtle time-is-almost-up signal. I don't know what to say.

• • •

Lake Tahoe in the fall is a rainbow of colors: the leaves a shock of red and yellow against the cerulean blue of the lake. The air is crisp and clean, and our New York lungs are a little shocked from it, high, like we've been sucking pure oxygen. The canoe bobs and wheezes in the water, aimless; the weight of all three of us may be too much for it. Lydia pulls her life jacket around her, checking and rechecking buckles. Cash eyes me, wary and nervous.

Sometimes I catch him looking at me when he's *not* wary, *not* nervous and all I see is love. In those moments I can see myself loving him back. One day. For now, I mostly feel guilt that he's fallen for someone so ruined. Most of the time, I'm a fragile bird to him. He is gentle and scared and loving and skittish. I don't know when it happened, when he fell in love with me. Somewhere between the diner and the hospital room. One day, I'd like to ask him.

He paddles us out to the middle of the lake, until the shore is a simple hazy line on the horizon, white sand and yellow trees, the lights of our resort glittering in the sunset. Evelyn would have loved this place. *Oh, the money!* I imagine her in my ornate room, with the plush carpeting, the high-rise view of the lake from our wooden balcony, the large, looming gas fireplace that comes to life with the flick of a button. She'd dance around barefoot, scrunching the deep pile between her toes.

Her smile, lipstick on her teeth. The dimple in her right cheek. Her weathered hands, with large knuckles, working hands but painted nails. How she'd touch her nose when she laughed. The way she'd tie her hair in a knot at the base of her neck.

Before we rowed out to the middle of the lake, I'd dragged Lydia and Cash around on a goose chase in our rented car. Up a private drive, on the North Shore of Tahoe Vista until Lydia had gasped.

"This is the house we stayed at. The one Evelyn got from a friend or something." I stared at the sleek gray lines of the "cabin" and realized she never could have afforded anything like this. No one she knew could have. Where did it come from? The images come to me unbidden: thick, juicy steaks on the pink side of gray, just about to expire. This house, the glass front, the breathtaking views I neither noticed nor appreciated as a teenager. The beaded dresses she'd bring home and try on, and we'd parade around our small living room, only to have it *poof!* disappear the next day. The "borrowed" convertible, the wind in her hair.

In the passenger seat, while Cash and Lydia watched me warily, I started laughing. I laughed so hard until tears squeezed out my eyes. Cash touched my shoulder.

"It was . . . stolen," I hiccoughed out. "She stole it all."

Lydia gave a soft, "Ahh, Zoe," like she was about to console me but I waved her away. "She so badly wanted to live the life she saw every day. She tried to give it to me. With vacations and dresses and steaks and wine, and oh, God—" my voice was strangled and the pain in my stomach was so hot white in that moment, I doubled over. I imagined Evelyn, sliding the keys to Mr. Miska's Tahoe cabin into her purse, the last second before her shift ended, on a weekend she knew he'd be away. I envisioned her saying, "Of course I'll get that dress dry cleaned," or slipping the slightly slimy paper-wrapped rib eyes into her bag.

I think of these things as I lift the lid to the wooden box. All the memories of Evelyn mix and mingle in my mind; she becomes ageless and timeless and less like a real, once-living person and more like an amalgam of childhood memories. Evelyn, floating free.

A breeze picks up and I gently turn the box over, scattering her dust into the water. At first it coats the surface, then slowly sinks. I think that now, the last thing I ever did for her was out of love. I hope she will never feel unloved again.

"I can't take back the last five years, Ev. And I know you always said *sorry was for sissies*. You didn't do apologies, you forgave without being asked. Well, I'm asking."

I try to track each speck until it all disperses and I can no longer see anything at all. *Mingle amongst the rich,* I think. She'd always wanted to. The water is calm and sparkling.

We sit awhile longer, till the sun fully sets, the blue lake turning an inky black. Lydia hums "Amazing Grace" and I tell one story, a simple one. My favorite story of my mother, the one that shows who she was as a person, the day she brought Rachel home for dinner.

"Sometimes it's the people who have the least that give the most," Lydia says, which is the most perfect thing to say.

I think that it's just about as fine a memorial service as a person could ever ask for.

"Ready?" I ask them, and they both nod. They're so patient with me, my friends. As it turns out, I am not, as Henry said, unlovable. Cash paddles us back. Lydia makes a joke about him sinking the canoe, and Cash lightly splashes her with water. I try to pinpoint my feelings. *Content.* I feel content. As Evelyn would say, *Well, I'll be.*

Sometimes life gives you a third chance. Who knew?

ACKNOWLEDGMENTS

Thanks to Mark Gottlieb, without whom this wild ride would not have been possible. Seriously, best agent ever. Endless thank-you to the Atria team, especially Sarah Branham and Sarah Cantin for your smart guidance and advice.

For my writing posse: Kimberly Giarratano, Ann Garvin, Elizabeth Buhmann, Sonja Yoerg, Mary Fan, Aimie Runyan, and all my Badasses: you have all read and brainstormed and been my saving grace and my cheerleaders and my tough critics when I needed it. To my Tall Poppy Sisters: LOVE YOU ALL, poppy power.

For my beta readers: Jamie Raintree, Rachel Jarabeck, Bridget Lynch, Sarah DiCello, Betsy Kirkland, Becky Riddle, Abby Polozin, Stephanie Bradley. Your feedback was invaluable. Thank you Teri Woods for your terrifying understanding of sociopaths and Carl Palmeri who gave me the ending from a small piece of undertaker trivia.

Gratitude to my entire family, who are the most supportive people I've ever seen: Mom and Dad, Meg, Becky, Molly, Mary Jo and Jeff, George and Lori, Judy and Audrey, Dottie, Chuck and Lauren, who cheer me on relentlessly. You must all be exhausted.

And finally, and foremost, thank you to the loves of my life: Chip, Abby, and Lily. You've certainly taken the backseat to this writing gig on many a day, with minimal complaining. You're my biggest fans and it means the world to have you in my corner.

Love my village.